THE NORWOOD NANNY CHRONICLES:
Book One

THE
AGENCY

MONICA McGURK

THE NORWOOD NANNY CHRONICLES:
Book One

THE AGENCY

RIVER GROVE
BOOKS

This book is a work of fiction. Names, characters, businesses, organizations, places, events, and incidents are either a product of the author's imagination or are used fictitiously. Any resemblance to actual persons, living or dead, events, or locales is entirely coincidental.

Published by River Grove Books
Austin, TX
www.rivergrovebooks.com

Distributed by River Grove Books

Design and composition by Greenleaf Book Group and Mimi Bark
Cover design by Greenleaf Book Group and Mimi Bark
Cover images used under license from ©Shutterstock.com/Anabela88

Publisher's Cataloging-in-Publication data is available.

Print ISBN: 978-1-63299-478-3

eBook ISBN: 978-1-63299-479-0

First Edition

For my parents

"The hand that rocks the cradle is the hand that rules the world."

—*William Ross Wallace*

PROLOGUE

It was the most basic of things, she knew.

Ruby had even said it once, in class.

And she'd tried so hard. She'd struggled through all the courses and practicums, learning all the roles of nanny—cook, teacher, entertainer, nurse. Even moral compass. Protector.

She'd handled tantrums and baths. She'd made snacks and tea and smuggled them treats, earning her way to the inner circle of their happy family through their little bellies. She'd clasped their hands to dance, built pillow forts on the floor, and tucked them in, one by one, pretending not to hear when they asked for just one more bedtime story.

Secretly loving it when they asked for just one more bedtime story.

She'd won their hearts, and the belief of their parents. So much so that those parents had entrusted their children's four little bodies—these miracles of life who were flesh of their flesh—wholly to her. To keep them safe.

And willingly, innocently, they'd come.

They had not questioned her when she'd led them away from their school. When she'd whisked them away in cars and vans to strange places, promising them adventures. When she had unspooled majestic tales and stories, weaving distractions so profound they had lasted them through days of captivity, they'd gone along, closing their eyes and imagining they were there—that they were anywhere else but in the belly of a ship, headed to someplace unknown and frightful. And, with their imaginations at play, they'd overlooked how parched their throats had become, and the stench of their own waste, trapped in the bottles she'd tucked and piled into corners, and the aching hunger that was becoming more pronounced with each passing day.

It's sort of a nanny job requirement to be able to handle bodily fluids and all manner of unpleasant things. The only other thing more fundamental to the job is to not lose the children.

That's what Ruby had said.

And now she'd lost them. She'd lost them, maybe for good.

FIRST YEAR

Chapter One

ORIENTATION

Bath, England

"Pardon me."

The lanky boy paused expectantly, looking past Bree to the empty seat next to her. Bree inexplicably flushed. He was the first person actually to speak to her, to even acknowledge her existence, since she'd snuck—an hour early—into the campus auditorium to await the convocation ceremony. She'd chosen what she'd thought to be an inconspicuous spot on the side of the wood-paneled room. Now, with the compact space filling up with her classmates, every seat was being claimed.

Clutching her backpack, she pressed her legs awkwardly against the chair and made room for him to squeeze through the row.

He smiled, one crooked tooth marring an otherwise perfect, glossy row. "Many thanks."

She blurted out nervously, "No problem."

He brightened as he tumbled, book bag and all, into the chair next to her, peering at her with heightened interest. "Ah! An American, are you? But how can that be? Has the old battle-axe Dean Albourn altered her stance toward the inclusion of residents from the wayward former colonies?"

She blinked at him, trying to parse the meaning from his big words and toothy enunciation. "You can tell I'm American from the two words I spoke?"

He chortled with delight. "With that gorgeous accent, which I take to be Southern? Of course I can tell." His eyes sparkled. "I'm right. Do tell me I am right. It would be such a relief to find another unicorn with whom I could share the burden."

"Unicorn?" she asked, feeling herself blush, ashamed at her confusion, again.

He waved a hand around the cozy auditorium, the seats of which were rapidly filling in, bringing life to the stern gothic stone and soaring ceilings. "I'm Norwood's first 'manny'!" He waited for her reaction, but she gave him her blankest look. "Yes, yes, I know. Dreadfully poor from the point of view of punning, but it seems the media have taken a liking to it and so here I sit, stuck with it."

He cocked an eyebrow and looked at her quizzically. "You don't know, do you? That's brilliant! Absolutely brilliant!" He reached over and clutched her hands. "It's like you've just come in out of the wilderness. You and I will have so much fun together. We will be outsiders, together. Splendid. I'm Dashiell," he rolled on, oblivious to her discomfiture as he shook her hand ceremoniously. "Norwood's first male matriculant. Ever." He gestured at the crowd again and waited for her reaction.

She blinked once more as she realized that, indeed, Dashiell was the only man in the entire room.

"And you are . . .?" he prompted.

"Bree. Bree Parrish. From Florence, Alabama."

"Bree Parrish. Why, with a name like that you almost sound British. But here you sit, Norwood's first American pupil."

"What?" she blurted. "I'm the first?"

"Surely you knew?" he chortled.

A bustle from the stage drew his attention away from her before she could deny having known anything of the sort. In fact, it seemed implausible. Suddenly, the bright chirping of the assembled young women diminished to a low murmur. He leaned over and shushed. "It's the battle-axe herself," he indicated, as a woman with a very impressive bosom mounted the steps to the lectern. "Brace yourself, my dear Bree. You are about to encounter one of the most fulsome displays of Britishness you will ever have the pleasure to witness in your entire life. Watch, and be amazed."

A straight-backed woman just slightly over five feet, to Bree's best estimate, gripped the neck of the microphone, adjusting it from atop a stepstool behind the lectern. "Ahem. Ladies. Ladies," she repeated, a shard of steel infusing her voice with authority. Instantly, the crowd silenced. "And gentleman," the woman acknowledged with a tilt of her head toward Dashiell, her nose wrinkling slightly as if she had just taken note of a particularly bad smell.

Dashiell nodded back to her, with a quick wink to Bree.

"Welcome to this opening convocation of this, the one hundred and twenty-fifth year of the Norwood College, where we build not only careers, but families, constructed from the foundations of academic rigor, discipline, sacrifice, commitment, and empowerment. Norwood offers more than just the most preeminent undergraduate degree in child development in the world; if you work hard enough, you may be accepted into its caregiver preparatory program and graduate in parallel with a coveted Norwood Diploma. The diploma, as you know, unlocks the door to unimaginable opportunities—diploma holders care for the children of CEOs, royal families, diplomats. They run their own caregiving institutions and schools. There is nothing else comparable to it in the entire world.

"You are here—one of only one hundred students accepted this academic year, in our most brutally selective admissions process ever— because you have demonstrated, through your academic achievements, a commitment to excellence that is the hallmark for which a Norwood graduate is known, and indeed, revered. Your striving has only just begun, however."

She paused dramatically, peering over the top of her reading glasses to skewer various members of the student body with an icy stare.

"Look to your classmate on your left." She waited for the rows of women to obediently swing their heads to one side. Bree surreptitiously noted Dashiell's jutting jawline and the faint hint of a five-o'clock shadow.

"Now, look to the student at your right." Row after row of heads swiveled in turn. A few nervous titters split the awkward silence. Bree was conscious of Dashiell taking in her quite average appearance—only a blaze of tangled red hair distinguished her from any of the girls in the room.

Albourn made her point. "Statistically speaking, one of you will not be here by the end of this school year. Moreover, a scant thirty will likely be admitted into the certificate program—into a guarantee of lifetime employment through affiliation with the Norwood Agency—later this year. The standards of Norwood are the toughest of any school in the realm, befitting the sacred duty with which our graduates are entrusted."

Anxious whispers skittered through the hall as the students looked around, and Bree wondered which of them would be the ones to be shamefully dismissed.

"As evidence of this, I give you Gul Avci, one of our recent graduates and an exemplar of a successful alumna."

A compact woman stepped forward from the line behind Albourn.

"Avci was an early admit due to her exceptional academic record. She garnered numerous merit citations and led as Head Girl during her time in these halls. More importantly, she has extended Norwood's reach into her native Turkey, demonstrating how British childcare norms are relevant the world over, taking an almost diplomatic zeal to her efforts."

Gul nodded slightly, as if this praise was simply her due, and fell back into line.

Looking satisfied, Albourn continued. "As your dean, I will not rest until I am satisfied that each and every one of you has proven yourself worthy of the Norwood name and the grave responsibility entrusted to you. Just like Gul Avci. Our faculty," she added, gesturing to the row of uptight-looking women behind her, "are here to ensure that you are given every opportunity to succeed. In the next forty-eight hours, you will have ample time to settle in to your quarters, complete registration, and gather the materials indicated in your syllabi."

Dashiell looked over at Bree and gave an exaggerated eye roll.

"Upon leaving this hall, you will find your first-year study group assignments posted on the wall. These groups are an essential aspect of the Norwood experience. Your group has been carefully assembled to maximize your exposure to the diversity of your fellow students so that you might equally learn from one another." She dragged the "I" in "diversity" out, unnaturally emphasizing it and rhyming it with "pie." "For first term, you are expected to work together, helping one another through your assignments and completing group work as designated by your professors. This year, we introduce a new element to the group method: Each of you will have the opportunity to grade every member of your group on every assignment, according to your perception of each member's preparation and contributions to the group's efforts."

A groan ripped through the hall before Albourn continued.

"There will be no exceptions to this rule. There will be no waivers granted for participation in Study Group and no changing of group assignments. Collusion on peer grading will be punishable by expulsion." She pressed her lips together with grim humor. "By this method, we hope to impress upon you the importance of rules and order, which you will find so instrumental in the development of a sound character in the children with whom you will work in the future.

"Due to the closeness of their working relationships, study groups will naturally be structured as living groups. You will be given your housing arrangements once your entire group has assembled. While we recognize that, in this age of social media, many of you would have preferred to be in contact with your group members in advance, or I daresay even to have chosen them yourselves, we find this method much more in keeping with the Norwood experience. So, too, is the required departure of your parents last evening. Meeting the unforeseen challenges of setting up your new home represents exactly the sort of valiant struggle that will help us forge you into a useful instrument of child instruction. Miss Montoya-Craig, a representative from the upper class, will assist you with locating your group once we have adjourned."

A dour-looking young woman sporting a pearl-buttoned cardigan emblazoned with the Norwood crest and an equally staid plaid skirt stepped forward on the stage, peering at them with dark eyes.

Dean Albourn raised herself up to her full, tiny, terrifying height. "Now, we shall sing of our sacred alma mater. Margaret?"

Montoya-Craig pulled a tuning fork from the deep pocket of her sweater and struck it neatly, letting the sonorous tone vibrate over their heads. Simultaneously, as if pre-orchestrated, the massive wooden doors to the hall burst open and two neat rows of upper-class students, a mass of beige, floated in along both sides of the auditorium, their voices already raised in song.

In the shade of watchful tree
Near sight of sacred vale

Our forebears trod the path to thee
With vows to never fail
O! Norwood, O! Norwood

"Oh my," Dashiell muttered. "This is quite syrupy and distressing."

"What are they wearing?" Bree hissed, appalled at the mass of dumpy khaki that now surrounded the room.

"Ah. That, my dear, would be the infamous Norwood nanny uniform. Mandatory. Yours for the next three years."

"They all look like nurses from World War II or something." She took a closer look and sighed. "Hats? Capes?"

"That would be the formal version. We'll have a more casual option for everyday." He snuck an appreciative glance at her. "It's a pity. Your hair is beautiful. Once your uniform is issued, you'll have to tuck it away, just like them. No loose locks on our nannies, here at Norwood. You must be prim and proper."

Bree blushed, and changed the subject. "What is that around their necks?"

"Whistles, I believe. Good for recalling your naughty charges should they escape your watchful eye."

With vigilance
And perrrrr-sistence
We pledge ourselves to thee
Norwood, O! Norwood
Du-ty, un-ceas-ing-ly!

Silence descended upon the room as Montoya-Craig drew a sharp hand before her, cutting off the warbling choir.

"Dismissed," Montoya-Craig barked, and the singers filed away.

The students themselves surged out as well, rushing the doors in their haste to see with whom they would be spending nearly every waking hour of the impending semester.

Bree sank back in her seat, stunned. "This is more like joining the army than going to college."

Dashiell flashed her a dashing smile, rising to offer her his arm. "What did you expect?"

"I didn't really know what to expect."

Dashiell looked at her with intrigue.

"It's a long story," she demurred.

"I'm sure you'll have time later to tell me all about it. For now, come, young American Bree. Let us determine what the Fates have in store for us."

In a courteous fashion, Dashiell led the way through the throng until Bree found herself face-to-face with the piece of paper that spelled out her assignment. She dragged a finger down the lists until she found her group.

"Oh, look—is that you?" she enthused. *Dashiell Heyward*, it said, typed very discreetly under *S. Susie Hilvale* and *Ruby Fripp*, and right above her own name, *Briana B. Parrish*.

"The one and the same," he said, bowing a half-bow. "The Fates have smiled upon us. And I see we have the House of Fewersham joining our team as well."

"Fewersham? I don't see anybody named Fewersham."

"Miss Hilvale. That is the name of her family's barony. Her surname is Hilvale. A very old and very, hmm, shall we say . . . interesting family, the Hilvales."

"I don't understand," Bree said, furrowing her brow.

"The muck of the gossip sheets. We can discuss it later."

"How do you know all this stuff?"

He smiled a sad smile. "When you are of the same fallen ilk as the Hilvales, you tend to cling to the stories. They make you feel less alone in the world."

"You're a baron, too?" she gasped.

"Err. Not quite," he said, looking a bit uncomfortable.

"Group 12! Group 12, approach the podium!" Montoya-Craig's voice rang out above the crowd.

"That's us!" Bree said. "Come on!"

They pushed through the crowd until they found themselves at the end of the hallway before a makeshift podium upon which the upper-class head, the same one who had led them in singing, now reigned. Bree peered up at her, taking in the tightly pulled bun of nearly black hair and the way she thrust her shoulder bones behind her, her back so straight it made Bree wince.

"Um. Group 12 reporting . . . sir?" Bree stumbled over her greeting while Montoya-Craig shot her a look of disdain. "I mean, ma'am?"

"*Ma'am?*" Montoya-Craig mocked her, drawing out the a's, rhyming with "jam," in exaggeration. "What do you think this is? Iowa?"

Bree blushed, unsure how to handle the reprimand.

"Come now, Miss Montoya-Craig," Dashiell began with his most buttery accent. "Surely you can be gracious to our colleague from America. This is her first time to the United Kingdom. Perhaps her first time away from home." He turned to face Bree. "Is it your first time away, Miss Parrish?"

Bree nodded, tongue-tied.

Montoya-Craig scoffed at his attempt at gallantry. "Oh, and we are to treat her with kid gloves, are we?" She took Bree in with a dismissive sweep. "Tell me, Miss Parrish. What exactly are your qualifications to join us here at Norwood?"

Bree flushed. "Qualifications?"

"Qualifications. The personal attributes and experiences which have prepared you for entry into the most rigorous program in child development in the former empire."

Bree stared. She had no qualifications, she thought, beginning to panic.

"Shall I use smaller words?" Montoya-Craig jabbed.

Bree flushed more deeply as she stammered on her reply.

"For goodness' sake," Montoya-Craig exclaimed. "I thought they spoke some form of English in our former colonies." She sat, smugly, a snicker of amusement escaping her. It was clear to Bree that she wasn't about to let up—not with such an audience. "So you are not, shall we say, academic. You must have some skill or experience with children, then?"

Bree gulped. "I was raised in an orphanage. I was one of the older children there, so I often helped with the others."

"An orphanage? How tragic and noble of you. So show us," the proctor insisted. "Sing us a lullaby, Miss Parrish."

Everyone turned to stare at Bree.

"Go on then," Montoya-Craig urged. "We're getting bored waiting on you. Give us a show."

Bree cleared her throat, digging deep into the recesses of her brain to find any song, any one at all.

With a deep breath, she began in a wavering, halting voice. She didn't get more than a few stanzas in before the crowd about her let out a collective gasp.

"Well!" Montoya-Craig cut her off. "I should say that is not a lullaby, Miss Parrish. Indeed, it is most unsuitable for young ears. I wonder that you are not even more embarrassed than you appear. What I want to know is how you managed to worm your way in here," she fumed, tapping a fountain pen insistently against her clipboard. "You clearly are not qualified. Not by my standards, anyway, which are one and the same as Norwood's. Furthermore, the rules are clear: English applicants first.

British second. European Union member applicants given third precedence. All others barred from attending Norwood."

Bree struggled with the distinctions Montoya-Craig was making. "English? British? I don't understand. And that can't be right—I held my admittance letter in my own hands."

"Of course you wouldn't understand. That said, the rules are the rules," Montoya-Craig stated.

"But—" Dashiell started.

"For one hundred and twenty-five years. No exceptions," Montoya-Craig cut him off with a spiteful smirk as she slammed her clipboard down upon the lectern. "I'm advising you not as your *colleague*, as you so artlessly put it earlier, but as your *superior*. For even though I am a student, I am not just *any* student. I am Head Girl. As the dean's right hand, it is my duty to enforce the rules that make Norwood so special."

Done with Dashiell, she peered over the lectern with barely concealed glee, pinning Bree with her stare.

"I am afraid we've had a huge misunderstanding, Miss Parrish. I am sure you'll agree with me, upon consideration, that Norwood is simply not the right place for someone like you. A dreadful mistake, to be sure, but one you will want to help us clear up, straightaway. Unless you are in fact British?" she offered in feigned hopefulness. She fingered the whistle chain around her neck, waiting for Bree's response.

Bree stared at her with a sense of mounting confusion. How did she win admittance, if those are the rules? She had not applied herself—her application had been submitted on the sly by a school counselor who hated to see her "waste her potential," without her knowledge. When the thick manila envelope of acceptance had arrived in the mail, proffering a full scholarship, both the orphanage director, Rodney, and its wealthy patron, Judy, had insisted she attend. What sort of strings did Judy have to pull to get them to bend the rules?

And could this fellow student really have her removed?

"Her admittance is not in error." From the side of the podium, Dean Albourn placed a dainty but firm hand upon her bulldog's elbow. "Move along, Montoya. You're slowing down the process and you know how that makes me feel."

"But—"

"You heard me. Your line of questioning is out of order. Move on, then."

Montoya-Craig screwed her mouth up in barely contained frustration. "Yes, Dean Albourn."

The dean stepped away to continue her rounds through the enthusiastic crowd—which, in a mixture of awe and terror, obediently parted before her—leaving Bree to push her questions to the back of her mind for later consideration.

"Where is the rest of your group?" Montoya-Craig snapped, her face a particularly nasty shade of purple.

"Susie Hilvale, here."

Bree turned to see the owner of the sweet, high-pitched voice behind her. A tiny curvaceous figure, crowned by a halo of honey-kissed curls, stood in a stray beam of light that trickled down from the peaked windows above. Her dewy complexion held a hint of cinnamon; her cheeks, bountiful as apples and supported by the kind of soaring bone structure most associated with cathedrals, were stained with a rosy, almost overripe tinge. Her azure eyes sparkled, their exotic almond shape fringed with impossibly long, black lashes. She was almost laughably demure, dressed out of a fifties sitcom—a neat circle skirt sticking out pertly below her knees, a string of pearls hanging decorously across her perky chest.

"Oh," Bree and Dashiell breathed as one.

"My dear Lady Fewersham, I presume?" Dashiell bowed over her hand smartly, quickly collecting his wits.

She giggled. "I'm no lady, sir, as you well know."

Montoya-Craig rolled her eyes.

"This reunion is quite touching, but I'm sure Your Lordship and Your Ladyship can catch up on the comings and goings of the peerage on your own time. Where's Fripp?" snarked their upper-class overseer.

"Here, miss." A regal, ebony-skinned woman stepped up to loom over them, her abundant braided hair neatly tied back in a bun. "Ruby Fripp."

"Fripp? What kind of a name is that?" Montoya-Craig frowned over her clipboard.

"A bit of this and that, Miss Montoya-Craig."

Montoya waved a frustrated hand. "No matter. You're here, that is all that I need to worry about. The administration has placed all of you scholarship students together for housing. You saw your rooming assignment?"

Scholarships? All of them, even the lord and lady? wondered a bemused Bree.

"Jaguar House," Ruby responded, neatly filling the awkward silence that followed the disclosure of the ill fortune of the families Hilvale and Heyward.

"Good. It's a bit of a walk, but it is more affordable and likely more comfortable for some of you, though it may require some adjustment by those of you accustomed to more regal accommodations. Here's a map," she said, thrusting some papers at them. "Uniform retrieval on the morrow. Make sure you make your assigned slot, or you won't have time for a proper fitting."

They stood staring at her.

"Well? What are you waiting for, then? Off with you. Find Jaguar House and mind the schedule. *Group 13!*" Montoya-Craig roared, dismissing them.

They shuffled off, contemplating their next move.

"Right, then," Ruby said, nodding resolutely, wrapping her trench coat more tightly around herself.

"Right," Dashiell agreed. "Off to Jaguar House we go."

Bree trailed after him. "We get a whole house to ourselves, Dashiell?"

He laughed. "No, silly. That's just the name of the building. It will be apartments."

"Then why do y'all call it a house?"

He tilted his head, looking at her with amusement. "You are a fine one for questions, Miss Parrish. But if you must know, the tradition of naming houses started with the rich and noble. They often named their edifices with important family names. Before street numbering became the norm, it was a good way to fix a location."

"It's so odd. As if a jaguar would ever be found here, in England."

He laughed. "Duly noted. Just be thankful we escaped some of the more tragic animal names."

"Such as?"

With exaggerated horror, he whispered, "Beaver's Cottage. Chipmunk's Croft, and the much maligned but misunderstood Mole's End. I'd rather be deposited in a place named after a cunning beast of prey than one christened for a foul-smelling rodent. Wouldn't you?"

Before she could reply, he switched topics.

"Now, you must tell me," Dashiell said with an appraising grin. "What is the name of that song you were singing? It was most suggestive. And whatever possessed you to sing it?"

Bree squared her shoulders, bracing herself for more ridicule. "It's called 'Mustang Sally.' I couldn't think of anything else. It was recorded in the town I grew up in—and is sort of famous. It just popped into my head."

Dashiell chuckled. "Intriguing. Montoya-Craig is bound to think you did it on purpose to mock her. If I were you, I'd let that be the story. We'll need our heroes in our first year, just as anybody else does, I imagine. You can teach me the words one day. I, for one, will have no problem cooing it to my future charges. Now, come along—we don't want to fall behind, do we?

———

A bit of a walk was an understatement. Of course, the fact that Dashiell misread the map and sent them in the opposite direction, past the Botanical Gardens and out to the M4 motorway, leaving them wheezing in fumes, did not help matters. Hours later, after retracing their steps and winding their way uphill past the commercial district, they found themselves standing before a distinctly seedy and dilapidated building. The fact that the dingy plaque on the wall reading "Jaguar ouse"—the H clearly long gone—did nothing to improve the building's sense of respectability.

Bree dragged an arm across her sweaty brow and frowned at Susie, who only seemed to glow in the aftermath of the humidity and car exhaust they'd all endured.

"This doesn't exactly look historic and charming," Bree muttered, staring at the graffitied walls.

"I'm sure Miss Fripp will be the first to tell you that graffiti have quite a storied past in the urban-built environment of England and is itself considered a modern art form of the highest esteem," Dashiell opined, winking mischievously at Bree.

Ruby harrumphed. "I'm from Notting Hill, you idiot," she said, pushing past him. "Not the Housing Councils. Come on, let's see what we got."

"I was thinking of the street artistry of Shoreditch, Miss Fripp, I assure you!" Dashiell called after her. Bree didn't know what they were talking about, but she was sure Dashiell had been rude. She scurried to catch up with Ruby. She found her in the superintendent's office, dangling keys around her finger.

"We're numbers six and seven. Let's go."

They trotted through the courtyard, scattered with the detritus of forgotten drinking bouts, cigarette butts, and discarded food wrappers, until they found the apartments they were seeking. Six and seven shared a vestibule, two entries facing each other under a caged light with a burnt-out bulb.

"Norwood rules. New for this year, obviously," Ruby said, shooting Dashiell a dirty look. "Boys and girls separate. You'll get an apartment to yourself, Heyward," she frowned, flipping him a key.

Bree found Ruby's accent, with her sing-songy, melodic rhythms, even while going over something as mundane as their rooming arrangements, fascinating—now that Ruby's nerves had settled after her encounter with Montoya-Craig, it had mellowed a bit to what Bree supposed was Ruby's more natural, London-blended sound. The hint of languid island rhythms in Ruby's voice was misleading. With its clipped consonants and shortened vowels, it had a relentless efficiency to it, made for winning debates and putting people in their place.

"We girls will have to crowd together. Let's see how bad it is." Ruby inserted the key, jiggling it until it clicked. She gave the door a hard shove with her shoulder, easing it open as its hinges whined and groaned.

"Welcome home," Dashiell muttered as they stepped into the musty room. He flicked on the light.

Susie sucked in her breath. "Well."

They looked around. They had entered into what could only be considered a common room, connecting directly into a tiny galley kitchen. The floors were dingy linoleum, the corners of some squares beginning to peel back in places. Pockmarked cinderblock walls surrounded them, stray cable wires hanging forlornly, the only window being the barred one that faced out into the neglected courtyard. A vinyl sofa and chair sat haphazardly in the center of the room.

Unfazed, Ruby strode purposefully through the room, taking stock of every detail. Bree followed, resolutely ignoring how the soles of her shoes stuck to the filthy floors as she walked, giving a faint pop every time she lifted her foot.

"What is the bedroom situation?" Ruby demanded of no one in particular. She turned into a corridor, the flickering fluorescent light above her turning her skin a strange shade of green before she disappeared to investigate.

Susie began inspecting the kitchen while they waited. It did not take long to inspect, though some aspects of it, like the presence of an absurdly small washing machine tucked under the counter next to the stove, fascinated Bree. A washing machine, but no drier. She would have to ask Dashiell or Ruby about that later.

Susie lifted a gritty piece of aluminum foil from the mini range between two fingers.

"How long do you think this has been here?" Susie asked.

Before anyone could speculate, Ruby reappeared. "One loo—attached bathtub and shower."

Bree rolled her eyes as Dashiell conspicuously mouthed the word "toilet" to her. Ignoring him, Ruby continued her inventory. "One bedroom with bunks and a single."

"You mean all three of us share a bedroom?" Susie sniffed. "Preposterous. Uncle Roger would definitely not approve of these arrangements."

"If your uncle is like my stepmother, he will turn a blind eye to anything so long as your tuition and board is covered, no?" Dashiell grimaced. "The perils of the impoverished peerage. Beggars can't be choosers. All such stuff." He looked down at his wing-tipped shoes and kicked at a loose tile.

"How much would an apartment like this run, anyway?" Bree asked. "I mean, under normal circumstances, if we weren't covered by scholarship."

"Two hundred, three hundred pounds, I suppose," Ruby speculated. "With a surcharge for us being so many people."

"Per month? That doesn't seem bad."

"Per week," Ruby snorted at her ignorance. Bree did the quick math in her head and gasped. It was hard to swallow such a huge expense for so little space.

"There's another door," Bree suggested brightly, hoping to divert herself from her disappointment. "Right off the kitchen." She gave the doorknob a shake. "Locked. Dashiell, try your key. I bet this connects to your suite."

On the other side of the door, they found a parallel layout of the same institutional drabness.

"See? It's really twice as big, if we combine our spaces by keeping the door open," Bree said optimistically as they circled back to the kitchen.

"Only he gets a whole bedroom and bath to himself," Ruby pointed out undiplomatically.

Dashiell inclined his head in mock sorrow. "Alas. I do not make the rules at Norwood. I simply adhere to them."

Susie turned on Dashiell, closing the space between them until she was uncomfortably close. Her eyes flashing with coquetry, she looked up at him through a halo of hair and trailed a well-manicured finger up his chest. "What is more important to you, my dear Lord Marquess? The stodgy rules of Norwood, or your sense of gallantry? Surely, you would not leave a lady such as me to suffer while you enjoy the largesse afforded you by accident of sex?"

Dashiell gulped and stared down at Susie, who even in her dainty heels barely rose to his chest. He straightened imperceptibly at the call upon his honor.

"What do you propose, my lady?"

"Simply that you and I, being of a common class and understanding, undertake to share your quarters. In a proper way, of course. Creating a better outcome for all concerned." She smiled magnanimously over her shoulder, batting her long lashes. "Just because our families find themselves in these dire straits," she posed ever so delicately, "does not mean we cannot strive to uphold the standards of our class."

"Oh, lord," Ruby muttered, doing nothing to stifle the Caribbean lilt that now surged to the forefront as she spoke. She crossed her arms and jutted out her hip. "Here we go."

"Well. I mean—" Dashiell stuttered as Susie turned back and gazed into his face, adoringly. "When you put it *that* way." He peered over Susie's mess of curls at the other women. "So long as you are amenable, of course."

Ruby snorted. "You two can keep to yourselves if you want. More space for all of us that way."

Susie clutched Dashiell's hands. "You've made a good decision, Dashiell. You'll see! Now let us discuss arrangements in our suite." She pulled him down the corridor, discreetly closing the door behind them.

"What was that all about?" Bree blurted, confused.

Ruby shrugged, her brown eyes sparkling with derision. "Classic manipulation. Combined with a good dose of class guilt, it looks like. She laid it on a little thick, I thought, but he seemed to go for it. Right suck eye, he was. She is pretty, after all."

"Suck eye? Class guilt? What do you mean?"

"'Suck eye' means he's an easy mark," Ruby laughed. "That's right. You Americans find it all so peculiar, don't you? I do, too, but I guess growing up here, I've gotten used to it. See, our Lady Fewersham is not an actual *lady*. She is the youngest daughter of the would-be Baron of Fewersham, who was dispossessed of his inheritance and passed over for the barony in favor of his younger brother."

"Passed over? Why?"

"According to the tabloids, he was a little too entrepreneurial for his daddy's taste. Things like selling porn subscriptions to the National Health

Service's sperm donation clinics." Ruby's eyes lit up with amusement, her face animated as she recounted the former lord's misdeeds. "Gambling debts that could have threatened the family holdings. Nothing illegal, just a bit unsavory, shall we say."

Bree blushed and tried to think of something to say. "Dispossessed means what, exactly?"

"He lost his title, and most of his inheritance, other than what his father settled on him at the time of the transfer of the title to his younger brother. So, our Miss Hilvale and her immediate family find themselves poor. Well, poor by their standards—probably quite above average by those of the rest of us. Nonetheless, they have a stink of unsuitability, of distastefulness, upon them. I imagine she's here because she needs to find respectable employment, something that will reinject her into high society but from a different angle, where she might wash away the sins of her father." She grinned mischievously. "Though after seeing how she went after Dashiell, I wouldn't put it past her to have grander designs."

"And Dashiell? She called him Lord Marquess. What is that?"

"Even mightier than a baron. Our Dashiell, he's the eldest son of a duke. Sadly, for him, his father is on his fourth marriage and with each divorce, the family estate has been reduced. His current stepmother apparently has quite the penchant for selling off the family chattel to fund her passion for horses and yachts."

"Chattel?" Bree was beginning to think that even a simple conversation here in England would be a series of vocabulary traps.

Ruby sighed, warming to her subject. "Oh, the bits and bobs they've accumulated over the centuries. Antiques. Jewelry. Artwork. It's been quite the scandal, all over the papers. She tries to sneak her sales past the stepchildren, so she doesn't get anything properly appraised. Giving it all away for a song. Tragic. Rumor has it the duke will need to sell off his lands and the family will lose its title."

She paused, a glint of speculation illuminating her face. "I would have assumed Dashiell would try to be a barrister or something. What do you call it in the United States? A lawyer. A very respectable profession for a family hit with hard times—he could even leapfrog into politics from there. Why he'd ever choose to be a nanny is beyond me."

"Is he really the first male to be admitted to Norwood?" Bree prompted.

Ruby nodded emphatically. "Yes. 'The Manny,' they call him in the papers. Maybe that's why he does it, for the celebrity aspect. The press has raked his father over the coals for being a dimwit ruled only by what's in his trousers, so I wouldn't put it past him to seek his revenge on the media. Use them to peddle tales from inside of Norwood and tell-alls from high-placed nannies, sell a boatload of exclusive interviews to *The Sun* or something and get the last laugh, making money off the slavering coverage."

Bree was slightly uncomfortable knowing so much about her roommates' private matters. And Bree definitely wasn't comfortable spilling the beans on her own, so she shifted the conversation.

"So, Susie is here because she has weak options. Dashiell for similar reasons. What about you, Ruby? Why did you come to Norwood?"

Ruby shrugged. "My mum's a private nurse, primarily caring for elderly shut-ins. My dad's an entrepreneur. Built himself up a series of mechanics shops throughout London. He specializes in imports, high-end things. They've worked hard, ever since they came from Trinidad, and I've learned from their efforts. I've always been the one to care for my siblings. I'm good at it. I like it. So, it seemed like a natural thing to do. I think I'd like to focus on special-needs children."

Bree's curiosity was piqued. "Do you have a lot of experience with them, then?"

Ruby snorted. "Nah. But I've done a market segmentation." She noted Bree's confusion and grinned. "I've identified which sort of families are willing to pay for what level service, and how many of them there are. It seems like all the rich people these days have their kids diagnosed with this and that—such special snowflakes now. Johnny can't tolerate noise. Pamela can't tolerate anybody touching her. Danny cannot eat anything that hasn't been blessed by a virgin riding a unicorn under a waxing moon. It takes a firm hand, I suppose, but these special-needs children can't be any more challenging than the senile old ladies I used to help my mother deal with. I wager it's the parents who are the difficult ones. That said, those high-society families, they'll pay good money for that kind of special service." Her soft chuckle did not take the edge off her naked ambition. "I aim to make enough to open my own agency—all special needs. It's a very practical choice."

"You seem to know a lot about rich people. And the nobility."

"For someone from the working class?" she scoffed. "I'm no *maco*. That's Trinidadian for 'gossip,'" she explained. "But watching the nobles' follies play out in the press is a pastime for us regular folks. You'd better get used to it, too, girl, if you plan to spend your life nannying out of Norwood. You think our new roommates are peculiar? You haven't seen anything yet. From the stories my mother tells . . ." She shook her head in disbelief. "Anyway—what's your story, orphan girl?"

Bree winced. "Not much to tell. My parents passed away when I was little. Car wreck."

"And you were never adopted out? Usually the young ones get snatched up quickly," Ruby mused, eyeing Bree speculatively.

"There were some irregularities with paperwork. Anyway, it doesn't matter. The orphanage has been my home, and Rodney, the director, has been like a father to me—the only dad I've ever known."

She pulled a photo of him, standing proudly next to her in her cap and gown at graduation, out of her wallet.

Ruby took it and squinted at it, tapping her finger on the image.

"That's him? You've got a black dad, then? I've seen black kids placed with white families, but never the other way around. That's brilliant. Maybe we'll get along even better than I thought."

Bree smiled weakly as Ruby placed the photo frame back in its place.

It was hard for her to put into words, exactly, how much Rodney meant to her—how much she owed him. She picked up her story, trying to keep it to the minimum.

"Well, it wasn't exactly a placement—after all, I was never adopted—but it is home. I wasn't even really planning to leave for college, but everyone seemed to think this degree would be good if I were to stick around and help, sort of transition to running the place down the road. Rodney is getting old, and his wife passed away when I was just a child."

"So, that business about being British—are you? British, I mean?"

Bree shrugged. "I guess it is technically possible, though I'm guessing there was some error. I didn't complete the application myself—a school counselor did it for me."

Ruby cocked her head, curious. "Why don't you ask her, then?"

Bree shook her head. "She died, just before graduation. It was very sudden, a shock to us all. She never even knew I was accepted."

Ruby shrugged. It was clear to Bree that she had no interest in sob stories and had more practical matters in mind. She turned to survey the kitchen, its walls covered with a thin sheen of grease. "Time to roll up your sleeves and turn this mess into our home."

The next forty-eight hours were a whirlwind. Multiple trudges up and down the fumy hill, going back and forth between the college and Jaguar House—for fittings, registration, shopping for groceries, books, and supplies—left her sore and out of sorts. She'd tried reaching Rodney but got the time zone difference wrong and was stuck leaving him a message on Thornton's ancient answering machine.

"What am I doing here?" Bree wondered as she stood on a block, being folded and pinned and tucked into a perfectly fitted khaki uniform, the armor she would bear to go out into the world as a Norwood nanny. The anachronisms of the white gloves, the silk tie with a pin through it, and the heavy woolen stockings only amplified the sense that she'd fallen through some sort of time warp. The pile of khaki skirts and trousers—"trousers," not "pants," she'd been corrected at her fitting, for "pants" referred to under-garments in England—polo shirts and cardigans, all emblazoned with the Norwood crest, were hardly attractive, if a little more practical and comfortable. She'd held her own, arguing with the tailor, that, given the coldish climate of England, she'd have all long sleeves, thank you very much. But she'd blushed when warned once again that her hair was unsuitable.

"A Norwood nanny is *never* seen in public with loose locks," the tailor scolded with a heavy Scottish burr, saying the words with such an expression of distaste she could imagine the visions of depravity running through his head. "From now on," he clucked, "you must pin the hair back tidily."

It was just as well. None of her hairstyling tools worked here, anyway, she'd learned that morning. After searching for twenty minutes for a light switch in the bathroom and finding it and the sole power outlet outside in the hallway—to prevent electrocution, Ruby had explained, as if the overblown British fear was perfectly reasonable—she'd plugged in her blow drier and blown it out due to the unanticipated voltage difference. The stench of the fried motor and burnt hair had wafted through their apartment and she'd resigned herself to having a more natural look.

"What am I doing here?" she thought as she scanned her courses after registration. There were two types of courses: those that qualified her for an undergraduate degree in child development, and her provisional courses for the Norwood Diploma. For the former, she had enrolled in *Introduction to Child and Family Psychology, Concepts of Learning, Physical Development,* and *Influencing Family Communications and Dynamics.* Or, as the upper-level students called them, *Brats and Spats, Junior's No Genius, Expending Excess Energy,* and *Dodge the Airborne Vase.* She'd also been forced to pick up a language requirement. They'd hustled her into Turkish, of all things, upon learning to their dismay that she had no foreign language background already. It couldn't be practical, she supposed, but they'd tutted and fretted and promised her it was phonetic and her "best choice at this juncture."

For the more hands-on certificate track, she was also taking *Food, Nutrition, and Health* (aka, *Navigating Nasty Nappies*) and *Children's Crafts* (aka, *Don't Eat the Glue*).

Dashiell, Susie, and Ruby, of course, were following the same track, all being issued the same schedules, schoolwork, rules, and clothing. Except Dashiell—what his manny uniform would look like remained a mystery. With that one exception, she had the sense that they were being turned into little automatons, the rough edges of individuality smoothed as they were prepared to go forth, deftly weaving the ideals of the long-vanished British Empire in the warp and weft of their young charges.

She looked around the apartment she would be occupying for the next year. A housekeeper had come to perform a deep exorcism on the decades of grease and dust that had accumulated into a patina on every surface of Dashiell and Susie's suite. When Dashiell had offered to have her purge their side, too, Ruby had viewed the generous offer with suspicion, but Bree had gratefully accepted before Ruby could refuse it. Somehow, the dispossessed nobility next door had found pieces of furniture that looked museum-worthy (probably out of some family vaults) and jerry-rigged a neat dividing wall to carve out two bedrooms in their cramped space. With an espresso machine and a tiny, mirrored Art Deco bar cart, their apartment had been transformed into something approaching elegant.

"I'm surprised the school didn't try to force them to part with a few of these lovelies," Ruby sniffed, trailing a finger over a beautiful inlaid wood box that Dashiell had carelessly strewn on a side table, "rather than fund them on scholarship. But I suppose that's one of the privileges of being of their class."

"What's that?" Bree asked.

"Having people look the other way," Ruby muttered, her lips pursed in disapproval. Bree tactfully ignored her, deep down thinking it all looked perfect, despite whatever unfairness that seemed to annoy Ruby.

With little to offer from her tiny pool of possessions, Bree had deferred most of the decorating of their half of the suite to Ruby. The newly clean walls were swathed in warm tropical and African fabrics. Cheery, colorful masks and a voluminous feathered headdress fanned in splendor across the walls. At first, it had puzzled Bree. Ruby was not exactly the cheery type.

"From Notting Hill Carnival," Ruby explained. "I'll take you there next year. You'll see a real spectacle then. If there's one thing all of us from the Caribbean have learned living in merry old England, it's that we've got to make our own sunshine."

The entire place was transformed into a cozy spot of warmth, defying the drizzle of Bath. All of Bree's things fit neatly inside the desk and cupboard—or "wardrobe," as Ruby dubbed it, the British alternative to a built-in closet—with which the room came outfitted.

Over her tiny single bed, Bree carefully taped up the movie poster, album covers, and postcards of her own home.

Ruby peered at them, impressed. "Your hometown is famous, then?"

Bree shook her head. "A little. Technically, though, it's the town over—Muscle Shoals—that's famous. Everybody knows the music that comes out of it. But almost nobody knows about the town itself. It's sort of a secret, outside of the industry and real music aficionados, even though the recording studios have been there for ages."

Ruby smiled and squeezed Bree's shoulder. "We'll find you some good music in London, on a break. Then you won't be so homesick."

The mention of home and the unexpected kindness from Ruby brought a momentary tinge of sadness. Even though it had only been a few days, Bree was learning that her best efforts to stay in touch with the children back at the orphanage would be stymied by time zone differences and busy schedules. She had the sinking feeling that she would soon be a hazy memory to most of them—even to sweet little Ollie, her favorite. It didn't matter, she reminded herself. They'd all be gone soon, anyway, whisked away into adopted families, their memories of Thornton and Bree vanishing along with those of too-tight shoes, hungry bellies, and night terrors—memories that Bree herself wished she could leave behind.

She shrugged off the feeling of self-pity that threatened to engulf her. None of that mattered anymore, now that she was here at Norwood.

As for the adults, Judy had never been a great one for talking, nor for any form of communication. She simply showed up when she willed, somehow knowing everything that had transpired in her absence—a commanding presence who was invariably swathed in Chanel, like a coat of armor. Even though she'd always taken a particular interest in Bree, Bree would be as likely to run into Judy on campus as she would be to receive a letter or a phone call from the orphanage's patron. Rodney's emails—he'd never learned to text—were brief, scattered with the sort of typos that came from two-fingered pecking at his ancient secondhand keyboard. And he would never waste precious cell phone minutes on a call to her.

Before she could feel sorry for herself all over again, Bree's reverie was interrupted by Ruby standing up and checking her phone.

"Right, then. Time to go, if we want to make the tour of the grounds. Wouldn't want that ninny, Montoya-Craig, to get on your case again."

Bree groaned, flopping over on her bed. "Really? It's raining. Can't we just stay in?"

"You call this rain? This is barely a drizzle. Up with you, girl. You of all people should be on this tour. Classes start tomorrow." She grinned a wicked grin and strutted toward the door, stopping with her hand on the knob. "This is your last chance to be awed by the campus, to revel in the glory of all that is Norwood, before you become an officially embittered and cynical student. Shall we?"

Bree sighed, diving off her bed and reaching for the umbrella that had practically become an appendage to her body. "All right. Let's go, before I change my mind."

Montoya-Craig gave a mean tour, punctual and informative, still commanding even in her Norwood casual uniform, whistle gleaming where it dangled from the chain about her neck. The campus itself was compact, enabling them to cover the ground in no time. From the auditorium where they'd begun orientation, seven lecture halls radiated out. An additional cluster, a state-of-the-art model day care, serving children from infant to age six, opened out onto an extensive park and playground area. Upstairs, a high-tech kitchen adjoined a laboratory that was outfitted with nutritional testing equipment. The other side of the kitchen opened into a nursing station, which itself housed a pharmacy, a phlebotomy station, a dormitory-style patient recovery area and a bevy of monitors. A discreet bathroom from which one could take and pass samples was tucked in a corner.

A separate recreation center housed a full gymnasium, pool, and exercise room, a cavernous basement for the teaching of defensive arts signaling its seriousness of purpose. Another building stood as the Arts and Crafts Annex. A central room with craft tables, lined with closets full of supplies, was surrounded by smaller cubbies where one could squirrel away and work on needlepoint, knitting, crocheting, quilting, decoupage, model building, or any of the other more solitary arts. Long arches of string crisscrossed the ceiling, ready with clips to display the artwork soon to be forthcoming. Bree noted with dismay the neat stack of first aid kits mounted on the walls, attesting to the potential for crafting accidents. A separate studio was set up for drawing and painting, a second with a phalanx of sewing machines, while a third area housed pottery wheels and kilns.

The library seemed unimpressive after the amount of space dedicated to the crafting. It was a plain concrete and glass structure, clearly a rather late addition to the campus. Study desks took up half the main floor. A few dusty card catalogs and microfiche readers, the marks of an earlier era, lined the walls, supplanted by the more modern computers that now took pride of place. Cozier chairs, sofas, and coffee tables dotted the basement, which hosted its own coffee shop. A big-screen TV took up the entire wall outside the shop. A rotating set of photos of beaming families seemed to be playing on continuous loop.

"That's sweet," Bree noted absentmindedly as she and Ruby trailed behind the tour group.

Ruby snorted. "It's not sweet. It's a marketing piece, done up for tours of prospective students. Can't you tell who those families are? Look here."

She drew Bree closer to the screen and pointed. Discreet labels in the bottom of each frame named the families in question. Ruby rattled them off without even having to look.

"The Royal Family of Sweden. The grandchildren of the American ambassador to France. The CEO of ClavisCorp with his extended family. The CEO of the biggest company in India, with his children. Robbie Davis, the cricketer, with his wife and children. Hugh Smothers, the fashion designer, with his husband and kids. The Prime Minister." She peered at Bree. "Don't you get it?"

Bree shook her head.

"These are the kind of families that, if you're lucky enough, you'll get placed with. It's what everyone at Norwood dreams of and why everyone tries so hard to get into the certificate program. We'll all get good placements if we graduate, but these . . ." she whistled low, "these kind of jobs catapult you into celebrity status."

She nodded at a billboard in the hallway. *Alumna Sharon Bergeron, Class of 2009, Nanny to the Grand Ducal Family of Luxembourg!* it proclaimed in bold-faced letters. *Lessons from The Other Side.* An eight-by-ten glossy of a beaming Bergeron was mostly obscured by a paper sign that had been stuck on with scotch tape. *Sold Out!* it read, hand-lettered in red.

"Sold out? But it's a whole month away," Bree said. "And school hasn't even started."

"I guess we'll have to be faster to get our spot next time," Ruby said, looking around at the empty lobby. "Come on. Let's catch up to the others."

The tour group had moved on, skipping the administration building to finish at the chapel. They could hear Montoya-Craig's officious voice booming over the group as they came closer.

"Of course, every student is expected to attend chapel services on Friday morning, as well as full Sunday services. Only officially excused absences will be permitted," Montoya-Craig intoned as she marched backward up the stone stairs leading to the vestibule. "Once inside, we will be in the Memorial Narthex, where you will be able to see tribute to those alumnae fallen in the line of duty."

The iron doors groaned as she inched them open, swinging them wide enough to permit the group to shuffle in.

Bree blinked, letting her eyes adjust to the dim light. A massive candelabra, now electrified, shed its watery illumination over the stones, darkened with the dust of one hundred years. Its weak light was amplified by vaulted skylights above—though in today's drizzly gray, they were of little help. A massive marble statue—a stern woman, holding up a burning torch to guide three young children clinging to her skirts—stood on an iron pedestal, taking up the greater part of the space between doors that led into the church proper.

"What's this? A shrine to Mary Poppins?" Ruby breathed seditiously into Bree's ear. Bree coughed to disguise a laugh.

Behind Poppins, row upon row of gilded plaques filled the walls. Each plaque was bronze, engraved with a name and two sets of dates: the years of the alumna's attendance at Norwood, and the years of her life. More recent plaques featured photos behind a heavy laminated plastic sheath, the fallen nannies staring gravely out from under the brown hats of their official Norwood uniforms. Some of the engravings left clues as to the alumna's untimely demise: *Threw self before oncoming vehicle, nobly sacrificing herself as she pushed the pram carrying her charge out of harm's way of a drunken driver. Drowned while testing, on behalf of her employers, a recently acquired personal submersible meant for family use. Trapped in debris while rescuing charges from fire. Prevented attempted kidnapping, losing life in process.* They stretched as far as the eye could see to the top of the wall and had begun to creep around the corner, onto the next wall. In the center of the wall, a simple sign declared: "Killed in Action."

Bree gulped. Maybe those coveted placements were not so desirable after all. Next to her, Ruby whispered, "I didn't know being a nanny could be so dangerous."

Montoya-Craig, overhearing, grinned maliciously. "Well said, Fripp. Nannying to the elite is not for the faint of heart. Your first and most sacred duty is to protect the lives of the children in your care. Sometimes simple accidents caused by carelessness—whether that of the nanny, or that of another member of the household—will claim a life. Sometimes, given the upper echelons of society in which we work, the work our employers do at the highest levels of diplomacy, government, and business, and the natural avarice of a jealous populace, our charges are targeted. And we are their first and last defense. Those not prepared to make the ultimate sacrifice should leave now."

She scanned the tour group, waiting for a cowardly soul to throw in the towel. But Bree imagined that they were far more afraid of her ridicule than of any imagined terrorist attack, kidnapping, or crisis. As they sat in silence, Dean Albourn emerged from the chapel itself.

"That's right, Margaret," she solemnly intoned, catching the last part of Margaret's challenge. "It will be hard for you all to appreciate the danger until you are further into your own training. But those who would harm the children entrusted in your care learn at their own peril how fiercely Norwood defends its own. Even when it costs one's own life, as one of our second-years so nobly experienced herself, sadly, just this past summer."

The dean's head inclined toward the doorway behind her and all heads swiveled, following her gaze. Workmen were dragging an easel into position in front of the door. The easel itself was festooned with an oversized wreath drooping with lilies. Propped inside of it was a massive headshot of an unsmiling young woman in formal Norwood uniform. *Alice Clark Memorial Service, 7 p.m. Sunday*, read the poster.

Ruby gulped.

"I still think we have more to fear from poopy diapers. I mean—nappies," Bree whispered to Ruby, attempting to lighten the mood.

"What's that, Parrish?" Albourn demanded. "Something to share with your class?"

As if watching a tennis match, the heads of the touring group swiveled to watch how Bree would parry Albourn's question.

Bree scrambled to find a suitable response, scanning about for a distraction. "Why are some of the plaques missing?" Bree asked, pointing back to the wall behind Poppins. Up in the middle rows, probably representing memorials twenty or more years past, two empty rectangles stood outlined in a rim of dust, the walls behind them darker from lack of exposure to decades of sunlight.

"Out for restoration," Albourn responded, looking at Bree with an arched brow. "Their photographs were damaged by a vandal. Why anyone would do such a thing . . ." Her voice faded. "Very observant of you, Parrish," she grudgingly acknowledged. "Your future charges—and their parents—will appreciate your eagle eye."

Bree sank into a deep breath, the temporary surge of adrenaline dropping as she realized she'd successfully avoided Albourn's admonition. Then the dean, looking up at the skylights and noting the fading light, drew her tiny body up into a taut bundle of officialdom for one last pronouncement.

"I hate to break up this gathering, but you all have a big day ahead of you tomorrow and I'm sure you'd like to go review your books so you are fully prepared for your first day of classes." She gestured grandly at the wall of dead nannies behind her. "Take inspiration from their lives, my dears. Do not disappoint their memory. And enjoy your first day of the Norwood experience. Good night. You are dismissed."

Chapter Two

FIRST TERM

Bath, England

"Miss Hilvale, your attire is completely unacceptable. Explain yourself."

Bree watched as Susie lifted her head from her lab table, her eyes amplified into wide, blurry pools through the snorkeling mask she was sporting.

"Whatever do you mean, professor?" she responded with a nasally high pitch.

"Why are you wearing athletic equipment in my laboratory?"

"I kept gagging at the last lab because of the smell," Susie explained, gesturing at the sodden nappy that was opened up on the table before her and Dashiell. "I thought this would help me complete the lab." Susie beamed, clearly pleased with herself.

"You do have to give her credit for trying," Dashiell interjected.

Unfortunately, Professor Harris was immune to patrician gravitas and overwhelming politeness. "I do not have to give her credit for anything. She looks ridiculous. What's more, such nonsense will not be possible when one is working with actual children."

"I doubt we will have to pick kernels of corn out of nappies to identify potential allergens once we are in a real placement," Dashiell muttered.

"Twenty points off this lab to both of you," the professor retorted, turning on her heel to stomp down the row. "And off with that ridiculous getup, this instant!"

Susie had barely pulled the rubber headpiece off when she clutched at her face and ran for the bathroom.

Dashiell sighed, abandoning his work to confer with Ruby and Bree.

"Poor thing has such a sensitive stomach," he commented, looking over his shoulder toward the bathroom.

"It's sort of a nanny job requirement to be able to handle bodily fluids and all manner of unpleasant things," Ruby noted drily. "Probably the only other thing more fundamental to the job is to not lose the children. If she can't hack it, why is she here?"

"Oh, you know," Dashiell responded, waving a hand in the air. "She's convinced she'll get placed with some handsome widower and wrap him around her finger to become the next Lady Blah Blah Blah."

Bree laughed. "Is that why she carries that book around all the time?"

He nodded with a sparkle in his eye. "Oh, yes. Don't ask her about *the book*. You'll get a full treatise on *Jane Eyre* and whatnot. Quite distressing, her interpretation of it, frankly—she's convinced herself it is an early precursor of that horrid American dating book, *The Rules*. Gets all gaga over the romance of it too. The gothic melodrama is entirely lost on her. She seems to completely overlook the crazed woman in the attic and all the nasty bits."

Ruby rolled her eyes. "Is she aware that her career plan is at odds with your current romantic situation?"

Dashiell chuckled. "No, I'm afraid not. That's one of the bits she overlooks. She is more hopeful than logical, our dear Susie. Nor is she gifted in the arts of childcare." Indeed, Susie's grades were atrocious. The only thing keeping her afloat at this point was the generous peer grading they'd all been assigning her, along with her foreign language course in Chinese, which, after ten years of earlier instruction, she was acing. "But at least she's consistent in her world view." A fond smile broke across his face. Bree thought he looked quite handsome, his face bright with affection—not mooning after Susie, but clearly taken with her. "I'd best go check on her and make sure she's all right."

"Why do you even bother?" Ruby challenged, clearly exasperated by Dashiell's easy acceptance of Susie's selfishness.

He mockingly clutched his heart. "Cupid's arrow has struck me! How can I resist?" He winked, a stray lock of dark, wavy hair falling across his forehead.

Ruby sucked her teeth. "Widowers don't fall off trees. What's to stop her from throwing herself at the first rich man who crosses her nannying path—married or not?"

Dashiell's face turned dark. Anger rippled across his features and, just as quickly, vanished, replaced by his normal veneer of politeness.

"She'll be wanting me, I suppose," he muttered, his voice a touch brusque, and walked off to fetch Susie.

Ruby shrugged off his anger. "I don't know why he's wasting his time with her. She won't make it past the semester. Mark my words," Ruby warned, tutting as she returned to the assignment in front of them, oblivious—or not caring—how her sharp tongue had vexed Dashiell.

"Maybe things will pick up for her," Bree offered.

"How? Shall we go over the litany of failures she has brought down upon our group so far? Let's see, where do we start?" She sniffed at the nappy and winced, marking a few items on the score sheet in front of her.

It was a long list, ranging from eyebrow-raising lack of common sense to outright catastrophes. In *Dodge the Vase*, Susie had asserted that a good way to calm a child having a tantrum at bedtime was to give him a hot toddy with a couple extra shots of whisky and trundle the child off to sleep, intimating with confidence it was what her father had always done with her. Susie had followed up that bit of brilliance by suggesting that if it didn't work, one could always threaten the child's inheritance as punishment. Their group had been forced to write 5,000-word essays on both the risks and warning signs of child alcoholism and the psychological impact of penia-phobia—the irrational fear of poverty—in young children as a punishment.

Then there had been their time attending a day care class as part of their "applied learning"—a regular requirement for *Junior Is No Genius*. An articulate five-year-old had cornered Susie, culling her away like a weak deer from the herd of more astute grownups, snowing her into thinking he was allowed to play with power tools from the Crafts Building. Her gullibility resulted in a trail of holes drilled through all of the cubbies and furniture in the Nursery, and a hysterical mother at pickup time.

In what was probably her worst moment, Susie had driven staples into Dashiell's hand when she lost control of the industrial staple gun during *Don't Eat the Glue*. That his wound hadn't become infected was a testament to Ruby's first aid skills.

Bree shook her head, reflecting on Susie's overabundant and slightly exotic brand of English beauty.

"I don't think Dashiell is drawn to her for her smarts, Ruby. Though she may be smarter than we're giving her credit for, if you think about how she always manages to get her way," she mused, thinking about the division of space in Jaguar House and how consistently Susie was able to manipulate Dashiell into writing her papers.

Ruby snorted with disgust. "She's barely able to function on her own. And she is using him."

"Using him?" Bree said, flipping over her worksheet and rapidly ticking off her answers—there was nothing in this diaper she hadn't seen before.

"He's a dalliance. A distraction until the Main Event—who will be someone with way more money than our Manny here."

Bree looked at him as he emerged from the bathrooms, cooing over Susie solicitously as she leaned heavily on his arm.

"Well, it looks to me like he doesn't mind being used."

"Humph. English people can be so stupid sometimes."

Bree arched a brow, amused by Ruby's outrage. "Aren't *you* English, Ruby?"

Ruby pulled a face on Bree.

"Class!" Professor Harris clapped her hands at them, trying to get their attention as if they were four-year-olds. "A brief announcement before dismissal! This weekend, we will be holding a special series as an adjunct offering to your *Physical Development* class, which, as you know, focuses on the growth and robustness of the child. Your ability to steward their physical growth depends, however, on your own physical fitness. This weekend's exercises will offer you, and us, the opportunity to assess your strength, agility, stamina, and hand-eye coordination so that you might have a realistic perspective on your own readiness for harnessing the energy of a child. Though it is not mandatory, we strongly encourage your participation. Your voluntary participation—and results—will be given special weighting in the selection of applicants for the certificate program at end of term. More information is posted on the bulletin board in the main hall."

Groans filtered through the lab as the first-years considered the prospect of another weekend ruined. Bree, on the other hand, felt a surge of adrenaline and confidence—perhaps the first she'd experienced since her arrival.

There was no point in being at Norwood if she didn't get into the certificate program, Bree reasoned. With Susie's scores weighing down the group's midterm grades, Bree wasn't as certain of success as she wanted to be going into the final stretch. But after years of minding the younger orphans and doing odd chores around the orphanage farm, she knew she was up to a physical challenge, so the weekend's extra exercises were definitely on her agenda. They might be just the thing to make the difference and get her into the certificate program after all.

—

"You can't possibly go to bed early," Dashiell pooh-poohed when she turned down the invitation to hit the finer spots in Bath on Friday night, preferring to get a good night's sleep in advance of the next day's drills. "We haven't been anywhere since the term started. You're coming with us."

"But aren't y'all attending the outing tomorrow?" she reminded them.

"The biggest physical challenge I am planning on tackling tomorrow is walking my bag of laundry to the door so the service can pick it up," Dashiell smugly responded. "And then stirring my martini."

"Are you sure you're on scholarship?" Ruby retorted.

"We all need to do it," Bree reasoned with them. "We are all aiming for the certificate program, right?" She included Susie in her statement, knowing in the bottom of her heart it would be tough for Susie to be a viable candidate. But they had to at least try. After all, they were a team.

"What's your point, Bree?" Ruby growled. Ruby had top marks and she knew it. Her admittance into the certificate program was a certainty. It was after six and everyone could hear her stomach was gurgling. It was obvious she was eager to get out of the apartment and enjoy a night out.

"Y'all heard Professor Harris—participating will only help our chances. We should take it seriously."

Ruby sighed. "She has a point. As much as I hate to admit it," she acknowledged. "And Susie's unending mistakes could still screw things up for us."

"But that doesn't mean we have to be sticks in the mud," Susie averred, rolling her eyes. "We can still go out. It will help loosen us up for tomorrow. Besides, Bree," she purred, tucking her arm into Bree's, "wasn't it you who shared the inspiring words of your orphanage director as he sent you off into the great unknown Britain?"

"'Beauty. Charm. History,'" Dashiell quoted back at her. "You can't go back at Christmas and tell him that all you've seen of Bath's graces is the inside of a dirty nappy."

She'd always been too serious. Rodney had told her that, time and time again. She thought of the allowance that Judy had set aside for her so that she might enjoy her time in Bath, when her studies allowed. She counted every pound and pence, worrying out the exchange rate daily to be sure she wasn't wasteful, planning her meals down to the half piece of toast to meet her budget. Perhaps she had earned herself a break.

"All right. I'll go. But it has to be an early night. Our wakeup call is six a.m."

———

The crowd at the pub spilled out into a patio area packed with picnic tables, here and there dotted with umbrellas. Along the building itself was a large swathe of tables covered by a striped awning. Dashiell flashed something out of his wallet at the host managing the crowd. The host broke into a wide smile and led them past several waiting groups, directly over to an empty table rather near the makeshift stage.

"What did you have to do to land a table so fast, mate?" Ruby asked, impressed.

"I'm a shareowner," Dashiell said quietly. "The Bells is community owned, sort of like a cooperative. When it did a share raising and opened up its ownership scheme, I jumped at the chance. Just a few quid, mind you."

"Figures," Ruby retorted, rolling her eyes.

Bree listened to their exchange, wondering what it would be like to have extra money about to invest in things like bars. It didn't seem consistent with being on scholarship, but what did she know?

She was quickly distracted by her surroundings. The leafy outdoor setting was already jumping. From the accents she could overhear, the crowd seemed local, rather than tourists, and there was an odd bicycle parked behind them.

"The Pizza Bike," Dashiell explained, noting her confusion. "Some of the best pizza in Bath, on wheels. They'll be packing up soon, I imagine. Maybe you can grab a slice before they are done."

She shook her head. She hadn't budgeted a lot for entertainment and didn't know how much a drink would cost her—she wanted to watch her spending carefully tonight.

Susie poked at Dashiell. "Get our server's attention, would you? I'm dying for a gin and tonic."

He made a *tsk* sound, disapproving. "Why would you get a G and T here? This is a proper pub, Susie. They have ale here."

Susie demurred. "I shan't drink it. A nice, pure gin will keep me clear-headed for tomorrow."

Ruby snorted. "As if academic performance ever came into your calculations, Susie. I'm guessing you have another reason."

Susie smiled. "Ale makes me bloated."

Dashiell laughed. "Gin it is. Ruby, ale for you, then?"

Ruby nodded briskly.

"And you, Bree? Shall I pick you one of the local brews?" Dashiell paused, waiting for her answer.

She hesitated. "Sure. I guess. Something inexpensive," she added, blushing.

Dashiell smiled kindly. "Never fear. Ale flows like a river here. It's plentiful and cheap. Even the good stuff." He flagged down a server who, after wrapping up an order, wound her way through the tables to help them.

"Three Summer Lightnings and a Scout and Sage, please," Dashiell said efficiently.

"Scout and Sage *Pink*," Susie interjected.

"Got it. Any food?"

They shook their heads.

"Suit yourself. I'll be back in a jiffy with your drinks."

The ale went down easy.

A little too easy, Bree thought to herself as she counted the empty pints crowding the center of their table. The crowd was raucous now, hooting and cheering on a televised soccer match along with the band that now occupied the little black steps that stood in as an outdoor stage. She couldn't follow the sport, and the band was eighties-style hair metal, nothing that Bree liked. It was making her head hurt.

"Where's our server? We haven't seen her in ages," Ruby wondered aloud.

"Why don't I go into the bar and order another round?" Dashiell offered.

"No, let me," Bree insisted. "I haven't even seen the inside of the pub yet. I'm curious. Susie, do you want another gin and tonic?"

She looked at Susie, who was still nursing the gigantic glass globe that was her first drink.

"No, but some water would be lovely. Maybe ask for ice cubes? They'll give them to you, since you're American."

Bree headed into the pub.

It had a close feel, the ceilings low and festooned with vines that hung down, creating an almost secretive atmosphere. The brick fireplace was empty—too hot a night, with this big a crowd—and papered over with hand-lettered bills advertising different drinks, concerts, and other local events. The bills, posters, and framed photos covered all the walls, layers of history that spoke to the deep roots the pub had laid in the Bath community.

Small round tables packed with drinkers were crammed onto the floor. Somehow, another stage was jammed in as well. More people crowded the bar. Behind the long, polished counter was a thicket of pulls and bottles, the blinking computer screen used to ring up customers' bills the only nod to the modern age.

Bree took in the three-deep crowd.

"You'll have to push your way through. Or make eye contact with the barkeep. Otherwise you'll sit here for hours, waiting your turn. Americans always do. You're too polite—rule followers."

Bree turned to see who it was who had understood her dilemma so quickly.

"You!" she exclaimed. "I recognize you! You're the alumna from the Norwood convocation." Bree had almost overlooked the woman, who seemed so different out of uniform. The woman from the convocation stage was now dressed in black form-fitting jeans and a black turtleneck that highlighted her muscled physique. Her hair hung down heavily, a shiny sheet of blue black that curtained her face. Her pointy boots, tipped in steel, sported an aggressive three-and-a-half-inch block heel, giving her a good half-head over Bree.

"Gul Avci," the dark-haired woman introduced herself, proffering her hand. "Just a few years ahead of you."

Bree grasped her outstretched hand. It was a firm shake, business-like. Controlled.

"Watch," Avci said. She shifted subtly, her body seeming to take up more space and her chin jutting forward. She cocked her eyebrow and, just like that, drew the bartender's eyes like a magnet.

"Summer Lightnings, is it? Three?" Avci asked.

Bree stared. "How did you know?"

Avci laughed. "Lucky guess. I'll make it a double order. Service is slow. And I'll throw in a round of shots. On me."

She took care of ordering and turned back to Bree.

"What's an American doing at Norwood?"

Bree flushed. "I could ask the same of you. Turkey is not in the EU, is it?" She didn't like the note of defensiveness in her own voice, but the rounds of ale had wiped out her ability to filter.

Avci smiled. "Touché. But technically, I am British. I was adopted out as a small child."

Bree paused, her alcohol-induced fog making it hard for her to process. "You were an orphan?"

Avci dismissed the question. "Ancient history. I consider myself a Turk, for all intents and purposes. My British background just got me a leg up. What about you? You never answered my question."

Bree was struggling with what to say but, with the way Avci's eyes fixed on her, she felt compelled to answer. She needed to say something.

"I was an orphan, too. But I don't know how I got in, to tell you the truth," she blurted, instantly regretting it.

"Another lucky break," Avci interjected smoothly. She eyed Bree intently. "That makes us a pair, doesn't it? Have you gotten into your trials yet?"

"Trials?"

"No, then."

"Do you mean the physical strength tests for extra credit? They start tomorrow. We're all going," Bree added, strangely eager to win this woman's approval.

Avci nodded. "Are you prepared?"

Bree was baffled. "What do you mean, prepared? How can we prepare for something that was just sprung on us? We don't even know what it is we'll be doing."

"I mean, are you prepared to do what it takes? Whatever that may be?"

Bree didn't know how to answer.

"Ah, look!" Avci clapped her hands with fake cheer, effectively changing the subject. "Your drinks have arrived." Avci watched as the server passed the loaded tray over to Bree.

"Go back to your friends. Have a shot or two. You'll need it. Liquid courage and all that. Oh, and before you go, head to the Back Room. That's where the real music will be. Something decent, not that stupid eighties tribute band you're suffering through outside. And no tourists," she said, pulling a face.

Despite her fog, Bree felt she had one shot to ask a decent question, to learn something important from Avci. She struggled to find the words as she balanced the weight of the sloshing pints.

"See you around, American Bree."

Bree opened her mouth to stop her. But before she could say anything—before she could ask, *What's going to happen tomorrow? Why will I need courage? What do you mean, whatever it takes?*—Avci melted into the crowd, gone.

The insistent droning of her alarm clock perfectly matched the throbbing of Bree's head when she awoke the next morning.

"Oh, God," she moaned, wanting more than anything to pull the covers back over her head and go back to sleep. She swung her arm helplessly at the clock, trying to make it stop.

"Wakey, wakey, Sleeping Beauty," Dashiell chirped at her as he whisked the comforter away to expose her to the early morning chill. "You'll be needing this, I shouldn't wonder." He thrust a steaming cup of espresso in front of her nose and left two ibuprofens discreetly next to her clock, smugly hitting the "off" button. "Suck that down and you'll be feeling better in no time."

"What happened?" she groaned into her cup, inhaling the bracing aroma of scorched coffee beans.

"It appears that we miscalculated your ability to pace yourself, dear Bree. And I must say, the pub was no match for your enthusiasm for dancing, or whatever it was that you were doing."

Bree buried her face deeper in the coffee cup. She'd warned them that watching endless matches of soccer—no, no, *football,* as they kept correcting her—was not her idea of fun.

"It would have been less embarrassing if it had been my kind of music," she muttered into her cup, trying to remember exactly what she'd done once the singing had begun.

Dashiell chuckled. "It was quite charming, actually. I'm glad you convinced us to check out the Back Room. I must admit, your performance last evening has raised my curiosity to see this music nirvana you call home. But no matter. Thanks to us, you will be on time for the Great Trials, or whatever these things are called, regardless of last night's indiscretions. On your feet. You don't have much time to waste."

She watched him leave over the rim of the cup and considered going back to bed one last time.

"Don't you dare!" Dashiell shouted from down the hall.

Sighing, she rolled onto her feet and stood, instantly regretting her decision. The movement to upright jolted her brain as if she were standing inside a ringing church bell. Desperately, she grubbed after the two pills and bolted them down, and then moved on to dig through her dresser in search of her official Norwood physical education kit.

An hour later, they stood assembled in the mist on the green lawn of the main quad, the soft puffs of their breath floating in the frigid air before them where they joined with forty others in their class.

"There will be three tests over the course of today and tomorrow," their *Physical Development* instructor, Miss Kent, began. A murmur of surprise went through the class and a number of students, heads shaking, picked up their gear and walked off, unprepared to surrender their entire weekend to the enterprise. "If you are here with your entire group, you will be kept in that team. Broken groups will be reassembled to create new teams for these two days. Teams will rotate through three exercises designed to test your strength, endurance, coordination, and agility. These exercises are not on campus, so it is imperative you follow the instructions provided you by the proctors and remain with your larger group at all times. You will not be back until well past dinnertime"—another ripple of muttering tore through the group—"at which point we will review logistics for the morrow. Sustenance will be provided throughout the day. Any questions?"

A bevy of hands shot into the air. Bree ignored the low hum of questions and responses, breathing deeply to cope with the unfamiliar battle between modern medicine and hangover that was going on within her brain. Her head let loose one last tremor of throbbing protest before going silent, conceding defeat to the ibuprofen.

"Very well. Good luck today. I cannot underscore how important physical prowess is to your future as a Norwood nanny." Miss Kent paused dramatically. "I don't have to tell you how Alice Clark's struggle, indeed, her very ability to ensure that, while she perished, the family in her care survived, depended upon the vigor and vitality we begin to instill in you today, through these exercises. I beg of you, take them seriously. If not for me, for Alice." She sniffed, holding a crinkled lacy hanky up to her nose.

Bree caught Ruby rolling her eyes. The constant pleading to *please, do it for Alice*—emotionally blackmailing their entire class into such mundane tasks as learning the known food allergens in alphabetical order—was getting old for all of them.

Kent cleared her throat, clearly stricken, before wrapping up. "And please, remember to report any medical emergencies immediately to your proctor."

Dashiell looked over at Bree. *Medical emergencies?* he mouthed, cocking one eyebrow.

"The only medical emergency we should worry about is Bree chundering from her hangover," Susie whispered, clearly enjoying, for once, the upper hand.

"She's fine," Ruby intoned, slapping Bree heartily on the back. "Look! The pills have kicked in. Just keep her hydrated. No problem. Right, Bree?"

Bree smiled weakly. "Right."

"Group 12? Are you all participating?" Bree followed the ringing voice from where it came, far across the quad, and gave an inward groan of disappointment. Margaret Montoya-Craig was walking briskly toward them, clipboard in hand.

"Who died and made her queen?" Bree muttered.

Ruby snorted and then hurried to whisper back to Bree. "Well, she *is* practically Norwood royalty. She's third generation. And three of her sisters and cousins have been placed with the royal families of Denmark and Spain, plus the Lauderstones in the United States. Though by all accounts they find that family too nouveau riche and want her to land something better."

Before Bree could comment, Montoya-Craig was upon them.

"You're all here?" she asked again, suspiciously. "No shirkers?"

"Not a one, miss," Ruby responded in full seriousness.

"Excellent. Excellent. Though surprising," Montoya-Craig intoned, shooting an unsubtle gaze at Susie and Dashiell before crisply checking their names off on her clipboard. She had chosen to dress in her formal uniform this morning and looked as if she were about to lead them into battle. "You'll join with Groups 11 and 13. The bus is waiting over there," she said, gesturing toward the parking lot that stood outside the glossy black scrolled-iron gate. "We will depart in five minutes." She looked at Susie with distaste. "Any business you need to take care of, such as vomiting and the like, do it now. There are no loos on the bus."

She marched off to corral the other groups.

"Good to know your reputation precedes you, Susie," Ruby smirked.

"It's Bree she should be worried about today, and not me," Susie responded with a toss of her silken ponytail.

"Yes, we know—you're an experienced sophisticate who can hold her liquor. Too bad that's not a prerequisite for the certificate. Right, then— let's board the bus," Ruby said dismissively.

The minibus lurched out of the lot and headed toward historic Bath. The cinderblock and brick of the town's working-class neighborhood gave way to the limestone and gold of glorious buildings glowing in the early morning light. Their symmetry and precision promised a world of order and progress, predictability and sense. The bus swung past the tiered columns of the famous Royal Crescent, skirting a wide expanse of lawn, and wound its way through a labyrinth of streets, abrupt starts and turns making it difficult to discern any direction.

One intrepid classmate broke the silence. "Where are we going?"

"To the train station," Montoya-Craig responded, offering up no further information.

Their ride ended abruptly before the "Bath Spa" sign. Their proctor herded them efficiently off the bus, shooing them inside the cozy station, itself a mash-up of Victorian whistle-stop, ancient Roman aqueduct, and boho office building. Montoya-Craig pressed a ticket into each of their hands.

"The next train's for London," she urged, pushing them forward. "We must be on it."

"Where are we going?" Bree asked.

"And in what class? Please tell me we aren't in standard," Susie added.

"You'll see," Montoya-Craig barked, obviously preferring to keep them in the dark and ignoring Susie's whines of displeasure at not being in the first-class car. They settled into their seats, the tired among them jamming in earphones to drown out the ambient noise with music, while the more industrious took advantage of the hour-and-a-half journey to study.

Bree fiddled with the construction paper, glue, and colored pencils she'd stowed in her backpack, an upcoming craft assignment for *Don't Eat the Glue* looming on her to-do list.

They connected to the underground in the cavernous mouth of the next station. Though Bree had taken the Tube on her way to Norwood (marking herself as an immature tourist when she giggled at the unfortunately named stop Cockfosters), it was still quite new and overwhelming to her.

"Keep up now! Mind the gap!" Montoya-Craig tutted at her, pulling her back into the disciplined march through the station. Bree sped up, cursing the overpacked bag she'd slung over her shoulder, and merged in with her team, wondering what the gap to which the older girl referred was, and why she should mind it at all.

"You all have your passports?" Montoya-Craig questioned as they clambered up and down the stairs. She asked innocently enough, but it was a test—they'd been warned that a proper nanny was prepared for any emergency, including a sudden trip out of the country, and so had been commanded to keep their passports and other essential paperwork on themselves at all times.

"Oh, God," Dashiell groaned under his breath. "She can't possibly."

"What?" Bree whispered.

"Let's hope I'm wrong," he grimaced, and kept climbing, allowing Montoya-Craig to shoo him into the Tube car along with all the others without a protest.

When the Tube spit them out at their next stop, he hung his head dejectedly. He shuffled along in anticipated misery until Montoya-Craig saw fit to reveal to them the next stage of their journey.

"You may surmise at this point that we are taking the Eurostar to Calais," she announced excitedly. "That's in France," she added, looking pointedly at Bree, "for those of you who may be unfamiliar with our local geography. We will arrive there at approximately 12:05. Once there, we shall migrate to the camps. They are greatly reduced from what you have witnessed in the past year's television coverage, but a core of refugee containment and processing remains in operation. There, we shall spend five hours volunteering in the kitchen operations. This shall be your only exercise on this day. This volunteer activity, alongside our journey itself, shall be a test of endurance—you will be on your feet for the entirety of your time in Calais, with no rest breaks. If we remain on schedule, you'll arrive home at a very late hour."

"Thanks a lot, Bree," Ruby whispered venomously.

"Sorry," Bree whispered back contritely. She looked at Susie, who looked even paler than usual, and saw Dashiell patting her arm comfortingly.

"It'll be all right," he reassured her.

Whatever was in Calais, Bree was guessing it was going to test more than their endurance.

It was a pit out of the third *bolge* of Hell. A permanent sludge threatened to suck off their tennis shoes as they picked their way through the rows of tents and plywood shacks that composed what remained of the refugee camp at Calais. Bree couldn't identify what was in it—rain-induced mud, to be sure, but the muck of filth and disease as well—and it stank of death. She held back a gag, choking on the stench of sweat, vomit, and waste, a smell laced with things much worse than anything she'd ever faced in a nappy. Elsewhere, great mounds of earth were heaped over the wreckage of bulldozed shelters. Children played a makeshift game of cricket, clambering across the moon-pocked expanse that spread behind the barbed wire. Billows of smoke drifted above them—somewhere in the camp something was burning.

"We're just about there!" Montoya-Craig said brightly, her starched khaki uniform and sweeping cape looking sorely out of place in this landscape of grays. Here and there, men poked their heads out of the openings of their homes, faces gaunt, eyes set too large against jutting bones and the shadows of days without shaving.

"Who are these people?" Bree whispered, tugging at Ruby's sleeve.

"Refugees. Or intruders. Depending on whom you ask," she answered, careful to not fall off Montoya-Craig's brisk pace. "Mostly from places in the Middle East and Africa. I thought they'd shut this place down and sent the people away, but I guess it's still operating."

"It's operating, all right," Montoya-Craig interjected. "In diminished circumstances, but definitely still here, as you can see. But the press has forgotten about it. They've moved on to the next shiny object of the news cycle," she finished, her disapproval evident.

Bree swallowed hard. She didn't doubt the proctor was right, but she could hardly blame the press if they'd forgotten about this hellish place.

She'd scarcely been here ten minutes and she wanted to put it and its sadness behind her, never looking back.

"In here," Montoya-Craig gestured, pulling back the flap on a massive olive-green tent. Bree barely had time to register the stenciled sign outside the flap—*Cantine* in French—before ducking her head in to enter.

The instantaneous rumble, borne on a wave of heat, threatened to knock Bree over. Her head was filled with the cacophony of clattering pans and banging pots and the steady *thwack* of ladles hitting the sides of proffered trays, dumping their ambiguous contents into neatly shaped spaces. It formed a steady drumbeat against which murmured thanks, muted conversations, and shouted protests took place. The tin-covered lights, strung haphazardly across the ceiling of the tent with extension cords trailing behind them, cast harsh shadows, creating an atmosphere of suspicion and interrogation.

She held her breath, wondering. Hundreds of people were shuffling through the canteen. She recognized the looks on their faces. They were the same as those she'd seen on the new orphans who found themselves at Thornton, their expressions betraying them as they struggled to adjust to their new situation. Some waited patiently, the spirit in their eyes snuffed out. Some were agitated, annoyed with the injustice of the turn their lives had taken through no fault of their own. Some looked annoyed—perhaps at having to eat the same mush they ate yesterday and the day before and the day before, annoyed that their blankets were too thin and scratchy, annoyed with the constant queuing and paperwork and pointlessness of it all. Others looked around, eyes darting, watchful, waiting for the next threat—still not feeling safe, no matter the miles behind them.

Yes, Bree recognized those looks. They were looks of despair. She hadn't thought to see them here, imprinted on the faces of hundreds of strangers who had absolutely nothing in common with Florence,

Alabama. But then again, she'd had no idea what she and her classmates were walking into.

"With me," Montoya-Craig said through gritted teeth as she led them through the crowds toward the kitchen. The aid workers dishing up the food looked dead on their feet, their official status denoted by the sky-blue vests worn over their civilian clothes—the only thing distinguishing them from the run-down refugees.

"How long have they been here?" Bree prompted.

"The line never stops," the proctor answered. "This is the only canteen left open now. When they did the first sweep to shut down the main camp, they tore down all of the sanctioned stores, along with the meager grocery stores that had popped up. So, this is it. Thousands of people served through here, every day. All of it dependent on aid."

She turned to face them all. "The good news is you are here to give them a break. Grab a hairnet and a vest and you'll be briefed by Thomas, the supervisor on-site."

Thomas did not waste any time. He wasn't exactly unfriendly, but Bree could tell he was one, like Montoya-Craig, who wouldn't suffer fools lightly.

"The rules are simple," he began, without so much as a hello. "Keep yourself, your utensils, and your workspace clean. The last thing the camp needs is an outbreak of salmonella or some other foodborne disease. Not even a handshake is permitted. Serve only with your right hand, out of respect for the rules of the primarily Muslim clientele."

Bree was impressed that he used the word "clientele" to describe the refugees. She imagined that, after being left with so little, being on the receiving end of that sort of attitude—being treated like a customer, instead of someone who was trapped here against one's will—would restore a little of the camp dwellers' dignity.

"Whatever your station," Thomas continued, "one scoop only of meat, and one of vegetables. If someone doesn't like the vegetables, they can't double up on the meat, or vice versa. If a client wants to give their food to someone else, that is their business." He looked very stern on this point. "But they do it themselves, after they've been through the line—there is too much room for misunderstanding down the queue, otherwise. Plus we can't afford the slowdown. Maintaining our throughput is critical."

Ahh, Bree thought. *Now the dehumanization. Throughput. Like a machine.*

"Be polite, but do not encourage conversation. After what they've been through, and what still awaits them, many of the people here are on the edge of a meltdown. A simple query or kind gesture could be misperceived as a slight, or serve as a painful reminder of something lost and irretrievable. This camp is a tinderbox; the situation is too volatile to afford such breakdowns."

Bree internalized his advice as he reemphasized it.

"Just keep the line moving. Do not engage. If things seem tense, call for backup." He pointed across the tent.

She followed his gesture and looked over to where an emergency walkie-talkie hung on a peg.

"Two minutes," Thomas told them. "It will take two minutes once you sound the alarm for security to get here. Better safe than sorry."

Bree carefully went through the steps: stowing away her backpack, tucking her long ponytail inside the hairnet, pulling on the vest—yellow instead of blue, denoting them as guests—scrubbing her hands with sanitizer, and finally slipping into the thin silicone gloves that would prevent her from coming into contact with the food. She tucked the long ends of the gloves tightly up under her sleeves.

"You'll be more comfortable with your sleeves rolled up," Thomas warned. "It gets hot in here."

She shook her head, tugging her sleeves down more firmly to reach her wrists.

"Suit yourself," he shrugged.

When she'd passed Thomas's inspection, she took her place behind an immense bin of pita bread. The woman she relieved wearily passed her a pair of tongs.

"If you do deep knee bends from time to time, your back won't hurt so much," she advised as she slipped away, already fingering the pack of cigarettes in her breast pocket. Bree didn't have time to thank her for the tip as the line surged, the throngs of hungry mouths demanding her attention.

She tried to follow Thomas's rules, but it was hard. It felt impossible to not give a kind word to someone so obviously beaten down, ridiculous to think that you could be curt, when all someone sought was reassurance or even the simple recognition that they were human.

And so, as the line and the hours wound by, she loosened up. They all did, the cement of indifference and fear with which they'd built their stony wall of silence crumbling under the boredom and curiosity. It was rarely more than a few words—they didn't have time for much else, and the men (for it was mostly men) seemed suspicious or shy around the women, in particular. But it seemed to make a difference.

And then, as she yawned and stretched, trying to ease the ache in her lower back, she saw them.

The children.

They bunched together near the door, a knot of them beginning their journey to the serving station. As they inched ahead, more followed, ducking inside the tent flap as if wishing they were invisible. They moved in clumps—from what she could spy, they'd sorted themselves roughly by age and gender—their band periodically punctuated by a stray adult in a blue vest.

Her hand, still clutching the tongs, hovered over the bread, the sight of them jolting her.

"Parrish! Do we have a problem?" Montoya-Craig barked at her from over her shoulder. The line was bulging at her station as refugees waited patiently to be served.

"No, ma'am," she replied, wincing as she saw Montoya-Craig's displeasure. Bree had stumbled over the pronunciation again, rhyming it with "jam" in a way that was sure to remind the proctor of her American wrongness. And it was the wrong thing to call her, anyway. "Miss," she corrected herself, hurriedly shoving pitas at the waiting men, not caring if she accidentally overserved them. "I was just surprised to see all those children in the line. They seem mostly alone."

"Indeed," Montoya-Craig agreed with a solemnity that took Bree by surprise. "About half the refugees coming through are children, many of them orphaned in the fighting or even along the way. It's a sad thing, don't you think?"

A tight knot took its place in Bree's chest. It wasn't sad—it was tragic. She'd no memory of her own parents, but she'd spent plenty of long nights wondering about them, cursing them (even though it couldn't have been their fault) for the state of abandonment she found herself in, and worrying about what would happen to her. And she'd been lucky—kind strangers had found her, safely thrown from the wreckage of the vehicle in which her parents had died, and they, along with the authorities, had seen to her placement at Thornton. But to have gone through war and fled your country, and to be faced with this—alone? She shuddered.

"When do we get a break?" Susie whined from down the line.

"You don't," Montoya responded. "You're only halfway through your shift, Miss Hilvale. Soldier on," she commanded. She stepped away, but not before squeezing Bree's shoulder.

Susie had wilted. Even from down the line, Bree could see her mascara was runny, her face shiny with sweat, the hothouse English rose now seeming more like a sad bunch of weeds gasping for water. Bree idly wondered if she'd ever had to work at anything before and felt a stab of pity.

Dashiell shot a look over his shoulder, confirming that Montoya-Craig had disappeared. "Here, Susie. Let me handle it for you while you rest up a bit. Go sit on that crate over there," he suggested, tilting his head toward the setup area, "but just for a minute. We can't afford to get you in trouble."

Susie's face lit up with hope.

"You'll get us all in trouble if she's caught," Ruby warned, slapping some chicken onto a tray with especial vehemence.

Just as quickly, Susie's face fell, her bottom lip quivering as if she were about to burst into tears.

"She won't," Dashiell assured them. "I've been keeping track of Montoya's circuits. I don't know where she disappears to, but she won't be back here for another twenty minutes."

That was all Susie needed to hear. She thrust her ladle at Dashiell, who adjusted to straddle the two chafing dishes, filling the gap, and gratefully sank onto her improvised perch.

Then Group 12 settled back into somewhat disgruntled silence. Bree was on auto mode now, mindlessly serving each person as they thrust out a tray. Her attention was locked on the cluster of children, which had only grown larger in the intervening minutes.

They didn't jostle one another as they made their way to the front. There was no playful hitting or boisterous ribbing. And there were no whimpers or wails—not even from the toddlers. An eerie silence, reflecting shock and numbness, enshrouded them.

One girl caught Bree's attention. She looked about six, her closely cropped hair—hacked hastily, with a rough hand—accentuating her delicate features. Her enormous dark eyes shone with the kind of gravity that should never be seen in a child. She clutched a tiny notebook in her hand and stared from across the tent, locking eyes with Bree as if daring her to look away.

Bree felt like the girl could see her soul.

By the time she made it to Bree's station, Bree had already made up a story for her, had fallen in love with her brave little heart and seriousness of purpose. Her head barely reached above the table, forcing Bree to peer over the chafing dish to catch her face.

"Please, miss," she said, stretching out her tray.

Bree remembered Thomas's rules, but it was unfathomable to her to be addressed, to be thanked, to be called "miss" or "madam" and not look the speaker in the eye, fully acknowledging them. Especially this one, so young.

"What's your name?" she asked as gently as she could while still making herself heard over the din of the canteen.

"Amina," she whispered shyly, though never looking away from Bree's face.

"What is in your notebook, Amina?" she asked, trying to draw her out.

"My family." She offered Bree her tray, which Bree swiftly held aside. Both hands now free, the little girl solemnly opened the notebook she'd clutched to her side, brandishing its pages like a talisman before Bree. There, in pencil, images of her past life were scratched onto the paper. One side showed a crowded city block, Amina's family's apartment evident from the cheery curtains fluttering in its windows as it floated above the street below. The facing page showed a man, a woman, three children, and a dog, stick figures elaborated with careful details, like the long lashes on her mother's eyes and the bone at the feet of the dog, showing the press of memory.

"Are they with you here? Your family?"

Amina shook her head solemnly, her chin dropping.

Bree didn't know what to say. "They'll find you," she said, knowing that it was unlikely and that her words might only make it harder for the little girl. She dropped two pieces of pita onto Amina's tray, ignoring her quota. "They'll find you—I just know it."

Amina raised her chin and stared at Bree, eyes empty. "No, they won't. They're dead."

Bree gasped as Amina pulled her tray away from her hands and continued down the line. Bree stared after her, shaken.

How could one so young be so . . . so . . . hardened?

Maybe it was better that way, she reasoned with herself. Maybe it was better to accept the truth and move on. But here Amina was, a little girl by herself, with nothing but her notebook and painful memories to her name. Bree watched Amina move out of the line and slip through a crack in the tent, presumably to eat her meal alone, in peace.

On an impulse, she threw down her tongs and turned to Ruby. "Cover for me."

"What?" Ruby threw up her hands with exaggerated exasperation. "First Her Ladyship, now you? Has the whole world gone mad?"

"It will only be a minute. I promise," Bree vowed, already scrambling through her backpack to find the colored pencils and paper she'd brought with her. Clutching them, she ran across the tent in search of the little girl.

She slipped outside and looked around. This was a different entrance— not an official one, she gathered, the tents and tin shacks squeezed together into something that resembled an alley. The day had turned darker, clouds overtaking the sky and a steady drizzle enveloping the camp. The mud underfoot was thicker now. She cast her eyes down the narrow lane, looking for any sign of Amina. It seemed deserted, this part of the camp, just steps away from the canteen, ghostly quiet.

And then, something caught her eye. A scramble, a slight struggle, someone ducking behind the corner of a shack.

She trotted down that way and paused, seeing something in the mud. Stooping, she plucked it out with two fingers.

It was Amina's notebook. It had been left next to the abandoned tray, the precious food trampled into the mud.

Gul Avci's words came hurtling back. *Are you prepared to do whatever it takes?*

Anger reared inside her. Shoving the notebook in her pocket, she began running down the row of ramshackle shelters in earnest.

"Amina!" she called out, forgetting she wasn't supposed to be here, forgetting all of Thomas's warnings about security and safety. "Amina!"

She heard a shriek, followed by a smattering of harsh words in a language she did not recognize, and turned, running even faster. Rounding a corner, she saw them. The scrawny man was crouching above the child, pulling on Amina's arm, wheedling and threatening as he tried to shake her from her stance. The girl was resisting him, planting her feet firmly, leaning back to counterweight his force and battling him off with kicks that she aimed for his knees and groin.

"No!" Bree shouted, lunging for the man. She began pummeling him with her fists, not caring where they landed, just so long as he let go of Amina.

He drew his hands up to block her blows, giving Amina the chance to scramble away.

Bree darted a glance at her where she'd backed up against the dirty canvas of yet another tent. "Run! Run away!" Her eyes trailed after Amina, urging her on.

Then, a heavy force connected with her gut, driving fiery pain through her abdomen. "Oooph," she groaned. Her knees weakened and she slid to the mud below. She looked up to see Amina's abductor standing above her, smirking, his heavy boot poised for another kick to her stomach.

"Run, Amina," she urged, choking the words out as she tried to catch her breath.

He swung his boot, hard, connecting with her shoulder and sending her sprawling back deeper into the mud.

Listening to the silence all around her, the sounds of Amina's footsteps receding into the distance, she realized there was nobody else here. Nobody to help her. The knowledge made her instantly alert. She darted her eyes about, looking for anything, anything at all, that she could use to defend herself. Slowly, as she scrambled like a crab on all fours backing up toward the tent, she felt around on the ground.

Her fingers landed on a forgotten length of construction wood, a splintered two-by-four buried in the dirt. She would have only one shot, she knew. The man was creeping closer, confident now that he had her trapped. She waited until he was looming right over her and launched herself, swinging the wood with all her might.

It landed with a sickening thud into the side of his head. He collapsed to the ground, writhing in the mud.

She struggled to her feet, catching her breath while she decided what to do next. She knew she should take her opportunity to put as much distance between this creep and herself as possible, but that meant leaving him to escape. And that meant that he would come back for Amina, and probably other children, unchecked. She couldn't let that happen.

She looked at him, mired in the mud, clutching his head. She looked at the board where it lay on the ground. Wheezing heavily, she began to reach for it, bracing herself for what had to be done.

"What is going on here?" the crisp, commanding British accent rang out. Bree's body sagged with relief as a small army of UN personnel, machines guns drawn, surrounded her and her victim. A small but stern woman, shrouded in a cape, stepped to the fore.

"Miss Montoya-Craig," Bree acknowledged with a sigh of relief as she straightened herself up, raising her hands to show she was unarmed. "I am sure glad to see you."

"I wish I could say the same," Montoya-Craig said sourly, taking in the scene before her. "Stand down—she's one of mine," she gruffly ordered the guards. "Unfortunately."

One of them nodded and the men holstered their guns—all but one, who kept it trained on the man still writhing at Bree's feet. Bree let her arms drop to her sides while Montoya-Craig continued.

"Why are you not at your post? And what is the meaning of this melee?"

Bree took a deep breath to steady herself and gestured at her attacker. "I caught him trying to make off with one of the refugee children."

The man gave a little moan, clutching his head. "Noooo," he protested weakly.

Montoya-Craig skewered her with a frosty glare. "Really? You caught him red-handed, did you? You're sure he is not her guardian?"

Bree shook her head, picking nervously at her long sleeves while she tried to explain. "She'd told me her family was all dead, when she came through the canteen line. She was alone. I . . . I know it was against the rules, but I felt sorry for her. I followed her outside to give her some things for coloring. That's when I saw he was taking her against her will. I heard her screams and saw her fighting him off. I didn't know what he was planning, but I'm sure it wasn't good."

Montoya-Craig eased up just a bit, her wrath having found a more suitable candidate. "I suppose that was the little girl we saw running past us in the other direction, then," she concluded. She looked at the man on the ground in disgust and then turned, briskly, to the Blue Beret who seemed to be in charge, and who loomed nearly a head and half over her. "And I suppose this is one of the child traffickers your lot was supposed to be cleaning up," she rebuked, acid sharp. "What a cock-up, this. Take him in now, or whatever your protocol is, but get the problem under control. I won't have my people put in danger because of your incompetence."

"Your volunteer wasn't supposed to be out here," the commander protested, his color rising. The rest of his unit milled about, unsure what to do. The soldier still brandishing his weapon tightened his grip on it as he homed in on the trafficker, who was struggling to sit up, nonsensical from his head injury.

"You're right. She broke a lengthy list of rules—both yours and mine," Montoya-Craig conceded, not even bothering to hide her annoyance as she shot a glance at Bree. "That said, once confronted with what was going on in your camp, my volunteer took action," Montoya-Craig retorted, the edge in her voice daring the Blue Beret to contradict her. "However she came to be here, she did the honorable and brave thing in protecting that child. So don't talk to me of right and wrong. I'll deal with her transgressions. You deal with his."

Dismissing him, she grabbed Bree by the arm and began marching her back toward the tent.

Bree struggled to keep up as Montoya-Craig dragged her through the mud.

"What do you mean, traffickers? Miss Montoya-Craig, how could there be child traffickers in this camp?"

The older girl sighed dramatically, refusing to slow her pace as she explained. "It's a nasty business and refugees make easy targets. Think about it—parents so desperate to get their children safely out of a war zone they will pay smugglers to sneak them across borders. Lone children who have nobody to protect them."

Bree was stunned, pressing Montoya-Craig to continue as they scurried through the back alleys of the camp. "I thought he was just some creepy guy."

"It is a brutal business dealing in human flesh. Children are put to work in factories. On farms. Or worse. All of them are enslaved—no identity papers, no wages, completely dependent on their owners. They are too young to know that their lives are effectively over once they are trapped. They cling to hope for a while, until it is starved, worked, or beaten out of them." Montoya-Craig darted a curious glance at Bree.

"Really, Parrish, given your background, I'd assumed you might have seen some of these victimized children yourself. Maybe not refugees, but children who've been exploited in the same manner. It's quite common, you know, and parentless children are the most vulnerable."

Bree thought about this. She'd certainly seen troubled children come through the Thornton Home for Children—children who looked hunted. Children who would steal food from the refrigerator in the middle of the night, acting as if they didn't know where their next meal would come from. Children who'd run away, over and over, testing the limits of Rodney's patience. Maybe they'd been trafficked and abused in the way Montoya-Craig described. If they had been, Rodney had kept it from her—from them all—deliberately. Probably protecting their innocence—whatever of it still remained.

The crowds of the canteen were close to them now. Bree had one last question before she knew the proctor would end the conversation and turn her mind to how to punish Bree for leaving her station in the serving line.

"Why would the UN let that happen? Why aren't they stopping the traffickers?" she asked plaintively.

Montoya-Craig stopped abruptly. She stared at the darkening sky, contemplating Bree's question.

"It's like this whole camp," she answered, her voice harsh. "They, and the government, have already declared victory. It's easier for them to declare the problem solved than to acknowledge the inconvenient truth. So, they leave the children as sitting ducks in the camp and turn a blind eye to the fact that every day, they disappear. They ignore the problem and hope it will go away. So far, the press have been complicit. Meanwhile, they leave it to someone else to clean up the mess."

She turned to face Bree, her eyes glittering and eager, watching for Bree's response.

"But who? Who can they leave it to?"

"People like us," Montoya-Craig muttered, brusquely pushing Bree through the canvas, back into the waiting throng of people.

———

When, a week later, Montoya-Craig handed them the sealed envelope with their scores for the weekend's exercises, Bree, Susie, Dashiell, and Ruby braced themselves for disappointment. The Trials, as Dashiell had dubbed them, were tough. While they truly did assess their physical prowess, they seemed only tangentially related, if at all, to the duties of an actual nanny. Bree thought about the memorial chapel, but despite having seen the names and faces of the nannies fallen in duty, it seemed far-fetched that she or any of her classmates would routinely face such obvious dangers. Nonetheless, the scores mattered—more than she wanted to admit.

They managed passable scores on agility and coordination, the test of which was their participation at an Autumn Harvest Ball held at a local nursing home. Susie and Dashiell knew from a season or two of debutante balls how to waltz, foxtrot, and tango, giving them a leg up. Ruby got credit for her skills, picked up from her mother, at helping the more fragile residents navigate between the buffet, the dance floor, the bathrooms, and their wheelchairs. Bree—well, she'd never attended a cotillion or anything approaching a ball, but she was quick, and strong. She managed to do a mean whirl around the dance floor with the posse of wheelchair-bound partners she'd managed to round up. It could have been worse.

Their strength test was simpler, but less pleasant. In cooperation with the local fire department, Norwood had set afire an abandoned (and, of course, nonhistoric) cottage in the hills overlooking Bath. While firemen watched, and Montoya-Craig timed, Group 12 joined two other groups hauling sloshing aluminum buckets of water to fight the inferno, the goal being to stop the fire before the roof collapsed. A fire truck full of water stood on standby in case they failed. Susie's flirtation with the fire brigade—chatting them up about their future plans for a fundraising calendar—managed to finagle a few fire-fighting tips that gave them a slight edge. Though Susie hadn't lifted a pail, even Ruby had to grudgingly concede that she had chipped in well to earn them points.

When it came to their endurance scores, though, they had a surprise. They'd expected the worst, especially after the rampant rule breaking they'd shown in Calais. And indeed, Montoya-Craig was punitive. Group 12 received twenty demerits for Susie's rest break and a full fifty for Bree abandoning her post—fifty demerits being the biggest deduction handed to any of the groups over the course of the entire two days. But she granted forty extra credits each for Dashiell and Ruby's extra stamina in covering for them. And, in a breathtakingly unexpected bit of grace, she bestowed upon them a thousand extra credits for Bree's act of bravery in saving Amina.

"Do not speak of this to anyone," she hissed at them, sweeping past in a swish of khaki as they stared in wonder at the computer-generated slip of paper documenting their grades.

Now all of them were contenders for admission to the certificate program. If they could make it through the rest of the semester. And if they kept on Montoya-Craig's good side.

Chapter Three

SECOND TERM

Bath, England

Bree absentmindedly flipped the airmail envelope over and over on her desk. She supposed she should be grateful Rodney had found the time to even write to her—Lord knows he had his hands full with the mess of children he had to manage every day.

But no matter how much she had anticipated his letter, dashed out on the backs of abandoned coloring book pages and graded homework assignments, his words were hard to read. The scholarship Norwood had granted her did not cover travel expenses to and from the college, only a stipend to manage her tuition, room, and board during terms. And since she'd left, there'd been some belt tightening at the orphanage. There was no room in the budget to pay for the expensive ticket that would whisk her from London to Atlanta, just a hop, skip, and a jump, as Rodney would always say, from her beloved Florence and Muscle Shoals. She would have to stay in her apartment through the holidays—the American Thanksgiving and Christmas, both. The latter, alone.

She flattened out the drawing from Ollie that Rodney had folded in with his letter. With one finger, she traced the crayon trail of primary colors with which he'd laid out, with as much care as his stubby fingers could manage, a picture of the orphanage and the play yard beside it. A stick figure with long red hair that shot crazily from an overlarge, misshapen head was drawn next to a much smaller stick boy, their hands overlapping. O-L-L-I-E, he'd labeled the boy. B-R-E, he'd named the girl, forgetting the last E of her name. She sighed and pushed the picture behind Rodney's missive.

"Don't be so glum, Bree. It's not as if we would abandon you here. You'll spend the break with us," Dashiell insisted, patting her hand.

"You can come home with me, if you'd like," Ruby offered. "The city is lovely during Christmas. They drape the lights right across the streets—big swags, strings of angels and trumpets. And the markets are full-on, too, with gigantic, shiny Christmas bulbs and music, even. Oooh, and I can show you Churchill Arms—it looks like a fairy garden when they're all done with it. Twinkling Christmas trees, stacked all the way to the roof."

"Or you and I could stay in Bath. I might even be able to get the keys to a family friend's place on the Crescent. Wouldn't that be fun?" offered Dashiell.

"I'll be going to St. Barts, sadly," Susie mentioned, filing a nail with great vigor. "Living off the scraps from my uncle's tropical table."

"You better keep that from the bursar's office or they'll revoke your scholarship, Susie," Ruby cautioned, shaking her head, her loose braids giving off a faint rattle as they gently swung about her head.

Susie took a break from her manicure to consider Ruby's advice.

"You're so right, Ruby. I consider myself forewarned and shall be duly careful." She then shifted in her seat to fix Bree with a look of sympathy.

"I am so sorry I cannot be of help at your time of need, Bree. But I will send you a postcard, darling, I promise. I'll think about you the whole time. I shan't enjoy it at all."

Bree smiled at Susie's shallow kindness.

"Y'all are great to offer," Bree said, tucking the envelope away in her desk drawer. "But I would feel like a third wheel, horning in on your vacation plans. I'll figure something out. Don't worry about me." She pushed back her chair and grabbed her windbreaker and backpack. "I'm going to go on campus for a bit. I'll catch you around dinner."

The November days turned dark early now, so Bree found herself following the sidewalks and wide streets back to the college in a half-light, even though it was early afternoon. She knew the way by heart. Past the quaint church. Over the bridge that allowed the street to split underneath her feet. Around the bend, the imposing stone walls and wrought iron gates of the park beckoning her to step inside and linger on the dirt footpaths and the grassy expanse, which had been transformed from a leafy bower into a skeletal stand of gray trees. Along the way, she let her mind turn over the question she'd been brooding about ever since they'd returned from Calais and her meeting of the little refugee, Amina.

Was it better to have known your parents and lost them, or to know nothing of them at all?

Amina was haunted by memories. They might fade over time, acquiring the dim outlines and soft colors that would make them bearable, but they would never leave her. The beautiful ones—the recollections of loving arms and bedtime stories, the dog nestling next to her on the covers as her eyes drew heavy with sleep—would be a source of both comfort and longing. The painful ones—the ones etched deep by her loss—would make her beg the darkness to make her forget.

Bree, in contrast, had nothing. Her mind was free of the attachments of *mother, father, family,* and *home.* It was as if she had sprung, fully formed, from the Alabama dirt outside the front steps of the Thornton orphanage. She could not cry herself to sleep remembering what she'd lost. But there was an empty space in her, just the same—not quite loss, but incompleteness.

And always, the questions.

A movement in the shadows of an alley caught her eye. A homeless woman huddled in a heap, nothing but piles of rags between her and the rain. Bree stopped. The woman looked strangely familiar—was this her usual place? Had Bree walked past her, unseeing, every day on her way to class these past months? Ashamed, she moved closer.

"Can I bring you inside for a tea, miss? Get you out of the rain for a bit?"

The woman lifted her head and stared at Bree.

"It isn't safe," she stated flatly.

"What isn't safe? Inside? The tea?" Bree answered, confused.

"Du-ty un-ceas-ing-ly," she hissed, off key, through her teeth.

Bree was startled to hear the snatch of words from the Norwood school song on the woman's lips. "What do you mean?"

But the woman had hunched back over and ignored Bree.

An uneasy feeling overtook Bree. "Who are you?"

Discomfited by the woman's silence, Bree backed away and began walking, every now and then looking back over her shoulder to where the woman huddled in a lump, until she was no longer visible through the rain.

The drizzle had picked up into a full shower as she approached the Norwood campus. The library lights shone in the premature gloaming, beckoning her, but she did not want companionship. Not now. So instead, she turned to the chapel, seeking the solitude of the memorials and hard wooden benches.

The heavy door gave way to her and she slipped in, allowing her eyes to adjust to the gloom. The melodramatic statue gave a faint stone glow, amplifying what little light trickled in from above.

"Hello, Poppins," she whispered wistfully, placing a hand on the statue's billowing gown.

The door creaked behind her. She spun around to see its iron magnificence yield a ratty and broken umbrella, from which emerged a completely soaked Dashiell. He battled with the umbrella, trying to force its broken spine closed, finally throwing it down to the ground in disgust and shaking himself free of the wetness like a great collie.

"What are you doing here?" she blurted, dodging the water he scattered everywhere.

"It didn't seem a good idea for you to be alone just now." He paused. "A thank-you might be nice," he prompted, looking cross at what she could only assume was her nonreaction.

She felt herself turning red with both indignation and embarrassment. "That was very kind of you, Dashiell, but I didn't expect you to babysit me."

He huffed at her characterization, peeling off his wet mackintosh. "I'm not here to *nanny* you, Briana. Nor *protect* you from imaginary hobgoblins. I am here to *abide* with you, as you seemed as if a bit of company would do you good."

She bit her lip, considering his point.

"You haven't seemed the same since Calais," he said pointedly as he took a seat at Poppins's feet. "You never told us what prompted you to do what you did—what was going through your head then, or afterward—though I can imagine it has dredged up some difficult times from your past."

He waited for her to respond. Patiently, he stared down at his loafers, picking at a speck of dirt.

"Not that I would know anything about your past. You know all about me and mine, but you haven't divulged one iota about your own. Other than the bare bones, of course."

She threw her backpack down on the flagstone floor and collapsed into a frustrated puddle. "There's nothing to tell, Dash. And that's the issue. I don't know anything about where I came from. Not a thing."

He looked up from his shoes. "Surely you know something?" he asked, his curiosity piqued.

"All I know is that my parents were killed in a car crash when I was just a baby. The authorities were never able to confirm their identities—they had papers on them, but they led to nothing. The Social Security numbers ended up belonging to people who had died as infants. They could find no school records, no mortgages, and no bank accounts—nothing. The credit cards they'd used to rent the car they'd been driving led to a maze of dead ends. No surviving family stepped forth to claim me. The doctors did their best, but essentially had to guess at my age based on my physical progress. These gaps in my past—what Miss Judy, Thornton's biggest donor, called 'irregularities' in my paperwork—my birth certificate and the like—made my permanent adoption by anyone difficult. Nobody wanted to take a risk on long-lost relatives emerging and an adoption being revoked after the fact," she noted bitterly. "Or discovering a history of abuse that only emerged when psychological and physical trauma surfaced later in life. I got transferred around as a toddler until I wound up in Thornton."

"That's incredible, Bree. You really have no memories of anything at all?"

She stared at the flagstone floor. He wouldn't understand, even if she tried to explain, so she simply shook her head.

"You must be very angry."

She shrugged. "Sometimes. But mostly I'm just bewildered by it all. When I saw those kids at the refugee camp, I couldn't help thinking how much worse it would be to have a family and then have it all snatched away from you. And something about that little girl just struck me. I don't know why, but—"

"You wanted to help take the edge off her loss. After what you've been through, it's totally understandable. And this Miss Judy?" he asked, picking up the thread of her past. "What is she to you now?"

"She never adopted me herself," Bree half-laughed, shaking her head. "She was too busy." The bitterness in her voice as she spat out the word *busy* surprised even her. "She's some bigwig executive in Atlanta. She didn't have time to actually take on a child herself. But she sponsors Thornton and has always taken a special interest in me," she continued in a rush, ashamed lest she be seen as ungrateful. "I guess she feels responsible for how I turn out."

"Your name, then? Where did it come from?"

She gave a sad smile. "I survived the crash—thrown from the car before it exploded. Me, in my car seat, along with a little diaper bag. My name was on a metal tag attached to the diaper bag. Nappy bag. You know what I mean. Briana Bellona Parrish." She pulled the chain around her neck and drew out the little charm and fumbled at it with clumsy fingers. "Apparently, the authorities ran the Parrish name down in all the US databases and were never able to link the aliases my parents were traveling under to anyone named Parrish. And there was not enough physical evidence to pursue anything like dental records." She swallowed hard. "The fire, you see . . ." She shuddered, not wanting to think about how horrible of a death that must have been.

He nodded gravely. "If they were even your parents."

She tilted her head, acknowledging that she had considered this possibility, as well.

"And that fuss from Montoya-Craig, about whether or not you are British?"

"A mix-up, I'm sure," she said miserably. "But one that got me here, so who am I to question it? Especially with the dean backing it up."

"Curious," he murmured. He drew himself up, readying a good dose of British stiff upper lip. "Well, whoever your parents were, they named you with great care. Do you know the meaning of your name, Bree?"

She shook her head no.

"'Briana,' of course, is derivative of Brian. Celtic, it is. It means 'strong and honorable.' Not bad, certainly appropriate, from what I can see. But the more interesting part is your middle name. Bellona."

She looked up at him from the floor, curious. "Why?"

"Bellona is Latin, and it is a very fierce name. It is the name of the Sabine—and later, Roman—goddess of war, who was reputed to be quite vicious and bloodthirsty. It is the root of the English word 'bellicose,' as a matter of fact."

"Really?"

"Oh, quite. And she is famous. Shakespeare called Macbeth 'Bellona's bridegroom.' Milton refers to her storming with all her battering engines in *Paradise Lost*. Rembrandt and Rubens sculpted her. The World War I Victory Arch at Waterloo Station even bears her likeness. So, whoever christened you, they envisioned their baby girl as a great, fearless warrior. With a vast, conquering future. Whatever you do with that legacy now, though, is up to you."

"I don't think of myself as bloodthirsty," Bree noted wryly.

"Consider it more . . . mmm . . . aggressive? In a positive way," he laughed, rising up from Poppins's feet. "As that trafficker in the camp learned, much to his regret."

She gazed up at him, and then the wall of plaques behind him.

"They're still there," she noted, wrinkling a brow.

"What?" he wheeled to look at the wall himself. "What's still there?"

"Well, actually, they are still *not* there," Bree clarified. Then, remembering that only Ruby had been with her, she explained. "See the gaps in the plaques? When we took the tour before the start of term, Albourn said they were out for restoration. I'm surprised they haven't been returned yet." She clambered to her feet.

"Conservation can be tricky. Photographs are delicate and the restoration can require several processes, depending on the extent of the damage." He looked around the damp vestibule. "I wouldn't imagine this is the ideal place to keep them. But then again, it's not like they are rare Man Rays."

"You seem to know a lot about art," she noted, the reference lost on her. She picked up her bag and handed him his ruined umbrella.

"Another side effect of being raised in a virtual museum, I'm afraid. Whether you consider it a feature or a bug is up to your worldview," he added with a wink. "Shall we, Mistress Bellona?" He beckoned to her with an arm. "It sounds as if the rain has passed. Luckily for us, as this wretched device of Ruby's is utterly worthless."

She tucked her own arm under his elbow and gazed seriously into his eyes. "Thank you." She gave his arm a little squeeze. "For everything."

"Say nothing of it, dear," he said, squeezing her hand. "We are your family now. I hope in the future you'll let us show you in many ways. And not make us run out into the storm and dark of night to prove it to you."

The rush of end of term swooped in on them with ferocity. They just didn't realize it until the assembly called for the first-year class. They milled about, chattier than Bree remembered her classmates being at their opening convocation, a slight edginess the only undernote to their familiarity.

Dean Albourn approached the podium and the crowd settled into its seats, the conversation quelling to a low murmur and then, quickly, total silence. Bree idly noted how the dean seemed to embrace the same frumpy but expensive style favored by Judy—chunky tweeds, calf-length skirts, and high collars being their fashion armor of choice.

"Good morning, ladies. And gentleman," the dean began.

"That got old in month one," Dash muttered under his breath.

"I've called you here to explain a unique aspect of our end-of-term process here at Norwood. Because it will be instrumental in our determination of your suitability for the certificate program and, indeed, typically leads to the first culling of students from our midst, we thought it *fair*"—she paused, grimacing at the word that Bree presumed had been worked into the dean's script against her better judgment—"to inform you of its particulars."

Bree shot a sideways glance at Susie, who was busy filing her nails. She watched as Ruby and Dash exchanged an uncomfortable look.

"Each of your courses will, of course, administer full examinations, weighted as indicated in your syllabi. These examinations are traditional in nature. They will be administered in the hall, under the supervision of your upper-class proctors." She gestured behind her to a row of starched upper-class women sporting their full Norwood regalia.

"Should they detect any cheating, they will immediately expel you from the hall and refer you to Honor Code Hearing. Though it is regrettable, we have had a few trials on Honor Code violations over the course of our history. These trials are administered by the proctors and are judged by a jury of your peers. Experience has taught us that your fellow students are the harshest judges of such a crime, for, after all, in a competitive placement process, such violations have a direct bearing upon the success of others. The punishment for a guilty verdict is expulsion." She scanned the assembly, letting her cold eyes settle with gravity upon each of them. "Consider yourselves forewarned.

"But that is the simple part of our end of term," she continued in a brisk tone. "The more unique aspect which we wish to address today is your end-of-term project assignments. These projects are intended to be cumulative in nature, tying together all the concepts you have learned in your coursework and testing your ability to apply them in real-world situations. These assignments must be prepared on top of studying for exams." She smiled grimly, eyes sparkling with anticipation. "It is a brutal workload, and this year's projects exceptionally so.

"They are group assignments, as is our preferred mode during the first term, and will provide, in total, an excellent test of your workload management, multitasking, and collaboration skills. You will receive your project assignments, with complete rubrics, for *Children's Crafts*, *Concepts of Learning*, and *Food, Nutrition, and Health* upon exit of this auditorium. You may find the need to adjust your weekend plans accordingly."

A groan rippled through the hall. Bree watched as Albourn smiled archly, the pleasure of ruining her students' social lives clearly one of the added benefits of her position.

"Ah. And lest I forget to mention it: These projects will be worth an additional bonus of fifty percent of your total grade in each course."

A few of the young women gasped. Albourn's grin broadened.

Ruby elbowed Bree. "That means we could all fail, even if we have top marks going into the final exam," she explained in an outraged whisper. Bree tugged nervously at the sleeves of her sweater, pulling them to her fingertips.

"Good luck," the dean concluded. "You will need it. Ladies?"

And with that, Albourn climbed with steady decorum off the stage, leaving the proctors to launch into a weak version of the alma mater, the protesting whines of their classmates engulfing the song.

"They can take their *persistence* and—" Ruby threatened. Dash cut her off with a pat on the hand.

"Now, now, Ruby. It can't be as bad as all that. Right, Susie?"

Bree peered down the row to where Susie sat, a serene look on her face. "It will be fun," she shrugged. "Projects are always more fun than written exams. Remember the strength trials? Those were like a special project."

"In which you almost got us failed," Ruby muttered disconsolately.

Susie arched a brow. Before she could retort, Bree swooped in. "We might as well get our assignments," she said. "Come on, y'all."

As they pushed through the crowd, they saw their class was splitting into two groups, circling about two stations. They muscled their way through to the first, where they were handed two manila envelopes.

"When you've read the instructions inside, proceed to the second station," the proctor directed them with a knowing smile.

They split off from the crowd and huddled in a corner of the stone hall. Ruby ripped open the first envelope, drawing out their briefing papers.

"It's a collaborative project for *Don't Eat the Glue* and *Junior Is No Genius*. We need to plan an entire holiday break's worth of daily crafting projects, suitable for the completely incompatible ages of four, nine, and thirteen in our Hypothetical Families. Bugger all!" She sucked on her teeth. "Evil genius, that."

"A Hypothetical Family with that many kids? Must be a second marriage," Dash snarked.

"Give me them," Bree said, snatching the papers from Ruby's hand and scanning the second page. She emitted a low whistle. "We have just this weekend to complete it. We have to submit a comprehensive vacation curriculum, samples of each craft, estimated elapsed time for completion for a typical child, and total budget. The rubric grades us on each project's suitability for the stage of motor skill, cognitive, visual, and emotional development for each child—"

"How do they expect us to master that, with such disparate ages?" Dash interjected.

Ruby shot him a dirty look for interrupting. "Go on, Bree. Continue."

"As I was saying," Bree continued, "the suitability for each child's developmental stage, its distraction factor—"

"In other words, will it suck up enough time for mummy and daddy to hit the ski slopes or sneak in a cocktail," Dash observed.

Bree ignored him. "Its practicality—deemed a function of portability—"

"For surely our Hypothetical Family will take their holidays abroad," Dash opined. "I'm thinking Innsbruck. Or perhaps Chamonix?"

"—mess," Bree continued, unfazed.

"Which mummy tends to dislike," Dash warned, warming to his narrative.

Bree pressed on. ". . . flexibility . . ."

"To repurpose the materials in case of Child Meltdown Emergency," he added, on a roll.

"And total cost effectiveness."

Bree pursed her lips and fixed Dash in a stony glare, daring him to comment. He was unable to resist.

"Why ever they would care about cost when mummy is cavorting about the Alps wearing ridiculous twenty-thousand-pound mink-lined boots, only God and Dean Albourn can explain," he said, rolling his eyes.

"Dashiell!" Ruby warned. "That's enough." She turned to Bree. "Is that it, then?"

Bree nodded. "Assuming a two-week holiday, we'll need at least fourteen projects. Even more if we can't figure out how to accommodate their age differences in a single craft. Then we'd be talking one per day for each child."

Susie's eyes widened. "That's over one hundred projects," she said, awestruck.

Dash patted her shoulder distractedly. "Not quite, dear. But it certainly will feel like it. Especially as it's a group project. Now, what about the other packet? I assume that's for *Navigating Nappies?*"

Ruby nodded. "Shall I?"

They urged her on, so she opened the envelope and began to read.

"You have learned the science of nutrition and health at a conceptual level. We will now test your ability to apply your knowledge. As a group, you will receive a very lifelike virtual baby—one that requires feeding at regular intervals, can simulate fever and illness, and, of course, can cry. Your task: forty-eight hours of care in the environs of your normal daily life, journaling every feeding, burp, wet nappy, bowel movement, and notable occurrences, along with vital signs, all with the aim of returning your virtual baby in better shape than you originally received him or her."

Bree could feel her jaw dropping open.

"You've got to be kidding me," Ruby added, dumbfounded.

"We had to do something like this in my high school home economics class," Bree offered tentatively. "Only it was just with an egg. We just had to not crack its shell and we could get an A."

"How hard could it be?" Susie wondered, shrugging.

"Sure, she says. How hard can it be to watch an infant while developing a holiday curriculum of arts and crafts in forty-eight hours, all while studying for our exams?" Ruby fumed.

"No, she's right," Bree said, defending Susie. "I mean, how lifelike could these so-called virtual babies really be? There's only so much they can do with robotics and stuff. It's probably only a little more complicated than the egg babies."

"They must be at the second station," Dash offered. "Let's take a look. And hope that Susie's right."

The crowd had started to thin, teams scurrying away with envelopes, papers, and bundles clutched in their arms.

"We're here for our doll," Dash grinned as he swaggered up to one of Montoya-Craig's upper-class colleagues who was manning the proctor's station.

She fixed him with a stony stare.

"You'll have to call it by its proper name if you'd like to be issued one for your group," she said, arching a brow and making a mysterious check mark on her clipboard.

Ruby sucked on her teeth in disapproval. Bree opened her mouth to intervene, but the proctor raised her hand to cut her off.

"No. He has to do it. He must finish what he started, properly."

Dash flushed.

"Oh, fine, then. If you must be obstinate about it. Group 12, reporting to be issued a virtual baby for our final project. If you please." He gave a smart, tiny bow.

The proctor let one corner of her mouth sneak up in a self-satisfied grin. "Very well. You're among the last of the groups to check in. They're a bit picked over now." She slid a separate clipboard across the table toward Dash.

"What do you mean, picked over? Surely, the dolls—I mean, babies—are all the same?"

She looked at him with pity. "Indeed, no. They've been individually programmed by the professor to have unique characteristics and, shall we say, challenges?"

He picked up the clipboard.

"Damn," he said softly.

Ruby snatched away the clipboard and scanned the list, sucking on her teeth in disapproval.

"We definitely don't want the colicky ones," she tutted to herself, jabbing a sharp finger at the list. "I don't care if it's only forty-eight hours, with all this other work we have to do, we'll want to strangle that baby if we have to deal with a two-day sleep strike." She shoved the clipboard back at Dash. "I propose we gamble and take one of the ones programmed with the professor's choice of sudden illness. What do you say to that, Manny?"

"Err . . . okay?" Dash answered. "If Susie and Bree agree, of course."

Bree shrugged and Susie rolled her eyes.

"How hard can it be?" Susie wondered. "I mean, it's a baby, for goodness' sake."

The proctor snickered as she put a crisp checkmark on her list. "*She.* Not *it*. Your baby's name is Penelope." She passed the bundle, swaddled in a tight pink blanket, over her podium and waited. When nobody else stepped up, Bree came forward to claim the child. She pulled back one corner of the blanket and shuddered. The pale plastic was too lifelike. She could pick out the downy fuzz covering the infant's skin and swore as she sniffed the doll's forehead that she caught whiffs of milk and talcum powder.

"She'll be activated in twenty minutes by remote control. Gear and a full baby biography with medical history are in a separate duffel near the exit. Make sure you take the right one—number nine. Best of luck to you," the proctor concluded, fighting with the corners of her mouth as they threatened to curl up in a mocking grin.

"Do we have time to stop for a salad or smoothie on the way home?" Susie yawned as they hustled her out of the hall. "I'm famished."

"Did you not hear the woman?" Ruby snapped. "Twenty minutes until all hell breaks loose. We will *not* be stopping for snacks."

Dash looked at her reprovingly. "There's no need to be so stern, Ruby. She's just a little peckish, that's all." He peered at Ruby with knowing eyes. "I imagine we all might be hungry, and a little touchy, just about now. A bite to take the edge off wouldn't hurt."

"We can order takeaway, then," Ruby conceded in a grumble. "Who knows what this child will do once it—*she*—comes to life? And we have to plan our whole project. We need to get home."

———

They'd divided up responsibilities to be sure they could get everything done. The baby care had been split into four twelve-hour shifts, closely matching what might be typical for a real nanny assignment, drawing lots for each shift. Dash and Bree had drawn the first rotations, which had been relatively inconsequential after their initial adjustment. When Penny—as they'd come to call her—had sprung to life, catching them just outside Jaguar House, it had been with a shudder and shriek, her mechanized arms flailing against her swaddling. She was surprisingly strong, her movements no less jerky than those of a child first realizing that her limbs were actually connected to her own body. They hustled her indoors, hoping none of their neighbors had been disturbed by her outburst.

"Oh, my," Dash had intoned, shocked, as he inspected Penny's nappy, turning a shade of green Bree had never seen before. "It appears that the digestive functions of the robot child are fully functional. But a bit in overdrive. She is in dire need of a nappy change."

A quick scramble through her duffel had turned up a pacifier which she refused to accept, multiple changes of clothes, a spare blanket, some formula and baby food, but no nappies.

"I know that technically I am on duty for the duration of this shift," Dash began, "but I do feel I will be able to procure nappies more quickly, and with less incident, if I leave her in your capable hands while I attend to the drugstore. In the meantime, use this." He pressed a fingertip towel embroidered with his family's crest into Ruby's hands. "It will have to do until I'm back. She simply cannot remain in that dirty nappy or she'll get a rash all over her bum."

After Dash had worked a night of two-hour sleep cycles, Bree picked up, earning the opportunity to work through a nasty diaper rash—regrettably not avoided by the sacrifice of Dash's heirloom linens—and a bout of teething. They breathed a sigh of relief when the third shift revealed that the dreaded mystery illness was the flu, bearing down with full force upon Penny while she was in Ruby's expert hands.

Bree looked up at Ruby now. She had Penny cocked over her shoulder, rubbing her back in tiny, endless circles, and was wearing a bright yellow slicker. Bree grinned and Ruby pursed her lips.

"You think it's funny until you get covered in vomit yourself. You'll notice the child has stopped her crying. The worst has seemed to pass. That's what counts. How about you? Are you holding up your end of the bargain?"

Bree scanned the floor around her. It looked like a bomb had gone off inside a kindergarten. They'd been feverishly working on crafts, building prototypes, testing them against the rubrics, and dashing off instructions along the way. Bree had been quite proud of her greatest brainchild, a project to construct replicas of famous British monuments out of Popsicle sticks, with flexible levels of difficulty that could adapt to the different ages and capabilities of a family of children.

"We're nearly there, Ruby," Bree reassured her. "Just a few more to go. And then we'll need to photocopy all of our documentation for submission."

Ruby's eyes narrowed. "What about you, Susie?"

Susie was idly playing with the stringing beads from an incomplete project that she'd hung around her own neck. "I finished my project hours ago," she shrugged.

"Don't you mean *projects*?" Bree corrected.

"I could only come up with one. But it's a really good one, so it should count for a lot." She inexplicably held up what looked like a lump of cloth.

"What is that?" Ruby hissed, careful to not wake Penny, who had just fallen into a fitful sleep.

"It's a napkin-folding craft—you know, to get the children to 'help' with Christmas dinner." She held the fabric up higher for their admiration. Bree peered at it. She peered again. If she squinted, she thought she could make out of its lumps and folds a beaver. Or maybe a squirrel.

"I think you might have had a very odd childhood, Susie," Dash pondered, cross-legged on the floor, as he prepared his sample sock and paper-bag puppets—a brilliant addition to the curriculum, taking many hours to make but also promoting a further round of time-consuming play, practically creating a mummy/daddy space-time continuum warp.

Susie just giggled, flopping a linen blob at him, provoking him to kiss her on the top of her head.

"Over twenty-fours hours and all she has is a napkin," Ruby muttered venomously.

"Not a napkin. A swan," Susie corrected. "You have to use your imagination. And the children will like them because they can hide their veggies inside and dump them in the loo after they are excused from the table."

Dash saw the wild look of frustration in Ruby's face and interceded, speaking rapidly. "It's okay, Ruby. Bree and I did plenty of crafts for our whole team. We've got it covered."

Susie beamed. "Of course we do. Because we're a *team*. And speaking of team, isn't it time to hand off Penny to me? I can take over from here, Ruby." She reached out her arms for the virtual baby, now silent against Ruby's shoulder, her arms flung out in spent exhaustion.

Ruby eyed her nervously. "Are you sure, Susie?"

Susie rolled her eyes. "The worst is over. You said it yourself. Leave her to me and all of you can run out to the copy shop to get everything organized. I'll pick things up while she's sleeping."

"I could use a bite to eat," Ruby said, warming to the idea.

"Would you be a love and bring me back a matcha latte, Dashiell?"

Susie asked, scooping the child up onto her own shoulder. "Maybe I could even do one extra craft project while you're gone? I was thinking about creating a stacking game out of those tiny liquor bottles they give you on first-class flights. They're practically overflowing from our liquor cabinet, Dashiell. We might as well put them to good use."

Bree cringed. "That's okay, Susie. We've got it covered."

Bree, Dash, and Ruby painstakingly boxed up their creations and trundled off to the copy shop to print out the accompanying detailed calendar, description of each craft with links to the rubric, crafting instructions, and budgets. It was a short walk to the campus to drop everything off in the relative quiet of night, avoiding the risk that something would be smashed or lost if they tried delivering their work during the hubbub of morning commuting—a tradeoff they happily made even though it meant turning in their work before the deadline.

When they all converged back on the apartment, however, things had run amok. They could hear Penny's shrieks before they even got to the threshold. A sickly sweet stench struck them in the face as soon as they opened the door.

"Oh no," Ruby moaned, wrinkling her nose. "I know that smell." She charged through the door but then drew up suddenly, throwing her arm back to stop them.

"Oh my Lord!" she exclaimed. "Don't step in it," she warned darkly.

A dribble of greenish-brown ooze wound its way across the area rugs and linoleum, leading all the way through the kitchen toward Dash and Susie's suite.

They followed it, gingerly stepping around the mess itself, to find Susie. She was dangling Penny out in front of her over the bathtub. A frothy poop was running down Penny's bare leg, dripping steadily, and her skin had turned a pale greenish-yellow.

"Susie!" Ruby demanded. "What's going on?"

"I don't know," Susie admitted, a look of panic on her face. "It's been coming from *everywhere*. I can't make it stop." She choked back a gag. Bree remembered Susie's weak stomach and snatched Penny away just in time for Susie to vomit in the bathtub. Passing the baby to Dash, Bree went to comfort Susie.

"Let's clean this up," she soothed. She went to pat Susie's head, but found her hair matted with something vile. She patted her shoulder instead.

Ruby snorted. "I'll get my medical kit," she said, darting out of the bathroom.

Bree laid a towel out on the floor and gestured to Dash. "Shhhhh," he whispered to Penny. "Be a good girl now. I know, I know. It's yucky. We'll wash and change you and fix you up in no time." He methodically unsnapped Penny's onesie, gingerly pulling it over the doll's head. The robot's programming was merciful—Penny did not fight him, like a normal baby would have.

Excrement had smeared all the way up the virtual baby's back. Bree frowned.

"Susie? Did you dress the baby's nappy this way on purpose?"

"What way?" Susie croaked from her position, crouched over the toilet.

"Backward," Ruby interjected, having rejoined them at the bathroom door. "And what are these?" she demanded with narrowed eyes.

Susie lifted her head from the toilet to see what Ruby was talking about. In the doorway, Ruby thrust the remnants of a tin of baked beans and an empty plastic package of cherry yogurt parfait in front of them.

"It's what I gave her for her tea," Susie responded.

They took in a collective gasp.

"You forgot about the BRAT diet?" Ruby roared in disbelief.

"What?" Susie asked with a blank stare of nonrecognition.

"We learned about it during our first week of class, Susie," Bree gently explained. "What to feed a sick baby, once they are on solid food, like

Penny is. Bananas, rice, applesauce, and toast are all that a rumbly tummy can handle. Get it? BRAT?"

Susie sighed tragically. "She was hungry." She laid her head against the porcelain, studiously avoiding Ruby's anger.

"She had the right kind of baby food in her bag, Susie. All you had to do was use what was in her bag," Bree sighed, feeling defeated.

Dash opened his mouth to defend her, but Ruby cut him off with a sharp look.

"Before you say anything, you should know she left that baby on your family's white-and-champagne-striped velvet settee—the lah-di-dah one next to your bar cart. Let's hope Penny did not roll off of that sofa while we were gone. Bad enough her nasty diarrhea ran out the back of her nappy and stained the upholstery."

Dash blanched and rushed out the door. Bree, head down, attended to Penny, whose wailing went from airplane engine roar to freight train pitch as Bree began wiping her down.

"Everything is monitored digitally. They will know what she did to the baby," Ruby complained, her dark eyes burning holes in Susie's back.

"*We* did it," Bree gently corrected. "No use complaining about it now. Let's see if we can get her recovered by the time we check her back in tomorrow. It's going to be a long night."

"I'm not taking this lying down," Ruby raged. She stormed out of the bathroom. Bree heard the angry slam of the door as Ruby left the apartment.

When they returned Penny to the nursery checkpoint the next morning, she had lightened to a slightly off shade of green. Their progress—and all of their careful work for the first thirty-six hours of nannying—was not enough, however.

"Fundamental error," their professor sniffed. They glanced at their grading sheet. A bright red F, circled and underscored, stared back at them.

The only thing that made it slightly less painful was that Group 13 had managed to kill their virtual baby and earned the distinction of being awarded an F minus, along with an extended role-play of being interrogated by the police.

Ruby smiled surreptitiously when news of Group 13's plight spread through the classroom.

"What did you do, Ruby?" Dash demanded sotto voce.

"I did what I had to do," she stated smugly. "Just made sure we wouldn't be at the bottom of the grading pool."

"You sabotaged their baby?" he exclaimed in a whisper, his tone somewhere between disgust and admiration. "That's what you did when you left Jaguar House last night?"

"You'll never know," Ruby responded, pressing her lips together to signal the discussion was over.

Bree blanched. "Ruby, you could get us expelled if we get caught! Remember the honor-code speech Montoya gave?" she whispered.

"Who said I did anything?" Ruby shot back. "Besides, you'll thank me later."

They rallied for the afternoon, which they spent presenting their arts and crafts projects to the children in the experimental day care. There, their inventiveness was much appreciated, most of the activities engaging the children and receiving accolades for their ingenuity and practicality. Susie's napkin-folding exercise was met with puzzled looks, of course. Most of the children simply wrapped their heads in the napkins and ran around shrieking in an impromptu game of Blind Man's Bluff. They received points off for that—being cited for a "threat of broken china and crystal"—but other than that, sailed through unscathed and with high marks.

On Tuesday morning, they were issued the project for *Dodge the Vase* and given the remainder of the school week to complete it. Its requirements

were slightly less onerous. They were to be given role-play assignments for
a series of mock "Family Situations," for which they were each required
to rotate through the role of nanny, interacting with members of the
Hypothetical Family, or HF, to resolve the situation. The role-plays themselves—and their subsequent self-critiques—were to be videotaped for
submission. They had drawn a recording slot on late Friday afternoon,
leaving them to brood all week about their tenuous grades and what horrible situations they might need to deal with during the role-plays when
their turn finally came up.

Outside of the conference room where they'd be videotaped, they
drew their scenarios randomly from the envelope that had accompanied
the rubric.

"Me first," insisted Susie, who'd had her makeup done specially for
the occasion. Her assignment was to handle the unwanted advances of
the man of the house, tactfully, without losing her job. She warmed to
the task at hand.

"Remember, Susie," Dash cautioned her. "These are *unwanted* advances. You cannot encourage him at all."

"I'll play the father to help put you in the proper mood," Ruby
said darkly.

They bit their lips anxiously, watching Susie and Ruby at work, and
sighed with relief when they hit "end" on the recorder without Susie having done anything embarrassing or more inappropriate than wearing an
extremely low-cut neckline.

Bree's situation was fairly straightforward: an uncomfortable discussion with mummy and daddy to raise the possibility that Junior might
have a learning disability requiring professional attention. With all the
resources at the HF's disposal, Bree couldn't imagine this would ever be
too difficult of a challenge for her to handle if it came to pass in her future
working life.

Dash's was slightly trickier—negotiating punishment for a child caught lying about homework, with Hypothetical Family parents who refused to believe their precious Junior would ever do such a thing.

And then came Ruby.

"Oh, Lord," Ruby protested, rolling her eyes as she looked at the assigned situation she'd crumpled up in her fist. "I will trade anybody to not have to deal with this."

"Oooh, what is it?" Dash had loved *Dodge the Vase*. He said it reminded him of so many "good times" with his three stepmothers, and so far the project exercises had been like catnip to him. "Is it a 'Nanny in Trouble' scenario? Nanny accused of stealing? Nanny breaking curfew? Nanny caught asleep on a nannycam?"

"Are you a fool? Do you think I would have any trouble defending myself against such nonsense?" In her outrage, Ruby's Caribbean accent rose to the forefront.

"No, you're right, of course. It must be something juicier than that," he averred, furrowing a brow. "Tasteful day drinking by mummy, perhaps?"

"Let me see." Bree snatched the paper from Ruby's hand and quickly scanned it. "Oh, Ruby, you're overreacting. Besides, we can't trade. We each have to take a turn as the nanny on tape."

"Please! I'll do your chores for a week."

"Not a chance," Bree grinned. "I really want to see you have to play this with a straight face."

"Not funny," Ruby warned, biting her lip to keep from laughing herself. "Maybe I can trade it for another topic?"

She desperately shook out the envelope to find it was empty.

"Okay, spill it," Dash demanded. "What's got your knickers tied up in knots?"

Ruby cleared her throat dramatically before launching into a recitation of her situation. "*You are putting away the laundry and unexpectedly interrupt Mr. HF cross-dressing in Mrs. HF's closet. It appears he has also purloined a pair of your panties. Mr. HF is understandably very upset at being caught. What do you do?*"

"Do? Why do you have to *do* anything?" Susie asked innocently.

Bree shrugged. "I suppose they think there is some risk to the children? Like, um . . ." She struggled to pinpoint what, exactly, the professor would have in mind.

Ruby scoffed. "Moral turpitude is not the issue. The bigger risk is that I get sent packing by Mr. HF before I can spill the beans to his missus," muttered Ruby.

"Discretion is the better part of valor, Ruby," Dash counseled. "Live and let live. Can the nanny be trusted with all the family secrets, and all that. I'd wager this is a trick question—less about the kids, more about your honor. I'd play this one cool."

Ruby nodded, her common sense taking the fore as she followed Dash's advice, deciding to take the tack of having a frank, nonjudgmental conversation with Mr. HF while quietly asking for her unmentionables to be returned.

On tape, Bree played the cross-dressing employer.

"Shall I be wearing your underwear, do you think?" she pondered. "I could put some on over my clothes. It might make it more real."

"He only took my underthings. It doesn't say he's wearing them. He's wearing his wife's clothing," Ruby pointed out.

"Maybe Dash should be the one dressed up. We have an advantage having the only manny," Susie pointed out.

"Fine," Dash said. "I've done it for Halloween parties at my horrid boarding school—might as well do it for this, if it'll help our grade." He sized them all up. "It will have to be something from your wardrobe, Ruby. You're the only one tall enough. Perhaps a nice wrap dress?"

Ruby grumbled about having to go all the way back to the apartment, but an hour later returned with a bag of clothing.

"You showered today?" she eyed Dash skeptically, holding back the bag.

"Oh, come on, Ruby," Bree chided good-naturedly. "Be a sport. We'll be done in a jiffy if you just hand over that satchel."

Ruby unhappily thrust the bag of clothes at Dash and he ducked into a restroom to change.

"Try not to stretch them out," Ruby called out after him. "He should pay for his laundry service to clean them," she continued.

"It's not as if he's full of germs, Ruby," Bree admonished.

"Easy for you to say," Ruby laughed. "He's not going to be fondling your underthings."

"He fondles my underthings all the time," Susie said with a wink. "And they're no worse for the wear."

"How do I look?" Dash burst back into the conference room. He'd settled upon a fuzzy angora sweater and skirt set. He was not able to zip or button the skirt all the way, and the sweater, straining across his broad chest, was too short, exposing a big gap of pale, hairy stomach. He spun around, twirling a massive pair of cotton underpants from his index finger.

"Oh my," Ruby groaned.

"Just imagine me as your employer, Ruby. Now then, shall we begin? Bree, man the camera. Ruby, I'll stand over here. You walk in, pretending to find me in the proverbial and literal closet. Ready?"

Bree found the whole process to be frustrating and ridiculous. For something that was so trivial in the scheme of things to take so much effort seemed in some ways to epitomize the essence of their nanny training. On the first, second, and third takes, Ruby could not get the pained, disapproving look off her face, refusing to look her employer in the eye, ruining the whole thing.

On the fourth take, her extreme reversal into faked understanding and earnestness made Susie break out into a snorting laugh, causing both Ruby and Dash to break character.

The fifth take, Dash's skirt fell down around his knees. He gamely continued on, pretending nothing had happened, until the underwear he was twirling flew off his finger, landing on the camera.

It took ten takes before they managed to get a decent cut for submission.

In the end, the professor told them that while she appreciated the apparent "enthusiasm" with which they had approached the scenario, Ruby would have been better off turning around silently and pretending it had never happened. They received a low B for their group submission, Susie's inordinate show of cleavage suppressing their grade even further than they'd expected.

After that dispiriting result, they were apprehensive, but hopeful, about their final assignment for *Expending Excess Energy*: One of them was to design a scavenger hunt through London, and the others were to test it out, keeping in mind the needs and capabilities of hypothetical ten-year-olds. *No Harry Potter–related activities allowed*, the instructions sniffed with an air of superiority. They were to suck up at least three hours of time in the search—enough time for the HF's mummy to get in some serious shopping or a trip to the salon.

"I nominate Susie to design the hunt," Dash announced as they read over the rubric.

Ruby and Bree shot each other worried looks, and then gazed past Dash at Susie, who'd wandered away and seemed engaged in the complex task of operating a pair of safety scissors she'd purloined from the Crafts room.

His eyes trailed theirs and his shoulders sagged. With a steadfast resolve he turned back and launched into his defense of Susie before Bree could even protest.

"She has lived practically her entire life in London. Including portions of her childhood. And she deserves an opportunity to redeem herself after the nappy incident with poor Penny. Please?"

Bree mulled over his request, locking eyes with Ruby, who looked less than pleased.

"I'll be with you to decipher the clues," he pressed on. "And besides, how many places in London could she think of to take a bunch of ten-year-olds?"

"What if she comes up with something ridiculous and wildly age inappropriate, like the races at Ascot?" Ruby challenged, pursing her lips with doubt. It was hard to argue with that, as Bree recalled the napkin-folding craft.

"They wrapped up in October, and they're not in London. So, we should be safe," he retorted. "But if I'm wrong, I know the dress code," he added with a wink. "Please." He fixed them both with a pleading look. "She needs the extra points awarded to the designer if she's to have a prayer of making it through to the certificate program. We can't let her fail—we're a team."

Ruby rolled her eyes, but Bree felt guilty for having been so selfish. "Okay, fine. Right, Ruby?"

"Yeah, I suppose," Ruby acquiesced, grudgingly.

"Brilliant!" Dash said, slapping the table. "Let me go tell her."

They sighed, nodding, and he bounded off to Susie, delicately extracting the scissors from her fingers before she mangled something. They watched him share their decision and saw how she threw her arms around his neck, stretching up on her tiptoes to reach him, beaming with genuine delight.

"Lord, help us," Ruby intoned, raising her eyes to heaven. "What have we gotten ourselves into?"

———

"*If all the world's a stage, and all the men and women merely players, to find your path and your part, you could do worse than this for a **START**.*" Ruby recited the first clue as they stood at the Piccadilly Tube entrance.

"Oh, look, she made it rhyme," Dash said with a note of pride. "Is that all it says?"

Ruby peered at the small type and then flipped the paper over to ensure she hadn't missed something. "Just says to check the dead letter box."

"Well, that quote—it's Shakespeare, right?" Bree asked, not quite sure.

"*As You Like It*, to be precise," Ruby confirmed. "The monologue about the ages of man. How we all play different parts, from infancy to the second childhood we revert to in old age."

"There's a sculpture called *The Seven Ages of Man* in the city," Dash speculated. "Do you think she'd send us there?"

"I doubt she'd be that tricky. And no ten-year-old would want to traipse about to see a statue. No," Ruby pondered. "I am guessing she meant it quite literally. A stage. To start our adventure. Probably one of the first stages in London."

"The Globe, then!" Dash announced.

"No," Ruby said, pursing her lips as she thought. "Too obvious. And, incorrect, as it was not nearly the first. Not to mention, it's not even in its original location. I'm thinking it's the Curtain, in Shoreditch."

"You're giving Susie too much credit, dear," Dash said, not unkindly.

"I don't think you're giving her enough," Ruby countered, the words coming out of her in a quick staccato. "She capitalized Start, and bolded the S. She meant for us to read into it. The Curtain is where many of

Shakespeare's best works debuted—including *Romeo and Juliet*. It's the place that started his legacy." She slapped the paper, sure now. "She must have meant the Curtain."

"Would a ten-year-old want to see a stage? Or a stuffy old play?" Bree questioned.

"We've already determined Susie had a very unique childhood. Besides, it's not an actual operational theater now," Dash corrected her. "It's a big archeological site, a pile of spooky ruins. Perfect for that age."

"Okay, ya'll. Let's get going," Bree agreed, starting down the stairs.

The others had to drag Bree to keep up with them as they hustled themselves down the buzzy streets of Shoreditch. Everywhere she saw distractions—the acid-bright murals calling her to action, the funky shops, and the over-the-top hipster pedestrians; the of-the-moment menus mounted in windows, offering brunch and drinks and trendy appetizers. She wanted to stop and stare and soak it all in, wondering why anyone would be willing to pay that much for avocado toast. But the clock was ticking, and they had little time to spare if Ruby's hunch about the Curtain proved wrong.

The Curtain excavation was a construction site more than anything else. Entire swathes of the street front were cordoned off with temporary chain link fence, and the entire city block was surrounded by high walls that had been plastered with posters that boasted of the forthcoming delights of mixed-use development and chastised workers to not harass the women walking by. From the street, they could spot cranes and backhoes, silenced for a day of rest, waiting amidst piles of dirt and forgotten rubbish. They crossed the street.

"Give me a hand," Bree asked Ruby. Ruby knelt and Bree took a hoist to peer over the fence. The site was scarred with massive holes—foundations in progress for forthcoming apartments and shops. In the middle, a temporary structure festooned with caution tape and plastic, joined with a series of half-demolished brick walls, covered what Bree could only assume was the dig. Temporary lighting had been rigged around the place to allow round-the-clock excavation, but all was quiet now. Bree paused, reddening before clearing her voice.

"Um. I'm not sure what I'm supposed to be looking for. What exactly is a dead letter box?"

Ruby snickered. "It's the deposit box for delivering the mail."

Bree hitched herself up higher and spied across the site. There, toward the back past the dig, a bright red postbox beckoned to them.

She hopped down. "It's beyond the fence. We have to go inside to get the clue."

"It says 'Danger! Do Not Enter,'" Dash pointed out, gesturing to the poster in front of them.

"If we want to keep going," Bree said, "we have to break the rules, Dash." She looked down the street. "Nobody's watching. We can be in and out in a few minutes." She began walking the perimeter, finally finding a door that had been left ajar.

"Come on, then," she said, disappearing behind the wall. Her companions slipped in behind her, jogging to catch up.

They converged on the red mailbox. Dash reached inside the deposit slot and extracted an envelope, brandishing it for them both to admire.

"Well done, Ruby. Perfectly interpreted. It appears we've achieved our second clue."

"Open it, then," Bree urged, impatient to hear it.

He tore into the envelope and began reading. "*The home of this Holmes will be perfect for you to continue your sleuthing. And sleuth you must.*"

Ruby scoffed. "Too easy. 221b Baker Street."

"What's that?" Bree asked.

"The fictional home address of Sherlock Holmes," Dash answered. "Now site of the Sherlock Holmes Museum. Onward, then." He turned on his heel and began walking for the wall, skirting the plastic-swathed behemoth of the archeological dig.

"Hold on," Bree said, stopping short. "Since we're here, shouldn't we at least take a peek?"

"A peek? A peek at what?" Ruby demanded.

"At the actual ruins of the theater. Isn't that the whole point of being here? It seems sort of a waste to have come all this way and not take a look."

"I thought the point was to get this," Dash responded, waving the envelope in the air. "*Veni, vidi, vici.* Time to go."

"It will just take a second," Bree protested, picking up the plastic and ducking underneath into the site, leaving her friends with the words, "Think of the kids!"

The light was muted inside. The brick walls of the demolished build-ings—or, what was left of them—loomed over a large excavated pit. The pit itself contained a warren of excavations below the ground, some knee-deep, some well taller than a full-grown man. More scaffolding and fencing had been thrown up to protect the site. From where she stood, it was hard to make sense of any of it—half-dug rooms, lined with ancient cobbles and bricks, were linked by makeshift wooden walkways and wide expanses of plain dirt. She could guess at what might have been the entry—or would that have been the stage? It was mind-boggling that an entire building could have fallen into ruin and rubble, hidden beneath layers of sediment and the busy streets of Shoreditch all this time. She walked the perimeter, carefully skirting its crumbling edges, a careful hand on the scaffolding to steady herself while she peered into the gloom, hoping for a sense of history to overtake her.

When it didn't, and she felt it was time to go, she jumped over a slight trench, swinging on the scaffold for leverage, and felt something give. She looked up to see a torrent of bricks tumbling down on her. She jumped under the scaffold just in time to see them skitter past her head and tumble into the trench below, bouncing off the walls.

"Bree?" Ruby called after her, her voice muffled by the plastic. "What was that noise? Are you all right?"

Bree waited to be sure the avalanche was done and then crouched down, peeking into the trench to consider the trail of dust and debris. She looked back up, and tilted her head, wondering. Why would anyone store cobblestones *above* the dig site? *No matter*, she thought, rising and brushing her dirty hands on her khaki trousers.

"It was nothing!" Bree answered. "I'm fine. There's not much to see in here, after all. I'm on my way."

She'd satisfied her curiosity. It was time to go find Sherlock Holmes.

The young lady operating the cash register in the museum gift shop kindly handed over their next clue after obligingly taking a photograph of them posing in their replica Sherlock Holmes deerstalker caps, jauntily holding pipes.

"Kids would love this," Dash enthused, handling the magic trick sets and replica magnifying glass. "You could spend loads of time with them here."

"And drop loads of money in that gift shop," Ruby tutted as she dragged him away from the shelves and handed the envelope to Bree. "The HF's parents would not like that. We'll be sure to get points off our score. What's next, Bree?"

Bree pulled out the next clue. "*The OED has identified at least a hundred words for rain in the British English language, but London has only one definitive defense against drizzle and downpour. If you ask the shopkeeper nicely, he may open up the brolly and its secrets.*"

Dash scratched his head. "Well, that's quite odd."

"She's going all out, isn't she?" Ruby agreed. Bree, too, could only find the clue to be quite perplexing.

"It sounds like she's sending us to an umbrella shop," Dash reasoned. "It must be James Smith & Sons." He typed something into his phone and then brandished the screen. There it was, right at the top of the search results. "James Smith & Sons—Victorian Umbrella Shop. The best in the nation, if not the world. Many custom-made and built to withstand a hurricane. I don't know what this mention of 'secrets' is all about, but I gather the shopkeeper will enlighten us. Maybe you can replace your wreck of a brolly while we're there, Ruby."

"I seem to remember mine was just fine until you took it without my permission, Dashiell," Ruby harrumphed at him.

A half-hour later, they stood in a veritable thicket of umbrellas, being treated to a lecture on the finer points of raingear design. Bree peeked around the shop while the sprightly proprietor explained how the choice, shape, and treatment of materials determined the umbrella's ability to withstand different wind velocities. Every window, bin, and shelf was filled with umbrellas of different sizes and colors. Some sported handles fused onto a shaft to create a custom design. Here and there she spied walking sticks and canes, to boot. Nowhere was there a computer, just a row of ancient logbooks documenting every order, going as far back as the store's opening in the 1800s.

"Why would a ten-year-old like this?" she whispered to Ruby.

"Are you kidding?" Dash interrupted. He pulled a tall umbrella out of a stand with a dramatic flourish. "*En garde!*" He struck an outlandish fencing pose for their amusement.

"Yes, we get a fair bit of that from our younger customers," the shop-keeper said, a tinge of exasperation in his voice.

Dash straightened up, chastened. "I suppose that wasn't very mature of me. Do forgive me. What I would like to know, however, is whether you have any umbrellas with, er, secrets."

The man looked at them quizzically. "Secrets?" he repeated. "What sort of secrets?"

"Well, sir," Bree interjected. "We don't exactly know. But the clue we received said if we asked you nicely you might show us."

"Do you think it might have been referring to something like this?" He reached below the counter and pulled up a specimen made with what looked like highly polished bamboo. Swiftly, he pulled apart the handle to reveal a secret chamber. Reaching inside, he extracted a small flask that ran the length of the rod, two shot glasses, and a pair of dice. He held them up for inspection. "This is for our more social clientele."

"Oh, that's marvelous!" Dash enthused. "May I?" He reached for the contraband and held it up to the light to admire it.

"Do you have lots of brollies like these, then?" Ruby asked.

"We have some in stock, and do some made to order. The drinking and gambling kit are popular, to be sure. But there are other items we've stashed away in little hidey-holes like these. Binoculars. Magnifying glasses. Bird whistles. Extra sets of car and house keys." He leaned over the counter conspiratorially. "Even the odd dagger and miniature pistol." He winked as their eyes widened. "Those only on commission, of course."

He leaned back and cleared his throat, extending his hands until Dash turned over the drinking paraphernalia. Admiring his own handiwork, he returned it deftly under the counter and wiped his hands on his apron. "What more can I do for you young folk?"

"The next clue would be great, sir. And I believe the gentleman here will be purchasing an umbrella for his friend," Bree laughed, poking Dash in the side.

Dash rolled his eyes. "Of course. Ruby shall have her brolly. On me. Or, rather, on the duke. You can put it on the Heyward account," he mentioned sotto voce.

The shopkeeper rang up Ruby's choice and then pulled an envelope out of the logbook, handing it over to Bree. "You enjoy your little game, young ladies. Sir."

They wandered out onto the stoop to read the clue in the open air.

Ruby scanned the gray sky. "I have to hand it to Susie. She really found some out-of-the-way, spectacular things for kids. The hidden compartments were incredible. But we need to get going. From what she said, we'll have at least two clues to go."

Bree tore open the envelope. "*Your first three stops have been about mysteries, secrets, and identity. This site, once a hospital, Found these themes entwined.*"

"That's an awkward turn of phrase," Dash commented.

"She meant us to pay special attention to the word 'Found.' See?" Bree showed them the paper.

Ruby eyed Bree speculatively. "The Foundling Hospital," she declared authoritatively. "Just beyond Regent's Park. That's got to be it."

"Foundlings? You mean . . ." Bree let her voice trail off.

"Orphans. Or abandoned children. Why she'd send us there, I have no idea," Dash noted, sympathetically. "But we'd better go."

"No," Bree stated flatly, backing away. "No way."

"Bree," Ruby chided gently. "It's not a functioning orphanage. It's a museum. Did you think we were going to meet actual orphans? There will just be some boring exhibits and the like. Don't be silly. Come along."

Bree brooded, trailing behind her friends as they wound their way through the crowded street. Identity. Secrets. Mysteries. Leading to a former home for abandoned children? She had a feeling this was no innocent fluke. This trail was leading to something that had great potential to distress Bree. What, exactly, had Dash shared with Susie about her own murky past? And why would Susie try to upset her?

——

"It's not the same as what happened to you," Dash whispered, leaning a hand up against the glass as they read the exhibit's explanation of the hospital's founding. "People had to hand their babies over in person. Can you imagine?"

She shook her head numbly, overwhelmed by the information in the exhibit. She was shaken by the thought of the thousands of children who'd been received and raised between these walls when the building operated as a functioning orphanage. She was moved by the magnanimity of the artist community that took the hospital as its own cause—Handel even coming himself, personally, to perform *Messiah* at Christmas every year. She was also overwhelmed by the spare, itchy fabrics of their clothing, the hard iron beds, and spartan furnishings of the institutional surroundings that were painstakingly reconstructed in the galleries. An entire display was given over to the collection of "love tokens," most of them hand-made, that teary-eyed mothers had left with their babies, hoping to one day be able to identify their children by these trinkets and reclaim them.

She shook her head, pushing away the thoughts that were creeping into her brain. "Where did it say we should look for the next clue?"

"Under the donation box," Dash answered, showing her the paper clue again while he pulled her along behind him. They found the box, and their next clue, near the exit. Ruby read it aloud.

"*The kids can get Shirley Temples. We'll have ours shaken, not stirred.* She's sending us to a bar." Ruby checked her watch. "It *is* after five o'clock. But which bar? It must be something to do with James Bond, no? Dash, you've got to have this one."

He grinned. "Let me guide you to the hideaway that inspired Ian Fleming's judicious use of the martini to establish the raffish character of the most famous of Britain's literary spies."

Bree rolled her eyes at his pomposity.

"After you, ladies," he said with a bow and a flourish.

Within the hour, they'd ensconced themselves inside of Duke's Bar, hidden off of Bond Street, being attentively cared for by the Italian wait-staff. Dash was in his element, explaining exactly why the martini, as described by Fleming, was such a telling choice for Bond, and directing the staff as to how to prepare theirs.

"Everyone knew that, if you shook the martini, you'd bruise the gin. And nobody would consider mixing a martini with both gin and vodka. It was quite shocking. It sent a clear signal to readers that Bond was a rebel. Very anti-establishment."

Ruby snorted. "Only the nobility would consider one's approach to mixing drinks as a sign of rebelliousness."

Bree was only half listening, her eyebrows furrowed in concentration.

"What's wrong, Bree?" Ruby asked, placing a hand on her shoulder. "I'd think you'd be chuffed. We avoided disaster and it was actually a bloody good scavenger hunt. I almost wonder if Susie got some help."

"That last clue, about the foundling hospital. It's almost as if she knew." She fumbled under the neckline of her sweater and drew out something on a long chain, pulling it over her head. "She knew, Dash," she insisted, depositing the item in Dash's hand. "What did you tell her?"

"What is that?" Ruby asked, sharp-eyed.

Dash inspected it, running his thumb over the scuffs and cracks, and then drew a deep breath. "It's the name tag from the nappy bag Bree's parents used when she was a baby. It bears her name—Briana Bellona Parrish. Her own love token." He passed the chain to Ruby, letting the gravity of his revelation settle around them. "I didn't share what you told me about your past with her—or anyone, Bree. I promise you. It's just a coincidence."

Ruby cocked an eyebrow. "A fairly large one, don't you think?"

"Maybe she was trying to get a dig in at you with the visit to the Foundling Hospital, but I honestly have no idea why. And the tokens? Purely accidental."

Ruby deposited the nicked and worn piece of plastic, strung on the cheap chain, back in Bree's hand.

"Maybe you should ask her yourself, Bree," Ruby prompted. "Here she comes now."

Susie was coming in through the main entry, winding her way through the café tables that littered the bar. She looked happy and self-possessed, wrapped tightly in a smart, midnight-colored trench coat, her hair perfectly coifed, towering heels clicking lightly on the tiles as she crossed the floor. Here, she was in her element—no, in command of it—with nothing suspicious about her air.

Bree watched her, unable to help but admire her confidence, and shook her head, shoving the chain deep in her pocket.

"No. I'm sure you're right. And if she did mean to upset me, for whatever reason, I don't want her to know it worked."

Ruby pursed her lips in disapproval but said nothing.

"Hello, my dear," Dash said brightly, cutting off their conversation as Susie approached the table. "You made a marvelous hunt for us. Really well done."

She beamed down at him and proffered her hand. "I'm so glad you think so, Dashiell." She turned with a mischievous air to Bree and Ruby. "You two, don't look so gobsmacked. I do have *some* talents, after all. Now, ladies, you won't mind if I steal His Lordship away from you? I have more surprises in store for him this evening . . ."

Bree's cheeks blazed red as she thought of what Susie meant.

Dash laughed and rose, carelessly scattering some bills on the table for their tab. "Come on then, you naughty hussy. Take me away and do with me what you will. You two have enough cash to cover the rest, do you?"

Susie laughed at him. "It's covered. I paid it before I came over."

Relieved, he scooped his money back up a little too quickly—Bree imagined he was grateful to have avoided exposing his actual budgetary situation.

With that, the couple left Bree and Ruby to contemplate the stultifying train ride back to Bath and another boring Saturday evening in, alone, hitting the books in preparation for finals.

Thanksgiving came and went, the roommates roasting a small bird in their kitchen and doing their best to approximate for Bree the kind of feast she'd have had back at Thornton. They'd festooned the apartments with garlands made of feathers and leaves (procured from where, Bree didn't know), crowning her with a construction paper diadem adorned with turkeys they'd carefully made by tracing their own handprints. It was a lovely afternoon, punctuated by a short email from Rodney, but it was barely a speed bump in the run-up to exams. At Ruby's practical insistence, they later turned in both activities, along with a short curriculum entitled "Myth and Reality in the American Retelling of the First Thanksgiving," for extra-credit points in *Don't Eat The Glue*, assuaging the guilt they all felt from having taken a break from their studies.

The tests were grueling, four-hour-long affairs designed to have them regurgitate all that they had learned of child psychology, family dynamics, nutrition, and health—the whole gamut—often sneakily intermingling topics from the other courses to test the full ability of the students to internalize and apply their knowledge in a more realistic context. The study groups had been distributed through the various lecture halls for each exam. Their group had been proctored by Montoya-Craig, who walked the aisles pounding a hiking stick, snapping an anachronistic pocket watch open and closed to keep track of the time, and mercilessly enforcing the "no breaks—no snacks" rules at every turn. They emerged from the last test feeling wrung out, more apprehensive now that they understood the difficulty of the exams, and wondering if they'd done enough to make it over the bar for the certificate program.

"Shall we hit the pub?" Ruby suggested as they dragged themselves off campus.

"I'd rather nap, to be quite honest," Dash countered with a yawn. "I don't think I've had a good night's sleep in weeks."

"Same," Susie concurred, dragging her backpack behind her like an errant child.

Ruby and Bree exchanged sideways looks—Bree could see that Ruby didn't think their groupmates' sleeplessness was entirely due to studiousness, either. Though of course, Bree reminded herself, it was really none of their business. Unless their late-night activities pulled *all* of their grades down. Or they got caught breaking the rooming rules.

"I don't know if I'll be able to sleep, to tell you the truth. Not until we get our grades. But we can go to the pub later," Bree agreed. "A stiff cup of tea might be good for now."

"There's our girl. Becoming a proper Brit already," Dash joked. "Next thing you know, she'll be asking for crisps at tea and her teeth will turn into a natural color instead of that ghastly fluorescent white."

Bree ignored the jabs at her American foibles and vocabulary. A good ribbing meant you were among friends. *Mates,* she mentally corrected herself.

They arrived at Jaguar House and stumbled like sleepwalkers to their stoop. They paused to let Ruby fumble in her bag to extract the keys.

"Wait," Bree cautioned as Ruby dangled them toward the lock. "Look."

The door wasn't locked. It was ajar, by an almost imperceptible smidge.

"You didn't forget to close it behind you this morning, did you, Susie?"

"Why do you assume it was me?" Susie snapped, irritated. "And no, I did not. I made sure to lock the deadbolt, too."

"It's probably just the cleaning lady," Dash reasoned.

"Not her day," Ruby responded in a whisper.

"Shhhh," Bree insisted. Cautiously, she pushed the door open, grimacing as it squealed on its hinges. They filed through, Bree leading the way with keys in her fist, ready to fight.

"Hello, Bree," an American accent greeted them. There, in the middle of the living room, stood Miss Judy and Rodney.

"Miss Judy! Rodney! What are you doing here?" Bree bounded over, nearly knocking them over with her book bag.

Rodney laughed, enveloping her in his arms. "Miss Judy had reason to be in London for business and offered to take me with her so we could see you. Oh, how we've missed you, Bree! Thornton is not the same without you."

Bree took Rodney in. He had aged during her brief absence from the orphanage. The worry lines were etched even deeper into his ebony skin, and the tight curls of his hair had all turned gray.

Bree reached for Miss Judy, squeezing her hand to extend the circle. "That was so kind of you, Miss Judy. You don't know what this means to me. But how did you get in?"

"Your landlord is not the most security conscious. He was quite easy to persuade—you should have a word with him. And you shouldn't have come in the front door all together like that," Judy scolded. "It would have been safer to split up and come through the other suite, as well."

"You probably awed him into submission with your big pearls and fancy purse," Bree laughed, squeezing Judy's hand. "But it was you, so it all worked out."

Behind her, she heard Dash clear his throat. "Ooh, I almost forgot," she said, disentangling herself from Rodney. "Let me introduce you to my study group and roommates."

"We've enjoyed getting to know you through Bree's letters," Rodney shared as the introductions were made.

"Where are you staying, and for how long?" Bree asked.

"A few days at most," Judy said vaguely. "We're at the Gainsborough, near the old Roman Baths. I thought we'd want to take advantage of the Christmas Market while we're here. Have you been yet?"

"No," Bree admitted. "We've been hunkered down, studying. I haven't even been to the Baths yet."

"Well, I've made the three of us reservations at the Pump Room this evening. It may be a bit touristy, but everyone should experience it at least once, and since the dining room is only open for dinner during the Christmas season, it should be quite special. Why don't you meet us in the hotel lobby in two hours?" She inspected Bree's attire of official Norwood gym clothes. "Wear comfortable shoes but something present-able for dinner. We'll walk the Market before we dine, and our dinner reservation includes a candlelit private tour of the Baths themselves."

"That sounds great, Judy," Bree enthused. "What a treat!"

"Then it's a plan," Judy said emphatically. She turned to Bree's room-mates. "I'm sure we'll see you all again before we depart. Congratulations on finishing your first two terms. We'll leave you to yourselves now. Thank you for indulging our interruption."

She breezed out of the apartment, Rodney in tow. Bree was struck with the sense of how small the room had seemed with Judy in it, and how empty it seemed now that she was gone. She was finally able to take a deep breath, and release it.

The yellow stone building of the Gainsborough, with its entrance at the top of a set of stairs and the door crowned by a fluttering Union Jack, was austere. Inside, the cream-and-black inlaid floors, punctuated by pillars, led away down long corridors and yielded to curving staircases. Bree felt insignificant, barely a speck in all the magnificence, waiting for Judy and Rodney in the lobby, and out of place, like a child playing dress-up, in the dress and stylish boots she'd borrowed from Ruby.

"There you are," Judy said, her presence immediately filling up the space. She had come from outdoors, dragging shopping bags behind her. Rodney carried another armload, grinning.

"We decided to hit some of the shops early," Rodney explained. "Look at these handmade toys. They're beautiful." He extended a bag for Bree to take a peek. She had to agree. Hand-carved and painted with a delicate eye, the toys were unlike anything she'd seen before.

"They're lovely, Rodney. The little ones will love them."

"Judy's being very generous, as always," he acknowledged.

Judy waved a hand, dismissing the compliment. "At these prices, they are a steal, and they'll last forever. Let's have the valet take these up for us so we can get you out to the Market, Bree. We've got plenty of stalls left to hit."

They bundled themselves up and walked the short distance past a vast, glittering glass-and-stone edifice that promised spa-like delights within. Then, with a quick right turn, they found themselves on Bath Street, the magnificence of the Market yielding itself to them.

"Ohhh," breathed Bree, as she stopped to take it all in. The entire street had been filled with little chalet-like structures, each peaked-roof abutting the next to form a continuous alley of tiny shops. Row upon row of them filled the space—a virtual village of craftsmen and tempo-rary restaurants. Strung with lights and illuminated from within, the wood lean-tos twinkled with a homey cheer that matched and magnified the glow of the illuminated yellow stone buildings that lined the street. Shoppers bustled about, laughing and calling to one another, and the smell of roasting chestnuts and mulled wine filled the air. Here and there, she caught a snatch of a merry carol.

"It's beautiful," she whispered.

"Wait until you see the abbey. That's the best spot. We'll run into it if we keep going this way."

They wound their way through Stall Street, then Abbeygate Street and into the Abbey Yard, stopping here and there to consider the shopkeepers' wares: sheepskin gloves, botanical gins, hand-knit blankets, hand-carved birdhouses that looked like fine mansions, countless soaps, scrubs, and scents bursting with essential oils, as well as pies, cakes, and candies. Anything under the sun, it seemed, could be found in the Market, the shopkeepers eager to share their story and the provenance of each item with you if you cared to linger long enough.

They buffeted their way through the cheery spectacle and milling crowds until, as Judy had promised, the Bath Abbey soared above them, gigantic spotlights illuminating every nook and cranny of its magnificence. Buttresses, pinnacles, battlements, and parapets were scattered about the structure, enabling it to reach to a staggering height. The vast expanses of stained-glass windows glittered in the spotlights, matching the twinkling lights of the gigantic Christmas tree that had been set in the square below.

"Can we take a closer look?" Bree enthused to Rodney.

"I don't see why not," he responded.

"How much time until our tour of the Baths, Judy?" Bree glanced back to confirm they had long enough to linger. Judy was turned around, watching something.

"What is it, Judy?" Bree asked.

Judy turned abruptly. "Nothing," she responded absentmindedly, her eyes scanning the little city of chalets. She checked her watch. "We need

to circle back to the Baths now, I'm afraid. But it will be just as spectacular, I promise, if a bit quieter. Come, walk with me, Bree—we haven't had
a chance to really catch up."

"You must tell me everything," Judy commanded as she tucked her
arm under Bree's and swept her down the street. Judy walked briskly,
not seeming to care that Rodney was loitering behind. Bree would have
liked to peruse the wares on offer as they passed shop after shop, but Judy
seemed intent upon their destination.

"I know I haven't written much," Bree admitted sheepishly. "It's been
a bit overwhelming. Preparing for the certificate program is like a whole
second major. I don't think any of us realized what we were getting into.
I'm sure your research into the program didn't bring up half of what I've
discovered since I've been here."

"Humph," Judy said, noncommittally, seemingly still preoccupied.
"But you're keeping up?"

"Yes, of course," Bree confirmed. "I'm doing quite well, overall, though
the group work certainly leaves some of that out of my control." She grimaced a bit, thinking of all of the semi-disasters attributable to Susie.

"Your group, then, they don't pull their weight?"

"That's not what I meant!" Bree protested, blushing. "I just mean, we
all try our best, but we have different strengths and weaknesses based on
our backgrounds."

"Such as?"

"Well, Dash is a nobleman himself, so he has a natural feel for the
way to best approach the family dynamics of the upper-class client.
Ruby's mom is a nurse, and Ruby spent a lot of time raising her younger
siblings, so she is really good with all of the health-related things we are
learning and knows a ton of ways to keep children distracted and happy.
Not to mention she's motivated. She wants to be top girl and named
proctor next year."

"And this Susie? What about her?"

Bree paused, choosing her words carefully. "She's got good team spirit. And has been killer in the language portion."

"But that doesn't help your group scores, does it?"

"No," Bree admitted reluctantly.

"Does she have a knack for the foibles of the upper class, like Dash?"

"Um . . . I think her upbringing was a little more unusual."

Judy arched a brow, seemingly on the verge of probing deeper to understand the meaning of Bree's comment, when she pulled up short. "Ah, here we are. The Roman Baths." Bree drew up her head, surprised at how quickly the walk had gone. The building before her did not stand out in any particular way from the street upon street of yellow stone edifices she had come to know as characteristic of Bath. In fact, its doorway was rather nondescript.

Judy darted another look over her shoulder. "Let's get inside and hope that Rodney catches up with us."

The lights in the great lobby were already dimmed for after-hours. A solitary suited figure waited at a large oval ticket counter. Upon seeing them enter, he tucked his cellphone into his jacket pocket.

"Ah, you must be Ms. Roberts?" the man smiled, swiping a clipboard off the ticket stand and walking toward them. "I'm Charles Pendergrass, your guide to the Baths this evening. But I thought you were a party of three?"

"One of our party is lagging behind a bit," Judy explained as she extended her hand to shake his politely. "We can start without him and hope he joins us along the way. I don't want Miss Parrish, here, to miss her opportunity to see the Baths at night." Bree, at her side, held out her hand as well.

"Pleased to meet you both," Pendergrass smiled. "The security guard over there will be certain to let him in when he arrives. As for us, given we are a tad behind schedule, I suggest we skip the terrace and head down immediately to see the main attractions—the Sacred Spring and the Great Bath."

"Isn't the terrace the best view?" Judy protested slightly.

"The view from the Bath itself is spectacular, if not as broad of a vista. And, honestly, the statuary on the terrace is Victorian, dating to the period right before the restored Baths were reopened to the public. Not nearly as exciting as treading upon two-thousand-year-old stones. Come, let me show you."

He led them across the hall to an elevator, ushering them in to begin their descent.

The elevator doors whisked open to deposit them in a large gallery. Exhibits about Roman people and worship, the construction of the Baths, and bits of broken pottery and statuary stood waiting, spot-lit for their inspection.

"Another time, should you come back to Bath and have more time, you can explore these parts," Charles explained. "To be honest, those exhibits are a bit stuffy—not worth it when you are on a tight schedule. Come around this corner instead and you can see the thing that makes this place so special: the Sacred Spring."

They followed him, ducking through a row of arches that opened onto a large green pool. An arched walkway surrounded the interior lower level, while windowed galleries stood above. Vaulted ceilings covered the pool in its entirety. It was dimly lit, a slight gurgling sound emanating throughout. A mineral tang filled the damp air. Bree felt the uneven cobbles under her feet and ran a toe over them.

"Careful, they can get a bit slick," Charles warned. "The spring is not normally open this time of night," he continued. "But I wanted you to see it first, because this is the heart of the entire complex. For thousands of years, natural spring water at a hot forty-six degrees Celsius has bubbled up on this site. It is the source for the entire bathhouse, and we believe it spawned its own religious cult. There was once a temple to a healing deity, Sulis Minerva, adjacent to this site. People came from great distances to worship and hope for some intervention from the spring itself. When restoration was underway, the archaeologists uncovered the largest cache of Roman coins ever found on British soil, as well as an impressive collection of curses engraved onto metal sheet work and dumped into the spring, which supposedly held the spirit of the goddess."

"Curses?" Judy questioned. "I didn't remember that part. Do tell."

"Yes," Charles chuckled. "Some quite creative and nasty ones, I must say. These things had an entire pattern and ritual to them. The texts themselves greet the goddess, name the perpetrator—usually a thief, a suspected witch, or in some cases, an adulterer—and then propose a contract with the goddess in exchange for either recovery of property or simple punishment of the wrong-doer. A very elaborate engraving of the tablet, which then was rolled and nailed, sometimes with ephemera associated with the accused thrown in, was quite typical. We've found them all over Britain, but the ones here were quite special. Lots of mentions of double-crossing politicians and spies, which is quite unusual—though certainly a known feature of Roman politics. So you see, this bathhouse held a unique place in the working of Roman society. It was more than just a place for socializing, or to maintain one's hygiene. It was an epicenter for justice. For revenge. To understand its scope, however, you must see the Great Bath. This way."

He ushered them back out and cut through the gallery toward a lone archway built into the stone. "After you," he smiled, gesturing them forward.

Bree stepped through the arch, feeling her way over the rough stone walkway, and gasped as she emerged into the Great Bath.

Steam, ethereal but thick, rose silently from the cyan depths of the water. A colonnade of stone surrounded the entire pool, spotlights warming the cold walls and recessed niches, lending a glow to the fog that birthed where frigid sky and damp steam met. Great tongues of flame, shapeshifting and writhing, turning yellow and blue and green, danced from the wide bowls of the metal torches affixed to each column, illuminating the entire bath in gold and studding the waters with little orbs of reflected fire. Above, statues of Roman generals and long-gone British politicians punctuated the stone rail of the terrace, silhouetted against the darkness.

They were the only ones there, intruders in the ghostly scene.

"Oh," Bree sighed.

"Indeed," Charles whispered. "Quite breathtaking, isn't it? Can you imagine actually taking your bath here? Of course, now we don't allow it. Too great a liability. Now only special tour groups, or guests such as yourselves, can even get this close." A jingling of electronic bells split the night, echoing off the stone. He dug in his pocket and extracted his cell-phone, annoyed.

"Yes?" he snapped, turning away from them slightly. After a few moments, he sighed. "Very well, then," and turned back to them, returning his phone to his jacket pocket.

"I'm afraid something has come up on the main floor," he explained, apologetic. "It won't take but a minute—I'll leave you two to explore and be back to fetch you to the Pump House for your dinner, if that's all right?"

"Of course," Judy acquiesced. Bree didn't mind at all. She wanted to simply breathe in this place, the feel of its ancient, moss-stained stones, etched by water, and let it fill her up. She turned away to explore the nooks and crannies of the perimeter as Charles scurried off.

She laid a hand on a pillar and peered down into the pool. Beneath the surface, she could just make out the steps that lined each side, leading long-ago bathers in to plunge and purify themselves.

"Judy, how did you even know about this place?"

Judy laughed. "From my old M&A days. Bankers always go all out to wine and dine you, especially if a deal closes. It's been years, but it's just as I remember. It's usually only open for evening tours in the summer, you know."

Filled with a sudden surge of emotion, Bree danced across the cobbles to hug Judy. "I can't believe you did this just for me," she enthused. "Just look at this place!" She twirled, nearly giddy, along the edge of the pool, looking up to take in the star-studded sky.

"Bree, be careful," Judy warned, but Bree couldn't keep herself from spinning. It had been months since she had felt this light.

"It's like being inside a jewel box," she laughed, as she began to slow to a more sedate waltz, "or the inside of an agate sliced clean."

"Bree!" Judy shouted sharply.

Bree heard the grind of stone against stone and felt the immensity of a shudder that bounced off the emptiness of the colonnade and came from everywhere at once. She snapped her head up to see something huge hurtling toward her. Automatically, she dove to the ground, rolling away until she was able to regain her hands and knees, skin scraping against the cold cobbles while shards of marble and stone cascaded about her, showering her with splinters. Instinctively, she covered her face.

Judy was shaking her about the shoulders. "Are you hurt? Did it hit you?"

Bree raised her head and looked over her shoulder. There, where she'd stood just a moment ago, lay a gigantic statue, broken in pieces, half of it submerged into the hot water of the bath. The ripples unleashed by the violent splash of the statue's fall were just now reaching the steps at the far end of the pool. She leaned back and peered overhead and saw a broken gap in the rail that guarded the perimeter of the terrace.

Judy had dropped Bree's arms and was trotting about the perimeter of the pool, heels clacking against the stones, scanning the terrace, eyes cutting back and forth as she kept a protective hand on her pocketbook.

"I asked you—are you injured, Briana?"

Miss Judy only called her that when she was angry. Or frightened.

"I'm fine, Miss Judy. I don't even think I have a cut. What happened?"

"I saw a movement out of the corner of my eye. Somehow that rail gave way and the statue tumbled over. You dodged out of the way just in time," Judy explained. "Quickly now. Get up and get under the walkway, out of range of anyone up on the terrace."

"But there's no one there, Judy," Bree said, her body protesting the effort to pick herself up as she stared up at the deserted terrace. "Is there?"

"Now, Briana. Do as I say."

Confused, Bree scrambled to her feet and took shelter in one of the niches, next to a giant pot. Just then, Charles burst through the arch, with Rodney emerging just behind him.

"My God, what happened?" Charles cried out.

"Apparently, we had a little issue with a structural weakness," Judy answered tartly, pointing to the collapsed terrace barrier. "One of your so-called liabilities—I believe that was the term you used?"

"But that's impossible," Charles objected, flustered. "We inspect it routinely. Everything up there, as well as here, was completely sound not even a month ago."

"There can be no other explanation," Judy countered smoothly. "Unless there were other people in the museum of whom we weren't aware?"

Baffled, Charles shook his head. "In this part? No. Just your party, me, and the security guard in the lobby. Besides, who would want to do that deliberately? Or even could? It's solid stone."

"Yes, I suppose you're right," Judy said, seeming to relax just a bit. "It was just an awful accident," she reasoned, her brow troubled as if still trying to convince herself. "A lucky near miss—she would have been crushed by that heavy stone."

The blood drained from Bree's head as she began to understand what Judy was saying. She leaned back against the stone wall and took a deep breath, trying to force her knees to stop shaking, while the chill of the stone seeped through to her bones.

Rodney came over and wrapped her shoulders in a comforting squeeze. "I think we've had enough adventure for one night. That fancy dinner can wait. Let's get you home, Bree."

———

Bree groaned. Her entire body ached. Whether it was the letdown from the adrenaline, or the bruises she'd given herself when she threw herself onto the timeworn cobblestones, she didn't know. But it hurt to even think about moving.

She rolled over in her bed, stifling a moan so as not to wake Ruby, and thought.

Eventually, she pushed the events of last evening from her mind and instead considered the envelope that Ruby had left neatly on her pillow, making sure she'd see it before bed.

Miss Briana B. Parrish, it read in elegant script. Inside was a summons, engraved on creamy stationery, the official Norwood College crest emblazoned at its top. She was to report to the faculty lounge library in the administrative offices at seven p.m. that evening, in full formal uniform. No explanations. No phone number or email to enquire for further information. She held the envelope up to the light.

"We each got them," Ruby croaked as she thrashed through the tangle of covers she'd awoken in. "What do you make of it?"

"Some sort of academic recognition?"

Ruby grunted. "Wouldn't have invited Susie, then, would they have?"

"A faculty dinner?"

"Then why the secrecy?" Ruby heaved herself up, throwing her stockinged feet to the cold floor. "I don't like it. But I guess we'd better show up."

"In all our glory," Bree breathed, inwardly groaning at the thought of finally having to put on that formal Norwood nanny uniform.

Her own fashion shame was nothing, however, compared to Dash's.

"You've got to be kidding me," Ruby said, dumbfounded, when he sheepishly emerged into their common space to reveal himself.

While the ladies' uniform was an exercise in blandness, all khakis and browns, the faculty had conferred a tweedy dignity upon their male student, the field of brown broken up by a dull green-and-red windowpane plaid. If possible, the outfit looked even more restrictive than that worn by the women. It consisted of a full suit—trousers, waistcoat, and jacket—topped by a swooping cape in the same monotonous tweed. Where the ladies sported silk ties and pins, Dash bore an ascot. And in lieu of their nurse-cap-like hats, he bore a deerstalker cap plucked out of the Sherlock Holmes museum.

He bowed neatly, drawing the cape out for effect. "A far cry from a smart tuxedo, but the higher powers of Norwood have spoken, and it will have to do."

"Do they want you to watch babies? Or solve mysteries?" Ruby wondered aloud. "You look ridiculous."

He feigned a wounded look. "I think they were rather going for 'trustworthy' and 'serious,' not 'ridiculous.'" He pulled at his collar. "It is a bit warm, though. I hope I will be allowed to remove the cape once we are safely settled indoors."

Susie patted his elbow kindly. "Hopefully, you won't have to be seen in it too frequently, dear."

He smiled down at her. "Ah, ever so supportive, Susie. Thank you. Though I fear your hope is in vain. Brace yourselves as you leave the premises, ladies. You may want to raise your umbrellas as a precaution. I believe our friends from *The Sun* may be here for a photo opportunity with their friend 'The Manny.' Shall we?"

Indeed, a small stand of tabloid photographers were awaiting their emergence from Jaguar House. Forewarned, the women shielded their faces with official Norwood umbrellas while Dash, undaunted, posed gallantly for their cameras, letting them get a good look at his official formal costume.

"Your Lordship!" a particularly enthusiastic female journalist shouted. "What's it like being the only man at Norwood? What's it like, being the minority, working in a largely female environment?"

Dash spread his arms in good-natured humor. "What could be better than to be surrounded by the attention of lovely ladies such as these, twenty-four-seven?" Bree cringed. "Seriously, though—Becca? It is Becca, isn't it? I think you're the one I spoke with on the phone, are you not?"

"He *arranged* this?" Ruby hissed. "How dare he?"

"I'm sure it was for the money; he means no harm," Bree found herself making excuses for him. "I'm sure it is quite embarrassing for him."

Dash continued, oblivious to their outrage. "Just so. As I was saying, Becca, I have nothing but the utmost respect for my colleagues. After all, we all have a shared mission, which is the care of our nation's most precious resource: its children."

Ruby feigned a great gagging noise from behind her umbrella.

"Now, you must excuse us. We have official Norwood business to which we must attend." He began steering the reporters away, humoring them with a few more poses of him flexing in his manny uniform. Bree breathed a sigh of relief when she realized that, thankfully, he'd arranged a car for their group—they were able to quickly escape once his duties as media darling were over and make their way to the administrative offices of the college. They pretended not to notice when he shoved the envelope of cash one of the reporters had passed over to him—presumably a payment for letting the media get a sneak peek at him in his new Norwood gear—into his cape pocket.

"Y'all, I honestly don't understand what the big deal is," Bree mused to Ruby. "So he's a male nanny. The first one at Norwood. Who cares? Why is that newsworthy?"

Ruby rolled her eyes, carefully minding the starched pleats in her Norwood dress as she ducked into the cab.

"I told you. It's the novelty. And the fact that it's him, with all the baggage and drama of his noble family. It's simply not done." She grinned, her enjoyment of discussing the foibles of the upper class soothing her indignation over the rigged photo opportunity. "You'll never get it until you're one of us, Bree," she pronounced. "And by one of us, I mean a Brit," she clarified. "But mark my words, there will be a big picture of him swanning about in that ghastly cape in the paper tomorrow. Hopefully, none of us will be in it with him." She hushed up as soon as Dash climbed into the front seat, next to the driver.

The Administrative Building was the one part of the campus that had not been on their tour. Tucked behind the chapel, it was one of the oldest buildings, where the college had held its original classes upon first opening. Covered in ancient ivy, it stood watchfully, foreboding in its silence. One rarely breached its confines. It was the site of academic discipline, ejections from the school, humiliating discussions of financial difficulties—nothing anyone ever willingly wanted to encounter.

And now it hosted this, their mystery meeting.

The door had been propped open. They shuffled in, momentarily quieted. Behind a cluttered desk, a frumpy woman in a mohair sweater sat checking them off one by one as they entered the vestibule. She peered over her glasses, through a thicket of yellowing, sickly plants and photos of cats, to greet them.

"No trouble with your account today, m'lord?" she chuckled.

Dash blushed. "Not today, Mrs. Framingham, thank you."

"Go on with you, then," she said indulgently, waving them past her station.

They followed the flickering sconces and other students down the hallway to what they presumed was the faculty lounge. A prim woman in a Norwood uniform stood at the doors, collecting cell phones before allowing the students to funnel in. Bree did a double take. It was Gul Avci, the alumna from convocation who'd approached Bree at The Bells Inn; the one who'd left Bree with so many questions.

"You made it," Avci said, a slight curve to her mouth as she held the strongbox out to Bree.

Bree dropped her phone in the box. "Through the strength trials? To the meeting tonight?" Bree was confused.

"You'll see," Avci said enigmatically, gesturing to Bree to move along into the lounge.

It was a wide room, paneled in rich, polished walnut that reflected back the high sheen of brass lamps scattered about the place. Stern portraits of former faculty members stared down at them, as if disapproving of their very presence. Heavy velvet drapes in a deep scarlet had been drawn over the windows, ensuring them privacy. No one had dared to take a seat at one of the plush Jacobean patterned sofas or high wing-backed chairs that had been artfully arranged into conversation groupings along the walls. Instead, about thirty students had packed themselves into the rows of stiff-backed wooden chairs that filled the center of the room. Bree noted they were all first-years, just like her own group. She did a head count and quickly calculated they were about the right percentage of

the class to be among the select few chosen for the certificate program—
if, indeed, that is what this was.

Hands clasped in silence, their classmates waited, khaki birds in rows,
surreptitious feet shuffling and the occasional clearing of throats the only
indication of their inner nervousness.

"Over there," Ruby whispered, pointing to a row in the back of the
room. They hastened over to claim their spots, facing the sole lectern, which
had been stationed at the far end of the room before a roaring fireplace.

Dash pulled at his cravat and began unwinding himself out of his
cape. "It's stifling in here," he complained beneath his breath.

"Shh," Ruby warned through her teeth. "It's starting."

A door, barely visible in the paneling, had opened, letting Dean Albourn
and a small klatch of other people into the room. The dean took her spot
at the podium while the others filled in the spaces behind her. Montoya-
Craig was there, looking smug. The head of the Physical Development
department was there too. Bree did not recognize the others.

"Miss Avci," Albourn ordered, her voice soft. Swiftly, the alumna
closed the heavy doors with a thud that resounded through the room.
They heard the solid click of metal upon metal as she slid the ancient bolt
through the lock. She moved to where the others stood behind the dean,
and watched.

Albourn eyed the assembled students, thoughtfully appraising them.

"You'll all be curious as to why we've invited you here this evening, I'm
sure," she began, her voice firm but soft, forcing them to strain to listen.
"You will have many questions, some of which we will be able to answer
tonight, many of which will only be addressed as time unfolds. So, I ask
you to bear with us as we reveal our purpose.

"I will be to the point. On the basis of academic merit, character, and
other qualifications, each of you has been deemed suitable for admittance
to the Norwood certificate program."

A murmur of joy and excitement flitted through the room. Bree and Ruby clutched each other's hands under the table, turning to each other with barely suppressed smiles.

Ruby arched a brow and tipped her head to the side, toward Susie, who was gleefully bouncing in her seat. "Her too?" she mouthed, unable to contain her shock.

Bree squeezed her hand, hard, giving a quick nod. They'd done it. They'd gotten their whole team through.

"Before you celebrate, though, we must share with you what this honor means. The full depth of this commitment, its very challenge, is beyond what you perceive, and will require significant sacrifice. Montoya-Craig?"

The painting over the fireplace split down the middle and opened itself up to reveal a projection screen. Albourn continued, slides appearing to punctuate her remarks.

"Norwood's certificate program is not merely a nanny training ground. And upon enrollment, your preparation and duties will not be confined to those of childcare."

Click. A shield bearing a rearing lion and rearing unicorn surrounding a royal crown flashed on the screen.

"We are a secret division of the Secret Intelligence Service, more commonly known as the MI6."

Click. A world map, punctuated by red dots, filled the screen. Bree felt a ripple of shock.

"Our graduates are highly trained spies, placed around the world in the homes of diplomats, military officials, government leaders, and business executives to provide intelligence in the interest of Her Majesty and our NATO allies. These placements give us an unprecedented level of access to intelligence. Your placements—so close to the seat of power, yet unsuspected—are at the very heart of our strategy for Western security."

Click. A blue and white star, emblazoned with the words "North Atlantic Treaty Organization," popped into view.

Murmurs of confusion now competed with the dean's presentation. She paused, waiting them out, until the rumblings petered out into discomfited silence.

"Should you accept this opportunity, you will have no choice in your future placements as a nanny. You shall serve as an instrument of the Western order, acting on our command. It is a dangerous job. You may find it easier to distance yourself from your families, for their protection. Marriage and children are frowned upon. You may be injured. You may die. And if you are caught or killed, the Agency shall never acknowledge you or the existence of any intelligence operation. You shall be known as nothing other than a sadly fallen nanny."

The slides shifted into a snapshot of the Memorial Chapel wall, displaying the hundreds of photographs of fallen nannies—no, *agents*, Bree reminded herself—bringing into vivid relief the risk they now all faced.

Her mouth went suddenly dry, and she fought the urge to vomit.

"The nerve," Dash muttered from three seats over. Ruby shushed him; just like Bree, she, too, was leaning forward, straining to hear every word that fell from Albourn's mouth.

"You will, on the other hand, have the opportunity for travel," Albourn boldly stated, as if she were describing a cushy office job or the role of a manufacturing plant engineer. "You will have the full benefits of civil service. And, most importantly, you will lead a life filled with honor and duty beyond what you have ever imagined." She nodded at Montoya-Craig. As the painting slid back to cover the screen, the group that had entered with Albourn—agents, she now realized—took their places along the perimeter of the seating area. Bree shifted uneasily in her seat. Her fingers were white and numb where Ruby's grip had only tightened.

"You do have a choice," Albourn continued. "You will have twelve hours to consider our offer to you. As you can imagine, continued secrecy is of the utmost importance. Our success is entirely dependent upon our agents being unsuspected." Bree watched in horror as the agents began to move amongst them. She struggled to push out of her seat but was shoved down, roughly.

"Sorry," Avci whispered in her ear. And Bree felt a sting in the back of her neck.

Protests, shouts of pain, and minor scuffles filled the room. Bree looked around, rubbing her neck, fingering a newly formed bump.

Albourn raised her voice to be heard above the din.

"You have been implanted with a GPS device that will enable us to track you." More protesting bubbled up, but Albourn continued, undaunted. The chaos quickly converted to silence as the students strained to hear her explanation. "You will not regain access to your cell phones until the close of the twelve hours. Any means of communication in your living quarters has been temporarily disabled. You are not to speak of this to anyone, and certainly not to your family. You will return here tomorrow at seven a.m. with your decision."

Bree scanned the faces of her classmates, hoping she had misunderstood what Albourn had said. Their faces betrayed the same confusion and distress she herself felt. She'd made no mistake, she realized with a sinking feeling.

"Should you accept our offer, you will begin training immediately following Christmas break," Albourn continued "The GPS device and communications tracking will become a permanent fixture in your life to enable us to ensure your safety and compliance. In order to preserve the secrecy of the program, you will be physically separated from those members of your current group not chosen to join the program. To encourage healthy emotional separation, any such former roommates will be informed that this reshuffling of group assignments is at your request." A murmur of dismay went through the room. "Unfortunate, but I'm sure you can agree, a sensible and necessary step if we are to protect your identity. From this point forward, you will exist in a parallel world within Norwood. Your true purpose can never be exposed to those who exist merely as nannies.

"Should you decline to join the Agency, you will be injected with a zeta inhibitory peptide, an experimental drug that will erase your memory. We cannot control the exact degree of memory loss—a risk you will need to bear. We have found that certain triggers in the Norwood environment may stir up memories, overriding the drug's effect and causing you to question your circumstances. *To remember.* To ask uncomfortable questions. This is a risk we cannot accept—not for the program, nor for your own safety. So, following the administration of the inhibitor you will be dismissed from the college, your departure attributed to academic failure. Regrettable, but the only way we can guarantee the integrity of our intelligence program."

Her face was stern. "Do not try to leave Bath. Every means of public transport is guarded by our agents for the next forty-eight hours. Our operatives are watching all roads leading from the city. Your every move will be under surveillance. You will be taken in and immediately injected with the zeta drug if we catch you in the act of escaping. Consider your options carefully." She gazed at them dispassionately. "You are dismissed."

Albourn abandoned the lectern and strode through the paneled door, her agents—Gul Avci among them—following behind her without even a backward glance.

The students sat in stunned silence.

"They can't do this," Ruby declared, talking more to herself than anyone in particular.

"They just did," Dash said tersely. "Damn battle-axe."

Bree disentwined her fingers from Ruby's. She couldn't breathe. She could barely even think. "I've got to get out of here," she mumbled, pushing her chair away brusquely and standing up. She stared about blindly, stumbling to the door, where she fumbled with the old-fashioned lock until she managed to swing it open.

"Bree, wait!" Susie called after her. But it was too late—she was running down the hallway, gasping for air as she thrust herself out the front of the Administration Building into the frigid night.

She looked about wildly. The lights were on in the chapel. There. She'd go there.

She expected to be alone, but when she burst through the door, she was startled to see somebody was already there, seated at Poppins's feet. She jumped back in surprise, then did a double take. When she saw who it was, she knew it was no accident. It was not happenstance that she was not alone in the chapel. For the figure that sat there was no stranger, and she was waiting. Waiting for Bree.

"So now you know," Judy said simply.

"You," Bree began, her breath still coming in heaving gasps, as she circled the statue. "You knew?"

Judy nodded.

"How?" Bree snarled.

Judy evaluated her with unemotional reserve. "Please, Bree. There's no need for theatrics. Everything I did, I did for you. If you calm down, I'll answer all your questions."

Bree stood still, catching her breath. She crossed her arms, narrowing her eyes at Judy. "All of them?"

"Yes, yes," Judy said, a note of impatience creeping into her voice. "Anything you want to know."

Bree cocked one eyebrow. "Okay," she said, taking a seat on the bench, keeping a careful distance between herself and Judy. "Who are you? For real."

Judy reached into her handbag and pulled out a long cigarette. She held it lightly between her elegant fingers, drawing on it until the tip glowed red, catching the flame from the gold-plated lighter she'd also extracted.

Bree ogled—she'd never before seen the lighter, or ever witnessed Judy smoke.

Judy sighed, her head tilting back to exhale a wreath of smoke, which wound its way around Poppins.

"My name is Judy Roberts, as you know. I was affiliated with the Norwood Agency for much of my adult life. I was a handler—running teams of agents out in the field. But I fell out with them years ago and had to assume a different identity. My telco jobs have been part of my cover, enabling me to move in and out of countries seamlessly, as needed. I'm not really American, but I work quite closely with Langley, which has supported my cover."

"Langley—that's the FBI?" Bree confirmed.

Judy shook her head, sucking in on her cigarette before answering, her words escaping her mouth in puffs of smoke. "No—CIA. The Bureau only handles domestic issues," she clarified. "As you'd imagine, with Norwood being a NATO-backed operation, the Americans are closely involved. It enabled me to make connections. But I'm really a Brit."

Judy waved her hand above her head, leaving a trail of smoke behind her long fingers.

"Those missing photos on the wall? They were me. And your mother. She was Norwood, like me. Hopefully, like you. And I was her handler.

I'm the one who vandalized them. I couldn't take a risk on you learning the truth until you were ready."

Bree stared at the dark squares on the wall. She'd been manipulated at every turn.

Her mouth was dry. "How can that be? All those people on the wall . . . they're supposed to be dead. But you're alive."

Judy shrugged. "After the botched assignment, I had to disappear. Faking my death and assuming a new identity was easy enough. Your mother, though . . . her death was real."

"What happened?" Bree whispered hoarsely, her eyes never leaving the space where the photo of her mother was supposed to be.

"It was a car wreck, as I've told you. She and your father were in the field and were set up. They weren't supposed to marry. They weren't supposed to have you. You were an inconvenience to me while they lived, but a debt to be honored when they died. I had to make sure you survived, that you were kept safe, or I wouldn't have been able to live with myself."

"My father," Bree whispered. It was all so new. "He was a spy, too?"

"MI5." She noticed Bree's confusion and explained. "British domestic intelligence. Counterterrorism, that sort of thing. He had a cover, of course. That was how your mother and he met. He was a widower and needed help, you see. She was placed in his home. If she kept a little eye on him while she was there, so much the better." Judy took another drag on her cigarette. It had burned down almost to her fingers. Adroitly, she snuffed it on Poppins's foot.

Bree frowned. "That means . . ." Her voice trailed off.

"It means you're British, yes. That's why your citizenship was not an issue for your admission. It was easy enough to manipulate your counselor into writing your application. The powers at Norwood knew who you really were—*are*—all along. If they thought there was anything strange about you happening to apply, well, they kept that to themselves. Though, of course, it means you are likely being watched by someone on the inside."

Bree frowned, setting aside the flare of anger she experienced at the realization that her problematic paperwork had been a lie all along—a lie designed to deliberately keep her from being adopted out of Thornton. A lie constructed so that Judy could keep her under watch—and under her thumb, Norwood bound. Her ultimate destination quite possibly a lie in which someone else at Norwood was complicit.

She could deal with that later. Other questions warred in her head. Her mother had been sent to spy on her father? Why? How did that work out? Was their marriage simply a pretext for continuing to spy on him, or were they really in love? And if he was MI5, did that mean he was spying on her, too? Were they both British? Or did her mother have an American connection that facilitated Norwood extracting Bree to Alabama? Did Rodney know? Was Rodney a part of it?

Amidst all these questions, though, there was one that was more pressing, one that rose to the top. Bree shook her head, pushing aside all the other questions to clarify her statement.

"If my father was a widower in need of a nanny, it means I have a sibling. Doesn't it?"

Judy acknowledged Bree's reasoning with a nod. "A half-sister."

"She survived, too?"

"She's alive."

Bree began to rock in her seat. It was too much. "I need to meet her."

Judy shook her head swiftly. "I'm afraid that is not possible. You were split up for your own protection. I couldn't keep you out of Norwood's clutches, but I was able to make it look like she perished in the crash with your parents. It would not be wise for her to resurface now and ruin all the good work I've done to keep you both safe."

Bree bolted upright at Judy's refusal.

"Why did you have to protect us? From what? What harm's way did you put my parents in front of that could have extended to me, a child?"

Judy seemed unperturbed by Bree's outburst. "There were people who wanted them dead. I couldn't take a chance that they would eliminate you, or your sister, as well. Your mother made me promise."

"She made you promise?"

"It was the only way she'd agree to take the mission."

Bree snorted in disgust. "So, you really had no remorse for what had happened. It was just part of the deal."

"Deals are everything in this business. Keeping your word is paramount. Until, of course, you need to break it." She smiled grimly. "You'll come to learn." Judy stood up, a hand snaking through her sleek bob to ensure it was in place.

"But you're the one who thrust me into this . . . this snake pit," Bree spat, unable to think of another word that fully captured her new disdain for Norwood. "This isn't about the children. And it isn't about Thornton. It never was, was it? You have some purpose for me, some use. What is it, Judy? Why did you bring me here? If it wasn't safe for me all those years ago, why thrust me back into the center of—"

"The business?" Judy pressed her lips into a taut line, crossing her arms. "Because there's something rotten here. Something that has been a slow drip, building to a deluge that could cause countless more deaths. Something which, if I can uncover it, may explain why that mission went so badly for your parents seventeen years ago. You see, Norwood doesn't know I am alive." Her eyes glittered, hard and determined. "They stuck you in the middle of nowhere, using various methods to keep the occasional discreet eye on you, and forgot about me, writing me off as dead. But I didn't forget. Even though it's been nearly twenty years, I can't forget that someone set us up and dragged my name through the mud, throwing the mission and blaming me for it. This is something I can fix, if I have a source inside, with a fresh set of eyes. I need you, Bree. You're the only one I can trust with this mission. I need to root out whatever it is that has insinuated itself into Norwood, Bree. You, and me. We need to root it out and hopefully, along the way, resolve this business with your parents. Once and for all."

"You couldn't have planned this all along," Bree stated, dumbfounded by the chain of events that had led her to be standing toe-to-toe with a deadly spy.

"No. My initial thought was only to keep my promise to your mother. To make sure that when they hid you away, out of harm's way, you stayed that way. To make sure they didn't have other designs on you. To monitor your progress, from a safe distance.

"But I couldn't stay away. And over time, I saw in you the things I saw in her. The sharpness and dexterity. Your quick reactions, the way you'd intuit the reality of situations and adjust. Your determination and stoicism. How, as the children came and went from Thornton, you could reshape yourself to fit in with the shifting nature of whatever cohort happened to be living there at any time. The idea that you could be even better than your mother seemed so obvious. And she was my best agent, ever, Bree. You could be that gifted. If you wanted to. I need someone like you now, more than ever."

The compliment confused her. She had always basked in Judy's praise—the fact that she still longed for it, wanted more of it, angered her. She shook it away and refocused.

"What's going to keep me safe now?" Bree challenged.

Judy reached into her bag and extracted a pistol. "I'll protect you."

"I don't believe you," Bree startled, backing away from Judy as she stared at the cold black hunk of metal. It didn't belong in a Chanel bag. It didn't belong in Judy's hand. None of this made sense, Bree thought. Everything about it was wrong.

Judy stood her ground. "The incident at the Roman Baths—that wasn't the first near miss for you, was it?" Judy pressed. "Tell me—what other 'accidents' have nearly befallen you?"

Bree thought for a moment. The confrontation in the Calais refugee camp. The falling bricks at the archeological site. Bree considered these unlikely events, and a chill ran up her spine.

"Coincidences," she whispered, shaking her head.

Judy shrugged, tucking the gun back into her purse. "Can you trust them?" Judy continued, hand on hip.

"Trust who?"

"Your groupmates, of course."

Bree thought about the scavenger hunt and Susie's uncanny clue about the Foundling Hospital. Remembering, she fingered the chain around her neck. Susie wasn't that savvy, she reminded herself. But Dash . . . What if it had been him, all along? And Ruby—what did she really know about Ruby? Was she so driven that she'd stop at nothing to make her mark at Norwood and secure her future—even if it meant selling out Bree?

She shook the doubts from her head.

"Of course I can trust them," she whispered. "They're my friends."

"Don't underestimate them, Bree. Nor anyone. You have to put yourself first. You understand me? From now on, you can trust no one. No one."

"Not even you?"

Judy pressed her lips into a thin, humorless line. "If you can't trust me, at least obey. You'll need someone to guide you. I can be that guide, Bree—if you let me."

"They would kill you if they knew you were here. Wouldn't they?"

Judy didn't bother to answer her question—it was too obvious. Instead, she returned to the heart of the matter. "I need to know if I can count on you. Eventually, my past affiliation with Norwood may come to the knowledge of your classmates, but I need to know you won't divulge it yourself. And no matter what they do learn, my real purpose here—this conversation—they can never know about."

Bree dropped her head to stare at the worn flagstones beneath her feet and nodded. What choice did she have?

"Very well," Judy sighed, the tension seeming to seep out of her body with Bree's acquiescence. "Let's get you back to Jaguar House. You'll have an early start of it tomorrow."

"One thing, Judy," Bree interrupted, her voice cracking. "My name. Is this my real name?"

Judy's eyes looked sad as she looked over her shoulder, poised before the open chapel door.

"Does it really matter, Briana?"

———

Her groupmates were huddled around the kitchen table. Susie was nursing a martini. Dash looked to be on his third whisky. Ruby had worked her way to the bottom of a Guinness. They looked up at her, expectantly.

"Where were you?" Ruby asked in a harsh tone, her latent Trinidadian accent coming to the fore in her emotion and exhaustion.

Bree immediately felt guilty. "I'm sorry. I needed to be alone. I was in the chapel."

"This whole time?" Ruby pressed.

Bree took a deep breath. "Yes."

Dash patted the chair next to him. Bree sank gratefully into the seat and reached across the table to grab a sip of his whisky. Unpracticed, she gulped and sputtered, grimacing and coughing as she thrust the glass back at him.

"You'll get used to it," Dash said, pouring a finger into a waiting glass and sliding it over to her. "You'll need to, after tonight."

They all stared at the table. Bree imagined that they were all feeling as duped as she was, though it seemed no one had the heart to say it out loud. Susie drummed her fingers on the table restlessly.

"It makes more sense to me now," Dash began.

"What does?" Susie tilted her head, curious as to what Dash could mean.

"Why admit a male pupil now, after all these years? The only reason to break with tradition is to keep the regulators out. An investigation into sexism or something like that would risk exposure. Bowing to public pressure keeps their secret safe."

Susie patted his hand. "It doesn't make you any less qualified, Dash. Nor groundbreaking." Dash smiled wanly. It was thin comfort now.

"Alice," Ruby blurted. "That student, Alice Clark."

"What about her?" Bree said, swirling the whiskey around in her glass.

"All those times we were told to do something for Alice. She didn't die because she was a nanny. She died because she was a spy."

Bree set the whiskey glass down on the table and watched the tiny golden whirlpool come to a stop. Another realization jolted her. "I don't think she's dead."

"What? What are you talking about?" Dash demanded.

"I saw her. At least, I think I did. That night you followed me in the rain to the chapel. I saw a homeless woman in an alley and went to help her. She quoted a part of the Norwood song back at me." Her voice cracked. "She told me it wasn't safe. It was her. I'm sure of it now. I couldn't place her then, but she was familiar."

"Oh my God, they wiped her memory," Dash murmured, his face looking unusually pale. "She must have wanted out. Or threatened to expose them somehow."

"What are we going to do?" Bree broached the question with which they were all struggling.

Ruby snorted, cocking a derisive eyebrow. "We don't have a choice, do we? If we don't join up, they kick us out and wipe our memory with some experimental drug. Who knows what kind of damage that will do?" Her face darkened. "Nor what else they may go on to do to our families. We'll wind up like Alice. Unless we can escape."

"What do you mean, Ruby?" Bree pressed. "We can't possibly escape. You heard them—they've got every way out of Bath monitored."

"Not now—later. After they think they've got us cowed. I have some forceps and scalpels in my medical kit. I'll dig the GPS out of our necks so we can run away without them realizing it."

Dash shuddered. "Sounds bloody. And what about you? You can't operate on the back of your own neck."

"I'll teach you how to do it."

Dash shook his head. "Too dangerous. What if one of us severs your spinal cord? Or you ours? Besides, knowing them, they're likely to have booby-trapped the damn things so if we try to tamper with them, we all get blown to smithereens."

"It can't be deep enough to pose a risk to the spinal cord. We have to try something," Ruby insisted, a desperate tinge to her voice.

"They'll find us no matter where we go," Bree said simply. "They have the full resources of NATO behind them. How could we ever get away with it? Even if we managed to dig the trackers out without hurting ourselves, we would buy ourselves some time, but that's all. In the end, we'd wind up the same."

"Maybe it won't be so bad, being a spy," Susie added hopefully. "It would actually be more exciting to be a secret agent than a plain old nanny, wouldn't it?"

Dash enclosed her hand in his grip. "Exciting. But infinitely more dangerous, sweetheart. I'm not sure it's something I would have signed up for knowingly. I'm afraid my volunteer bona fides run more to charity auctions and the like—my patriotism more of the bunting and fireworks type. Taking bullets was not in my plan." He sagged in his chair and took a hard gulp of whisky. "But I agree with where you started, Ruby. I don't want my memory wiped. If I were to flunk out of Norwood, I would become even more of a laughingstock. And my stepmother would force me to join her decorating business. Though I'm loath to admit it, as much as my family pains me, I don't want them hurt. I cannot knowingly put them at risk. I see no other choice." His mouth twisted bitterly as he said the words.

"Ruby?" Bree pressed.

Ruby finished her Guinness and grimaced. "Yeah. I guess you're right."

"So, we're all in," Bree stated flatly. "Even you, Susie?"

Susie tilted her chin and smiled sweetly at Dash. "I'll go wherever Dashiell goes." He leaned down and deposited a kiss on the top of her head.

"Thank you, sweetheart. I appreciate the sentiment."

"Then it's settled," Bree declared. "Seven o'clock tomorrow, we join up. But we join as one. Together." She stared hard at each one of them. Friends or foes, she needed to keep them close. "One team, keeping each other's backs. Right?"

Under the harsh fluorescent light of their humble kitchen, they mumbled their assent and glumly raised their glasses, clinking to their future as spies of the realm.

"To Alice," Ruby intoned.

"To us," Susie added.

"To surviving," Dash added grimly.

"Yes, to surviving," Bree echoed, wondering just how they would when so many before them—her parents included—had failed.

They gulped their liquor, feeling it burn as it went down.

Chapter Four

THIRD TERM

Bath, England

"Such a shame you spilled on your uniform—I suppose you'll have to go home and change. After all, a certificate girl can't be seen looking like that."

Bree pushed herself up to her knees, surveying the aftermath of being tripped by yet another first-year whose ego had been bruised by not having made the cut and who resented the ruthless efficiency with which the chosen had been hived off and elevated, leaving the rest of them to lick their wounds.

"Be sure to pick up after yourself," the bully snipped, stepping over Bree where she knelt on the floor, surrounded by a puddle of coffee.

Bree sighed. Everything had gotten so much harder since that night when they'd learned the truth. And the January weather had turned biting, the wind slicing through them as they trudged to and from campus in the dark.

The artificiality and danger of their newfound circumstances had acted as a strange aphrodisiac to Susie and Dash. What had been a flirtation turned into a serious infatuation, their 24-hour preoccupation with one another just an added stressor, in Bree's opinion.

The merciless separation of the certificate program students from those in the regular course had happened swiftly, in a manner designed to inflict the most hurt feelings. Rooming assignments were broken and rearranged. Students were tracked into parallel, but segregated, courses—ostensibly to accommodate the much busier schedules of the elite certificate program, but really to isolate them from any prying eyes. A wall of hostility now stood between them and their former friends, increasingly strangers on the same campus.

The regular college coursework had continued, of course, with new courses for the new term—*Infant and Toddler Assessment and Early Intervention, The Role of the Parents, Language Development,* and *Supporting Schemas of Play.* A weekly community internship to get practical experience, tailored to the background and skill of each student, was also introduced. For Susie and Dash, this meant serving as children's docents in the local art museum. Ruby was placed in a day care, finally getting her chance to work with special-needs children. Bree was put into a children's party-planning outfit called Mommy Poppins and soon found herself dealing with Ozzy Whizzpop and his annoying performing pet, Bonkers the Monkey. A full course load, in and of itself.

But the certificate requirements—in reality, spy training—were shaping up to be even more intense, in keeping with the stakes.

The administration waited until a few weeks into the semester to introduce the fledgling agents to this part of their program. Montoya-Craig walked up and down the rows of desks in the small classroom in which they'd been ordered to assemble for a ten p.m. roll call. She passed their curricula out, and Bree watched as everyone flipped frantically through the photocopied pages, sagging in their chairs, already defeated by the crushing workload. Montoya-Craig eyed each of them critically, as if already guessing who would need to be weeded out.

"Because this is a three- versus a four-year college program, we load our students up each term. That is to be expected. This term, however, will be particularly challenging, as we are trying to prepare you for field-work that will take place over the course of the summer break."

A young woman whom Bree did not know shot an anxious hand up. "My family already has summer vacation plans in France—"

"Miss Johnson, you will have to say au revoir to your family to complete your requirement, or you will have to say au revoir to Norwood—and your memories," Montoya-Craig cut her off with a poisonous smile. She turned to address the entire group. "That goes for all of you. From now on, you will have to do as Norwood directs if you are to retain your spot. Fieldwork is essential to your readiness as an agent. Skipping or delaying it is not permissible." She resumed her pacing, bouncing a pencil off of her chin. "Now, where was I? Oh yes, the course load.

"Most of the courses this semester are practicums—that is, they are applied learnings. The good news is that they will require minimal read-ing or writing—no papers or reports, for which you can thank me later. The bad news is the extensive time in hands-on learning, which will eat into your late-night and early-morning free time."

Bree eyed the course list, reciting each course's title in her head as she tried to recall the nicknames that Ruby had already ferreted out of the older students. *Practicum in Cybersecurity, Encrypted Communications, and Technology,* aka *Snap-Spy. Introductory Geopolitics*—aka, *Pin the Tail on the Banana Republic. Practicum in Defense, Terrorism, and Physical Security*—known colloquially as *Wonder Woman 101,* with apologies to the resident manny. Continued language requirements. And then the course Bree dreaded: *Practicum in Social Graces and Charm—Smile and Sneak,* or, as Bree thought of it, *Wrong Fork.*

"Do not be lulled into thinking that the applied learning courses will be easy. They will be mentally and physically daunting, by necessity. Or, as course reviews last year indicated, 'killer'—just like you, our young spies, are meant to be."

She let that sink in. A nervous cough from one of the students in the back of the room was the only sound. Montoya-Craig continued.

"The back of your handout includes a release, holding Norwood harmless for any physical injury you may incur during the course of this semester, and our Anti-Terrorism Policy, in which you testify you are not affiliated with any known terrorist organization. Both forms must be signed and returned to your *Defense, Terrorism, and Physical Security* instructor tomorrow, before you commence class. You can look it over now. While you do, I'll welcome back Gul Avci. She has graciously agreed to join us this evening to answer any questions you may have—bestow you with a bit of alumna wisdom, as it were. She'll pop in and out as her schedule permits throughout the term, acting as a mentor of sorts as you go through your initial training."

Avci had entered the room dressed in the more casual Norwood uniform. She tagged onto Montoya-Craig's statement in a tone that Bree took as an attempt to be reassuring.

"Don't worry, class. You won't usually find spy craft to be so bureaucratic and dull." Susie giggled and Ruby shushed her.

Bree, for one, was grateful for Avci's attempted lightness, even if it was a bit tin-eared for their true feelings. Because through all the formality and forced normality of registering for spy classes, her classmates' collective consciousness was infused with the understanding that the GPS tracker had never been, and would never be, removed from the soft spot at the base of their necks where it had been so brusquely injected. That night in the faculty lounge had marked the end of their freedom. Their every movement was visible to their handlers, who as of yet remained anonymous to them, as was their performance on every test and evaluatory exercise. Their identities were already being subsumed into those of instruments of the state, no matter their official status as students. They were to be machines, their value reduced to spreadsheets full of numbers and coordinates and the ability to kill at will.

And they were not even twenty years old.

Avci and Montoya-Craig seemed to have come to terms with and even embraced this reality. For Bree and her classmates, it was too soon . . . too fresh a wound.

⸻

"Who will go first?"

They were in the basement of the recreation center. It was ten p.m., the twenty or so students in this section assembled for their first bout with *Wonder Woman 101*.

"Don't be shy," Professor Shadduck urged from the center of the mat where she stood in a comely track suit, whistle round her neck, looking for the life of her like a gym teacher and not an instructor to would-be world-class spies. "You won't be graded on this, but I do need to see how each of you naturally approaches a combat situation so that we establish a baseline from which to assess you." Bree looked to where Miss Kent stood with the tripod on the side of the mat, and then to the additional cameras mounted on the ceiling. "Your vitals will be transmitted from the chip in your necks. Come on, then—who's ready to give it a go?"

A thick-necked, beefy woman stepped onto the mat, raising her hand. Shadduck beamed and tossed her some protective headgear.

"Well done, you. Name?"

"Anya."

"What's your fighting experience, Anya?"

Anya shrugged, broadening her stance on the mat. Bree could see how her muscled thighs stretched taut against her yoga pants. "Played some rugby in school. That's about as close to it as I ever came. That and keeping my younger brothers in line." She grinned.

"Brilliant. And who will take on the brave Anya this evening?"

A tall, lean brunette joined Anya under the fluorescent lights. "I will, professor. The name's Vivian." She smartly caught the headgear Shadduck tossed at her without warning. "I took a self-defense course to earn my Street Wise Girl Guide badge," she mentioned. As a few snickers flitted through the assembled class, she hastened to add, "But that was a long time ago."

"Excellent," Shadduck enthused. "Gear up, you two, while I explain the rules." She addressed the group lined up on the perimeter of the mat.

"In this course you will learn personal defense in the form of the most advanced martial arts training available—namely, *krav maga*, which is taught to the Israeli Defense Forces, and Brazilian *capoeira*—as well as skills to enable you to defend the children you may be guarding. We expect you to be able to significantly disable, if not kill, your opponent. In the field, you will come to learn, anything is fair game. Broken bottles can be weapons. Other people's bodies can be shields. For right now, however, I want you to avoid targeting the face or head. Try not to bend anything to the point of breaking. Your goal is simply to overcome your opponent and bring her—or him," she said, with a slight nod to Dash, "to the ground. We will know you surrender when one of you cries, 'Mercy.'"

She turned back to Vivian and Anya. They had tucked their ponytails inside the headgear and stripped out of their sweatshirts, down to some sporty tank tops. "You have your mouth guards in place?" They nodded. She paired them up in the circle at the center of the mat, where they hunched over awkwardly, not sure of what to do.

Shadduck held her hand between them. "On my count, then, you may begin. One . . . two . . . now!" She jumped out of the ring and watched them begin to circle one another. Kent worked the tripod, clicking a remote to set the other cameras recording to capture every angle.

Anya and Vivian wheeled about the mat slowly. Every now and then, one of them feinted as if they were about to charge, but something was holding them back.

"We're going to be here until two in the morning if this holds up," Ruby complained under her breath.

"Ladies!" Shadduck screamed from where she crouched beside the mat. "We don't have all night. Show me what you can do!"

It was all the encouragement Anya needed. She let out a great roar and barreled head on at Vivian, arms outstretched as if to envelop her in a gigantic bear hug. Vivian sidestepped her and stuck out one foot, deftly tripping Anya, who promptly smacked face-first down onto the mat.

Vivian threw herself on top of where Anya lay in a heap and neatly pulled her arms and legs back as if to hog-tie her.

"Do you yield?" she shouted between gasping breaths.

"I yield," Anya conceded, wheezing through a painful grimace. "Mercy."

A shrill whistle called them to a halt. "Wonderful, just wonderful," Shadduck proclaimed, reaching a hand down to heave the both of them up from the mat. "Ice is in the cooler over there, if you need it. Who's next, then?"

Dash raised his hand. "Ahem. Dr. Shadduck. I would volunteer myself, but I wonder how I might participate in this . . . exercise, given it is hardly sporting to have me square off with one of the fair ladies?"

Shadduck laughed. "Do you think the bad guys will nicely pair you off by sex when they send their agents out to get you in the field, Heyward, so that your sense of noble honor is not distressed? I think not. You'll have to fight just like the rest of your classmates. Who will take on Mr. Heyward?"

"I will," Susie answered promptly, stepping into the ring. Her blonde hair was pulled into a pert braid that swung low down her back; her yoga pants and top clung to every curve.

"Susie," Dash whispered urgently to her as he came onto the mat, "this is a *very bad* idea. You're what—half my size?"

Susie scoffed at him as she began stuffing her bounteous hair into the helmet. "Just promise me you won't break one of my nails. Miss Kent, make sure you capture the moment he concedes in full close-up."

Kent shot her a cheeky thumbs-up. Dash stared at her as if she were mad.

"Just . . ." He shrugged and picked up his own headgear, his eyes full of concern. "I promise not to hurt you, my darling girl. Just don't be rash. If you fall, don't fall on your hands, or you may break a wrist. Try to *roll*," he added with exaggerated care. "And—"

Shadduck cut him off. "Now is not the time for your coaching. I think she's ready. Are you, Heyward?"

He nodded, misery visibly suffusing his every pore, as he hitched the buckle on his helmet and took a half-hearted stance facing Susie, who had posed herself in the center of the mat. When he and Susie were poised and ready, Shadduck blew the whistle.

Dissatisfied, Dash shook his head and turned to plead with Shadduck, ignoring Susie. "It's no good. If I hurt her, I'll never forgive myself." Finding Shadduck implacable, he pivoted to address Susie, who had not moved from her ready stance.

"Please, dearest, don't make me—"

"Hiiii-yaaaa!" Susie bellowed, turning out her leg for a massive flying roundhouse aimed right at Dash's head. He flinched, bringing up both hands to block her. While his arms were still raised, she landed sprightly on one leg. Before he knew what was happening, she'd closed the distance between them and grabbed his shoulders, bringing her knee in for a solid blow to his groin.

The whole world seemed to stand still.

"Ohhhhh," the class all breathed in unison. Kent zoomed in for the close-up.

Dash's face turned a nasty shade of red, then purple. His knees crumpled and he sank to the floor.

"Ooof," was all he managed to whisper before collapsing sideways onto the mat, where he lay, clutching his groin.

"I think 'ooof' is noble-speak for 'mercy,'" Anya snickered from the side of the mat.

Shadduck blew her whistle, a sharp V furrowing her brow. "I said no aiming for the head, Hilvale. But other than that, well done," she added grumpily.

Susie poked Dash's leg with her sneaker-clad toe. "Maybe next time, you'll take me seriously, Your Lordship," she said sweetly before turning and walking off the mat.

"It's a good lesson for you all," Shadduck began, warming to her subject. "The reason Norwood nannies are so effective undercover is that the world at large underestimates us women. They look at us and see someone innocuous, soft, *nurturing*," she said, sneering at the words as she spoke them. "That is, if they see us at all. Even right in the heart of their household, the scions of power are blind to our influence and capacity . . . blind to the fact that we are human beings with our own motivations and drive, not simply cogs in their domestic machines. The only time they perceive us as threatening is when the lady of the house fears we will wield our sexuality. Those uniforms we make you wear—yes, they stamp you as a professional, they mold you in our image, but they also make you colorless and shapeless. Asexual. Benign. Invisible. When you are a nobody, a nothing, then—and only then—can you stride with impunity in the very halls of power and take what you want, acting as our agent. For after all, who could be so harmless as a nanny?

"Use it. Use their sexism and blindness to your advantage. And don't ever make the same mistake yourself."

She cast one last look of disdain at Dash where he lay helpless on the ground.

"Someone help him off the mat," she said, dismissively, as she turned to prepare for the next bout. Ruby and Bree scrambled to Dash's side, pulling up one arm each and aiding him as he hobbled off the mat.

"And find an ice pack!"

———

From this inauspicious beginning, Bree came to love *Wonder Woman 101*. The laconic outline of the course syllabus could never hint at the adrenaline-inducing thrills that became a normal part of her Thursday evening routine. The ballet-like choreography of the deadly *capoeira*. The force and brutality—and beauty—of *krav maga*. Rappelling—from ropes, initially, but then from the makeshift bonds of bedsheets and blankets, curtains and electronic cords, the sorts of things one would be forced to use to escape a luxury hotel taken over by terrorists. How to bind an intruder so that he couldn't escape—using whatever was handy, including the incredibly tensile materials of a disposable nappy. How to fold origami to entertain the children—building in plain sight a cache of razor-sharp paper tools that could seriously damage an eye if thrown just the right way, like a nunchuck.

"Tonight we're going to strap it on!" Shadduck shouted across the gym, clearly excited.

Susie and Dash, who were back in a lovey-dovey phase, snuggled together. She giggled and stretched to whisper in his ear. His eyes grew wide.

"I sincerely doubt that is what Shadduck meant, Susie, you minx," he admonished her. "Really, wherever did you learn such things?"

Shadduck was pushing something that approximated an oversized ball cart on wheels to the middle of the floor. When she stopped, she flipped the lid open. "Pair up. When you have your partner, come grab one of these for the two of you and start getting into it. You'll take turns wearing it."

Bree and Ruby didn't even look at each other—they nearly always paired up for these things—and instead began walking to the cart. They were first to reach it. Ruby thrust an arm inside and fished out the object of their exercise.

It was another virtual baby. With her other arm, Ruby pulled out a baby carrier, the sort that allowed for the baby to be carried close to the chest, or on one's back.

"You'll be testing the progress of your defensive skills in a more realistic environment today," Shadduck began explaining as the other students pulled their own virtual baby out of the bin. "You'll need to fight off an attacker—played by your combat partner—while protecting the baby, which will be strapped to your chest. This simulation will give you a better sense of the balance, agility, and awareness you will need to have at your disposal when the safety of one of your charges is at stake. Attackers, you have your choice of weapons in the kit that Misses Kent and Montoya-Craig are wheeling in."

Bree watched as Ruby shimmied into the carrier, the fabric contraption with all its straps and snaps a bit unwieldy. Bree left her, rummaging through several toolboxes full of weapons while she half-listened to Shadduck's ongoing instructions. She fingered the gadgets lightly, all of them more or less familiar to her now. Some were replicas of real weapons, with all the heft and weight of the real things, designed to help practice disarming an opponent—a rubber Glock, a rubber hunting knife. Some were real. A salt gun. A stun gun. Brass knuckles. A policeman's baton, like the kind a British police officer would use. Pepper spray. And then there were the improvised ones. A box cutter. A corkscrew. A chef's knife. A glass bottle. A sharpened pencil. Lengths of cords, severed from various electronic devices. She slipped her choices into the back of her Norwood-issued track pants and stepped aside to let the others make their picks.

"Presumed age of VB, Professor Shadduck?" Ruby queried, balancing and slightly tossing the model infant in her hands to assess its weight.

"Good question, Fripp. Six months."

Bree watched Ruby nod and lift the VB into the carrier on her chest, facing inward.

"Note what Fripp has done, class," Shadduck bellowed over the excited chattering of the students sorting through the weaponry. "Fripp, why is the VB facing in?"

Bree listened, impressed by Ruby's almost-dismissive reply. "An informal assessment of weight suggests the VB is quite large for six months of age," she answered. "Hence, forward-facing runs the risk of stress on its spine, especially in situations of sudden movement, twisting, or leaning. Further, at six months, a typical infant will not have full head control to handle forward-facing movement. Finally, the stimulus anticipated from the impending combat would be too much for the neurological development of the VB. Not that one would necessarily anticipate a combat situation when loading the child."

Shadduck jutted out her lip and gave Ruby an appraising, satisfied nod, then turned to help one of the pairs that was struggling with its baby carrier.

"Bravo, Ruby! Three points for Hufflepuff," Dash mock-whispered as he unbuckled and flipped the VB on Susie's chest to be facing in.

Johnson, a girl who was watching their group from the sidelines, snorted in appreciation.

Bree rolled her eyes. "Shut it, Dash. You're just jealous because you're getting a D in *Infant and Toddler Assessment* and Ruby is top of the class."

Dash feigned being hurt. "I cannot believe you would bring that up, Bree." He fiddled with the baby carrier fasteners, ensuring they were snug. "I'm sure all is forgotten, when it comes to our marks, once we are in our first family placement. Besides, I have a feeling this"—he waved a free hand about the gym, pointing to the general ruckus—"is the sort of skill that will end up being more important to our future advancement." He turned back to Susie. "Ready, dear?"

Susie shifted the VB around a bit, testing the solidity of the buckles and straps. "I suppose I am."

Bree turned from them to face Ruby. "Let's get on with it, then. Ruby, pretend I'm a gigantic Russian baddie coming at you now." She grinned.

Ruby laughed.

Shadduck scanned the group and then shouted instructions. "Attackers, your goal is to disable the nanny sufficiently to be able to snatch the child. This is a kidnapping scenario. I stress, *kidnapping*. You need to come away with a living and preferably uninjured child if this is to be considered a success. It should not go unremarked that this could easily be a rescue scenario, where as a nanny you would have the same exact goal.

"Nannies, your aim should be obvious. Do not allow the kidnapper to seize the infant, and do your utmost to keep the child injury free."

Susie shot up a hand. "Professor, in most situations, one would have access to one's mobile, a panic button, or an alarm system to alert security and call for assistance. These steps would of course be our first line of defense. Are we to presume these steps have already been taken, or are they unavailable to us?"

The class shifted, unexpectedly impressed by Susie.

"Excellent question, Hilvale, which tees up my last point. Presume you have called for help and security is on its way. This means you must outlast the invader until said help arrives. Plan on three minutes."

"Show-off," Dash said with affection as he squared off to face his love, this time giving her the space and respect he'd learned from hard experience was her due. Susie blew him a kiss.

"I'll be timing you," Shadduck finished. "Montoya-Craig here will man the first aid station, along with the medical staff." Bree's eyes tracked to the first aid kits that Montoya-Craig had neatly laid out after clearing away the weaponry. Among the shiny white boxes emblazoned with red crosses, she spied one still sullied with bloody fingerprints. Five somber medics in pristine white lab coats stood in a line next to the proctor, who looked like she was enjoying the prospect of injury just a little too much.

"How can *she* have so much time to put into torturing us?" Bree moaned, noting that Montoya-Craig's bun seemed a little tighter than usual. "Doesn't she have her own training to attend?"

"She's being groomed for handling duty. So they're using this to assess her leadership skills. That's why she's the Head Girl. She could end up running all of Norwood one day," Ruby answered, rolling her eyes at the implausibility of it.

"Is that what you want now, Ruby?" Bree prompted.

Ruby shrugged noncommittally. "I'd rather be the one giving than taking orders. That's all."

"You may begin." Shadduck's whistle blew shrilly, and the gym went silent as everyone at once turned to the life-and-death struggle with which they'd been tasked.

Ruby wrapped a protective hand around the VB's neck and nodded with sudden gravity toward Bree. "Go for it, girl. Let's see what you've got."

Bree's range of vision narrowed as she focused on Ruby, highlighted in a pool of light from the wire-caged lamp that hung high above them from the ceiling. She could feel the weight of her weapons pulling at her waistband, could feel the weight of each passing second as the gym clock ticked them off, one by one. The varnish of the polished hardwood floor stung at her nose as she considered her options.

Fake or not, the baby must come away alive.

She could hear the frustrated grunts and choked-off breaths of combat around her, but still, she waited. A veil of silence fell upon her as she saw her opening.

Slowly, she stalked toward Ruby. She wanted to get her moving, off balance. Ruby licked her lips, starting to ease backward, looking over her shoulder for somewhere safe to take a stand.

Swiftly, Bree pulled the box cutter out from her waistband and flicked it open to reveal the blade, accelerating toward Ruby. Ruby wheeled and began running for the wall of the gym. *I see what you're doing*, Bree thought with a note of respect. *But it won't help you*. She sheathed the blade and tucked the box cutter into her bra and with a hop, bolted after Ruby, arms pumping hard.

She gained on her, arms outstretched, just as Ruby broached the wall. Bree wrapped her hands around Ruby's neck, shoving her hard from behind. Ruby managed to brace herself against the wall and wheeled on Bree, breaking her chokehold with a well-placed elbow to her arm and hammering a fist forcefully into Bree's jaw. Stunned, Bree stumbled back. Ruby grimaced, already breathing hard. She yanked Bree's shirt collar and shoved her headfirst toward the cinderblocks. Bree twisted herself so that her back would absorb the impact instead of her skull as she slammed hard into the wall. The breath completely knocked out of her, she slid to the floor. Gasping for air, she swung her free leg to cut Ruby's feet out from under her. Ruby's protective instincts kicked in—rather than crush the VB, she threw her arms up to wrap its head in a sturdy embrace, taking the full impact of the fall herself.

Ruby was face-down on her knees now. Bree scrambled on top of her and pulled the lengths of severed lamp cord out of her trousers. Roughly, she bound Ruby's legs. While Ruby tried to buck her off, Bree flipped her over onto her back and wrestled her arms away from the VB, binding her wrists in a solid handcuff knot. Ruby wriggled, but she could not get free. Holding her down with one knee, Bree extracted the box cutter and slid the sharp blade out. With a swift move, she jerked the steel through the straps of the baby carrier, severing them, and then tossed the box cutter away. Carefully, she pulled the VB away from Ruby's body and stood up, sidestepping Ruby's attempted kick. Her heart pounded in her ears as she tucked the VB up against her shoulder, cradling its delicate neck.

Shadduck's whistle screeched.

Three minutes. She'd just made it.

Bree looked around. The gym floor was a mess of fallen comrades and abandoned weaponry, bloody skid marks marring the glossy shine of the polished wood. The silence that had settled around Bree as she focused on taking down Ruby was shattered by an onslaught of groans and muffled cries as those who'd failed writhed on the floor, clutching their injuries. Shadduck appeared entirely unperturbed by their pain.

"Attackers, if you've managed to extract your target, make your way to Montoya-Craig. She will confirm your successful kidnapping. If you're injured, go see Kent or a trainer and, for God's sake, keep it down. You're making enough noise to wake the dead."

"Help a girl out, Bree?" Ruby asked between heaving breaths. Bree looked down to see Ruby waving her bound-up hands in the air. "I can't get out of these on my own. You did a damn good job on the knots."

"I'll need to cut you out. I'll find a knife on my way back from Montoya. Hold on."

Bree limped to the check-in station, looking around as she did. A group was huddling around first aid. Anya was near the back of the line, cursing while she tried to stanch her spurting bloody nose, while a self-satisfied Johnson sat smugly to the side, watching. Bree was impressed—Johnson was skinny, but she apparently was tough—tough enough to best hulking Anya, at least.

Bree was first in line to check in, and only a few others straggled in behind her.

"Well, well," Montoya-Craig said, her eyebrow cocking in skepticism. "You lifted the VB, did you? Let's see how you did." She held out her hands and Bree dutifully deposited the doll. Montoya flipped it over and took out her mobile to scan the code implanted on the underside of the VB's melon-sized head. Her phone beeped. She glanced over the readout and pushed the VB back at Bree, disgusted.

"Blunt-force trauma equivalent to shaken-baby syndrome. Your infant's brain dead, if not actually dead. Let's hope you do better keeping the VB safe when it's your go as nanny, eh, Parrish?"

Bree took the lifeless doll back in her hands, cheeks burning.

"Reboot it before the next bout. Next?"

Dismissed, Bree dragged herself away.

What if she couldn't do it? What if, when it actually came to it, she couldn't protect a child in her care? Bree pushed the thought down and squared her shoulders, ready to try again, vaguely aware that in the recesses of the gym, Avci was shaking her head in disappointment.

———

Bree thrust herself up through the ice, gasping for breath. Her hands gripped the sides of the deep soaking tub to which she'd been assigned for physical therapy. Here, in the bowels of the gymnasium, the Agency secretly kept trainers on staff to bind the wounds and sooth the aches of the spies in training. Nursing them back to perfect health was not the goal. Getting them up and about was. Nothing was to interrupt their training, and testing their mettle—seeing just how much damage they could work through without collapsing—was instrumental to the assessment of their readiness for fieldwork.

The dermatologists and makeup artists on staff did their best to hide the abrasions and black eyes, teaching each pupil how to dab and blend makeup so that the aftermath of a steely fist could pass the next morning before the uninquisitive eyes of the regular students as the puffiness of a long night of studying or one too many drinks.

The trainers had left the last few of them to haul their weary bodies out of the cold water and trudge home on their own, licking their wounds and brooding over another evening of failure.

Bree sighed and leaned her head against the edge of the tub. She tried not to think about how tired she was as she let her eyes flutter closed for just one minute.

"You'll turn into a prune." Dash's voice bounced off the tile floor.

Instinctively, Bree jerked her hands from the edge of the tub, sliding them below the water. Steadying herself, she smiled, opening her eyes and tilting her head to see him. "I thought I was the last one."

"I lurked about until almost everyone was gone," he explained from across the room. He was swathed in towels, evidently fresh from the sauna. "I'm not squeamish, but even I recognize that not everyone is comfortable with my presence when there's flesh to be seen." He paused. "I trust you don't mind?" He took her answer for granted as he waddled gingerly toward a bench along the wall.

"Don't be silly," she smiled ruefully, acknowledging his dilemma. "We ground-breaking unicorns need to stick together. Come sit and talk with me. I'm not ready to get out yet."

He eased himself down, grimacing.

"Did you save your virtual baby?" she asked.

He winced, shaking his head. "Susie defended it brilliantly the first round. When it was my turn to nanny, she seemed to be less intent on kidnapping the baby than on beating me senseless. She killed it and very nearly me, I'm afraid. My body is black and blue from the waist down." Gingerly, he whisked aside the towel covering his thigh to reveal a massive purple mark.

Bree frowned and shifted in the water, the ice swirling about her body as she turned to face him, trying not to look too hard at his injuries, nor the way they stood out against his well-formed muscles. She wrapped her arms around herself and rested her head on the edge of the tub.

"What'd you do to earn the wrath of Susie this time, Dash?"

He covered himself up and shrugged. "I would own up to it if I knew. I would. But I am truly bewildered this time. It seems, lately, that sometimes the very sight of me annoys her. I thought things were getting better, but after tonight, I'm not sure."

Bree bit her lip. She'd seen how quickly Susie's mood could shift, but she had not observed any pattern to it. Not yet. "I'm sorry, Dash. That must be so frustrating."

He laughed ruefully. "Serves me right, I suppose. After all, I did try to call things off a bit ago. She became clingy and weepy and I relented. We've made up, but she is probably just punishing me for that. Again." He shrugged, sheepishly. "My bad judgment. The House of Fewersham has always been known to be full of difficult personalities. Maybe, next exercise, I'll foist her off on that Johnson—a nasty little thing, she seems. And you? You seem to be nursing your arms a bit. Pull your wrists, did you?"

"It's nothing," she averred through chattering teeth. "Old injury acting up, is all." She cast about for a different topic. "What do you think our field trip next week will be?"

He leaned back thoughtfully. "We've only traveled for things that cannot be accomplished safely—or without observation—on campus.

Shooting range? Night trekking? More rappelling? Underwater plane crash simulation? Who knows? We'll find out and be terrified all over again, soon enough." He pushed himself up, being careful to maintain his modesty. "I'll retreat to give you some privacy. But when you're ready, I'll be waiting for you on the front steps."

"You don't have to do that, Dash," Bree protested, but he waved her off as he hobbled off to the locker room.

"We unicorns stick together, right? I'll see you in a few minutes. Make sure you dry off properly and bundle up. There's a sharp chill in the air—you wouldn't want to catch a cold. And if you find yourself too sore to climb stairs, remember, there's a lift in the back of the hall."

"A lift?" she asked.

He smiled. "An elevator. I'd thought you'd have gotten that one by now."

———

He stood outside, stamping his feet and rubbing his hands together, when she emerged. All signs of the brutality inflicted upon him by Susie were now wrapped under layers of cotton and wool. To the outside world, he looked every inch the Lord of the Manor. She watched his profile as he stared toward the gate—his broad forehead, the perfectly straight nose that defined "patrician," the way his jaw jutted, square and assertive. It was a wonder his face had emerged unscathed from tonight's melee. Her own face was puffy under the eye socket, angry red splotches streaking over the seemingly permanent gray bags and threatening to turn into something more sinister where Ruby had stuck her with a well-placed elbow.

Bree stood for a moment, shoving her bandage-wrapped arms deeper into her pockets. Then she trotted over to him, testing out her soreness, clearing her throat to alert him to her presence.

He turned, brightening at the sight of her, his impossibly correct posture becoming even more upright. Deftly, he tucked a long strand of her curling bronze hair up into her stocking cap.

"Loose locks, Mistress Bellona. How very unprofessional of you." Tugging the collar of her coat closer about her throat, he continued. "Don't want you to turn into a Popsicle now—that is the American term for it, isn't it? Do you think you can manage a brisk walk?"

She laughed. "I think between the two of us, you took the worst of it. I can keep up with you. Let's go."

The trek back to Jaguar House was different at night. This part of Bath was quiet after dark, shuttered like a tiny country village. They trudged up the hill, Bree wincing every now and then as a misplaced step revealed a new sore spot to her, her breath coming in puffs against the inky sky.

Along the way, she snuck a look at the alley where'd she'd spotted Alice, hoping to get a glimpse of her again, and a chance to ask more questions. Even though she glanced down the gloomy corridor each time she passed, which was just about every day, she'd yet to find her. She'd disappeared. If she even was Alice. Stifling her disappointment, she turned her curiosity to Dash.

"Dash, what are you doing?"

He looked at her curiously. "Whatever do you mean?"

"I mean, everything," she said, the words pouring out of her. "What are you doing here at Norwood? I mean, I know why you're here *now*. You're trapped like the rest of us. But before—why'd you come? It makes no sense. You act like you don't care, like this is all a big joke to you, but I know deep down you do. How can you and Susie be on scholarship when you so clearly come from wealth? And, speaking of Susie, why are you wasting your time with her?"

She saw his body tense at her words. She didn't mean for it to feel like an attack, but, when she slowed down to think about it, she supposed that that's how it would seem to him.

"Didn't Ruby explain it all to you? I'm a profligate waste of space, here to have a good time and prey on the vulnerable women of Norwood." He meant it to sound good-natured, but he couldn't disguise the tinge of bitterness.

"Oh, come on now," Bree scolded. "You and I both know Ruby can be judgmental. Why don't you just tell me?"

He sighed dramatically and rubbed his brow. "What you see at Jaguar House is the little I've managed to scrape out of back rooms without my stepmother noticing. So, that is how I can maintain the appearance of being a gentleman while qualifying for a scholarship."

He added, "I know it must irk you and Ruby, both."

"I just never understood," Bree clarified. "I'm not sure I do, even now. Your world is very foreign to me."

He laughed grimly. "Would it were to me, my dear. But that brings me to your second question—why Norwood? I mentioned to you my father's penchant for new wives. My mother was his unfortunate first wife. Would it surprise you to know that his second was our nanny?"

Bree gasped. "No!"

"Oh, yes," Dash confirmed with a bitter laugh. "A proper Norwood alumna. They planned it quite cleverly. She accused my mother of being unfit—planted evidence of it, in fact. He had her removed as a danger to me and my sister, quietly divorced her with a nice settlement, provided she stay away from us children. After a suitable period of time, he slipped a ring on the charming finger of the second Duchess Rowland.

"I was too young to understand what was going on at the time. But imagine, adoring your nanny and your mother and then being forced to choose—no, wait, that's not right. Having the decision thrust upon you, being told you can only have one. It was Solomonic. And, when I later came to realize what had really happened . . . Ah, Bree. It is a hard day for a child when he realizes that just because someone loves you doesn't mean they won't be brutal and ruthless in their own self-interest."

Bree thought back to the exchange between him and Ruby during the nappies lab. His violent reaction to Ruby's suggestion that Susie might focus her gold-digging on a married man now made sense. Ruby had touched a sensitive nerve, one that clearly was still raw.

"Your father didn't love you if he'd put you through that," Bree insisted.

Dash smiled wistfully. "He loved me. He still loves me. Just not more than he loves himself, and his self-image." They walked another block, Bree very deliberately giving careful inspection to every darkened store window, before Dash picked up the story. "I take every opportunity I have to needle him. I was a complete cock-up at school, though I aced every entrance exam and IQ test ever administered. Norwood is my way to embarrass him. The duke's heir, dandling little babes on his noble knee. The fact that the media eats it up is a bonus. If I don't stick it out, though, he'll get his own—he's threatened to force me to work at my stepmother's interior design business as punishment. I don't doubt he'd follow through with it. It would give him an extra set of eyes on her."

"So, how does Susie fit into all of this? Did you know her before Norwood?"

He shook his head. "Susie? No, we'd never met. I really should let her tell her own story. Suffice to say, she emancipated herself from her father two years ago. She really is poor. As for why I bother with her . . ." He shrugged. "I should think it obvious. I'm perhaps a bit soured on the idea of romance and any institution such as marriage. A dalliance with Susie, knowing she has her eyes set on greater heights, is perfect. At least for me."

"And the fact that her family is notorious gives you one more thing to use against your father."

Dash pulled to a standstill and bowed neatly. "Your powers of deduction are quite keen, Miss Parrish. Have I satisfied your curiosity?"

She nodded. She had a million questions she would like to ask him, but she knew she had tried his patience enough for one night.

"Good," he said, firmly closing the subject to any further discussion and beckoning her to continue walking. "Now I have a few questions for you. Why haven't you been sleeping?"

Bree bit her lip. "Who says I'm not sleeping?"

"It wouldn't take a genius to notice the shadows under your eyes. But it *would* take a deaf man to not hear you thrashing about and crying out in your sleep. I've noticed you've taken to the couch at night, after we've all turned in. Trying not to disturb Ruby, are you?"

Bree hesitated.

"Go on, then. Spill it, Bree," he urged. "What's bothering you so much that it's giving you nightmares?"

She shrugged and sighed. "I've started dreaming about my parents again."

"Again? But I thought you said you have no memories of them?"

She nodded. "I don't. But I used to dream about them when I was little. It's started up again. I dream about the car crash. It's as if I am older, and watching it from the side of the road. I always see my mother, trapped inside. She bangs on the window, begging me to help. I can see my father, slumped over the wheel. I can't see their faces, but somehow I just know it's them. And I can't move. I can't do anything. I can only stand there and watch them burn to death, unable to look away."

"Dear God, Bree. That's horrible. You dreamt this as a child, you say?"

She nodded, wondering if she should tell him the rest. "I was probably six or seven, maybe a little younger. Judy had just shared with me the story of how my parents died. It was when Rodney's wife was dying from cancer, so he was gone most nights, sleeping at the hospital to be with her. The church sent a temporary assistant to help him. She . . ."

Bree hesitated.

"She didn't understand me the same way Rodney did. She saw it as a weakness, I guess, that I was afraid, and an inconvenience that I kept waking up the other children, screaming. So she started locking me at night in the barn behind the main house."

"What? All night?"

Bree nodded. "She tied me to one of the old rings that you would've tied a horse's lead to, so that I couldn't run away. Gagged me with a handkerchief."

"Bree!" Dash stopped in the middle of the sidewalk and stood to face her.

"It's okay," she smiled with the best false brightness she could muster, her eyes watering. "She always came to get me in the morning, before Rodney arrived back from the hospital."

Dash wiped away the sole errant tear that had escaped her eye. He placed heavy hands on her shoulders and looked at her, searching her face.

"You never told him, nor Judy—did you?"

She shook her head. "How could I? I didn't want to cause Rodney more trouble, not when his wife . . . And the woman . . ." She couldn't even say her name. She cleared her throat and made herself continue. "That woman threatened she'd have me sent away if I ever told anyone. I was too young to know any better." She blew out a deep breath. "Anyway, eventually, Rodney came back and that woman went away. I never saw her again."

He frowned, staring at her intently.

"Take your hands out of your pockets, Bree."

She hesitated.

"Bree. Show me."

She tried, but couldn't drag her eyes away from his. Slowly, she pulled her balled up fists from her pockets. Dash took her hands in his and turned her arms over, pushing up her coat to expose her inner arms. The stark white bandages stood out in the dark.

"May I?" he asked gently, waiting for her permission. She nodded once, quickly.

Delicately, he began to unravel the bandage on her right arm. Bree could not help but admire the deftness of it, the way he stripped the cloth away, twisting it into a neat ball as he slowly exposed the tender skin of her wrist.

The raised scars caught the errant moonlight and seemed to glow.

"That bitch." The vehemence in Dash's voice startled Bree. He squeezed her fingers in his, his own hand shaking with anger. "The other is the same, I take it?"

She stared at the sidewalk, unable to speak.

"I can understand why Rodney would have been too preoccupied, but Judy? How could she have failed to notice?"

"She wasn't there that much," Bree protested half-heartedly, before shrugging it off. It was a question she'd managed to avoid thinking about, herself, for a very long time.

"And here, all this time, we thought you had a strange Southern temperature disorder that prejudiced you against short sleeves." His voice was gruff now as he cupped her hand between his, warming it against the chill. "You must know you don't have to hide this, don't you? Nobody would ever dare judge you for it. On the contrary, anyone who knew would be—"

She shook her head. "I don't want my whole story to be a tragic one, Dash. I can't be that person. I just want to be me."

He pulled her into the crook of his arm and kissed the top of her head.

"It's a wonder you didn't have nightmares your whole life after what she did to you," he murmured against her wooly hat. "And the dream itself—it's the same now as it was then?"

"Mm-hmm. Except now, near the end, when my mother throws herself against the glass, it's not her I see. I used to just see a blurry spot where her face would be. But now, it's not blurry. It's Alice Clark. It's her face from the memorial poster. The second-year student whose memory was wiped."

"I remember," Dash muttered. "Bloody hell." He released her shoulders and shoved the bandage into his book bag as they resumed walking, continuing in silence for a block or more before he questioned her again.

"Has Judy contacted you?"

Bree sighed and shoved her hands even deeper into her coat pockets. "No. I haven't heard from her since the day before we were implanted. She left town unexpectedly on business."

"You haven't heard anything at all?"

Bree stared resolutely ahead. "No."

"Do you think she might know more than she has shared with you, Bree? Aren't you curious? Your subconscious is practically screaming at you every night."

She shrugged. "She doesn't know anything."

"I don't believe you," he whispered, pulling her to a stop. He lifted her chin, forcing her to look him in the eye. Her heart skipped a beat.

"In your nightmares, you keep calling to Judy. Why would Judy be in your dream about your parents' deaths, Bree? What are you not telling me?"

She tried to twist her face away, but he tightened his grip, ever so slightly.

"Tell me."

Judy had warned her not to trust anybody. But Dash was the one person who'd been completely honest with her. The one person who'd looked out for her.

"Judy. She's one of them," she whispered, watching the words come out in puffs of breath to avoid looking him in the eye.

"What?"

"She's Norwood." She tore herself out of his grip. "Or ex-Norwood, to be precise. She was my mother's handler. My father was a spy, too—MI5. The crash that killed them was a mission gone bad—Judy's mission. Oh, so I guess I am British." It bubbled out of her, and she laughed a little, relieved from finally speaking the words aloud. "Judy thinks there's some sort of conspiracy and only I can help her solve it." Bree took a shaky breath, steadying herself, before giving him a weak smile. "I think I beat you on true confessions."

Dash's hand, still frozen in the air where she'd wrenched away from him, dropped to his side. "I should say so." He paused, then delicately posed his question. "Did she tell you any more about your parents?"

Bree shook her head.

"But what she did share with you—it could mean the accident that took their lives might have happened right here. They were British, after all. Did you ever think of searching the local records to see what you can find? You've only ever searched in the United States."

"It's not as if the headlines are going to scream 'British Spies Killed in Crash.' Would they? I'm sure the government covered it all up." Her mouth twisted bitterly as she considered the difficulty of discovering anything at all.

"Worth a try, though, wouldn't you say?" They'd crossed the threshold into the dingy confines of Jaguar House's courtyard. He turned and searched her eyes. "I'll help you."

He strode to the front door and began deftly unlocking the jungle of latches they'd installed since their landlord's unfortunate lapse in judgment. He eased the door open just an inch and paused.

"We don't have to tell anybody else. We can use our class time and newfound *Snap-Spy* skills to dig around in the electronic detritus. If your mother was Norwood, I bet they have records of her attendance."

She wondered at the lump growing in her throat. "I'll think about it," she whispered, her body brushing up against his lean, muscular frame as she slipped in through the door. She grabbed his hand.

"Dash—you cannot tell anybody. I mean it. I don't know if I can trust Judy, but from what she's told me, I definitely can't trust anybody at Norwood. If they found out what I really know—"

"Tell them what?" He winked, squeezing her hand hard. He gave her a little push, then let go of her hand. She felt the sudden yawn of separation as he closed the door, leaving her to her thoughts.

She didn't want to get her hopes up—not now. But a thrill ran through her at the thought of maybe, just maybe, finding out something new.

"Your collective education regarding the non-Western portions of our world is remarkably limited. Our course assumed at least a rudimentary knowledge of the origins of the Chinese empire, its successive dynasties, the Opium Wars, the Civil War, the Cultural Revolution . . . But clearly, as these abysmal essays illustrate, you do not have it."

Professor Simmons slapped the papers before each student with the angry force of disappointment. A horrific red F, circled and underlined, screamed up at Bree. She quickly flipped her essay over.

Judging by the general reaction of the other students in her *Banana Republic* class, she was not alone. Bree's head pounded. It was only six a.m., and she found it hard to focus on geopolitics this early, especially after the bruising she'd taken last night. She longed for coffee, tea—anything to jolt her brain and infiltrate every weary cell with a burst of artificial energy.

"Except for Hilvale, of course." Simmons waved Susie's paper around in the air.

Even from her seat, one row down from the back of the room, Bree could see the wildly enthusiastic "A!!!" scrawled across the top of the page, next to a row of shiny foil stars Simmons had stuck on as a reward. Bree bit back her irritation. *Of course* Susie would know all about Chinese history—she'd studied Mandarin for years. And, *of course* Simmons retained some of her early nanny training, treating them all like imbeciles who could be motivated by something as trivial as a sticker.

Susie took the paper gleefully from Simmons's hands. "Oooh," she enthused, tilting the pages under the fluorescent light. "They're *prism* stickers."

Ruby kicked her seat. Bree didn't need to turn around to know she was rolling her eyes.

Simmons began droning. "I will remind you why you are required to take this course. In your position as nanny to the elite, you may be thrust into the upper echelons of diplomacy, global trade, and nation building. At a minimum, your employers will expect you to be up on current events, understand the nuances of history and circumstance that make their business and diplomatic dealings sensitive, and be of service in navigating the minefield of such delicate affairs—all so that you do not *embarrass* them. This is the only way for you to pass unobtrusively, in and out of the inner circle, whilst caring for their precious children."

"I'm sure the Spanish prime minister will just swing the door wide open in the middle of his negotiations with the Catalan separatists while we are wiping his grandchildren's bottoms," Dash whispered to Bree.

"You jest, Your Lordship," Simmons interrupted him sourly, fixing him with her one good eye, "but it is in fact your job to make such circumstances materialize. Even the split-second snatch of whispered negotiation you might overhear could be valuable to our allies and masters."

Dash flushed, glancing at Bree sheepishly. Simmons walked past him, continuing her lecture while she paced up and down the rows of desks.

"Furthermore, your ability to influence and interpret the events around you—indeed, your ability to fulfill your assigned mission—may very well depend on your intimate knowledge of the national and cultural histories, the aspirations and resentments, that underlie all diplomatic and military endeavors. How can you catch out the anomaly, the untoward, if you do not know the natural order of these things? The minimal underpinning in geopolitics this course is intended to give you is thus foundational to your future."

She wheeled upon the class. "A performance such as that demonstrated on this assignment suggests a lack of seriousness and that you are woefully unprepared for even conversational engagement on any topic related to politics or international business. To help bring the urgency of this to life, we have concocted a little experiment for you. A surprise, if you will."

Bree watched as the students all shifted upright in their seats. Surprises at Norwood were never of the pleasant sort.

"Your *Practicum in Social Graces and Charm* professor has graciously agreed to collaborate with me in hosting a ball at the end of this term. The ball shall serve as a final venue in which we can observe your ability to navigate a social situation fraught with danger—perils of the conversational, etiquette, and spy craft sort. Dancing. Dining. General knowledge of current and historic events. All of it shall be assessed to the most rigorous standard. In addition, you will be expected to engage in one conversation of deep expertise on a topic assigned to you. Mark your calendars for the thirtieth of May."

She smiled a venomous smile. "I must warn you—this will require the utmost attention to your etiquette and manners. We will be having a seven-course meal, not chowing down on greasy fish and chips.

"Your every move, from which utensil you select for each course, to how you actually dine, to where you place your napkin, will be evaluated." She looked with disdain upon Bree. "As a reminder, Parrish, as you seemed to have been confused in your last social graces exam: Yes, in the past, the term 'napkin' may have been considered gauche, when it more often referred to a feminine hygiene pad. Now, in the company of educated and upper-class people—the type of people who would be frequenting gatherings such as this—'napkin' is the preferred term. The use of the term 'serviette' when dining refers to paper, and is very lower-class. As well as vaguely French," she sniffed.

A titter of amusement went through the room. Simmons enjoyed it for a moment and then looked at them all with fake enthusiasm.

"Did I mention that the exam, as it were, will be graded on a curve, and is weighted such that it shall determine the entirety of your course grade? It will also determine where you land in the rankings for summer assignments. Those on top will receive the plum international placements, of which there are very few. The rest of you will end up in local day cares, no doubt." She chuckled, but Bree noticed her professor was watching, hawklike, most likely taking note of which students were dismayed and which seemed relieved by the prospect of being left behind for the summer. "You may draw your expert topic as you exit the classroom this morning. Miss Montoya-Craig will be happy to assist you. Dismissed."

Montoya-Craig stood smugly at the door, a large bowl in hand.

The panicked students surged toward her, hoping to secure one of the better topics, regardless of it being a matter of pure luck.

"How are we expected to dance when there's only one of you, Dashiell?" Susie pondered.

"I'll break out my finest orthopedic shoes so that I am prepared with the optimal arch support. I shan't shirk my duties. A gentleman never refuses a lady—no matter how many—a turn around the dance floor," he promised, gallant as ever.

"Oh, that would be just the thing to make everything right as rain," Ruby snipped, her sarcasm in full bloom now that the caffeine from her bottled coffee had kicked in. "But I'm guessing we'll just have to take turns leading." She gave an exaggerated sigh of resignation. "I suppose this means we'll have to all get formal gowns and the like."

"Oooh," Susie enthused, clapping her hands. "You're absolutely right. Floor length, to be certain. You cannot go shopping with anybody else but me. I insist. You too, Bree."

Bree winced at the thought of spending money on something she'd never wear again after the mock ball, where everyone, including herself, would be too nervous to even notice her gown She had continued to be thrifty with her spending money, but she'd been warily watching the balance dipping lower and lower and was loath to ask Judy for more. She didn't want to be any more beholden than she already was.

"I don't know if that's a good idea, Susie," Bree said as gently as she could, reluctant to dampen Susie's enthusiasm. "I think thrift shop is more my speed. Besides, the dress is the least of my worries. We'd better get up there to pull our topics."

Montoya-Craig was waiting for them. "Go ahead. Not much left."

"Ladies first," Dash offered, stepping to the side.

Susie drew first. Her eyes widened as she read her topic aloud. "Bitcoin and the threat to international monetary stability and national sover-eignty." She looked wildly at Dash, who simply shrugged.

"Maybe our *Snap-Spy* professor can help?" Bree offered hopefully.

Ruby went next. She smiled and shoved the slip of paper into her pocket. "Lucky me. The links between agrarian reform, soil conservation, and democracy in Haiti."

Bree pulled her topic and looked at it, confused. "The Senkaku/Diaoyu Islands dispute," she read.

Susie was nodding vehemently. "That's a good one. Very contained. And it will give you a chance to improve their perception of your grasp of Chinese politics. I'll help you." Surprised at Susie's sudden generosity, Bree tilted her head in agreement. *Maybe I was too suspicious of Susie, after all*, she thought. *Maybe the whole thing with the foundling hospital was a coincidence.*

Montoya-Craig looked slyly at Dash. "Go ahead. We've saved the best for last."

Dash reached into the bottom of the bowl and pulled the remaining slip of paper. Eyeing it, he groaned.

"This is written as if by an uninformed, simpleton sixth-former. Honestly, what am I supposed to do with this? Decades of debate on this topic have passed, mountains of ink spilled, to no avail. And I'm expected to come up with a coherent argument than can be shared between the salad and soup course?"

They pulled the crumpled paper out of his fist and moaned in sympathy.

Montoya-Craig shot him a triumphant look.

"Good luck reforming the UN, Manny. We'll be so interested to hear your plan. And all of you remember: Pass/Fail. You know what happens if—"

"Yes, yes, we know," Ruby broke in. Bree could tell Ruby was as frustrated as Bree by Montoya-Craig's excessive enjoyment of the pain about to be inflicted upon them. "We know what happens if we fail. It's a one-way ticket to medically induced lobotomy-land. We've got it. Come on, then—let's go before Miss Montoya here comes up with yet another way to get us ejected from Norwood."

She brushed by Montoya-Craig, head held high, pulling Bree, Dash, and Susie in her wake.

———

The shuttles wound their way through country lanes. Bree knew that if there had been light, she would be able to see the blades of grass, sparkling with frost in the morning air. But though only fifteen miles from Bath, the area surrounding Combe was deeply rural, with not a single street-light to illuminate their way.

She shifted in the half seat on which she perched, trying not to disturb the hulking form of Anya, sweetly snoring next to her, and pressed her face to the window.

The sweep of fields, studded with hillocks and clumps of trees, yielded to a quaint village. Homes and shops huddled together, pressing against the street. They passed a rectory, a silent tea shop, and then an arched bridge against which a cluster of dinghies waited. No fisherman or tour guide would be coming for hours, Bree knew, if at all. It was only three in the morning. The boats would wait until after breakfast, at least, if not for the fullness of spring.

The sleeping town faded behind them, the hills flattening to welcome them to field after field lying fallow in the chill.

Professor Shadduck stood up in the front of the bus, clinging resolutely to a bar as the vehicle took a corner a little too fast.

"Just a mile or so beyond these woods is our destination—the Castle Combe circuit track. You've been working your simulators on your own time, practicing safe driving techniques in slick and icy conditions. Today we will test your skills on a real course, against a higher standard—evasive driving. It could be paparazzi seeking a shot of your precious charges. It could be an enemy spy. Whatever the reason, we need you to be prepared to safely escape such a threat."

The trees fell away behind Shadduck. A blaze of lights illuminated a massive track.

"Three hours. Your instructors are former police, Formula One racers, and members of the Royal Air Force. Skid pads first, then full track. We'll save off-road for another day. Pay careful attention. We don't want anyone to die this morning."

Bree thought about the warning, and how quickly it had become mundane.

Beyond the track, next to a series of low-slung buildings, a fleet of red and black BMWs and Range Rovers awaited them. Staff, fully suited in orange and cream racing gear, stood at the ready to help them suit up.

Anya snorted and startled as the bus suddenly lurched to a stop.

"We're here. I'll fill you in, Anya," Bree whispered as Anya stretched awake. Bree tried not to wince as she was squeezed into an even smaller patch of seat. Slowly, the murmur of the young spies rose as they pushed out of their seats and jostled for position in the aisle.

The bus disgorged them into the parking lot where they huddled, stomping their feet and mumbling against the cold.

"I'm Retired General Gerard Smith," one particularly huge man began. He didn't shout—his voice was commanding enough that he didn't have to. The group intuitively quieted itself to listen.

"If you are like the Norwood classes before you, you already are aware of the basics of speed, taking curves, and turning into skids. You know the difference between front-wheel and rear-wheel handling, the dangers of antilock brakes. We will not be reviewing these. Instead, we will put you into situations of pressure to test these skills and add to them. You will detect when you are being followed—whether by car or by airborne

device. You will evade. You will fight off an attacker while driving. We
will learn first on these skid pads—short courses marked with cones and
slicked down with a special chemical treatment to simulate the most dangerous conditions you will face, all in a controlled environment. When
you have passed your time trial, we will take you to the full track. Some of
you will have the chance to play the aggressor, as well, which will prepare
you in the event that you need to recover an abducted charge. Sheila,
what did I miss?"

"That should about cover it. Now that you've been briefed, suit up,"
the petite woman standing next to him added, tossing a heavy white helmet into the air. She gestured behind her to a cart of uniforms. "Your
track suits are flame retardant. Your helmets are outfitted with radio
communications, which will be essential to our exercises today. Vehicles
are standard issue but reinforced with roll bars for your safety. Four to a
group. No time to waste. Who's first?"

Bree raised her hand. Susie, Dash, and Ruby's hands quickly joined hers.

Sheila nodded at her. "Fine. You, come with me. We're going to do
something special to kick things off. The rest of your group will be briefed
by Gerard while everyone gets their gear."

Bree had practiced *krav maga* with a baby strapped to her chest. She'd
learned how to test food for poisons. She'd learned how to trail someone
on surveillance without being seen and how to wipe out her own digital
trail. How to disarm a security system, break into a locked room, and
breach the protection of even the most invulnerable safe. How to burgle.
To scale walls and rappel cliffs. To detect and deactivate surveillance cameras, including the dreaded nanny cam. She knew how to interrogate a
reluctant subject; knew the subtle signs of when someone is lying; knew
even the tells one could not suppress when one was being unfaithful to
a loved one (useful knowledge for blackmail down the road). She'd been
briefed and trained on every spy gadget imaginable.

But ten minutes later, strapped to the undercarriage of Sheila's specially fitted Land Rover, Bree wondered if she had truly lost her mind.

"Trust me," Sheila yelled down to her. "If you can rappel out of a window with a bedsheet, you can do this. Are you ready?"

Bree tested the straps around her legs and back. With a reluctant thump against the chassis, she gave the signal to go.

The SUV swayed and settled a little as Sheila clipped herself into the driver's seat. The engine roared to life, the entire vehicle lurching as Sheila pulled out of the repair bay and headed to the skid pads course. Bree's gloved fingers gripped and regripped the frame of the car, every cell of her body acutely aware that beyond the fire- and skid-resistant bodysuit in which she was armored, a scant twelve inches separated her from the pavement.

Her team didn't know she was here.

If they remembered their training, they would check the underside of the Rover before climbing in to start the engine. If they didn't, her job was to cut the rear brake activator on the second turn, putting the car into an unanticipated spin and climbing out to attack.

As Sheila had said, easy peasy.

The SUV stopped. She listened to the muffled drone of instruction, felt the tension of opened doors and the sway of more bodies climbing into the vehicle. It settled down, just a little lower.

Then, with another lurch, they were moving.

The vehicle crept, weaving between the orange cones that were just barely visible in Bree's peripheral vision. She slid an arm out of its strap, carefully, and extracted the cable cutter. Underneath her, the sagging bottom of her jumpsuit dragged just a little against the pavement. Instinctively, she arched, pulling herself against the grime-coated underbelly of the Rover.

With the first curve, the SUV shimmied and slid. She felt the sharp jerk of a corrected steering wheel and froze, clinging to the undercarriage.

With a shudder, the heavy vehicle righted itself, smoothing its course over the artificially slickened road.

She stretched back even further, reaching beyond the axel. The cables blossomed from the actuator, winding their way to the rear wheels. She felt the driver swing wide, preparing for the next turn.

Gritting her teeth, she snapped through one, then the other cable, barely able to move her fingers through the heavy gloves. Then, as the car began speeding up to take the curve, she braced herself and closed her eyes.

Seeing would only confuse her.

Burning rubber assaulted her nostrils as the tires lost grip. She could feel the spin—whirling and whirling, reminding her of when she was a little girl and Rodney would twirl her by the ankle and wrist, swinging her body round and round under the huge live oak behind the orphanage's main residence hall. She'd rolled around on the ground afterward, giggling and dizzy, her world momentarily turned upside down.

There was no time for disorientation now. She squeezed her eyelids even tighter, forcing herself to focus. *Your mom probably did this*, she coached herself. *All the time.*

Her eyes snapped open at the same time she flicked off the buckled straps to begin climbing toward the rear of the Rover. With clips and carabineers, she hauled herself over the back bumper and, as the SUV began to slow, hurriedly climbed up its backside. Inside the vehicle it was chaos—her groupmates' heads bumping into one another, their loss of control clearly terrorizing them. She felt a warm sense of satisfaction that, as of yet, they had not detected her behind them. The Rover had been outfitted with a luggage rack on the roof. She pulled herself topside, shifting her rope to clip to the rack and mounted herself, catlike, on top.

The vehicle's pirouetting was coming to a palsied end as it bumped along the course. She kneeled, thumping the roof to alert them to her presence, and then raised a victorious fist, her thighs and shoulders shrieking in protest.

Underneath Bree, the Rover finally sputtered to a stop. The occupants tumbled out, tearing off their safety helmets and peering up at her in terror. From the other side of the lot, the rest of the group was running, jostling to get a closer look.

Bree took off her own helmet, for once not caring that her ponytail had come undone and she was in violation of uniform regulation. The long, unkempt strands of her hair radiated molten bronze under the skid pan lights.

"Booyah," she said with a grin as she looked down on her group. Their terror changed to awe, and then irritation, as they realized what she'd done.

"Good God, Bree," Dash blurted out. "You could have killed us all."

She slid down the front windshield and popped over the hood to the ground.

She shrugged. "Isn't that the point?"

Ruby snickered, unable to hide the fact that she was impressed. "Aren't you Little Miss Cool?"

From the edge of the crowd, their classmate Johnson tilted her head, appraising her. "Actually, she's hot. You're smoking." She pointed at Bree.

Bree darted a look behind her to see the reinforced pad on her uniform's bottom was shredded, a spark embedded in the fibers. She patted off her own behind. "Won't be the last time, I'm sure."

Sheila grinned. "Ace job correcting out of the spin, Susie. It was a nasty one, wasn't it? As for the rest of you"—she spun around to address the entire class with a stern eye—"remember to check under your vehicles before entry. Every time. No exceptions. This time it was a mate with a cable cutter, having some innocent fun. Next time it could be a bomb. Everyone, back to the starting line. Now you'll all get a turn, though nothing quite as dramatic as Bree's Spiderman act."

The group groaned as one and pivoted to walk back across the lot.

Bree tossed her helmet high as she walked past Dash. She just barely brushed him, coming close enough to whisper, "I'm ready. The records search. Let's do it."

———

"Mrs. Framingham," Dash oozed as he swept in, Bree trailing behind him. "How do we find you today? Well, I hope?"

The administration building's receptionist was swathed in fuzzy pink mohair, a knot of overwhelming fake pearls twisted about her throat. The unfortunate plants under her care had shed the last of their desiccated leaves, leaving nothing but sticks and stumps protruding from the cracked earth. She blew her nose into a delicately embroidered hanky, pushing away the detritus of lozenge wrappers and cough syrup bottles that littered her desk.

"Horrible, Dashiell," she moaned with dramatic, nasally flair. "I cannot seem to rid myself of this upper-respiratory congestion. I just hope it's not contagious to cats." She gazed lovingly at one of the several portraits that surrounded her computer. "I don't know what I would do if she took ill. She's like family to me."

Bree tried to suppress an amused smile. Dash shot her a disapproving look.

"Quite," he commiserated. "I know just what you mean. The creatures know us better than we know ourselves, don't they?" He leaned over the computer to get a better look at the photographs.

Framingham beamed at him. "I should have known you would understand." She leaned in conspiratorially. "She always knows my mood. And she can tell, just by the way I talk about someone, whether they are trouble or not. She's a very good judge of character."

Bree coughed to cover a tiny giggle and focused excessively hard on the student announcements pinned to the bulletin board on the opposite wall.

"Aren't they all?" Dash enthused. "She had the good sense to make a home with you, didn't she? And we wouldn't want poor . . . hmmm, what did you say your cat's name was, Mrs. Framingham?"

"Eartha. Her name is Eartha. Her mother's name was Ivy."

"Yes, yes. Eartha. As in Kitt? And Poison Ivy. Clever, aren't we? I wouldn't have taken you for a Batman aficionada." Framingham blushed with pleasure that he'd figured out her little joke. "Yes, as I was saying, Mrs. Framingham, we wouldn't want little Eartha to worry about you. You must have this tea. Earl Grey with a touch of lemon. Just the way you like it, no?" He swooped in to offer her a steaming to-go cup.

"Oh, heavens, Dashiell. You are so thoughtful." Framingham fell upon the cup with gratitude, sticking her nose into the rising steam and inhaling deeply. "This may just cut through the fog in my head. Dear me, I almost think you're trying to butter me up for some nefarious purpose." She let a peal of tinkly laughter spill from her throat until it broke up into a sound that would have been more appropriate to a honking goose. "Now, I know you didn't come all this way just to deliver me this tea. Tell me, what do you need?"

Dash paused, looking thoughtful. "I would hate to ask."

She laughed again, her fingers drifting up to clutch at her pearls. "Ask away. The worst I can say is no."

Dash looked over his shoulder to where Bree stood, as if confirming she was not paying attention, and then whispered, leaning heavily onto Framingham's desk, weary with his burden.

"Do you think the bursar would be willing to let me borrow against the funds my father put into my account? Just for a few weeks, mind you. I'd be able to pay it all back before the next term started."

Framingham was already tutting with disapproval.

"I thought I'd ask you before I approach him to inquire. I would hate for it to get back to my father."

She patted his hand sympathetically. "Not a chance, my dear." She pushed her glasses up higher on her exceedingly straight nose, then worried her necklace in sympathy. "Not a chance he'd let you, and not a chance he'd not immediately phone up Your Lordship. I'm so sorry."

Dash sighed, shoulders slumping. "I was afraid that would be the case. Well, Mrs. Framingham, I am so very grateful to have your discreet assistance on this matter. As always, you have been most helpful." He cleared his throat and rose to his full height, squaring his shoulders to stave off the disappointment. "Bree, my business here is finished. Come along."

As they descended the steps into the sunshine, Bree turned her face to his, an expectant question in her eyes.

"She has no idea what's going on there. She couldn't, or she'd not be so lax with her computer security. Her user ID was on a note taped to her desktop, right next to the kitty pictures. And I'll bet you her password is 'Eartha,' with some numbers and an exclamation point thrown on the end. I'll get it in under ten tries. And I'll be into the school IT system this evening. Just watch."

"What if you're wrong?"

"Then I'll try Ivy, and combinations thereof. Or maybe something having to do with Batman, if she was trying to be particularly clever with the Catwoman and Poison Ivy references. If all else fails, I'll send her some cat photos for her to click on and get her to download some spyware. But it won't come to that. I guarantee it. All lonely, middle-aged, single ladies use their pets' names as passwords. It's practically statistically proven."

Bree thought of Miss Judy. She couldn't imagine her securing her precious tablet with a sentimental pet name. Then again, she couldn't imagine Miss Judy getting all googly-eyed over a cat.

"If you say so," she said, keeping her skepticism to herself.

In the end, he got it on the first try: Eartha1!

"Now what?" Bree asked as she huddled over her *Infant and Toddler Assessment* books under the fluorescent light of their kitchen at Jaguar House.

"I placed a Meterpreter shell on their network. It will map all the terminals and start searching them for any file that looks like student records. So now, we wait."

She sagged a little, disappointed. Now that they were so close, any delay seemed interminable.

He peered at her, one brow arched.

"You've waited for eighteen years, Bree. I promise you, you'll know more about your mother than you ever have, in under a fortnight. Norwood has taught us well—if tonight's lax security is indicative of the rest of the network, you'll get anything left in the school's computer records, and we won't leave a trace. They'll never know what hit them."

Bree frowned, unconvinced. "Framingham mustn't be in on it. I bet the rest of the system won't be so easy."

"Oh ye of little faith," Dash said, feigning hurt. "Just watch."

"Say you're right and you get in. Will you be able to access the records of my mother's missions? Of her assignment to my father's home?"

He shrugged. "No promises there. I'd be surprised if those were as easy to breach. So, first things first. Let's find out who she was."

Bree fingered the little tag that hung about her neck. "Yes. Let's."

———

Bree, along with Susie and Ruby, was crowded into the tiny bathroom on the other half of the suite, Dash having been dispatched elsewhere as the women readied themselves for the Norwood Ball.

Bree was relieved when, even to Susie's critical eye, they looked stunning. Ruby had rescued one of the less risqué old Carnival costumes
from her neighbor's attic back in Notting Hill, refashioning the bodice
by trimming down the profusion of feathers that sprouted on all sides
and adding a new skirt. The majestic collar and long column of silk
made her look like a modern-day Cleopatra. Bree was much too tall
to borrow one of Susie's hand-me-downs and had stubbornly refused
to buy something new, despite all of Susie's cajoling. In the end, she'd
found a black, long-sleeved gown in a thrift store behind one of the
many churches in Bath. Its simplicity was the perfect offset for her pale
skin and burnished hair, which she'd piled lavishly on the top of her
head. To herself, she noted with satisfaction that the sleeves covered
her scars and the length hid her very practical loafers. She could dance,
should she be forced to, or chase down an errant toddler without fear
of tripping.

Bree and Ruby had drawn in a collective breath when Susie unveiled
her own choice. She twirled about in a brilliant emerald sari that had
been carefully wrapped and folded about her lithesome body. The fabric
was exquisite, a beautiful silk banded on the edges in gold needlework.
The cropped top underneath—the same vibrant green—boasted sleeves
worked in bold purples, oranges, and crimsons, edged in the same gold
embroidery, and offered just a glimpse of Susie's taut abdomen and faintly
visible rib cage.

"Susie . . . it's beautiful! *You're* beautiful!" Bree found herself gushing
as Susie twirled for their approval. "That t-shirt . . ."

"It's called a *choli*," Susie corrected her, giggling as she draped one
exquisitely manicured hand against her chest and struck a pose. "Do you
like it?"

"It would be hard to watch children in that," Ruby opined, eyeing
it doubtfully, "but then again," she conceded, looking down at her own

skirt, "none of this is very practical, is it? It *is* lovely. But I do have a question for you, and don't take this the wrong way, Susie, but don't you feel it is cultural appropriation to wear such a thing? Especially as the descendent of colonizers? I mean, it's not like we're attending a costume ball." Even though it was blatantly obvious that Ruby herself *had* dressed in a costume, she crossed her arms as if daring Susie to contradict her.

Susie shrugged, spreading out her arms to admire her finery. "I don't think so. It was my mother's. How can it be inappropriate for me to wear it when it is from her country?"

Ruby looked confused. "Your mother's Indian?"

Susie giggled and peered at herself in the mirror. "Silly. Didn't you know? I would have thought Dash had mentioned it. Or that you'd already picked it up out of one of your trashy gossip magazines. Though I guess it's a rather dated story now."

Bree watched in surprise as Ruby let the barb land, confused. Curious, Bree prompted, "No, I don't think we know anything about it, Susie. Why don't you tell us?"

Susie fussed at her fake eyelashes in the mirror while she talked.

"My mother and father met years ago at some charity function. She was a Bollywood actress. He—well, you know all about him, I'm sure. They had a torrid affair, apparently, of which I am the result. He says he would have married her, but she refused to give up her career— she went straight back to Bandra when I was not even two. Supposedly she couldn't take me." She squared on them, a glint of hurt and anger in her azure eyes.

"It was bad enough that she'd had a child out of wedlock. Her father could barely stand to be in the same room with her after that. What was worse was the way I looked. The older I got, the harder it was." She swept a hand along the side of her body, as if she was on display in a showroom.

"I don't follow," Bree said.

"An Indian girl—even one with an Anglo, English parent—shouldn't grow up to have blonde hair and blue eyes. The genetics don't work. Not unless there are Englishmen—two or three, I'd wager—in the family tree. In some instances, these might have been colonial bureaucrats or soldiers who raped, seduced, or kept secret second families and managed to sneak their DNA into the picture. Recessive DNA that was lurking in the background all along, just waiting for a chance to pop out into the open. For there is no record of intermarriage in my mother's family. We were supposed to be pure of caste and blood."

Bree swallowed hard. "They rejected you because you are proof of something unsavory in the past. Something they didn't want to acknowledge."

Susie smiled sweetly. "We'll never really know what happened, but whatever it was, my grandfather did not like it. My mother's brothers threatened her if she dared to show her child in Indian society. They had enough on their hands trying to explain away the disgrace of a daughter dancing and acting in films and being generally notorious. What could she do? She knew she would never fit in as the wife of a black sheep noble in England. She packed herself back to Bollywood and left me here, with my father. His bastard daughter. Poor me."

She laughed, a bright, cheery sound that echoed against the cracked linoleum and stained tile of the bathroom.

"Poor little rich girl. You see, Bree . . ." Susie placed a solicitous hand on Bree's shoulder. "I'm not so different from you, after all. I may not be an orphan, but I haven't seen my mother in over fifteen years. To her, it is as if I don't even exist."

Bree reached up to take Susie's hand. "I'm so sorry, Susie. I didn't know."

In the back of Bree's mind, two streams of thought worked in parallel. One was the surprise of hearing Susie talk so knowledgeably about genetics. The second was her realization of just how deeply compromising Dash's dalliance with Susie would seem to his father, if everything Susie had just shared was true. Illegitimacy, colonial privilege run amok, class and racial prejudice—no matter how far in the past some of it had occurred, there was no doubt in her mind that Dash's father would find it all, well, *lacking in taste*. Of course, Dash knew all along. For just a second, she resented how callously he was using Susie for his own ends.

Susie squeezed Bree's hand, giving it a little pulse, and shrugged.

"There's nothing for which to be sorry. But I do think, in light of the circumstances, it is perfectly appropriate for me to wear a sari to this evening's festivities. Ruby, do you agree?"

Bree watched as Ruby nodded vigorously, for once at a loss for words.

"Very well, then," Susie said brightly, the fire in her eyes now softened into simple excitement for the party. "Shall we?"

The budgetary hawks of Norwood had refused to rent out a real ballroom for the night. Instead, a special task force of first-years who had been passed over for the certificate track, but still hoped to regain the good graces of the Agency's Jobs Placement Committee, had worked miracles to turn the gymnasium into something that bordered on a transformation. The ceiling and walls were swathed in tulle and fairy lights. Great candelabra stood in each corner and in regular intervals along the banquet table, which was set with glittering crystal, china, and silver and backed up against the bleachers. The entire effect was one of ethereal glow, the warm light bouncing off the polished pine floors and radiating up to disappear in the rafters. If one ignored the smell of musty gym socks, it could have almost been a real ballroom.

Two tuxedoed gentlemen circulated with flutes of effervescent champagne and canapés, the soft strains of a string quartet masking the sounds of conversation.

"MI6," Ruby whispered to Bree. "I overheard Kent when she was discussing security for the party."

Bree raised an eyebrow, taking them in. They certainly looked older than her classmates—weathered, hard, and resolute.

Johnson and Anya wandered over to join them. Johnson looked just as mousy as ever, swathed in something nondescript and gray. Anya shuffled uncomfortably in a strapless gown, her hulking shoulders looking like she was about to burst from the seams of the dress.

"Did you check out those waiters? Easy on the eyes, eh?" Johnson noted, her eyes lingering appreciatively over them.

Bree looked again. She noticed the way their suits molded to their broad shoulders. She saw the manner with which the tails of their tuxedo jackets just brushed past their trim waists and buttocks, ending over muscular thighs, which were just barely hinted at through the elegantly draped wool of their trousers.

Anya snickered. "Don't be so obvious, Bree."

Bree pressed her lips into a grim smile and turned back to her friends. It wasn't appreciation that had kept her eye lingering, but incongruity. Yes, these were definitely not your typical waiters. She'd have to keep an eye on them, when she wasn't worrying about which fork to use—she had a suspicion they were meant for more than just security.

Dash swooped in, bearing champagne flutes. "Ladies, permit me to say you look most radiant this evening." He passed around the glasses. "Ruby and Susie, I must add, you look particularly exotic. Your presence is a timely reminder that too often, we English lack imagination, as well as full appreciation of our cultural heritage."

Ruby looked vaguely disgruntled at being labeled "exotic" but, Bree noted, she'd apparently decided to shrug it off, swiping a glass from his hand.

"You look quite handsome, too, Dashiell," Susie cooed, tucking her arm under his. "Almost to the manner born."

He smiled indulgently at her and brushed an imaginary piece of lint off his lapel. "I'm afraid the waitstaff are better dressed than me. But a shabby tux from my father's last wedding was all I could muster. I'm surprised it still fits."

"It's loads better than that wretched manny uniform of which you are so enamored. I half expected you to show up in it, deerstalker and all," Johnson noted tartly.

Bree had to agree with her. The cut accentuated Dash's lean frame and broad shoulders.

"I bet I could still outwrestle you, even in this dress," Anya challenged him.

Dash looked at her quizzically. "Well, I, ah—"

Their conversation was interrupted by Professor Shadduck parading through the gym, striking a set of chimes with a large wooden mallet.

"Time to be seated," Dash noted, his relief at having an easy escape from the awkward conversation evident. "I scoped the table in advance. I'm sorry to report, Bree, that you are seated in the middle, at the right hand of *la femme* Albourn. I hope you are prepared for a grilling."

Susie piped in, declaring, "Bree is perfectly ready to discuss the China-Japan island tensions. I've briefed her fully. She'll do amazingly well, even head-to-head with Albourn. Right, Ruby?"

"Uh, yeah, I guess so. Right." Ruby seemed surprised that Susie had asked her opinion.

"Good luck, then, Bree. We'll expect a full report when we break for dancing."

They all scattered. Bree took her seat, grateful that her dress lacked the fussiness of a train or hoopskirts, making it possible to negotiate the chair with some semblance of grace. The waiters descended upon them, their delivery of the first course—soup—a vast, orchestrated ballet. As they retreated, Albourn swiveled in her seat and pinned Bree beneath her eye.

Bree took a deep breath. Down the table, she spied Gul Avci, their alumna mentor. Avci raised a glass, urging her on.

"Parrish," the dean began, dragging out Bree's terror while she took a long slurp of the chilled melon. "Brief me on the Senkaku/Diaoyu Islands."

"The disputed islands are located—"

Albourn cut her off swiftly, violently ripping a piece of dinner roll and shoving it into her mouth. Apparently, the power of her office meant the dean had long since stopped worrying about whether her manners were appropriate for polite dinner conversation.

"I don't need a geography lesson," she declared, a shower of crumbs spouting from her lips. "Nor am I interested in your regurgitation of what the dispute is. I am well aware of what the islands are and the fact that Japan, China, and Taiwan contest their ownership. Put it in context for me. Why should we care?"

Bree fingered her silverware, thinking, vaguely aware of the clipboard-wielding assistant lingering behind the dean's chair and Avci staring at her from her spot at the foot of the table, both of them listening, hard, to everything she said.

"Well . . . as the People's Republic, China has aggressively pursued a policy of restoration of its territorial rights."

"Restoration?" Albourn pressed through a mouthful of bread, her disregard for their painfully learned social protocols underscoring her complete authority.

"Their term. They were able to negotiate the return of Hong Kong from the British, the Return occurring in 1997, widely considered the end of the British Empire. They scored another diplomatic coup in 1998 when, on his first official presidential visit to China, President Clinton stunned America's allies by voicing out loud as US policy the three no's, effectively shifting US foreign policy and parroting back Beijing's stance. In that announcement, he said the States would not support independence for Taiwan, that it would reject any solution that created 'two Chinas,' and that it would oppose Taiwan's admission to organizations such as the UN."

Albourn nodded as she scraped up the last of her soup with her spoon. "Nasty. The Brits in Hong Kong were already feeling abandoned by us and then he pulled the rug out from under the Taiwanese. Without so much as consulting us. A travesty. Go on," she encouraged, waving her spoon.

Bree was on a roll, her confidence surging. She'd been well briefed by Susie, and while others found the geopolitics they were pressed to learn dull, she found the hints of intrigue fascinating.

"Many observers see the disputed islands as another example of the PRC seeking to reclaim what they consider to be lost geographical ground. Others note that their interest in the islands surfaced only after surveys indicated the presence of oil reserves. But clashes with errant fishing boats and escalated military exercises have lately raised the stakes."

"So. China on the move?"

Bree leaned her head in assent. "Militaristically or culturally. Consolidations in Asia could be seen as consistent with its goals to unite the world in a new flurry of commerce and art through its recreation of a modern Silk Road, cutting all the way to the heart of Europe."

Albourn pinned her down with a curious look. "What do you think?"

Bree smiled, pressing her lips into a tight line. "I have no opinion, Dean Albourn. I am just a simple governess. But there are many who believe the United Kingdom, and indeed, the West, should tread carefully, lest our pursuit of good trade relations lead us down a path toward diminished influence in Asia and elsewhere."

Albourn leaned back in her chair and clapped. "Bravo. A nanny must show her intelligence but also demonstrate she knows her place. You were thoughtful without getting drawn into taking sides. Just the thing for a good spy. Now," she said, as she noted the waiter hovering discreetly behind them, "let him clear your bowl so we can all move on to the salad course. All right," she said, shifting in her seat to get a better view of her next victim. "You there, Miss Hogg, talk with me of the Quebecois Independence movement."

Bree let her shaking hands rest in her lap, grateful to have passed Albourn's test. From down the table, Avci mouthed, "You ace. Brava." But one more test remained—the dancing—a fact that she'd conveniently forgotten until three courses later, when the swell of strings into a graceful waltz caught Albourn's attention.

"You must go, dear," she said, stabbing her fork toward the gaping empty space of the gymnasium. "They won't serve dessert until after you young people have had a go about the floor. Mind yourself," she added, her dark eyes glittering sharply.

"Ma'am?"

Albourn shrugged. "I wouldn't want you to trip on that lovely gown of yours." She turned away, dismissing Bree.

A throng of students pushed away from the table and moved toward the center of the gym, milling about as they negotiated partners and determined who would lead. Bree stayed on the perimeter, watchful.

The tuxedoed men were not clearing the tables to make way for dessert. They were lingering in the shadows, beyond the dim light thrown by the candelabra.

They were watching, too.

Bree made her way to Ruby. "Eyes on the perimeter, Ruby," she muttered in Ruby's ear as she leaned in to give an exaggerated hug. "What do you notice about the waiters?"

"I saw it too. They're encircling us. As if to herd us."

Bree forced a laugh to disguise the seriousness of their conversation.

Some of her fellow students turned, surprised. One of the waiters pursed his lips together and tilted his head, muttering at no one.

"See that?" Bree whispered. "He's wired for communications. Do you see weapons?"

Ruby peered over Bree's shoulder as she pretended to pick an errant crumb off the front of her gown. "Negative. But that doesn't mean they aren't there. Let's find Susie and Dash."

They linked arms and began to work the perimeter of the crowd. The musicians were working hard to outplay the women's rising chatter, the excited aftermath of having survived their own geopolitical quizzing. Dash towered over most of the women, even in their heels, making him easy to spot. He waved as he noticed them, raising an inquisitive brow and giving Bree a very American thumbs-up. She shook her head, mouthing, "Threat. Level. One."

He looked at her, the smile instantly disappearing from his face. "Where?" he mouthed back.

She stared at him pointedly, eyebrow arched. "Look around," she mouthed to him.

She was dragging Ruby backward now, apologizing curtly to the colleagues over whom she tripped, scanning the room for danger. The waiters were moving toward them, trays arrayed in front of them, but the trays were empty.

"Gun!" Anya shouted.

Ruby dove for the floor, dragging Bree with her as they slid in one sweeping motion behind the banquet table.

"Gun!" Anya bellowed, her voice echoing in the high ceiling of the gym. Total chaos erupted.

Anya charged. The waiters immediately abandoned their pretense, tossing away the heavy silver serving trays to reveal the pistols they were now pointing into the crowd, barking orders. The music cut off abruptly, the strings shrieking crazily as the cellist and violinist abruptly stopped. Bree watched, peering over the banquet table with terror as they pulled the weapons they'd duct-taped to the backs of their instruments out, brandishing them at the second violinist and viola player, who each began shrieking hysterically as they abandoned their music stands and ran, panicking, into the general melee.

One of the waiters grabbed a music stand and unceremoniously swung it across Anya's windpipe, dropping her to the ground.

One of the waiters was attempting to take charge. "This is a hostage situation!" he cried. "If you do as you're asked, nobody will be harmed!"

Some students, remembering their training, ducked to the floor to avoid being caught in any forthcoming crossfire. The students who remained standing turned as if one to look back at the banquet table, seeking reassurance from the Norwood staff.

But Bree could see that they were already gone, somehow having abandoned the room unnoticed, nothing but dirty plates and silverware to attest they had even been there.

The sounds of panic echoed throughout the gym. Bree took one look at Ruby and, together, they pushed the table over, the crash of china and crystal splintering into a thousand pieces only adding to the confusion. They leaned against the table's underside, catching their breaths behind the barrier, until Dash and Susie darted around the corner, crawling.

"My apologies, ladies," Dash quipped through gasps for breath. "It appears our dance cards are full. I will regretfully ask for a rain check on our promised waltz."

"How many are there?" Bree demanded. "Five, maybe six? Including the musicians? We can take them out."

"Did you see them drop Anya? What if it's a training exercise?" he asked, pulling at his collar.

"If it is, someone at Norwood will stop us before we can hurt anybody. I'd rather not take the time to figure it out. If it's really a hostage-taking, we've seen their faces. They won't let us out alive. Weapons?"

They patted themselves down, shaking their heads. They'd been told countless times in *Wonder Woman 101* to never find themselves unarmed, but it wasn't until this moment they realized the truth in that advice.

Bree peeked back over to check their position.

"Anyone see Johnson? We could use one more."

They shook their heads. It was as if Johnson, ever their shadow, had evaporated.

"Mousy thing anyway," Susie sniffed. "We don't need her."

Bree shook off her momentary doubt to focus.

"They seem preoccupied with the group huddled on the floor," Bree said. "There's a chance we can go unnoticed by sweeping behind the bleachers. Ruby and Susie, you go right and deal with the two on that side. I'll go left. Dash, can you do something from the table and distract them, so we have the element of surprise?"

They all nodded.

"All right, then. Dash, give us maybe ten seconds to get around to the other side. We'll all do our best to improvise. Good luck. Now."

The blood pounded in Bree's head in time with the count. One. Two. Three. She was running as fast as she could, silently cursing the clumsy skirt that messed with her stride. Four. Five. Six. Her lungs were heaving now—it took everything she had to move with stealth and keep her heart from exploding in her chest. Seven. Eight. Nine. She had barely a second to look around the edge of the bleachers and set her plan.

From behind the table, Dash unleashed a barrage of broken plates, glasses, and candlesticks, attracting the attention of the hostage-takers.

Now.

Bree sprinted from the bleachers, diving quickly to scoop up one of the abandoned platters and rolling back to her feet with it in hand. Two quick strides and she was upon one of the men. He turned just in time for her to bring the platter crashing against his head with a satisfying thud. His head jerked unnaturally, as if it wanted to separate from his neck, and he staggered, a trickle of blood escaping his ear. But he still gripped his pistol. Bree swung the tray up, hard, against his shooting hand, sending the gun flying until it landed in the far corner of the gym.

She looked up. Across the way, Ruby was swinging a candelabra, buffeting the ribs of one of the men who appeared to have lost his gun. But the cellist was coming up behind her, brandishing the butt of his gun. Bree flung the tray she still gripped in her fists like a Frisbee, aiming for his throat. It hit its mark and he instantly fell to the ground, clutching his windpipe. Unaware of what was going on behind her, Ruby finished off her man with a well-placed swing that took out his knees.

One tuxedo-clad man still stood over the rest of the students, swinging his gun wildly while trying to artfully sidestep the detritus being flung at him by Dash.

"Don't get any ideas," the remaining MI6 man warned. "I've got a gun."

"For God's sake, people," Susie grunted out from where she was in hand-to-hand combat with the last remaining waiter, much of her sari ripped and trailing behind her. "We outnumber them. What are you doing cowering on the ground? Get up and fight!"

A general murmur of agreement went through the women seated on the floor.

"Don't listen to her!" Susie's combatant spat in between swings. "She's just a dumb, cute, bitty thing, isn't she?" he sneered. "Spoiled, too, I bet. You wouldn't follow her!"

Susie froze.

He paused, sneer frozen in place. Bree could see how he reveled in the hurt look on her face.

"Oh, shut up," she said, exasperated. "I'm had quite enough of you for one evening." In one swift move she kicked off her stiletto so that in spun, heel over toe, up into the air. Her perfectly manicured hand darted out to catch it as she bore down upon the man. Blisteringly fast, Susie dug the spike of her remaining shoe into his foot, bringing him to his knees with a howl, headbutting him for good measure, stunning him. With no hesitation, she swung the stiletto for his eye, her sculpted arm bringing its pointy tip toward him in a perfect, lethal arc.

"That's enough!"

Dean Albourn's hand snaked up, steeling itself about Susie's wrist, staying her arm just before impact. Bree watched as Susie's muscles trembled and twitched in protest, the ache to complete her attack and finish off her opponent too much to bear.

"That's enough, Susie. You've all shown your mettle against these gentlemen. The exercise is over. Montoya-Craig has captured your marks. You may relax."

Susie sighed and dropped her head in acquiescence as Albourn released her arm. Susie drew her hand in, staring at her shoe as if she didn't recognize it and could not piece together how it came to be in her hand. After grappling with the issue for what seemed like an eternity, she forced her fingers open, one by one, dropping her deadly stiletto to the floor. Her eyes seemed dead as she scanned the wreckage about her. Slowly, deliberately, she reached down and ripped the last shred of her sari's skirt, effectively leaving herself in a mini, and kicked off her other shoe. Her lip curled derisively as she looked one last time at her opponent where he huddled on the gym floor, nursing his wounds.

Then, and only then, did she return Albourn's commanding stare.

"Susmita," she said, blowing an errant wave of sun-kissed hair off her forehead.

"What?" Albourn asked, confused.

When Susie spoke again, her voice was strong and resolute.

"The S. in S. Susie Hilvale stands for Susmita. I want to be called by my real name from now on. Susmita. Not Susie."

The silence was overpowering as she glided barefoot across the floor and out of the gym. Bree, Ruby, and Dash followed quickly behind her, leaving Montoya-Craig to place tiny rows of green pluses next to their names in the exercise book.

Clinging to tradition, final term grades were posted on the side of the administration building the next morning. The pages fluttered in the brisk wind as the students—hopeful and fearful—huddled around them, searching for their student ID number and hence their fates.

"You look, Susmita," Ruby urged, her tongue thick on the unfamiliar name. "I don't think I can stand to do it myself."

Susmita burrowed through the crowd, ID numbers in hand, as the rest of them waited. In a few minutes she emerged, her face glowing in triumph.

With their performance at the ball, they had more than made up for their lackluster performance on finals. They had somehow secured the top marks. A summer international posting—their first fieldwork as actual spies—would be theirs.

From somewhere in the crowd, Avci emerged to congratulate them. "Are you ready to do whatever it takes?" Avci asked again.

This time, Bree—and her roommates—were certain. They were.

Chapter Five

SUMMER TERM FIELD SPY CRAFT

Istanbul, Turkey

"Eda! How many times have you been told? You cannot bathe the cat. She cannot come into the tub with you. She doesn't like to get wet!"

"But Bree," the four-year-old pleaded, her eyes brimming and bottom lip quivering, "I just want to see what will happen! Arslan told me all her fur will fall out and I want to see what she looks like naked!"

Bree hid her laugh behind the terry washcloth. At nine, Arslan was a typical big brother, and with three younger sisters, he had plenty of targets for his tricks.

"The only naked thing in this room right now is you, young lady," Bree said in mock seriousness. "Climb out now, so I can dry you off and get you dressed for your parents. You can have a sweet when you're finished."

The promise of a treat lured the little fish from the water. As Bree rubbed her down, she wondered at how swiftly her life had changed.

By rising against the faux kidnappers at the Norwood Gala, Bree's group had secured top marks for the term and locked in first position for summer term internships. While most of their classmates had won plum positions shadowing alumnae in regular celebrity placements or were working the resorts as temporary nannies for summering guests, they'd been chosen by none other than Gul Avci for something much more serious—and dangerous: field placements in the middle of a live operation.

Every night before she fell asleep, Bree recited the convoluted setup as it had been explained to them all. She was joining Agent Avci in her ongoing operation as "co-nanny" to the four children of Lieutenant Colonel Kemal Asker of the Turkish Land Forces' First Army in Istanbul. Their cover—coordinated with the Askers' full cooperation—was simple: Asker's wife, Handan, of a wealthy family herself, needed more help with the little ones, freeing her up to be the attentive hostess Asker required to advance his military career ambitions.

The reality was anything but simple. A secret faction within NATO seeking to remove Turkey's president from power had managed to recruit Asker, who was disillusioned with his own corrupt government. His participation had escalated from selling secrets to actively collaborating to illicitly funnel NATO arms to an insurgent rebel force right at Turkey's doorstep. Those behind the operation had assured Asker it wouldn't come to actual military conflict—the pressure would mount until the Turkish government fell, restoring democracy. Asker had blindly believed them.

Only now, someone inside the Army—or maybe even the president's office—may have found out what he was up to, and the threats against Asker's family were mounting.

Bree's mission was simple: to work with Gul to protect the children, at all costs, as their deaths or kidnapping would likely cause the lieutenant colonel to flee, ruining the most important asset they had inside the Army.

That, and find out who was selling out Asker.

Easy peasy.

Dash had been placed with the family of the German Defense Minister to monitor the fractious diplomatic relations between Germany and Turkey. With the skills he'd shown in *Snap-Spy*, he'd also be the one running any computer espionage they might need during the operation.

Ruby had been placed with the family of the NATO High Commander, placing eyes and ears to ensure that nobody at NATO had any official awareness of the operation.

And Susmita was at Norwood HQ, running overall mission ops and planning an emergency exit route for Gul, Bree, and the children, should they need it. After her aggressive performance at the ball, she'd been deemed the most intuitive choice for anything that might require quick thinking and brute force.

It did not pass notice amongst the group that this assignment also conveniently eliminated the need for her to tend to actual children.

Every day, Bree was to report on her status—and any discoveries—to her handler, Gul's parallel updates serving as a built-in mechanism to cross-check for accuracy and ensure the mole wasn't within the operation itself.

Eda flung her arms around Bree's shoulders, her long, soggy hair lashing Bree out of her reverie.

"Hurry, Bree! I want to see Baba and Anne."

Bree laughed, wrapping her in the towel and leading her out of the bath to get dressed. "Let's see, little one. If you can beat Isra and Gamze to be the first girl ready, I will cut you an extra big piece of baklava. I know your father and mother are eager to see you too." With a squeal of delight, Eda tore off streaking, the towel falling to the wayside.

Sometimes, the family sat to a joint dinner, but more often than not, the colonel and his wife's duties kept them away until later in the evening. Bree and Gul took turns attending the children during this part of the day, giving each of them a chance for their own break. The Askers might then come home to see the children for a brief moment before bedtime.

This nightly presentation of the children to the Askers was not as formal as Bree had feared. Perhaps it was because of the colonel's own humble beginnings. Perhaps it was just because of the love that suffused the household. Whatever it was, both parents seemed genuinely delighted to welcome their children as they scrambled to climb in laps, twist their mother's ropes of gold chains, and try to make Baba laugh, shouting above one another breathlessly to tell their stories from school or the latest escapades of the neighborhood cats.

Spurred by Bree's competition, the girls threw on their pajamas and robes in record time and raced to the sitting room of the apartment they shared near the Selimiye Barracks on the Asian side of Istanbul. They arrived to find their big brother, Arslan, already seated at their father's feet, listening raptly while his father tuned his *saz*.

"Sing! Sing! Sing!" the girls began chanting while they jumped up and down, led by the biggest, Isra, who dutifully remembered her father's admonition that they practice English whenever in front of their new foreign nanny.

Asker laughed, basking in the admiration of his girls.

Handan rolled her eyes. "You will make him have a big head, my daughters," she admonished with a smile.

"Daughters should think their fathers hung the moon," Asker teased. "I, for one, think my daughters are the stars twinkling in the firmament. It is as it should be."

"Very poetic, my colonel. Now let's see if your way with words carries over into a song that is worthy of that instrument of yours."

He bowed his head, acquiescing with a grin to her playful demand. His fingers danced over the strings, his eyes closed as he made the last adjustments. Bree found herself holding her breath—whenever Asker played, it reminded her of Rodney plucking out the old bluesy songs he loved to play back in Alabama. Asker waited until the antsy scrambling of the children at his feet settled into silence. Then he began.

It didn't matter to Bree that she could not understand most of what he sang. She didn't need to know the words. The passion Asker poured into each note sent her on a roller-coaster of emotion every time she listened to him play. He had a tendency to pick old folk songs drenched in the violence and hardship of his people's past. Tonight's performance seemed particularly mournful. Near the back of the room, she leaned against the wall and closed her eyes, too, feeling the shudder of despair, the soaring call for mercy, the quiet acceptance and grief that he conjured up, his voice breaking, then falling to a whisper, as he spun the tale.

When the room fell quiet, she opened her eyes to find him smiling at her, amused.

"It pleased you, Bree, this old song of mine?"

She nodded, feeling her face flush. "It seems so sad," she stammered, embarrassed. "I didn't understand it, of course."

"Ah, but you did," he insisted, shaking his head while he strummed the strings absentmindedly. "Our music calls to you. You feel its sadness in your bones, even if you cannot decipher the words. This one is the cries of a mother sending her son to war, never to have him in her arms again. You have a good soul, Miss Bree. A sensitive one, even, to recognize this sorrow. It is a good thing to have you here, with our children."

He and Handan shared a meaningful look.

"And you, my playful magpies! Even you are quiet for the sad songs, aren't you?" The children giggled, happy to be the center of his attention. "Let's play something more amusing now, eh?"

The children jumped to their feet, holding hands and dancing in a circle to his tune, which Bree now recognized as a wedding dance he'd played for them before. Around they twirled, their tiny feet making intricate cross-steps so that they nearly floated over the floor.

When they collapsed in a heap, laughing, exhausted, and hot, Handan took command.

"I have a special question for you all," she said, her voice gentle. "Do you think you are big enough to get yourselves to bed? Can I count on you all to follow Arslan's instructions so that Baba and I can have a word with Miss Bree?"

Arslan puffed himself up. "I can be in charge, Anne." He beamed at his mother as he addressed her.

"And Gul will be there to assist you, Mr. Arslan—not that you will need it," Bree winked.

Eda protested. "Bree said we could have baklava."

Handan smiled. "Arslan is big enough to cut you each a piece. Run to the kitchen and then be off to bed. Be sure to brush your teeth," she called after them as they raced down the hall.

Bree raised an eyebrow. "What's this? I gather it is something serious."

"Come, join us, Bree," Handan said, indicating a chair near theirs. "Sit down so that we may talk." As Bree settled into her seat, Handan peered down the hallway, listening to the diminishing shrieks of the children, to be sure they were alone.

"There was an attack at the *cem evi* in Gazi Istanbul today," she began, her voice trembling as she relayed the news.

Bree frowned. As religious minorities, the Askers downplayed their religion, but the children participated in activities at their own *cem evi*—a sort of cross between a mosque and a community center—weekly. This was an escalation their operation could not ignore.

"What happened?"

The colonel sagged into his chair, the charm he'd showered upon the children used up, replaced with the unremitting worry of a man backed into a corner. "It was a bomb—military grade, but it could have come from anywhere. Luckily, the building was fairly empty. No worship being held, just meetings. Only ten people were killed. *Only*," he repeated bitterly, the word twisting his lips.

Bree looked from Asker to Handan. "You want to discuss the plan?"

Handan nodded. "I don't think we can wait any longer. Not after all the other incidents in the past weeks."

Bree recounted them quickly in her head. An unmarked car had run a traffic light and narrowly missed hitting the car taking the girls to their school. Arslan's school had been plagued by a series of false fire alarms, disrupting classes and causing a general disarray that made Arslan, himself, extremely vulnerable. Handan, too, had been feeling increasingly insecure. Only a few nights ago, she had been walking home from a wives' event at the barracks campus and upon turning into the streets along the river had found herself being trailed in the dark. Her would-be assailant never closed the distance between them but had obstinately stuck with her the entire route—she had described it as a distinctly unsettling experience.

Yes, it was time they removed the children, for their own safety, and put Gul and Bree out of harm's way, too.

The colonel echoed her thoughts, his voice cracking with the same emotion that had overflowed in his song. "I couldn't live with myself if anything were to happen to them. But spiriting the children away without us? Maybe that is not such a good idea."

You need to calm him down, Bree, she thought to herself. *Remember, we need to keep the asset in place. He needs to be confident.*

Bree squared her shoulders and began reviewing with him in her most soothing voice. "We've been over the plan countless times. We've eliminated every weak point."

Handan nodded, folding her hands tightly in her lap to keep herself from wringing them. "We'll tell anyone who asks that I've sent the children for a visit to my sister in Malatya."

"Yes," Bree agreed, seizing on Handan's comment for momentum. "Gul and I will pack the children's bags. We won't talk of it again. We'll make our move when we've confirmed all the other arrangements. The less you know, the safer you'll be, too."

Asker's gaze wandered the room, agitated, his eyes settling on the old black-and-white photograph of his hero and namesake, Ataturk. "Our city was always a crossroads of the world. It had room for people of every faith. I do not even recognize it now. If this is what it is to be, I do not want my children to grow up here. It is not worthy any longer." Asker spat the words, his frustration plain.

Bree paused. She couldn't let him give up. Not now. His patriotism, his idealism, was the key to his role in the arms smuggling. From her briefing, Bree knew Asker was the most senior person they'd been able to turn inside the Turkish military. He alone could create the commands and the paper trail to cover up the diversion of weapons their broader mission relied upon. The only reason he did it was his belief that the government could be toppled, creating a better future. If he abandoned hope for his country, the whole thing could fall apart. She called up the words her handler had coached her on, over and over, in her nighttime communiques.

"This is temporary, remember?" she prodded him gently. "Handan will leave the country shortly after we do, to join the children, and when things have settled down, they'll all return. Your work here is too important to abandon. Right?"

Handan and Bree waited for his consent.

Finally, he sighed. "Yes, you are right. Of course, I must continue. If I don't stand up to them, who will?"

Gul and Bree conferred in secret each night over the kitchen table, double-checking their arrangements and confirming they'd executed every one of Susmita's directives. The extra set of backpacks and false documents they'd prepared for the children were stowed away under Gul's bed, waiting. The cars had been rotated out for repairs, allowing false bottoms to be installed. When, several weeks later, Arslan came home bearing a notice from the school that nearly half of the teachers had been accused of being traitors against the government, and so were stripped of their positions and thrown in jail, they knew the time had come.

Bree slept fitfully the night before. She spent long stretches awake, walking through each step of the plan. Nothing could go wrong. And why would it?

She supposed it was a vote of confidence from those back at Norwood, but somehow, she expected that the night before her first big operation she'd get some pep talk, some reassurances, something more than the terse order, *Report at Conclusion*, next to Susmita's name in her encrypted texting platform.

She kept checking the texts, mindlessly refreshing, until she was rewarded with a single word.

Ping.

She smiled. Dash. She checked the time—late night for him.

Ping back, she typed swiftly with her thumbs.

Ready? he responded, just as quickly.

She wanted to tell him she was nervous. Even afraid. But she knew there was a good chance her handler was monitoring their texting even as it was taking place.

Absolutely.

His words of reassurance filled her screen. *We've got your back here. Team ready to receive the packages in GE when delivered. S ready with backup if needed.*

She swallowed down another wave of self-doubt and typed more. *I know. All good.*

She watched the little dancing ellipses as she waited for his next message.

Sorry I have not attended to you properly.

She furrowed her brows, confused. He had been strangely incommunicado, but she'd thought that it might have been at her handler's instruction.

Think I may be nannying great-grandchildren of long-rumored spawn of Eva Braun and the Führer.

She snorted, trying to stifle the laugh provoked by his inappropriate joke.

Manny Suit better than Lederhosen they tried to foist on me

Living their twisted Sound of Music fantasy

Want to poke my eyes out with knitting needles but not sure what I'd do for craft activity next day.

She knew what he was doing. He was trying to distract her. And it was working. Tears rolled down her cheeks as she silently shook in her bed, trying not to crack up.

I will be a better correspondent next mission, I swear.

NP, she typed back. She hesitated a moment and then asked: *Any news re: kittens?*

It was the only safe way they'd been able to land on to refer to his continued data mining in the school records.

Sharp claws and won't come out to play. Yet.

She felt a long drag of disappointment.

Now get some sleep. We'll be cheering you on tomorrow.

She smiled to herself, wiping the tears from her face before signing off for the night.

Good night, D. And thanks.

———

"You must go," Gul insisted, crossing her arms across her chest as the definitive end of the argument. "You cannot have any deviation in your schedule today or it could generate suspicion. Colonel Asker, with all due respect, you must depart for the base now."

His eyes flashed with stubborn resistance. "I will not leave without saying goodbye to my children."

"You will see them soon enough, Colonel," Bree prodded gently. "They won't be ready for another thirty minutes. We cannot afford for you to linger. And we cannot afford to give your children any indication that today is unusual in any way. They need to behave normally if this is to work."

Handan cleared her throat and placed a hand on his elbow. "Kemal."

He shook his arm away, but the lines etched in his face softened. "You women are so strong. Is it childbirth that makes you so hard? Or your resentment at all the injustices that marriage forces you to accommodate? We men are such a burden upon you, I know. We are the reason for all these troubles to begin with." With an exaggerated sigh he threw up his hands. "All right. Have it your way. I'm going." He squeezed Handan's hand and turned to Gul and Bree, pointing a finger at them. "Keep them safe." Then he stalked out the front door.

The living room window was open to the street below. After a few moments, his angry voice floated up. "God damn pigeons! Always shitting on my car."

Bree grinned—it was the same frustrated outburst they'd heard every morning they'd been here. The familiarity of it was comforting. Gul chuckled, and Bree as well, appreciating the sense of normalcy it lent on such a tense morning.

Handan, however, didn't notice. She was still staring at the door her husband had slammed behind him, eyes fixed as if willing him to return.

"I cannot do it," she finally announced.

Gul's head jerked back in surprise. "What do you mean?"

"I cannot be here to see them off. I'm not like him, able to act all gruff to cover up my feelings. I won't be able to hide my tears." Handan began frantically gathering random things to her, eyes unseeing as she clutched at each piece—a scarf, her purse, a plastic shopping tote, a cat toy. "I must leave now. I must leave before they see me." Teary eyed, she stumbled toward the front door where Bree intercepted her. Bree held her by the shoulders, her firm but gentle gaze quieting Handan.

"Handan, you need to be here this morning. It's their routine. What you tell them this morning will be very important in getting them safely out of the country."

"We need you to tell them to obey us, no matter what," Gul interrupted bluntly. She darted a glance down the hallway, watchful for the children, who were about to wake. "This thing is planned to the second. We won't have time to cajole or answer a million questions. They must be obedient this morning. And we need you to remind them of this before we leave."

Handan sniffed, her chin quivering. But she nodded, tentatively at first, then resolutely. "You are right. I must send them off properly."

"Without scaring them," Bree added.

"Yes." Handan smiled a tremulous smile. "Without scaring them."

Bree squeezed her shoulder with encouragement, thankful that Handan hadn't noticed her own knees shaking. "Before you know it, you'll be meeting them in Berlin." She began taking the items from Handan's hands, steering her back into the living room.

Gul raised a hand, cocking her head toward the children's rooms. "They're up. No more time for talking. Now we execute the plan."

Thirty minutes later, Arslan, Isra, Eda, and Gamze were turned out in their school uniforms, book bags in tow while they jostled at the door, licking crumbs from their fingers. Eda had awoken cranky and whiny and was clinging to her mother, begging to stay home so she might visit her grandmother.

"Shh," Handan soothed her, holding her close and stroking her hair. "Your grandmother has doctor appointments today. And she only wants to see good girls who go to school and obey their mothers. Not whiny girls who cause trouble." Her words were deliberately harsh, the words of a mother steeling herself to let go, but her voice caught on them, nonetheless. Bree and Gul exchanged a long glance.

Handan pushed Eda away and turned a stern gaze on her children. "That goes for all of you. Make your grandparents proud—listen to Gul and Bree. Do exactly what they say, no arguments. They will tell me which of you behaves the best and whoever that is will get a prize!"

"Tonight, Anne?" Gamze demanded.

Handan pressed her lips together. "When you come home."

Isra and Gamze clapped their hands excitedly, while Arslan, ever the cool "big boy," rolled his eyes. Eda whimpered, twisting her skirt in her hand.

"Go now, or you'll be late for school," Handan commanded, her voice breaking.

Eda began to cry.

"Eda, we don't have time for this," Gul tutted. "Here, take this. It will make you feel better." She thrust a ratty teddy bear at Eda. Bree recognized it as one that had sat on the shelf in the bedroom the girls shared. Eda looked at it dubiously, sniffing dramatically, but quieted down. She grasped the teddy bear, tucking it under her arm, and held up her other hand to Gul.

Gul clasped it, sighing with relief.

"We'll see you later," she said to Handan. Handan nodded and walked to the door, swinging it open.

"Goodbye," Handan replied, sending them out. She stared hard at each child as they walked through the door. When Arslan brought up the rear, she hugged him fiercely. He wrapped his arms around her and earnestly promised, "I'll make sure the girls behave, Anne."

Handan gave out a strangled sound—half laugh, half cry—and pushed him out the door, closing it firmly behind them all.

The drivers—positions long ago filled by plants from the Norwood network—waited below. They split up as normal, Gul with Arslan and Bree with the girls. Before climbing into the back seat with Arslan, Gul nodded at Bree.

"See you at the meeting point."

The traffic was even worse than usual. As the SUV crawled forward, Bree found herself pushing her feet against the floorboards of the vehicle, as if she could force it to move faster by sheer will. She monitored the flow behind her, using the rearview and side mirrors to confirm that they were not being followed.

She forced herself to relax, melting into the seat. If they were late, it just made what they were about to do that much easier, she realized.

She kept up with the chatter of the children while, one by one, they passed the neighborhood landmarks that Bree realized she'd never see again. The old barracks, where Florence Nightingale once nursed the injured from the Crimean War and now held the headquarters of the First Army. The Maiden's Tower, beckoning from the strait. The entrance to Camlica Park, one of the first places Gul had taken her with the children so she could see all of Istanbul laid out before her. The children had darted among the flowers and trees of the manicured lawns, shyly giggling at the brides who'd come to have their pictures taken. They had sated themselves with honey and cream as they'd watched the sun set.

She pressed her hand against the window, wondering at how quickly a place could work its way into your heart.

When they finally made it into the neighborhood with the school, she turned to address the children. She had rehearsed this part over and over with Gul.

"Gul and I have a surprise for you and Arslan. We planned it with your parents."

"Is it a pony?" Gamze asked innocently.

Bree laughed despite herself. "No, silly, not a pony. Where would we keep such a big animal? The surprise is a trip."

"A trip?" Isra asked doubtfully.

"Think of it as a field trip. An adventure. Which means you will get to leave school today."

"Yay!" All three girls bounced excitedly in their seats.

Bree shushed them. "But it is a secret trip. And it requires us to play make-believe together for a little bit. Do you think you can do that with me?"

The girls nodded, giggling at the prospect. Bree sighed. *Maybe this won't be so hard*, she thought.

"All right, then. Listen carefully. Let's make-believe we are all famous magicians on our way to cast spells on mermaids to help save them from the evil witch. Because we are famous, we must disguise ourselves and mustn't tell anybody about our secret plans. Can you handle that?"

They nodded solemnly.

"Good girls. I know I can count on you. The first thing we must do is go into the school together. Since we are late, I'll sign you in and we'll pretend we're going to class. But instead of class, you will follow me so we can start our adventure."

"How will we go on our trip if Mr. Ocak leaves us at the school?" Isra, ever sharp, asked the obvious question, pointing to their driver.

"You'll see," Bree promised. "It's a secret. Part of the surprise. First, I must give you your wands." She reached into her bag and presented the girls with the homemade wands she and Gul had crafted for them. Each wand was different. Isra's was bright orange and green with a flurry of sparkly pipe cleaner curlicues at the end, as if the wand was caught in the middle of casting a spell. Gamze's was deep purple, covered in glitter, and sported a cascade of silver tinsel and wired stars at its tip. Little Eda's was red, decorated with stickers of mermaids, unicorns, and dinosaurs. Braided strings of red, white, and blue cascaded from it. The girls' eyes grew big as they took their wands in turn, cradling them like a treasure in their tiny, outstretched palms.

"Your wands have special powers. I'll tell you about them soon. For now, grab your things. Remember—no talking to *anybody*. If you tell our secret, we won't be able to go."

The girls tumbled out of the car, jostling to hold Bree's hand. The drop-off circle was deserted—as Bree had anticipated, they'd missed the first bell. She breathed deeply, reminding herself that if anybody had managed to trail them, this offered them a clear view of the girls arriving at school—another day, just like any other.

"I'll meet you in the pickup lot," she said to Mr. Ocak. He nodded and put the SUV into gear, pulling away from the curb. She then walked the girls into the school.

Everything went smoothly. She signed the girls in and was instructed to walk them to their classrooms on the other side of the building. The hallways were deserted, the students and teachers all occupied with their first morning announcements. Classrooms were extra crowded, as the teachers who had not been dismissed struggled to squeeze in extra students. Nobody had time to care what was going on in the corridors. Bree marched the girls right past the classrooms and down the hallway to the cafeteria, where they ducked inside the kitchen.

Eda hung back, dragging on Bree's sleeve.

"What is it, Eda?"

"We aren't allowed in there."

Bree squatted down to bring herself to eye level with the four-year-old. "Today, with me, you can go in. We will cut through to get to your special chariot, which will bring you to the sea. Okay?"

Eda looked at her older sisters, who were grinning.

"Okay."

The cooks, already busily preparing the noon meal for the students, barely gave them a glance as they ducked through the back of the kitchen toward the delivery entrance. Bree led the girls out, past the unloading truck, to where Mr. Ocak had parked the SUV.

"That's not a chariot—that's just our car!" Isra exclaimed.

"Wait," Bree said. "Look here." She popped open the rear gate and shifted the extra backpacks around before lifting out the false floor, revealing the hiding place. She lifted each girl in her arms, in turn, to let them each take a look. It was a tight fit, but she knew all three of them could lay down comfortably for the forty-five minutes she estimated it would take to get to the rendezvous point; knew the air holes that were not visible from the floor of the vehicle would be more than sufficient to keep them safe.

She and Gul had worked to make the hiding spot as enticing as possible—the floor was covered with a fuzzy faux sheepskin rug. Embroidered pillows awaited their heads. And the entire interior was painted like the night sky and studded with glow-in-the-dark stickers. She had gotten up early to shine lamplight on them, ensuring they would glow for the duration of the ride, and stowed the flashlight there as an extra precaution.

"Magicians cannot be seen entering the Mermaid Queendom," she intoned seriously. "This hiding spot will keep you safe."

"From the witch?" Gamze asked, eyes wide.

"Yes, from the witch. Now quickly, let me get you in. Isra first."

Swiftly she lifted each child and settled them inside, ever watchful that they not be seen. She peered over the edge at them, lined like sardines in a tin.

"I will command your chariot and when we get to the Mermaid Queendom, we will meet Gul and Arslan. In the meantime, I need you to imagine which spells you will use to conquer the witch."

The girls giggled, clutching their wands. *So trusting*, she thought wistfully. *That alone makes them worth protecting.*

"Okay. I am going to put the cover back on. I will see you in a little bit. Remember—practice those spells!"

Driving in Istanbul was a nightmare. Bree's international driver's license granted her permission to do so, but it was a privilege she'd rarely exercised. Between her difficulty with the Turkish signs, the crush of traffic, and the tangle of roads that crisscrossed the sprawling city, it had usually been easier to be driven everywhere they needed to go. But from this stage on, the fewer people who knew the details of their plan, the better. From the very beginning, she and Gul had used their free time to practice this route so that now they both knew it by heart, along with several alternatives should they run into trouble.

As she navigated the SUV, she winced at every pothole, every sudden braking, hoping the girls weren't overly jostled where they lay hidden in the back. And she watched the clock. They had a ten-minute window during which they would connect with a courier from their contact within the American Air Force. At contact, they were to transfer to the courier's vehicle so that he could smuggle them all to one of the bases in Turkey hosting NATO operations and then stow them all on an outbound military flight for Germany.

This was the trickiest part of the operation, but Susmita had insisted that the passport scan of all four children would alert the authorities if

they tried to fly commercial. It was safer, though infinitely more complicated, to move them this way. Colonel Asker had agreed.

She pulled the SUV behind a row of sky-rise apartments, aiming for
the bank of dumpsters at the end of the alley. A lone vehicle—a heavily
reinforced Raptor—sat idling behind them.

She slowed, coming up on the vehicle cautiously.

She opened the walkie-talkie app on her mobile and hailed Gul.
"Approaching vehicle now. ETA?"

Gul was only minutes away. Bree decided to park and check out the
courier. From the glove compartment, she withdrew her pistol, releasing
the safety and tucking it into the strap under her jacket before jumping
down.

She couldn't see the courier behind the darkened security glass of the
armored vehicle. She waved a hand, walking slowly toward him, waiting
for him to emerge.

When he didn't, she stopped and drew her gun.

"I need you to come out," she stated loudly. "I'm Roxelana," she continued, sharing the codename they'd agreed to use to establish identities
at this point of transfer. "Roxelana," she repeated.

Still nothing. Just the soft rumble of the idling vehicle.

Behind her she heard someone else enter the alley. She darted a glance
over her shoulder and saw, with relief, that it was Gul in the Mercedes.
She waited, gun still pointing at the Raptor, until Gul joined her.

"What's the problem?" Gul demanded.

"Where's Arslan?" Bree asked sharply, ignoring her question.

"He's still in the trunk of the car, hidden. Calm down, Bree. Why are
you so tense?"

Bree felt the muscles in her jaw spasm with tension. "The courier. The
Air Force guy. He hasn't responded to the hail."

"You shared the codename?"

Bree nodded. "Something's wrong. But we won't know what unless we broach the vehicle. That glass is impenetrable."

Together, they circled the Raptor, swinging as wide as the narrow confines of the alley would allow. As they did, they checked each of the passageways between the apartment towers.

"All clear," Gul confirmed.

"On my count," Bree stated. "One, two, three. Now!"

They charged the Raptor, each taking one side and swinging the doors wide. What they saw inside sickened them.

The man they presumed to be the courier was slumped over the steering wheel. A hole in his head oozed bits of flesh and blood. Behind him, and all around the driver's side, a splatter of blood and gore slathered and dripped off of the interior.

Gul pulled his lifeless body up off the steering wheel. He'd been shot at close range. It was a clean hole, ringed with a charcoal-like abrasion that Bree recognized as the imprint of a gun barrel. A pattern of gray and black tattooed the skin around the wound, the spattering of hot gunpowder. With a look of disgust, Gul let him fall back to the dashboard and wiped her bloody hand on her pants leg.

"It's an ambush. Secure the perimeter," she ordered Bree sharply. "Whoever did this knew we were coming and may try to take the kids."

Guns drawn, they swept again, this time scanning the banks of shiny windows in the towers above them, wondering if the shooter had retreated to the vantage point of the apartments.

Bree saw nothing.

"It doesn't make sense," Gul puzzled. "If they wanted to stop us from leaving, why wouldn't they stick around to snatch the kids, too?"

Bree had no answers. She couldn't think at all. She was concentrating too hard on not throwing up as the tangy, iron-laced scent of blood wafted up in the summer heat. She bent over and vomited into the weed-choked space behind the dumpsters.

When she finished, she drew her sleeve across her mouth and winced at the sourness.

"We need to get the kids out," she stated.

"Not until we know what to do," Gul insisted. She pulled out her mobile and initiated contact with the entire operations team. Bree looked over her should as she typed, eager for any bit of information. *Contact point compromised. Courier dead. Unable to initiate transfer. Advise additional intel and next steps.*

They waited, pacing the alley, wondering just what their team, scattered at a distance of thousands of miles, would instruct them to do.

Their handler's initial response confirmed their fears about the operation: *Air Force contact taken out. Original exit no longer feasible. Germany and NATO, any intel?*

Dash texted: *Nothing.* Ruby added, *NATO just informed of extra security at all public airports. Claiming terrorist threat.*

"*Kahretsin,*" Gul cursed, spitting into the dirt. "We're screwed now."

Bree tried to remain calm, fighting off a second wave of nausea. "Susmita has our backup plan. Probably more than one. Just wait and see what she says."

Susmita's text made them even more worried. *Safest route out now is with smuggled refugees through Greece.*

Gul swore again. "That's hardly safe! Especially with four children."

Bree's mind went over all the news stories—the overloaded boats, the swelling waves tipping them over, the children washed onto the beaches, dead. Not to mention the people who were promised safe passage and then found themselves swallowed up into forced labor, disappearing into the bowels of Europe never to be seen again.

As if able to hear their thoughts, Susmita continued. *Confirmed safe contact to take you over and smuggle you to Calais.*

Uneasy, Bree texted back. *Is this truly best option? Can't we be diverted before Calais?*

Susmita's response chilled them. *Only option. Can't interfere with trafficker route or risk ruining contact.*

Their handler cut in, settling it. *Returning to Askers not possible. Must remove children to safety. S will set up contact and send you instruction. Over.*

For the first time since she'd been implanted, Bree was grateful for the tracking device at the base of her neck, for she imagined it was easy for someone to be lost forever in the underground world she, Gul, and the children soon found themselves navigating.

Driving the Mercedes or the SUV was no longer an option. They'd managed to hot-wire an old van that had been parked down the road from the apartment complex, and with it headed to the location Susmita had directed them toward: the seedy district of Aksaray. The traffic was incessant and the van so poorly ventilated that the children gagged on gasoline fumes and whined about the heat from the back seats.

"Can't you occupy yourselves? Find something to do. Look out the windows and see what you notice," Gul ordered them, impatient with worry.

The children pressed their noses to the glass while Bree desperately tried to keep up with Gul's driving, struggling to understand their way on the Turkish navigation app she was trying to use.

"Give me that!" Gul snapped in frustration as they missed another turn, grabbing the phone out of Bree's hand. Bree felt herself flush, embarrassed that she couldn't figure out something so simple. Gul cut into an alley and swung past a market's beautifully arranged mountains of pomegranates and pumpkins, berries and grapes, as she sought another shortcut. She veered through another alley and emerged, once again, into heavy traffic.

"Bree, what's that?" Gamze called from the back seat.

Bree looked over her shoulder, and then out the window to where Gamze was pointing. There, nestled into the block of sterile cinderblock office building and hotels, was a door, set back into the concrete. Men hurried in and out, looking nervously over their shoulder. The dark window occasionally sputtered with a flickering neon sign, its brief flashes showing the unmistakable form of a naked woman dancing.

They had arrived in Aksaray.

"Let's sing, children," she called out, trying to distract the little ones from the windows. "You need to find us someplace decent to pull over," she muttered under her breath to Gul while the children launched into a Turkish nursery rhyme.

"I'm trying, I'm trying," Gul asserted, scanning the streets until she found signs pointing them toward a Western-style shopping mall. She followed the route until she found a quiet spot, far in the back of the parking garage, where they could hide the van. She hustled the children out before giving orders to Bree. "Pull the plates off. No sense in making it easy for them to find us."

"Them who?"

"Who knows? It doesn't matter, does it? Just do it. Meet us at the elevators."

Inside, they wandered the mall, skirting the food court and the toy stores until they found the relative quiet of the strange grocery store on the bottom level. They were killing time, trying to keep the children distracted and out of the way, where no one could recognize them, while they waited.

Their next move was critical. Gul was to meet with the smuggler Susmita had identified as being reliable, someone who'd been smuggling people into Europe for decades, long before the current refugee crisis—Abu Ali. Of course, his reliability came with a price—they would need to spend all of the cash they'd stowed away for their escape, nearly €20,000. And it came with risks. Aksaray was notorious as a sex trafficking hub, and they would need to watch their step. Abu Ali's network was only reliable because he was able to work with police, border patrols, intelligence officials, and other higher-ups to get them to turn a blind eye to his operation. If the official network was actively looking for the Asker children, there was nothing to prevent Abu Ali from selling them out. Keeping their identities secret was critical.

Gul shoved her gun into her hidden holster and slipped some extra bullets into her pocket. "Get them ready. If I'm not back in three hours, you need to get them on the move."

Bree nodded, looking at the children where they camped out on the tile next to the vending machines of the underground market, and wondered how long she'd be able to hold together the crumbling edifice of make-believe she'd worked so hard to build. The children's eyes were heavy, tinged with heavy blue shadows, the flickering fluorescent overhead lights only highlighting their exhaustion. Their hasty meal, procured hours ago from the street vendors of Istanbul while on the move, was not going to sustain them much longer. Their little bodies ached, she knew. But they couldn't rest. Not yet.

"Come on now," she coaxed, urging them to their feet. "We need to get you ready for the next part of our adventure."

"Can't we go eat, Bree? I'm hungry," Eda whined.

"Not now, Eda," Bree reprimanded, trying not to sound too harsh. "I promise later. Come on, then." Bree herded them into the public restroom. "You too, Arslan," she insisted, pulling him into the ladies' room. She looked under the stalls to be sure they were alone. "The witch has passed a magic spell blocking our entry to the Mermaid Queendom. We must wear disguises if we are to enter the realm."

She thrust plastic bags at each of the girls. "Go in the stalls and change into these clothes. Bring your other clothes out to me when you are finished." Isra, Gamze, and Eda obediently went into the largest stall and closed the door behind them.

Arslan looked up at her with wise eyes. "We aren't going on an adventure, are we?"

She touched his head gently. "We are. But not the one we had planned."

"Is Baba in trouble?"

She startled at how perceptive he was. She had always wondered how much of their late-night conversations he'd overheard.

"Not just yet. But we are getting you out of Turkey, just in case. Your Baba and Anne wanted you safe. And you are safe. We've just had a change of plans. It is very important that from here on out, you listen carefully and do exactly as Gul and I tell you. And be brave for your sisters. They will watch what you do and follow your lead."

He nodded, thinking things over. "I promised Anne that I'd make sure the girls behave. I will keep my promise. And I will behave, too."

She sighed, patting his cheek. It was still soft and round with baby fat. He was too young to shoulder such responsibility, too young to be so serious. And yet, here they were.

"Thank you, Arslan. I know you will."

The girls tumbled out of the stall. They were dressed in jeans and t-shirts, proclaiming them to be fans of this or that football club.

"We don't look like princesses or magicians," Gamze declared, turning up her nose at the gear she now sported.

"Exactly!" Bree beamed with false brightness. "The witch will never recognize you. We just have one more step and our disguises will be complete." She drew a long-handled pair of scissors out of her last plastic bag. If the authorities were looking for them, they'd be looking for three little girls and their older brother—not four boys. They'd also be watching for two female nannies. She unpinned her bun and let her shiny, auburn hair cascade about her shoulders. Regretfully, she grabbed a clump of hair and brandished the scissors. "Just watch."

When they met up with Gul at an open-air café later that night, it was as a small gaggle of boys, baseball caps hiding the raggedy unevenness of their shorn hair. Bree had packed away their magic wands, deeming them too girly for the time being, promising the girls that they'd be able to cast spells by closing their eyes and making a wish. Gul nodded with approval as they slid into chairs and ordered tea and sweets, the children at a separate table under Arslan's watchful eye, allowing Gul and Bree to talk.

"What did you do with their things?" Gul demanded in English, speaking in a low voice.

"You mean, their hair and clothes?" Bree whispered back.

Gul rolled her eyes. "Subtle. Yes, their things."

"I dropped them in various trash bins along the way. I dropped the hair along the way in little tufts. I figured the pigeons would take it away for nests or something and, *poof*, all the evidence will disappear." Finally, she'd thought, a good use for the pigeons. It wouldn't endear them any more to Colonel Asker, but given the circumstances, she thought it was quite clever.

"And?"

"I knocked out any cameras that might have us on surveillance, too. We're clean. No tails as far as I can tell. What about you?" Bree asked.

"We have spots on a container ship that leaves tomorrow night from Mersin. We should probably leave Istanbul now and drive as far as we can toward Ankara before we stop for the night. It will take us most of tomorrow to complete the drive."

Bree mentally calculated how much money they'd need to refuel the van and feed the kids along the way. They had just enough left to get them there. If they sold the van in Mersin, they should have a little more for bribes during the journey.

"You informed HQ?"

Gul nodded. She took a sip of her tea and set down her cup. Bree noted the delicacy of the tulip glass, which seemed so out of place with the conversation they were having.

"They will monitor our progress and do what they can to delay the ship if we are behind schedule. Meanwhile, they've cleared the body from the alley and hidden the vehicle," Gul whispered, hunching over the table, "which should buy us a little more time. If they can access the apartment building security tapes, they will try to determine what happened."

"And Abu Ali?"

"Shifty as hell. But according to Susmita, as trustworthy as we'll find in this business. So, we'll have to take our chances. We're probably lucky he had room on that cargo ship. It's an unconventional choice—I'm really curious how she even came up with it—but she's probably right. It may be the only way out of the country for us now."

Bree was certain the plan had its origins in their time at the refugee camp in Calais. She nodded, taking in everything Gul had shared and watching her with wonder. She seemed so calm. How was it that someone barely older than her could handle such a crisis? She felt a swell of gratitude that she'd been paired with this experienced operative for her first assignment. Then again, how could it be that she, only one year into her college experience and with less than nine months of spy training under her belt, was handling it, as well?

It was surreal.

Gul was staring at her. Bree stared back, suddenly smiling—somehow in the intensity of their conversation, she had failed to register that Gul's own hair had gone missing.

"Take off your cap, Gul," she asked.

Gul did, and Bree laughed out loud. Gul had shaved the sides of her head and somehow managed to fashion her hair into a bleached blonde fauxhawk. Freed from the restrictions of the Norwood regulation braid, her new hairstyle revealed the coppery auburn of her natural roots. Any of the reassuring softness of her nannydom had been ruthlessly carved away in her self-transformation. Bree was surprised to see, now that the buttoned, high-collared, and long-sleeved shirt of her mandatory uniform was gone, shiny scar tissue snaking up Gul's arm, continuing across her collarbone and around the back of her neck. Gul self-consciously fluffed her hair, which had been flattened by the hat. It was a gesture more Norwood nanny than Sex Pistols, and it endeared her to Bree even more.

Yes, everything was definitely surreal. Bree crumpled her napkin and pushed away from the table.

"All right, Gul. As we say in America—'road trip.'"

———

"No way. We'll suffocate in there." Bree crossed her arms, defying the trafficker.

They'd made it to Mersin. The sun had been setting on the miles-wide beach; the children pressed their noses longingly against the van's windows, begging to play on the sand, under the palm trees—but they couldn't take the risk and hadn't a minute to spare.

Once the sun had set, they'd worked their way through the forty-five piers of the port, the towering cranes and brightly colored containers forming an otherworldly atmosphere under the bright lights of the docks.

But now, as they completed the final steps of their transaction, Abu Ali's man had revealed they were slated to spend their journey in a hard-topped container—raising the stakes, for their access to precious oxygen could be at risk.

The man shrugged, the tattoo across his chest just barely visible under his wife-beater tank flexing with the motion. "Your choice. But I won't place anyone in the soft-tops anymore. There are so few of them. They are obvious targets. The authorities go straight to them, just rip the canvas off and pluck out the refugees. I can't guarantee your arrival, which is bad for business. So, it's the hard container or nothing."

Bree racked her brain. There had to be an alternative. She looked at Gul to confer.

"I don't have a backup, Bree."

The trafficker interrupted. "I should remind you that Abu Ali has a no-refund policy. Whatever you've spent so far is gone."

Bree sucked in her breath. She knew Norwood would be able to get them more cash, eventually. But they couldn't afford the delay. They needed to hurry things along. The children were restless, and the ship would be loading soon.

"Tell me about the precautions you've taken for safety," she said, begrudgingly.

He smiled. "Drill-holes throughout. Unless it gets stacked out of order, you should have free air circulation. We outfitted it with two small fans. Jugs of water, though you'll have to be careful to make it last. A portable toilet, but they tend to be temperamental. Your empty water bottles can also work in a pinch. Escape hatches cut into the sides, disguised in the seams and exterior paint job. So as soon as you dock, you'll be able to push out and climb down. We'll have someone waiting for you on the other end."

Bree frowned at the mention of making the water last. "How long do we need the water to last?"

"Ten days. You should be in port in Spain in just about a week and a half."

She bit her lower lip. She hadn't counted on it taking quite that long. They'd have to get more food, even if it meant emptying out the vending machines from the canteens on the piers.

Gul looked unhappy. "You said we'll have air if the containers are stacked properly. What if they're not?"

The trafficker pursed his lips. He muttered something in Turkish to Gul, who gasped and began arguing heatedly.

The man's face turned red, and he spat something Bree took to be an insult at Gul. Gul simply laughed at him, a cold, calculated thing, and made to reach for her gun.

He raised his hands, protesting in rapid Turkish, while he watched Gul gesture vehemently with the pistol. Finally, they reached some accord and Gul grudgingly tucked her gun back into the holster. He yelled at her one last time, throwing his hands up in the air as if pleading with some stubborn God, and then stormed off into the back room, leaving Gul and Bree to themselves.

"What was that? What did he say?"

"It doesn't matter what he said. I negotiated something different. You'll have your own container. Just you and the kids. That will maximize the odds of there being enough oxygen, even if there is a mistake in the load."

Bree narrowed her eyes. "What do you mean, me and the kids? You're coming with us."

Gul shook her head. "One less adult to suck up the air will help your chances. Besides," she said, brandishing her phone, "we got this just as we walked in. Susmita wants me to go back and help Handan get out. Her options just got infinitely more difficult."

Bree read the text, and then, just to be sure, checked her own phone.

Sure enough, Susmita had ordered them to split up to keep both parts of the operation intact.

"But Gul," Bree protested, "I can't take them by myself! I don't speak Turkish. Or Spanish, for that matter. How will I get us all through?"

"Do you think any of the refugees they smuggle on these things speak those languages? If anything, they speak Arabic or their old tribal tongues," she scolded. "Everyone from here on out will speak English. You'll be fine." Her face hardened. "You'll have to be. The children will be counting on you. We all will be."

Bree sighed and rubbed the bridge of her nose. She had barely slept last night and her head was throbbing. There was still so much to do before they snuck into the container.

"You'll have plenty of time to rest once you're at sea," Gul advised, as if reading Bree's mind. "Come on. Let's fetch the children. You have no time to waste."

"I don't know, Gul . . ."

"You don't have to. Our handler knows. Susmita knows. If they think you can pull it off, you're ready. Let's go."

It took expert-level storytelling to persuade the children to climb into the container with her. She wove a tale like Scheherazade, grasping at whatever she could.

"We are boarding a magic vessel that will take us to the heart of the Mermaid Queendom. See over there?" Bree prompted, gesturing to the cranes in the harbor. "Those are giant octopuses the Mermaid Queen had defeated in battle. As punishment, the queen has pressed them into service to aid us on our journey. But her spell will protect us, making their memories vanish with the rising sun, so they will never speak of us to the evil witch. We'll be safe, here in our own enchanted bubble, no matter how hard she looks."

In the inky blackness of the container, they huddled together in their sleeping bags, backpacks doubling duty as pillows, while Bree continued weaving her tale, calculating with every plot twist the careful balance between distracting the children and sucking up the precious oxygen.

It was dark.

With the flashlight as their only guide, she encouraged quiet activities—Arslan doing math problems with chalk on the walls of the container, Eda tracing her hands next to his solutions and turning the shapes into strange sea birds, fishes, and corals, decorating the imaginary seascapes of the Mermaid Queen's home. Isra and Gamze became adept at shadow puppets, populating their story with their own fantastical creatures, and so practiced at casting on their yarns that they were able to knit, even in full dark, so that within the week their handiwork wrapped all the way around the enclosed rectangle that was their temporary home.

Thank God for *Don't Sniff the Glue*, Bree prayed each night when the children fell asleep having been successfully occupied for yet another day; the activities she managed to pull from literal thin air helped them forget the rumble in their tummies. She prayed, marked one day off with her own private tally on the wall, and then she racked her brain again for the next crazy turn in the story that she knew must last until the very end of their journey.

She tried not to listen to the groan of the cables, straining with tension as the ship rolled. She especially tried to ignore the sounds of other human beings that occasionally floated up to them—the scuffling, the cries, the arguments. She reminded herself that even though she had no cell service, the implant at the base of her neck meant that her team knew exactly where she was. Maybe Dash, Ruby, or Susmita were staring at a little dot in the middle of the Mediterranean Sea right now, willing them on.

And so they passed the days.

The bickering started on day two, when the novelty wore off. In the dark, Bree couldn't see who was pinching whom; couldn't see the swift, stealthy hand of one of the sisters snake out to tweak the others' hair, pulling extra hard to compensate for the newly shorn shortness.

Separating them to the corners of their tiny space seemed meaningless, but it was all Bree could do.

Arslan became sulky, annoyed with his sisters and frustrated that the normal privileges and coddling he'd had as the only boy and oldest child were lost to him in this dark place. Bored, he entertained himself by tormenting his sisters.

"You're boys now," he mocked, teasing them over their lost locks and masculine clothing. "Anne and Baba won't even recognize you. They won't take you back when we get home," he taunted. "Not even Grandmother will want you. You're ugly now."

"Take it back!" Isra demanded, throwing herself against Arslan in the dark, thrashing her tiny fists against his chest. Eda and Gamze simply wailed, fearful that Arslan, their protector, their hero, might be right.

"That's enough, Arslan," Bree said sharply, pulling him apart from Isra and separating them yet again. He harrumphed and rolled over on his side, ignoring her while she drew the weeping Isra into her arms.

Inside, Bree felt like her grip on the situation—and her sanity—was tenuous. But she reminded herself that at least the bickering meant they were alive, that they had spirit left in them, even if misdirected. That they had air.

With each passing day, Bree added another tick mark to the wall. And with each passing day, Bree watched and wondered if it was just her imagination that the kids were seeming listless.

They could not run out of air.

On day five, the portable toilet's so-called temperamental nature displayed itself, clogging up horribly, forcing them to put their water jugs and bottles to use as an alternative. They cleared one corner of their tiny space, designating it for this purpose, and huddled closer together.

By day six, the smell of their rank bodies, the mingling of sweat and bad breath, the decay of stale food and rotten apple cores, was overcome by the stench of the malfunctioning toilet. Bree tore up a pillowcase to make tiny bandanas to cover their mouths and nose in an attempt to keep them from gagging. Eda, who'd been struggling all summer with night-time potty accidents, reverted and started wetting the bed, forcing Bree to expend precious water on rinsing out her panties and sleeping bag.

"Here," Bree soothed as Eda sniffled, the little girl's cheeks aflame with shame and frustration. "Let's learn some American songs. Come on now. All of you."

The promise of something foreign and exotic momentarily distracted them. They settled around her.

"These are nursery rhymes. This one was one of my favorites when I was your age," she explained before launching into "Little Miss Muffet."

"But what is a tuffet?" Eda prompted, rapt.

"And what are curds and whey?" Gamze added.

"Curds and whey are like Tulum cheese. And a tuffet is like a little stool," Bree explained, relieved to have commanded their attention. "Let's try another. This one is called 'Itsy Bitsy Spider.'"

"Are all American songs about spiders?" Arslan asked skeptically.

"No, silly," Bree smiled. "Now watch carefully. This one has hand motions." She propped up the flashlight and turned it on, her careful rationing of its batteries set aside for the moment as she sought to distract them.

"Itsy Bitsy Spider" occupied them for a while. The older children were incredibly patient with Eda as her chubby little fingers struggled to climb the spout and mimic Bree's gestures. She giggled delightedly every time she washed the spider out, her laughter infectious. Bree could feel the mood in their dark hideaway lighten.

I can do this, she thought. *Just keep going.*

"Now it's your turn. Teach me one of your Turkish nursery rhymes," Bree prompted.

A short debate broke out between the four of them as to which rhyme was the best, and which would be easiest to teach her with her fractured and limited command of the Turkish language. Finally, they agreed.

"*Fış Fış Kayıkçı*," Arslan pronounced. "You will like this one, Miss Bree. It's about a boat."

"It's not about a boat. It's about the person rowing the boat," Isra corrected.

Arslan rolled his eyes. "Same thing," he dismissed. "Who will row with me?"

Gamze and Eda jostled for his hands. He winked at Eda and pulled her in front of him. "Sit down and cross your legs, little sister."

They held hands and began swaying back and forth as they sang.

"Fış fış kayıkçı

Kayıkçının küreği . . ."

"Do you hear it, Miss Bree?" Gamze giggled, pulling Isra down to mime the nursery rhyme, too. "It is the sound of the oar in the water. How do you say in English? *Swish, swish?"*

"Hop hop eder yüreği

Akşama fincan böreği

Yavrum yesin büyüsün

Tıpış tıpış yürüsün . . ."

Bree watched the children swaying back and forth in the dim arc of the flashlight, pulling each other's hands in perfect imitation of an oarsman cutting his blade through the ocean waves. Their rocking slowly came to match the subtle swaying of the ship. Enthused, they got up and danced as best they could, gliding and swirling over the stack of crates in the shipping container—boxes of cargo that, together, formed the temporary floor where they perched and waited—hunching over to give themselves the illusion of room beneath the looming ceiling, as they launched into the second and third verses.

Bree let their chanting singsong mesmerize her as she caught snatches of the words, translating them as best she could in her head. Pastries for dinner. Beating hearts, thumping like a drum with the rhythm of the oars. A baby growing and toddling about.

It was a song of being free on the water. Free.

She swallowed the lump in her throat as they collapsed in a breathless heap of giggles. She could be thankful, today, that the irony was lost on them, and tried not to think too hard about the words of the song.

By day seven, the children's nerves were on edge, made worse by the constant itching that accompanied their uncleanliness and the over-powering miasma that now filled the entire container. Gamze and Isra ejected Eda from their little nest, claiming she was too stinky and would wet their bedding. They all refused to sing—not the Turkish lullabies, nor Bree's American nursery rhymes. Desperate to distract them, she dredged up the humiliation of her first day at Norwood and tried to teach them "Mustang Sally," but gave up when she couldn't find an explanation of what the words meant that was suitable for small children. "It's about horses," she averred, putting a stop to any further discussion.

In the end, Bree spent her day cutting off their bickering and soothing hurt feelings, doing her best to avoid the use of punishment. For what could be more punishing than what they were already experiencing?

By day nine, the little ones, Gamze and Eda, lingered on their sleeping bags all day, refusing to play. Bree held them on her shoulders so they could take turns pressing as close as they could to the air holes drilled into the walls, gulping in as much air as they could, fearful that their fatigue was a sign of something more sinister.

And then they waited. When they remembered, they recited the names on their fake documents to themselves, trying to remind themselves of their assumed identities so they would be ready the next time they were asked.

And Bree lay awake, terrified that if she fell asleep, the oxygen might run out and she might not ever wake up.

Sometime in the middle of the night—she couldn't be sure when—Arslan sidled up to her in the dark.

"Miss Bree?" he whispered, touching her lightly on the shoulder.

"Yes, Arslan?"

He sniffed. "I miss Anne and Baba."

Her heart broke for him.

"I know. I promise you, Arslan, your Anne will be waiting for you when we get to our final destination."

There was a long silence. "She will?" His voice had a tinge of skepticism that didn't belong with one so young.

"I promise," she whispered vehemently. "And then you can all go see Baba. Miss Gul is with them now, making sure that everything is okay. Now come here," she said, pulling him into the curve of her body, trying to comfort the brave boy who couldn't admit that he was scared.

Day ten passed in much the same way, except now the children were too listless to eat. The battery on the flashlight finally died, leaving them completely in the dark. Eda simply clung to her ratty teddy bear. At some point in their journey, she'd reverted to sucking her thumb.

Bree turned her phone back on, hoping she'd accurately gauged their timing and she wasn't wasting precious battery power. She dozed on and off, knowing she had to be alert if and when they made landfall. At some point in what seemed like the middle of the night, she registered a tiny bell go off on her phone.

She sat up—if cell service was restored, they must be close to land.

She clutched at her mobile, clumsy with it after such a long stretch of disuse.

It was a text from Dash. *Monitoring Maersk systems. U R 1 hour from port. Get ready.*

In the dim light from her phone, she looked over at the kids. Their tiny bodies swelled and fell. She let out her own breath. They'd made it. They'd survived. Now they just had to get out of the container and catch their ride from Spain to Calais, where they could, like so many refugees, slip through the cracks of the system and be done with their sojourn.

She felt a frisson of anxiety, worrying whether their one-day delay would complicate this part of the transaction, but pushed her concerns aside. Seedy as the traffickers were, they were professionals. They must deal with this constantly. And if Dash could monitor their ship's progress, surely they could too.

Now, to get off the ship.

They were at the top of the stack. They needed to sit out the unloading process, letting the massive crane pluck them from the hull, and slip out once the container had come to rest on the pier. If everything went according to plan, they would be met by Abu Ali's colleague and transferred to a truck that would take them on to Calais.

Timing would be everything. And if the people in the other cargo units slipped up and were discovered, their chance of escape would disappear.

"Everybody up," she whispered, crawling over plastic pallets on which they'd spread themselves to gently shake the children awake. They groaned, the omnipresent darkness giving their little bodies no cues to wake up. Arslan burrowed his head deeper into the wadded up sweatshirt he'd been using for a pillow.

"Get up," she repeated, jostling him again until he sat up, rubbing his eyes.

Isra yawned as she flopped over in her sleeping bag. "Did we sneak by the witch, Bree?"

Bree smiled. "Just about. We still have to sneak past her gate. If you use just a little bit of your imagination, you'll be able to see it. It is all the pearly underside of shells, just like you'd pick from the seashore at Patara Beach, and twined with seaweed. But you'll see. Just a little longer now. Pack up your things and I will give you a bar for your breakfast." It was the last of their supplies—she would have to remember to tell Abu Ali's people that she needed to get more food and water for the next leg of their journey.

"I'll keep my wand out, to be ready for the witch," Eda soberly vowed. Bree gave her chopped hair a tweak where it stood up straight on her head.

"You do that. Hurry now. Gamze, you too."

When the big blast of the ship's horn sounded, they were dressed, backpacks strapped to their backs. They listened as the smaller horns of the tugboats called back, and felt the ship slow. She could sense the ship's movements in her bones—felt it sidling up to the pier, felt the massive shudder that ran the length of it as it came to a halt.

Bree positioned the kids in front of the makeshift trap door that had been cut into the side of the container.

They sat in silence, waiting—for what, they didn't know.

Above them, there was a grinding of metal, an insistent *clank clank clank* of dragging chains, and a massive *whoosh*. It was the sound of the top being lifted off of their cargo bay, exposing their pod to the fresh sea air for the first time in ten days. She inhaled the bracing scent of salt, rotting seaweed, and fish, pushing closer to the air holes to greedily suck it in.

"Brace yourselves," she cautioned the children. "Hold on to one another."

Arslan wrapped his arms around Eda and Gamze. Eda gripped her wand, now ratty and tired, in her fierce little hand. Isra steadied herself against the wall.

They could hear distant shouting. The thud of something heavy landing overhead caused them all to flinch. The container gave a lurch, and suddenly, they were swinging through the air. The children gaped, their minds and bodies struggling to reconcile the sense of swaying motion with the solidity of the box in which they still sat. In the corner, the containers of urine and waste tipped over, flooding the stale air with one last overpowering plume of stench.

The physical sensation of suspension was unnerving. Bree crouched, carefully balancing herself to look through the air holes—blue sky and puffy clouds was all that she could see.

The motion was too much for Isra, who started gagging, trying to hold back her rising nausea. She bent over, throwing up in the little nest of trash they'd left behind. Arslan let go of the little ones to come and rub her back, cooing soft words to her in Turkish.

"Don't cry," Bree ordered, regretting how sharply the words came out. But they couldn't afford to be heard, and she needed all of them to mind her now.

The metal box twisted slightly at the end of the crane, its half-hearted whirling shifting the pile of boxes on which they were perched, each twist a little more contained until the crane deposited the container with a massive, echoing *boom*.

The boxes shook, one last time, as the cargo settled beneath them.

As the reverberations died out, Bree let out a sigh.

"Come away from the trash, Isra. All of you, come closer."

They crowded about her, their eyes huge with anxiety. Gently, she wiped the corner of Isra's mouth with her sleeve. They'd get water to rinse her mouth out as soon as they were safe.

Outside, she heard the roar of a truck engine coming to life. Underneath them, there was another lurch as the container started moving with purpose. While it hurtled toward its destination, Bree finally instructed them.

"Our container has been loaded onto a truck to bring it to a warehouse now. Once we are parked, as soon as it is quiet, we are going to slip out this door right here." She pointed to the trap door. "I will go first. Arslan will help each of you girls out and then he will come last. We will all be jumping down the magic rainbow to escape the clutches of the witch and then we will be safely out of the Mermaid Queendom. Can you be brave and do that with me?"

They nodded somberly.

The truck bearing them turned and they all swayed sideways. Then it stopped.

"Okay. Just wait for me to tell you when."

She stared at the door. She'd made up her mind to count to one hundred before opening the door, hoping that that was enough time for the men working the docks to clear away so they could slip out.

She was at fifty when the chains landed on the top of the container, dragging all the way across until they made contact with the hook and held rigid. The container gave a lurch, and Bree felt them pulling away from solid ground, soaring away in the wrong direction.

"No!" Bree cried, throwing herself against the air holes. Blue sky, again. She pushed against the wall, striving for another angle, and caught glimpses of the crane. And there, beneath her, another cargo ship, its massive hull opening like an empty maw to receive their container.

"They can't," she muttered to herself, desperately typing on her phone. "We're supposed to unload here."

As the crate sank ever closer to the freighter below, she watched Dash's text. *Container misrouted for São Paulo. Get out.*

Now.

She looked around wildly. Now? The drop to the sea would kill them all.

The dark hull was looming, closer and closer through the air holes. In a flash, the glow of warm morning sunlight and the bracing scent of saltwater were replaced by the dank, hollow darkness of the pod. Soon they'd be engulfed by it.

The crane unceremoniously deposited them, the scraping of metal on metal as the cables disengaged and the sudden stillness their cue that they'd come to rest inside the ship for their next, accidental, leg. Bree rested her head against the container's walls.

You can't give up. Not now, she reasoned with herself. *You promised Asker and his wife you'd keep them safe.*

She peered out of the holes. They weren't at the bottom, but they were far from the top. She could only imagine how long the trip to Brazil would be. They had no more food and water. They would run out of air and die before they ever reached another port.

That left her with only one choice.

"Everyone, unroll your sleeping bags." She unsheathed the jackknife she'd tucked into her pant leg and began systematically tearing the bags into long strips. She didn't have time to braid them, just knot them together. When she was done, she looped one end through the gaps in the plastic crate, tying the ends as well as she could.

"Sit back," she commanded the kids. They shrunk against the wall, giving her ample space to deal with the trap door. Bracing herself against some boxes, she began kicking out the tiny square, which was held in place with just a thin seam of putty.

After a few solid thrusts, the door scuttled off, glancing off the containers and clanking its way to the bottom of the hull.

She didn't bother to look—just unfurled her makeshift rope out the opening, praying that it was long enough to reach the floor.

When it did, just barely, she wanted to cry with relief.

The next part was tricky, she knew, for there was no way she could get all four of the children down the rope at once. She wasn't strong enough, and she doubted the bags could support all their weight. They would have to split up. And she'd have to leave some of them behind for she knew there was no way the kids would go down on their own. She would have to show them the way first.

"It's time for the rainbow slide," she announced, adopting a breezy, cheery manner that she hoped would hide her pounding heart and sweaty palms. "Who's excited?"

They all just stared at her, frightened.

She took a deep breath and smiled. "It's really quite fun. We're going to slide out the door all the way to the floor. I'm going to take Eda with me first, to show you how it's done. What do you think?"

Arslan looked at her, eyes questioning. "I don't think this is how we are supposed to exit. Isn't there a ladder?"

She feigned nonchalance. "Who needs a ladder? This will be much more fun. We do this all the time in America."

Isra, whose mother had kept up a constant litany cautioning her to *be careful*, found this dubious. "You do? From what?"

"From . . . from barns. And skyscrapers. All the time. Just watch, it will be fun. It's only as high as the diving board at the pool. Eda, come here, sweetie."

Eda dragged herself over to Bree's side.

"You're going to have to leave your backpack, honey. We don't want to be too heavy for the rainbow slide. Arslan will throw it down to us once we are on the ground."

"But what about my bear?" She thrust the soiled stuffed animal out for Bree's inspection. "He's afraid of heights. He won't like it if Arslan throws him from up here."

Bree sighed. "All right. You take your bear. Just climb on my back." She got on all fours, allowing Eda to scramble up. She shoved her legs through the opening in the wall, wrapping her hands around the makeshift rope and giving it a tug to test its hold.

"Here we go," she said, silently praying that the bags would hold together long enough to get all five of them down, and pushed herself over the edge.

She could feel the fabric stretch and give as she began half falling, half rappelling, using the walls of the container stack for momentum. Eda was clutching her neck, practically cutting off her windpipe, the bear in one hand smashed against Bree's face.

"Whee!" Eda shrieked, her hand now half covering Bree's eyes.

The fabric cut into Bree's palms, stinging, as they slid down, faster and faster, their progress interrupted every now and then by a thump against a container as they lost control. But then they were tumbling, their feet losing purchase on the floor beneath them as they made it to the bottom of the pit.

It was over. Ten seconds was all it had taken, and the rope had held. It was dangling there above them, waiting for the next child to descend.

"Arslan! Arslan!" Bree shouted as she stood up. "If you can hear me, throw down Eda's backpack and then put Isra on the rope. Now."

The tiny bag flew down and landed at her feet with a thud. Then, Isra's little legs popped out of the hole.

"Isra. Hang on to the rope. Wrap your legs around it at the bottom and slide yourself down. Don't try to go fast. Take your time." Bree coached her as she stood up and positioned herself below the trapdoor, readying herself to catch Isra should she fall.

Isra—brave, big sister Isra—shimmied down the rope, treating it just like the one they'd used for physical education at her school, and landed on her feet at the bottom.

Bree gave her an elated hug and made her stand with her sister.

"Arslan? Can you come down with Gamze? Do you think you can do that?"

He was big for his age, and strong. She tugged on the rope, testing it again. It would hold, even for the two of them.

She peered up at the hole. "Arslan?"

He popped his head out, his brown eyes widened in panic. "She won't come! She's crying and won't get on my back!"

They didn't have time for this. Above them, the crane was swinging in more and more of the massive shipping containers, piling them high and blocking the sky.

Bree told Eda and Isra, "Stay right here," and then began scaling the sleeping bags back up the container stack.

The strips she'd tied together were starting to fray, digging into her hands as she pulled herself back up the wall. Whether real or her imagination, she could feel the fibers in the fabric stretching and giving way.

Arslan scrambled to help her over the edge when she reached the opening in their crate. She knelt, breath heaving, quickly calculating what to do.

"Gamze, you must quit crying," she scolded. "I can't think with all that noise."

Gamze sniffled. "I want Anne," she whined before plopping her thumb in her mouth to stifle her own wails. Bree peered at Arslan. He was putting on a brave face, but the rims of his eyes were filled with tears.

Over the sound of the crane, she asked, "If your Anne were here, Gamze, she would want you to be very brave. She knows you can be, and so do I. Arslan, I will take Gamze. But I need you to go first. Can you do that for me?"

He squared his chest in a way that mirrored his father, shaking his head. "Yes, Miss Bree."

"Good little man," she said approvingly. "You remember what I told your sisters? I just need you to go fast, Arslan. I can't take Gamze down until you're off the rope. I'm not sure it will hold all of us at once."

She guided him onto the ropes, double-checking as many knots as she could before he began descending. She watched, anxiously, as he slid down, down, down, hitting the bottom and stumbling to his knees.

"Back away!" she shouted, not wasting any time. "We're coming down!" The spaces below were beginning to look like dark canyons as the cranes continued their work, blotting out the opening.

She swung Gamze onto her back.

"Hold on tight," she warned as she swung her legs over the edge. Gamze wrapped her arms around Bree's shoulders, her legs around Bree's waist, and sniffled into Bree's collar.

Bree shoved off.

They bounced against the crates, Bree's rappelling skills keeping them from too much damage. It was a careful calculus—the faster Bree went, the more she could feel the rope giving out under her hands. With the span of two crates left to go, she heard a violent tearing sound and felt the fabric giving way. She loosened her grip, allowing gravity to pull her faster with the rope as a guide. A knot slipped through her fingers, unraveling, and they began to fall.

Instinct drove her to wrap herself around Gamze's tiny body—she crouched, feet first, to absorb the impact. With a thud, she landed and rolled, cradling Gamze against her. She rolled to a stop at the children's feet.

"Ugh," she groaned. Gingerly, she rolled onto her back and boosted Gamze up to examine her. "Gamze, are you okay?"

Gamze burst into tears, her fingernails digging deep into Bree's skin as she clutched and scrabbled at her, trying to get even closer.

Bree winced, every shake of Gamze's body sending shock waves through her own. The children rushed to their knees, surrounding them where they'd landed, chattering with concern in Turkish and touching both Bree and Gamze to ensure they were unhurt.

"She's all right, I think, Miss Bree. Scared, but no injuries," Arslan opined.

"Help her up off of me, then," Bree moaned. The children heaved Gamze up from where she lay, clinging to Bree. Bree rolled over to her knees, grimacing with the effort. She'd sprained her ankle and probably her shoulder, at least. And every intake of breath felt like daggers in her chest. But it didn't matter. She couldn't stop until they were safe.

"Help me up, Arslan," she asked. He offered his hand. She leaned heavily against him, pulling herself up to her feet. Pain screamed through her leg. She could feel the sweat beading about her forehead.

"Quickly now. We need to get to the end of the pit. There's a ladder there—we can climb our way out." She wanted to laugh—the ridiculousness of having worked so hard to get down, now overshadowed by an even more Herculean task of going up. "Eda, don't forget your teddy bear."

They began running in the direction Bree pointed, Bree limping behind them. In the shadows, a ladder loomed. Bree looked at it with despair. There was no way she could carry any of them up it this time, not with her ankle. They'd have to make it on their own. But the rungs—they were so far apart. She wasn't sure if Eda could do it.

Arslan took charge of his siblings. "You heard Miss Bree. We need to climb. Isra, you go first. Gamze, you go next. I will follow you with Eda. Eda, you will need to climb onto my back." He looked at Bree, his eyes full of purpose. "Miss Bree will come behind us. We will go slowly so we do not slip. Eda, give your bear to Miss Bree."

Bree felt a twinge of guilt. He was too young to have to take such responsibility. But she was grateful at the same time. She knew by looking in their eyes that the spell was broken. All thoughts of the Mermaid Queendom, of magic wands and floating bubbles, were banished now.

The fantasy of their little adventure had been stripped away. The children sensed their safety depended on them getting out.

And so, they began to climb.

With every rung, Bree winced, worried that this would be the one where their little hands, sweaty and weak, would slip, sending them plunging to the ground. But they didn't. As she climbed, squinting into the sliver of sky above, the light grew more intense. They were making headway, climbing out of the hull back to the top of the freighter, the only sounds the continued clanking of the crane, now further away, Gamze's quiet weeping, and the pinging of her phone, a stream of insistent text alerts exploding in her back pocket where she'd tucked it away.

Bree's muscles were shrieking, the bruises and sprains from her fall protesting this new attack, new pains announcing themselves with a vengeance—a knee, a hip, and several ribs, making each breath excruciating. As the children drew nearer and nearer the top, Bree was falling further behind, her breathing heavy and labored now. The teddy bear, which she'd tucked inside her shirt for safekeeping, was itchy, a distraction she could do without, but she'd promised Eda she would bring it safely up the ladder.

As Isra approached the top, Bree shouted, "Find some place to hide, Isra! All of you, wait for me!"

One by one, they disappeared over the edge. Determined not to make them wait too long, Bree renewed her efforts, gritting her jaw against the waves of pain that threatened to overwhelm her. The texts, she reasoned with herself, must be from Dash, and would instruct her on what to do next—how to get them all off this damn ship.

Arms and legs shaking, she cleared the top of the ladder and rolled herself out onto the top deck. Panting, she forced herself onto her hands and knees. She was grimacing through the pain, gathering up her strength so she could rise and join the children, when a sharp *click* went off in her ear.

"Don't move."

The voice was accented, its way with English making the words sound strangely round and contorted in the speaker's mouth, but the thrust of the cold metal pistol against her temple made his meaning clear. Bree froze.

"Where are the children?" she murmured, fear seizing her heart.

"You don't need to worry about that now. They're safe with us."

They're not safe unless they're with me, she thought. She whipped her hand around to draw her own gun, but the pain in her shoulder made her slow.

The butt of his gun rammed into her temple, and she fell to the floor. The heat of the metal deck, warmed by the early morning sun, radiated into her skin. The man's final words ricocheted in her brain as he brought the butt of his gun down again, and her vision turned to black.

"You look just like your mother," the man said, but his voice was already so far away.

Chapter Six

SUMMER BREAK

Bath, England

You look just like your mother.

From the recesses of her brain, the words floated up to her consciousness.

She doesn't have a mother or father. Judy is all she has, the voice opined, its clipped British accent dismissive.

Someone needs to know. The words were melodious, but rapid-fire. *Someone besides Judy. Rodney, maybe? Does he even know the truth about Judy and Norwood?*

Her brain struggled to make sense of the conversation. They were talking about her. But they weren't the person who knew her mother. His accent had been different from theirs—what was it? She couldn't place it. But she longed to talk to him—she had so many questions for him. How did he know her mother? What was she like? How did he just suddenly appear in her life, placed so perfectly to disrupt the plans they'd carefully laid to lead the children to safety?

The children.

Her heart plunged, terrified.

Something had happened to the children.

She sat up, eyes wide open, gasping for breath, as she looked desperately around her.

Ruby and Dash stared at her, aghast. They were out of uniform—an unfamiliar sight—the heavy bags under their eyes telling of a long vigil. Dash shook his head and moved to the door, swiftly closing it.

Bree glanced down. She was in a twist of scratchy institutional-gray blankets, her limbs spread akimbo and tangled with monitors and tubes. One of her arms bore a cast. She swatted at the wires crossly, still trying to catch her breath, and felt a wave of pain.

"Don't be doing that, now," Ruby reprimanded her, jumping to her feet. "You'll only cause the machines to go crazy with their beeping. And you, you're all skin here. Let me cover you," she fussed, smoothing the bedcovers to shield Bree's bare legs.

Bree looked around, trying to make sense of her surroundings. By the antiseptic look of things, she was in a hospital—a private room. Even through the closed door she could hear noises from down the hall; she could hear the murmur of nurses and aides, the rattle of gurneys, and the distant beeping of other patients' machines.

"The children," she said out loud, her voice scratchy and coarse from disuse. She dragged her eyes away from the door and began reaching around her, looking for her clothing. She had to go. She had to go to them. Her leg was out, reaching for the ground, when Ruby pushed her back onto the bed.

"I have to go to them," she cried.

"Shh," Ruby soothed, gathering up Bree's hands. "Bree." She said her name softly, gently.

In that one word was all the grief in the world.

"Bree, listen to me." She cupped Bree's chin in her hand, willing her to be still.

"You cannot go to the children, Bree. They're gone."

It was like a punch to her gut.

"Gone?" she whispered, her eyes filling with tears. She twisted her face away from Ruby's grasp and looked imploringly at Dash, her eyes begging him to tell her it wasn't true and that she had somehow misunderstood Ruby.

"Missing," he hastened to clarify. "When the extraction team arrived to pull you off the cargo ship, you were alone and unconscious. They searched the ship, but the children were nowhere to be found."

"They're gone?"

Dash hesitated before confirming. "All they found was this."

From behind his back, he drew the ratty teddy bear that Bree had carried up from the bowels of the cargo ship. "It was Johnson who spied it. She and Anya were part of the team sent to get you." Gingerly he placed the toy at Bree's feet.

Bree began to weep, great, silent sobs that racked her body and sent spasms of pain deep into her bones.

It was the most basic of things, she knew.

Ruby had even said it once, in class.

And she'd tried so hard.

She'd struggled through all the courses and practicums, learning all the roles of nanny—cook, teacher, entertainer, nurse. Even moral compass. Protector.

She'd handled tantrums and baths. She'd made snacks and tea and smuggled them treats, earning her way to the inner circle of their happy family through their little bellies. She'd clasped their hands to dance, built pillow forts on the floor, and tucked them in, one by one, pretending not to hear when they asked for just one more bedtime story.

Secretly loving it when they asked for just one more bedtime story.

She'd won their hearts, and the belief of their parents. So much so that those parents had entrusted their children's four little bodies—these miracles of life who were flesh of their flesh—wholly to her. To keep them safe.

And willingly, innocently, they'd come.

They had not questioned her when she'd led them away from their school. When she'd whisked them away in cars and vans to strange places, promising them adventures. When she had unspooled majestic tales and stories, weaving distractions so profound they had lasted them through days of captivity, they'd gone along, closing their eyes and imagining that they were anywhere else but in the belly of a ship, headed someplace unknown and frightful. And with their imaginations, they'd overlooked how parched their throats had become; the stench of their own waste, trapped in the bottles she'd tucked and piled into corners; the aching hunger that was becoming more pronounced with each passing day as she carefully parceled out their food, trying to make it last.

It's sort of a nanny job requirement to be able to handle bodily fluids and all manner of unpleasant things, Ruby had said. *The only other thing more fundamental to the job is to not lose the children.*

And now she'd lost them, maybe for good.

Ruby said nothing, just held her hands and let her cry.

"How?" Bree demanded when the worst of her sobbing had subsided and her body was no longer shaking. She couldn't bear to look at them. Couldn't stand to see the looks of mingled curiosity and horror, blame, and doubt that she knew they cast upon her. But she needed to hear what had happened.

"We don't know," Dash said simply. "It would appear that whoever snatched them had advance notice of your whereabouts. Which would suggest that the transfer of that crate to the ship bound for Brazil was no accident."

Ruby nodded. The air in the hospital room was tense—Bree sensed that Ruby wanted to say more and had been about to elaborate on Dash's explanation but was holding herself back.

Bree raised her chin and looked at her, desolate. "What is it, Ruby? You don't usually mince your words. Don't hold back now. I need to know."

Ruby looked over at Dash. He nodded once. Ruby sighed and Bree braced herself.

"Someone knew you were coming. They knew the crate was misdi-rected—and maybe even made it happen themselves—so they could pick you off more easily. Which means they may have someone on the inside."

"Or that they have infiltrated our communications," Dash hastened to add. Bree didn't need to wonder why he seemed so eager to find an alter-nate explanation. If there was a mole, the odds were high it was someone in Norwood command, or even one of their group. The thought was almost unbearable.

Bree squeezed her eyes shut, willing herself to not cry.

Spy. Counterspy. An operation gone bad. Her mind instinctively turned to the subject that had preoccupied her so much of late: her mother. Was this the kind of trap that had led her parents to their end? Was death what they had intended for her, as well? What would her mother have done in this situation, if she'd survived?

Her mother.

"I don't know how many there were. I never saw them. I just heard one of them. He was waiting for me when I climbed out of the hull. Before he knocked me out, he said something." Bree gulped hard.

"Dash. Before I woke up I heard you talking. You told Ruby, didn't you?"

He looked at her, bewildered. "Told her what?"

"Don't play stupid. I heard you. Just admit it. I need to know."

He sighed. "Yes, I thought it for the best, given the circumstances. No secrets, all of that."

Fresh tears rimmed her eyes. "You promised me."

He shrugged. "She deserves to know."

"Who else?"

Dash didn't answer.

She squeezed her eyes shut, willing herself not to cry.

"Who else, Dash?"

"I told Susmita, too," he admitted. "Listen, I understand why you're upset, but why does it matter now?"

"It matters because of what he said. He told me I looked like my mother," she whispered, her eyes still pressed shut. "He knew my mother."

She heard Dash's sharp intake of breath, and heard Ruby suck on her teeth in disapproval.

"Are you sure?" Ruby pressed her. "You know, you took a pretty big whack to the head. Maybe you're misremembering?"

Bree opened her eyes. "No. I'm certain that is what he said. I didn't hallucinate it."

Dash rose from his chair, stretching the muscles that had stiffened from his vigil. "Well. Then we know we are dealing with a professional. And that's about all we can take from that. If I could get further in my little search of the archives, perhaps we'd know more about your mother to piece it together."

The way he mentioned their clandestine search of Norwood's computer records in front of Ruby—so casual and matter-of-fact—gave

Bree pause. Hadn't that been their secret, too—just Bree and Dash, working together?

Ruby followed Dash's cue and rose from Bree's bedside. "We can sit here all day speculating, but it doesn't change a thing. We were set up."

None of them said it, but Bree knew what they were all thinking: that the two people best placed to tip off an outsider and disrupt the operation were Susmita and their handler.

"You need to sleep," Ruby fussed, bending over to straighten and fluff Bree's deflated pillows. "We should go now. The doctors will be expecting us to notify them that you're awake. The officials at Norwood too. It wouldn't look right if a nurse came in and found us chatting away. We're lucky that you came to during one of their breaks and after the morning rounds. So we could fill you in."

As she and Dash made for the door, Bree cleared her throat. They paused, Ruby's hand on the doorknob, and waited.

"Susie. I mean, Susmita. Where is she? Has she been here?"

Dash shuffled his feet and looked embarrassed. "She hasn't. But, in fairness to her, she's been in interrogation a lot. She's taken the brunt of it so far. But I know she is very sorry about what happened. She feels just terrible."

Sure, she does, Bree thought, her heart hard. She was barely able to contain her irritation with Dash for yet again finding an excuse for Susmita's behavior. She sat in a room, far, far, away, making decisions that led them straight into disaster. How terrible would she feel if she'd been the one to hold the children's hands? To promise them everything would be okay? To look Handan and Asker in the eyes and tell them she would bring their children to safety? Bree pushed away any thought of sympathy for the position in which Susmita now found herself and steeled herself for her next question.

"Gul. What happened to Gul? Handan? Asker?" Her voice was flat. Deep down, she already knew.

Dash sagged a little.

Ruby answered gently. "Gul was shot, apparently trying to get Handan out. She's dead. We lost Handan. She just disappeared. Our analysts haven't been able to find any evidence of what happened on the video surveillance, but they're still trying. As for Asker, well . . . We have eyes on him now."

She looked at Dash.

"Suicide watch," he explained. "Also, we're waiting to see if the kidnappers contact him. So far, they haven't communicated at all. No demands. No explanation. As far as we know. For now, the arms flow has stopped. He's too unstable to be relied upon."

Bree sank back in her pillows, this new knowledge crushing her.

"Try not to think about it too much, Bree," Dash advised as he guided Ruby out the door. "And rest. You've sustained a concussion, four broken ribs, and contusions, sprains and tears in nearly every joint and ligament on your left side. Oh, and shattered part of your wrist, too. But they've already had you in surgery for that."

At his mention of surgery, Bree caressed the bandage on her wrist, wincing at the wound, which now seemed to pulse angrily, demanding her attention.

"You have a lot of healing to do. And you'll need to be alert when the Agency leaders come for the official debrief interview. Now that you've regained consciousness, it's only a matter of time before they will want to talk to you." He looked over his shoulder before continuing. "You may want to avoid mentioning what you shared with us. About your mother." A funny look passed over his face. "You may want to avoid mentioning we even had this conversation."

She nodded, feeling tiny in the bed.

"Whatever happened, it wasn't your fault. You did a good job." He paused. "Even Dean Albourn has said so."

He gave her a sympathetic smile and closed the door behind him.

Bree sank deeper into the bed, groaning. Now that her mind could shift its focus from what Ruby and Dash had been able to share with her, it became preoccupied counting up the aches and pains that radiated through her entire body. It was no surprise that she hurt, given what Dash had told her of her injuries. She wondered how much pain medication she could take without incapacitating herself. She wanted to be sharp when her questioning took place.

The door swung open. A cheery nurse clad in scrubs came bustling in, clipboard in hand. She smiled with false brightness.

"I hear we're awake! Brilliant news," she gushed, keeping up a rapid monologue while she checked the machines, noting everything down on her clipboard. "It's been five days, Miss Parrish. Of course, some of that time we held you under ourselves, just to make sure any brain swelling was under control. But we were beginning to worry you'd decided to take a little holiday on us!"

Bree shifted uneasily in the bed, trying to suppress a grimace. "Five days? That seems like a lot."

"No more than warranted for your injuries. And listen to you, with your cute little American accent. Even though you're hoarse, I can tell. Ooh, there, I see it hurts when you shift, eh? On a scale of one to ten, how bad is your pain, love?"

"What should a one or a ten feel like?"

The nurse tittered. "Well, normally I tell the ladies a ten is like childbirth, but you don't know anything about that, do you? Let's see." She crossed her arms and deliberated. "A one is like you stubbed your big toe. Irritating, but you know it'll be quick to pass and you're more annoyed with yourself than anything. A ten, you can imagine what it would be like to swallow broken glass, the shards tearing up your entire throat. Or being dragged over a bumpy, asphalt road full of potholes, naked, the hot tar stripping away your flesh. A pain so fierce you'd like to die."

"Vivid," Bree said drily. "I'd say I'm an eight."

The nurse whistled. "You're a tough one, then, love. Broken ribs are the worst. Or so I've been told. Do they hurt you when you breathe?"

Bree took a deep breath to test. Her wince was all the nurse needed to see. She began fiddling with the drip bag that hung near Bree's bed, its long tube coming to an end where it was inserted in the back of Bree's hand.

"We'll pump you up with a little morphine. Just a tad so you can rest."

Bree put up with the nurse's ministrations, accepting the indignity of having her bedpan and bandages checked, letting the woman fiddle with the angle of her bed and force ice chips upon her, while she waited to be left to her own thoughts. She was grateful for the steady stream of prattle from her caregiver; she didn't need to make any effort to converse, just let the noise wash over her, distracting her. She longed for the respite of sleep, where she could forget her shame and grief.

"There now!" the nurse exclaimed enthusiastically as she plumped Bree's pillows one last time. "You're all set. Oh—what's this?" She reached to the foot of the bed and picked up the forgotten teddy bear, letting it dangle from two fingers. "Nasty, this. In need of a good wash. It's yours, I gather?"

Bree nodded, unable to speak past the lump in her throat.

"I don't suppose you'll let me send it to the laundry? It looks like it's harboring all sorts of filthy germs."

Bree shook her head. "I'd like to keep it here, please. It's . . . sort of sentimental."

"As you wish. Just let me try to make it somewhat sanitary." From one of the cabinets, the nurse extracted a can of disinfectant spray. Holding the stuffed animal in the air, she doused it in a steady stream of aerosol before handing it to Bree. "I never truly believe these sprays work, but at least I can say we made an attempt. There you are, love. Maybe having it nearby will help you sleep."

Bree tucked it next to her in the bed.

"The doctors should be by later in the afternoon. The surgeon will want to check on your wrist, to be sure. And the neurologist will want to assess the extent of any head injury—check your reflexes, your memory, things like that. Right fun, that'll be," she said, rolling her eyes emphatically. "So, try to rest now. I will see you at the end of my shift," she said as she made to leave, "but if you need anything in the meantime, just push that button there. Don't get up on your own, now, after all those days off your feet," she warned. "You'll be too unsteady. Call us if you need us."

Bree watched the door close behind the nurse as she left, and sighed.

All she had now was the quiet whir and beep of her monitors, and her own thoughts.

She hugged the bear to her chest, choking back a sob. Absentmindedly, she began petting at its matted fur while she thought things through. She should have asked Ruby to contact Rodney—it sounded like Norwood had not yet done so.

But what would they—what would she—say to him? How to explain the extent of her injuries and how she'd received them? As far as he knew, she was spending summer term interning as a nanny for some family in Manchester. They could say it was a car accident—really, there was no way he'd know the difference. But could she lie to him? And should she?

She fidgeted with the bear's fur and thought better of her impulse. No, she couldn't drag Rodney into this.

Unless he was already a part of it.

She rolled to her side, cursing the uncertainty that plagued her every thought. At least the morphine seemed to be kicking in, she thought. The pain in her ribs was feeling dull and distant underneath the tight bandages, the aches where the sheets brushed against her bruises and wounds softer, as if swaddled in cotton.

She pulled the bear up closer to her face. "What did you see, little guy? Do you know what happened on that ship? You might be the only one who does." She gave it a squeeze and then stopped.

Her fingers felt a gap on its back. A gap at the seam.

She flipped the stuffed animal over to inspect it. Sure enough, the seam was pulling apart, a little tuft of fluff beginning to show. She stuck a finger into the gaping hole to try to restuff the bear. But instead of a big ball of stuffing, she felt something hard.

Curious now, she pulled and dug. There was something there, all right. She dug at it harder, trying to work it out of the hole in the toy. She had to stretch the seams further, pulling bits of thread out to widen the gap, extracting the cotton filling that was in the way, but then she had it.

There, in the palm of her hand, was a little camera.

A nanny cam.

She cursed her stupidity. She'd never bothered to sweep the children's rooms for cameras, one of the first things they'd learned to do, because she'd assumed Gul had already done so. But her mistake might turn out to be a blessing. She just had to figure out a way to download whatever recordings it had captured.

She peered closer at the device. It looked like one of the higher-end models—motion activated, with a removable SD card. She could remove the card or attach the whole device to her computer with a cable.

But she couldn't let it fall into the hands of the Norwood people. Not until she'd had a chance to look at the video herself.

She played around with the box until she was able to extract the SD card. Where could she stash it? She needed a place that wouldn't get inspected while she slept. Someplace nobody would look.

She glanced at her cast.

Why not?

Without thinking any more about it, she shoved the card under the fabric cuff. It hurt like hell, digging into her skin, but eventually she was able to work it far enough down the cast itself that it was no longer visible.

She shoved the camera itself under the mattress and tugged at the edge of the hole, trying to repair the bear as best she could. As she did, the door swung open. It was the same cheery nurse, but this time she looked a bit cross.

"You have visitors, Miss Parrish. I told them you might not be up for it, but they insisted." Bree watched silently, discreetly shoving the teddy bear to the side as Dean Albourn and Professor Shadduck strode into the room. The dean was in a tweedy suit, while Shadduck was in an official-looking navy blazer, a little patch bearing the Norwood crest emblazoning her lapel. Montoya-Craig trailed after them, a smug look on her face.

"Now, you just ring me if it gets to be too much. We can't let you wear yourself out." The nurse shot a stern look of warning at the women from Norwood. "I'll be back to check on you in a few minutes."

They each pulled up a chair, angling to get as close to her bed as possible, and waited for the door to fully close behind the nurse before greeting her.

"I hope you're not in too much pain," Shadduck began.

Bree shrugged. "Too much is relative. I'll live." *Unlike others on our team—unlike Gul.* She bit back the words she wanted to spit at them. She wasn't supposed to know, she reminded herself. So she held back, watchful.

Shadduck nodded knowingly. "Yes, you will. And for that we're very grateful."

Dean Albourn leaned forward in her seat, entwining her fingers. "Of course, we're thankful for your safety, Bree. But you've been unconscious for five days. We've lost five precious days. We need to know what happened. While I'm sorry to do this to you now, under the circumstances, we need to ask you a few questions. I hope you understand."

Bree closed her eyes and nodded. When she opened them, both Shadduck and the Dean were staring at her intently.

"Start at the beginning," Shadduck ordered. "And be advised we will be recording this conversation." Montoya-Craig pointedly pushed a button on her phone.

"The beginning of what?" Bree asked, confused.

"Tell us about your first day with the colonel's family. Your first meeting with Gul. Tell us everything you remember. Everyone who came and went into the house. Everyone you remember interacting with the children. Even people who simply crossed your path. Tell us all about that day, and every day after. Up until the day you ended up on that cargo ship."

Bree's eyes widened. She looked to Albourn for confirmation. Albourn's jaw was tense; she nodded slightly to indicate that Bree should go ahead. But Bree noticed something else: Albourn's hands were twitching.

So. Albourn was on edge. Albourn had something to hide, too.

Bree sighed, resigned, and leaned into her pillows. It was going to be a long afternoon.

———

She'd made it.

They'd interrogated her for five hours, initially. They'd ignored the tactful interruptions by the nurse. They'd waited patiently when the neurologist had come by, flashing his penlight in her eyes, asking her to count backward from one hundred in sevens, and checking her reflexes, until he declared her brain whole and functioning.

They'd sat aside as the orthopedist had twisted and turned her cast this way and that, gauging the pain in her wrist. When he'd stuck a finger inside the cuff to test for swelling, Bree held her breath, fearful he would find the SD card she'd stashed away, but he simply smiled, pleased with his handiwork, and patted her shoulder, congratulating her on what would soon be, he was certain, a complete recovery.

They'd stared blankly in response to the dark looks from the nurse when she came in to announce her shift change. She was nothing to them. And with a fresh nurse on staff, they would have hours more leeway, time with which they could pick apart every statement from Bree, looking for inconsistencies, clues, leads.

Bree had gritted her teeth through the pain. With each successive wave, it grew sharper and more intense. She used it to keep her mind sharp. She figured she could learn as much from their questions as they could from her.

"The soldier who was to courier you, Gul, and the children," Albourn pressed. "Did you recognize him when you found him in that alley?"

"He'd been shot at close range in the head," she told them. "But the shot was clean." She thought back to the tangy smell of copper and the lingering scent of gunpowder that had filled the Raptor, and wanted to gag. "I got a good look at his face. I don't think I'd ever seen him before."

"What did he look like?"

She shrugged. She forced herself to think past the splattered interior of the vehicle, past the gaping wound in the back of his head, trying to remember the details. "He was an Asian male. He seemed to be dressed in standard-issue military garb, though of course, I wouldn't really know. He had a flag of the United States and an American eagle tattooed up the side of his neck. No rings or jewelry that I observed. I don't recall seeing dog tags."

Shadduck perked up. "A tattoo, you say? On his neck?"

Bree nodded. "His collar was loose, so I actually got a pretty good look at it. It was partly obscured by his undershirt but seemed to be pretty big. And it came up to here," she said, gesturing with her good hand to a spot halfway up her neck.

Albourn and Shadduck exchanged a meaningful glance.

"Who handled all the communications with the courier, Bree?"

Bree swallowed her annoyance. "You know we didn't do anything directly. It was all handled through Susmita and the handler. We had no contact with the Air Force personnel ourselves."

Then, shifting in the hard plastic chair, Albourn changed the subject. "Tell us about Gul."

"What about her?"

"Anything you can think of that is relevant."

"Did she have any contacts with the Americans herself?" Shadduck prompted.

Bree crinkled her brow, annoyed. "I just told you that neither one of us had any direct contact with the Air Force."

"How do you know for sure?" Shadduck continued.

Bree was stumped. "Well, I guess I can't know for sure. Most of our days we spent together, but not always. We divided and conquered with the children sometimes. That gave her time to dig deeper into working out who was threatening the Askers—she was the natural for that, given my limited understanding of Turkish. She would follow up on leads under the pretense of running errands for Handan, or bringing something like a forgotten lunch to the colonel at his office. Sometimes she'd bring the kids in for a surprise visit and use them as a distraction. People got so used to seeing her around she was given pretty much the run of the place. And we alternated having breaks over the dinner and evening hours. We slept in separate rooms. So, yes, both of us had enough periods of privacy where we could have made contact with someone outside of, or inside of, the operation without the other one being the wiser. But surely, you don't think it was Gul?"

"Think it was Gul that what?"

Bree chose her words carefully. "That compromised the operation. After all . . ."

They leaned forward in their chairs. Bree remembered she wasn't supposed to know about Gul's death.

"After all, she considered herself Turkish, too, and shared Asker's political views. She would have no motivation for undermining us. And if she had, she could have done it at countless other times, in much simpler ways. It's too convoluted."

"She shared Asker's views?" Albourn asked sharply.

Bree nodded. "Yes. In our private conversations, she spoke disparagingly of the current government. It wasn't just about the job, her time in Istanbul. She was as motivated as Asker. She wanted to see the government collapse so that real democracy could return. I don't know what you are thinking, but it wasn't her. Just ask her. She'll tell you herself."

Bree dropped the bait, testing them to see what they'd reveal.

"We can't. She's dead."

Bree pressed her eyes closed. They trusted her enough to share that information. Perhaps she, then, wasn't under suspicion.

"She was alone," Bree whispered. "She went back to Istanbul and was alone. Do you know what happened?"

She opened her eyes to stare at them with frank curiosity and more than a little hostility. For hadn't it had been Susmita's orders that separated them to begin with?

"Why did she leave you, Bree?"

"What do you mean, why? We were told to. We both got the order. It came at the last minute, right before we were to climb into the shipping container. Susmita messaged us that Handan needed help and we were to split up."

"Divide and conquer," Shadduck muttered, looking disgusted.

"Show us," Albourn demanded. "Montoya-Craig, let her have it."

The older girl reached into her haversack, withdrawing an evidence bag. She tossed the bag onto Bree's bed.

"Show us the message," Montoya-Craig stated archly, not bothering to hide her skepticism.

Bree zipped open the bag and withdrew her phone. There was no point to this, she knew. At HQ, they could crack her passcode, bypassing her biometrics, to see her text streams. They could monitor their secure channels at all times. There was no point in making her do this herself.

Other than to make her scared.

She scanned her fingerprint and went to the secure text channel. With increasing apprehension, she swiped through the messages, reliving each moment. But the order to send Gul for Handan was gone. It was as if it had never existed.

"It's not there, is it?" Montoya-Craig stated. Her voice was cold, calculating.

Bree shook her head, her eyes filling with tears.

"Was it ever there, Bree?" Shadduck probed. "Did you lie to Gul?"

"No! It doesn't make sense! You all knew we'd split up. You had to have known."

"Look at your communications, Bree," Shadduck pressed as Albourn coolly watched Bree's reactions. "There is nothing there to suggest that anyone on the team knew you'd been separated."

She desperately scanned the comms that had come from the team. There were the messages from Dash, instructing her on the landing in Spain and the misrouted container. And that was it. Nothing more. No mention of Gul.

"But Gul had to have been in contact with you the whole time. Her messages must say something about it?"

Albourn shook her head sadly.

"When we recovered Gul's body, her mobile was missing. And none of our records show communications from Gul. We had ten days of silence from her. We assumed she was with you, on the cargo ship, and therefore out of range. It wasn't until we extracted you that we realized she was missing."

"How is that possible? The GPS implant should have shown you exactly where she was," Bree demanded.

Bree's interrogators looked at each other. "When we found her body, the implant had been . . . removed," Albourn said delicately. "We presume whoever abducted her rendered it inoperable immediately."

Bree tried to ignore the bloody images that popped, unbidden, into her imagination.

"So you see, Bree. Either you're lying, or we have a very deep problem inside of Norwood," Shadduck stated, leaning back in her seat. "Our job is to figure out which."

"I'll take that back now," Montoya-Craig said, nodding at the phone in Bree's hand. Bree handed it over, meekly.

The interrogation continued.

By the end, Bree had learned five things.

First, judging from Albourn's and Shadduck's reactions, something was off about the American soldier they'd found dead. Which meant that the removal of the children may have been compromised from the very beginning.

Second, their communications stream had been corrupted. Bree knew she and Gul both had received the orders that separated them. She'd seen the messages herself. But now, they were gone. Either someone inside of

Norwood had wiped them, or someone outside had deeply infiltrated and compromised their systems. Either way, it was a problem.

Third, much to her shock, she was now under suspicion of being the mole—if there really was a mole inside the Agency. Not only had they taken her mobile, they'd seized her pistol as evidence, too. It only made sense, she reasoned with herself, but it drew a sharp line under her status: not to be trusted. And it left her feeling strangely vulnerable.

Fourth, from the way the questioning had studiously avoided and steered around all mention of Susmita, she assumed Susmita was under equal suspicion and was, perhaps, even the lead suspect, along with their handler.

And finally, if she was going to clear her name, she'd have to find the children—and their kidnappers—herself. It was the only way. She still had two advantages—two secrets—that she knew would somehow aid in her search: the brief words of the man who'd knocked her out on the ship, and the SD card still hidden in her cast.

But first she had to get out of this hospital. The physicians had given her two days until discharge; she knew she'd be watched carefully until then, and the chip in her neck ensured that would continue even after her release. Her only hope was to get to the safety of Jaguar House, where, hopefully, she'd have some privacy. And some allies.

Hopefully.

She'd been exhausted after the marathon session of questioning and hadn't put up a fight when the night-shift nurse pumped her drip full of morphine. The deep, painless sleep that ensued was a welcome respite from the barrage of worries and questions that filled her restless mind.

She woke once, in the middle of the night, to find Dash sitting at the foot of her bed. She looked at him quizzically. Something about him was different—something she hadn't noticed earlier today, when he and Ruby had visited with her.

"You have a bald spot on your head, Dash."

He smiled. "Technically, it is not bald. It is the start of a fade, which is quite the trendy hairstyle. Or so I have been told by my more optimistic friends. And my barber."

She tilted her head, puzzled.

"Why do you have a bald spot, Dash?" Her tongue felt thick with drugs as she asked the question.

He sighed and gestured at his head with frustration. "My young Germanic charges thought it would be amusing to shave my head while I slept. I thankfully woke up mid-attack—the electric razor was quite noisy. Upon consultation with my barber, I've decided to let it grow in gradually rather than remove the remaining hair from my head. Satisfied?"

She grinned sleepily. "I would like to see you in a fade. Maybe with a pattern carved into it. Like a snake? Or something from your family crest—a dragon, is it? Or maybe you could shave down all the sides and leave the top long, and put it in braids, like Ruby?"

He snorted. "I shouldn't think so. Obviously, the medication you are taking is going to your head. Tell me . . . how did your interview with Albourn and Shadduck go?"

She yawned. "Well, they think I'm to blame somehow. So, I've got that going for me."

He nodded. "Yes. I'm afraid we are all under suspicion at this point. Though some of us more than others."

"You really shouldn't be here, Dash," she said, feeling guilty. "They'll be tracking you now. I'm surprised they don't have me guarded twenty-four-seven, in fact."

He looked at her with what she could only imagine was pity. "Bree. You are."

He paused.

"I'm your guard tonight," he added, delicately.

"Oh," she whispered simply.

She hadn't thought about that—about how they would try to turn them against each other, about the seeds of suspicion that must now be taking root between them. A stab of fear gripped her—had she already shared too much with him and Ruby? Did he really think she was to blame, not just for her failure to protect the children, but also as the architect of the whole fiasco?

Or was he the one to blame? After all, he'd been in charge of communications. It would have been easy, so easy, for him to manipulate them all.

Before she could contemplate it any further, the morphine reached up to reclaim its hold upon her and she drifted back toward deep slumber. As her eyes fluttered closed, she saw Dash settle into his chair, magazine in his lap, to keep watch over her.

She whispered one last question to him, so softly that he almost didn't hear.

"Dash, did you ever think it would be like this? That people might live and die because of what we do?"

"What's that, Bree?" Dash put down his reading at the sound of her voice.

"Nothing." A lone tear squeezed out of the corner of her eye. She hugged Eda's abandoned teddy bear to her side and kept her cast close to her body, hoping her latest secret was safe as she fell back to sleep.

Jaguar House was not, unfortunately, the sanctuary Bree had envisioned. When she'd hobbled out of the hospital, ribs wrapped tight, arm in sling, she'd hoped that once they were back together, everything would return to normal.

But instead, they moved in individual orbits, all of them circling around the sinking feeling that one of them had betrayed the others.

Bree felt her isolation acutely. There were no summer classes to draw her to the campus. She and her roommates were the only students whose fieldwork had ended precipitously early, bringing them back to Bath, and they'd been ordered to stay put. Her phone had not been returned to her and her laptop had been seized. On her budget, she simply couldn't go out and replace it.

She existed in a complete vacuum.

She endured the regular inspections from Ruby, who took it upon herself to nurse her wounds and keep track of her physical progress. It was a good use of Ruby's skills, Bree had to admit—she was observant and efficient in her caregiving. But she had the habit of falling into the nanny role for which she'd been trained, treating Bree like an ignorant child and ordering her about. Bree put up with it, grateful to have someone so capable to care for her and relieved to not have to spend any more time than necessary at the hospital.

Truth be told, being bossed around by Ruby was better than the alternative. So long as she was occupied discussing her aches and pains, gritting her teeth while her ribs were rewrapped, or having Ruby assess her gait, she was avoiding having to suffer through a stilted conversation with her roommates. It was awkward between them now. She had to learn to let the waves of hostility that emanated from Susmita, in particular, wash over her. *She's just afraid*, Bree reasoned with herself—*afraid that she'll be accused, in the end. My being found guilty is her best hope that her own worst fear won't materialize.*

Bree also swallowed the indignity of being called summarily, at any time of day or night, to the administration building for another round of debriefing, as they liked to call it. Each session found them going over and over the same questions, posed this way and that in hopes of tripping her up, finding an inconsistency, no matter how small, that could be the string enabling them to unravel the whole mystery.

And still, as far as she could discern, there was no word of the children or Handan.

A week passed. *You mustn't feel sorry for yourself*, she chided herself. She had work to do. She needed to get to it. So what if they kept her under surveillance? she reasoned. The more they watched, the more they'd see she was innocent, merely looking into leads that could help them resolve this once and for all. They wouldn't be able to pin her with anything. Except, perhaps, for not being forthcoming about the video from the nanny cam.

She fingered the SD card. She needed to find a way to view the video.

She was almost frantic with worry that every moment of delay was putting the children in danger—that there was something on the video that would aid in their recovery. She just had to get to it.

She could break the security codes on her roommates' computers, she knew, but the risk of being caught was too high, and if they found out, it would only deepen their suspicions. The computer lab at Norwood was out of the question. No, she needed to go to one of those printing shops and pay for time on one of their systems. And now was the time to do it—Ruby had left her alone to take her soggy clothes to the launderette for drying. She had a window right now to slip away.

She tucked the card back into her cast and grabbed her bag. She thought she remembered where to find the shop she needed—it was on the way toward campus. She ducked out of the front door and walked quickly through the courtyard, hoping she wasn't seen. Without pausing, she stepped from the curb to cross the street.

A horn blared, and a rough hand yanked her back painfully as a car bore down upon her.

"Do you want to get killed?" an angry Dash demanded, shaking her roughly. "You're beaten up enough already. Do you think you'd survive getting struck by a car in your state?"

"I'm sorry," she stuttered, overwhelmed as she realized the car had not even slowed. "I forgot. I forgot to look right. I just forgot." She fought back the tears that sprang to her eyes.

He sighed. He still held her by the shoulders.

"No, it is I who should apologize. I overreacted. You've just . . . given us all quite a scare, Bree. We—well, we didn't know what to think. That whole time you were unconscious, we didn't know if we would get you back."

He reached up and tucked a stray strand of hair behind her ear. She suddenly felt extremely aware of where his other hand still rested on her bare skin. She flushed and shifted her messenger bag.

Awkwardly, he let her go. She cleared her throat.

"May I accompany you, wherever it is you were headed?"

Disappointment flooded her.

"I was just headed toward campus. To take a walk."

He nodded. "Sensible for you to get some exercise, so long as you are careful. I'd be happy to join you. I could do with a bit of a stretch of the legs myself."

He pointedly looked both ways, took her by the elbow, and led her across the street. They began the descent toward Norwood, walking in silence as if unsure of what to say to one another.

Bree realized the wisdom of his caution. Even walking slowly, her body protested every step. She held herself carefully, aware that a slight twist of her torso, the merest bend, could trigger a spasm of pain in her ribcage.

She struggled for a topic of conversation, something to break the awkward silence.

"I'm surprised the media haven't circled around me like vultures," she offered hesitantly. "I bet you could sell that story for a lot of money."

He jerked his head back as if she'd slapped him.

"I wouldn't. How could we ever bundle that up for a newspaper without completely revealing the truth about Norwood?" He stared at the cobblestones as they walked. "Besides, after the gushing photo essays of us preparing for the ball appeared in the local tabloids, the college administration drafted a new policy entitled 'Standards of Confidentiality for Norwood Nannies.' It forbids us from having any contact with the media and threatens expulsion should a student be found to be accepting payment from any newspaper, website, or television program. They came out with it while you were in hospital. You'll have to sign it soon, just like the rest of us." Dash flushed a deep red, his set jaw the only indication of how angry he was at having his extra source of income cut off so unceremoniously.

"Oh," Bree said, not knowing what to say. She shifted her bag to her other side, trying to manage the strain on her hip.

"Here, let me take that," Dash offered, lifting it from her shoulder to ease her burden. He added, "I found something today. Something that might interest you."

She turned to him, curious, and winced from the pain.

"No, no, keep looking straight ahead," he ordered. "It won't do you any good if you wear yourself out. I'd describe it to you, but I think it best if you see it for yourself. And for that, you'll have to make it all the way to campus. Do you think you can do that?"

Her chin lifted a little. "Of course. I'm not made of glass, Dash."

He chuckled a little under his breath. "Yes, of course. You're quite right. Carry on, then, Mistress Bellona, and we'll see what we can see."

It took them twice as long as normal to make it to the Norwood courtyard—Bree had to stop and rest several times, catching her breath and letting the pain subside. But they made it with the summer sun still hanging low in the sky. The fluttering oaks and weeping willows caught the light summer breeze, their susurrus filling the quiet yard.

"It's in the library. Come," Dash instructed as they crossed under the gate.

They swiped their ID cards for entry. He led her past the reading room, through the stacks, and into the furthest part of the library shelves. He took her through a door into a stairwell and they began to descend.

"I was thinking," he began as their footsteps rang against the metal treads. "About my tactics in finding your mother's identity. I've been very frustrated that my spyware wasn't working, but I suppose I shouldn't be surprised at the level of security. Though with everything that's happened with our, um, Istanbul case, it does seem a little inconsistent. Be that as it may, I've been unable to find anything meaningful through technological means."

He paused, tactfully stopping on the landing to let Bree catch her breath.

When they resumed their descent, he picked up his story.

"But then I started thinking about what you said in the hospital."

"What's that?" Bree asked, unsure where this was leading.

"What your attacker told you. About you looking just like your mum. And I thought, maybe I'm going about this all wrong. Maybe we need to do some old-fashioned sleuthing. So I came here."

They were at the bottom of the library now. He swung open the door and led Bree into another set of stacks, this one mustier, with the smell of old paper and ink. Bree took a deep breath, reveling in it.

"I came to the stacks and found the old Norwood yearbooks and started looking through them. Searching for someone who looks just like you. And this is what I found."

He led her to an empty study table scattered with books. He pulled the one off the top and opened it to a page he'd bookmarked with a tiny slip of paper.

Bree followed his finger to the image in the center left of the page.

The colors had faded with time, but there was no mistaking the coppery hair that cascaded over her shoulders, nor the greenish-blue eyes. A smattering of freckles covered the bridge of her nose and cheeks. A slight grin of amusement, barely held back, hovered on her lips.

She seemed familiar, Bree thought. Like looking in a mirror, but just slightly off—as if the image was turned around, somehow, or sideways, or maybe just an echo of a memory.

"There's no other redhead in the entire class," Dash commented, "nor any in the adjacent classes." His delight in his discovery was evident. "Set aside that unfortunate nineties hairdo and you really are, as they say, her spitting image."

"I don't know, Dash," Bree commented. She squinted at the photo, trying to see herself in it. "It may be just a superficial resemblance."

"I know you don't want to get your hopes up," Dash insisted. "It's natural, after all this time. But it must be her. It simply must."

"Margaret McCarthy," Bree breathed, reading the inscription below the photo. She allowed herself to feel a little thrill. "Her name was Margaret McCarthy."

"Irish, by the sound of it. Which could explain the Celtic aspects of your own name. And look—she was Head Girl."

"Does it say anything more about her?" Bree was rifling through the pages, looking randomly, hoping something would jump off the page at her.

Dash stilled her hands. "No, I'm afraid not. But now that we have a name, I can do a different kind of search. I can target the Norwood records more precisely. And we can search outside of Norwood as well. See if we can find marriage records, things like that."

Bree gripped his hands and looked at him. Her eyes were shining with excitement and tears.

"You don't know what this means to me, Dash."

He blushed. "Of course, I can imagine. I know how important it is to you to learn about your past."

She shook her head and gripped his hands more firmly. "Yes, but that's not what I mean."

He looked at her, confused. "What do you mean, then?" He'd lowered his voice to a whisper.

"That you would still do this . . . do this now, after everything that happened. It means you believe me."

His eyes softened as he gazed at her. "Of course, I do, Bree." He pulled her down into a chair and sat beside her. "I don't for a minute think you are responsible for what happened in Turkey and Spain." His face darkened. "I wish I knew who was. I have my suspicions, of course, but that's all they are. Suspicions. And, unfortunately, the powers that be are deliberately keeping us in the dark."

She swallowed hard. She needed to take the chance.

"I have to show you something."

She let go of his hands and reached into her cast, pulling out the card. She brandished it in front of him.

"There was a nanny cam inside of the teddy bear. One I didn't know about. The stuffed animal was up on a shelf inside of the girls' room in Istanbul. Gul gave it to Eda the morning of our escape attempt, to quiet her down. But it wasn't one of Eda's normal toys. I'm beginning to wonder if Gul chose it deliberately—if there's something on the video that will help us. We need to find some way to view it without anyone at Norwood knowing what we were up to."

Bree set the card down on the desk. She tapped her fingers against the wood, waiting for Dash to say something.

He stared at it for a long time. Finally, he spoke, sliding the card across the wooden desktop back toward her. "You need a coffee, I think. We both do. Come on."

She tucked the card back in its hiding place. When she was finished, Dash pulled her up and slammed the yearbook shut.

He made as if to go, but then, thinking better of it, he scattered the yearbooks about the basement level of the library, tucking them randomly into shelves, carrels, and carts.

"Better to leave nothing anyone can discern a pattern from," he explained. "Now, shall we? I know just the place."

They emerged, blinking, from the cool dimness of the library.

"Hey, Bree. Dash."

They were startled to see Johnson leaning against a pillar, as if waiting for them.

"It's good to see you up and about, Bree," Johnson continued when they didn't respond. She scanned Bree, taking in her injuries, and waited.

Bree smiled weakly. She looked around to be sure they were alone. "Thanks. I mean, really thanks. I heard you were one of the team sent to extract me."

"I'm surprised you're here, Johnson," Dash interrupted. "Didn't you get sent back to your regular assignment?"

Johnson shrugged and pushed away from the column. "Anya did. Mine ended early. I thought we might hang out a bit?" She eyed them speculatively. Bree cringed inside, guessing how badly Johnson wanted to pump them for information.

Dash placed a protective arm around Bree's shoulder. "I need to get her back. She's not fully recovered, you know. Maybe another time."

Johnson shrugged. "Suit yourself. I'll see you around."

Dash stared, pointedly waiting for Johnson to leave. She smirked at him before descending the steps. Dash stood still, waiting until she was out of sight.

"Lurker," he muttered under his breath, and guided Bree away in the opposite direction.

They walked away from campus, going deeper into the warren of backstreets that made up Bath. They might be tracked by chip, but the chips couldn't tell what they were actually doing, the way a human could. They might be paranoid, but they'd reasoned the more distance they put between themselves and Norwood itself, the less likely the place they settled in would be under surveillance. Soon, skin covered with a faint sheen of sweat, they were ensconced in a buzzy internet café, each of them nursing a cold mocha as they faced a computer. They'd been careful along their walk to ensure they weren't being followed.

"You first," Dash prompted. She withdrew the SD card from its hiding place and inserted it into the adapter. The computer quickly recognized it, enabling her to open it. The files were in chronological order.

"Let's go backward," Bree suggested, scrolling to the last recording. It was dated the night before their departure. Bree clicked on it and the video, a head shot of Gul, sprang to life. But there wasn't much to look at.

"What's she doing?" Dash demanded, irritated. "She's just staring at the camera. She isn't speaking at all."

"She is speaking," Bree insisted, resizing the image for a better view. "Just not with her mouth. She's blinking, Dash. She's put a message in Morse code."

"My God," Dash whispered. "You're right."

It was a short message, a mere two minutes. It took them twenty replays and nearly two hours to be certain they'd deciphered it properly, all the while thanking their *Snap-Spy* professor for the brief overview of historical encryption techniques he'd forced-marched them through in third term. In the end, it came to this.

Arms not reaching Syrian rebels. Being diverted to China. Asker does not know. Source of diversion unknown. Suspect internal. Repeat. Suspect internal. Operation compromised. Be careful.

Be careful.

"Shut it down," Dash breathed in her ear once they were certain they'd captured it all. "Close out the video and remove the card."

Her nerves were shot with caffeine, adrenaline, and fear.

"She knew," Bree whispered. "She knew something was wrong."

Dash nodded absentmindedly. "China? That seems so random."

Bree thought about it. "There are plenty of people who are upset with China's policies. Including people inside China." She paused. "I only know any of this because of Susmita. She taught me as part of my preparation for the ball."

Dash sighed. "Well, in light of what is on that card, I think I need to show you this."

He extracted his wallet and pulled out another SD card.

"What's that?"

He pressed his lips together, frowning. "I set up a security camera to observe Jaguar House."

"You've been spying on us at our own apartment?" Bree hissed. The outrage in her whisper caused a couple of people to turn and stare at them.

He shrugged. "Not really all of you. Susie. I mean, Susmita. Damn, I find it hard to call her that." He ran an exhausted hand through his hair. "I set it up to keep an eye on things while I was in Germany. I thought that something was off. And I was right."

He played a series of recordings for her. Repeated evenings showing Susmita greeting a man who was not Dash—a man they did not know. They kissed, and lingered, and she pulled him inside the apartment. In some of the recordings, he left the same night. In others, the time-lapse counter showed that he'd spent the night, creeping from the apartment around dawn. Despite the heat of the summer, he was usually shrouded in some sort of overcoat, his face shadowed by a hat. Only in the final frame did they get a view of his face. The still shot upon which Dash hovered showed a man of unmistakable Asian descent.

"I'm sorry, Dash," Bree whispered. She took the mouse from him and closed the file.

He shrugged. "I knew it wasn't love. It never was. But I thought something could explain how hot and cold she'd gotten with me. She's probably been seeing him from nearly the beginning of our relationship. And with us all out of the country, she got sloppy."

"Is it a coincidence?" she pressed, voicing her thoughts to Dash, being careful to keep her conversation with Judy secret. "He looks Chinese. She is the most advanced Chinese speaker in the entire program, with a great command of Chinese history and politics. And now, we have this Chinese connection suggested by Gul. What do you think?"

He extracted the SD card and tucked it back in his wallet.

"I don't know what to think anymore. But Susie—I mean, Susmita—is very insecure. Those airs of confidence she puts on? They're simply a cover to mask how horrible she feels about herself. It's hard for us to imagine the level of rejection she's had to withstand—from her father, her mother, indeed, her entire family. She is constantly seeking validation. That's all I was to her, I know. It's all this entire Norwood program is, at the end of the day—one massive opportunity for her to prove she means something. It's not so hard for me to imagine her being groomed to be a traitor and somehow finding it a twisted reassurance of her worth. She wouldn't need a massive political or financial motive. She'd do it just to feel good about herself. She would."

Something struck Bree then. Something both exciting and terrifying.

"The man who knocked me out. When he spoke to me, it was in English, but I thought his accent was strange. What if he was Chinese, Dash? I think he might have been."

He looked at her oddly, then turned his attention to the computer. Systematically, he began erasing their search history and log of use.

"I hope he wasn't, for your sake. But, I must say, I don't believe in coincidences. They are just the spasms of the universe, trying to spawn the truth into the bright of day. If what you're saying is right, and he was Chinese . . . if this conspiracy somehow reaches back all the way to your mother's death, it's a very twisted plot, indeed."

He proceeded delicately with his next comment.

"What if he wasn't Chinese? Did you ever stop to consider whether he recognized you and your resemblance to your mother because he was your father?"

Her heart lurched.

"They never found any bodies in the crash, did they?" he asked.

She shook her head, too choked up to respond.

If he had been her father, why had he left her alone all these years? And why would he hurt her?

Dash patted her hand.

"Just wild speculation, dear. But something to think about. In any case, we need to be very careful from here on out, Bree. We've uncovered something very disturbing. I'm not sure how much of it we should share with anyone else. At least for now, let's let it lie."

"How can we let it lie? How can we let it lie when the children are still out there?"

"We must, Bree." His voice became stern. "I know how upsetting it is, to not have closure with the Askers. But you've got to accept it—they're gone. We may never find out what happened to them." He was blunt—deliberately so. Only the slight shaking of his voice gave away that he, too, might be struggling to deal with the children's disappearance. "We have to acknowledge that we don't even know if they are alive."

"That's not true!" In her vehemence, her voice had risen, drawing looks from across the café. Dash shook his head in warning. She dropped her voice to a whisper.

"The man who knocked me out—he said they'd be safe with him. They're still alive. And I have to find them."

"You can't trust the words of an assassin, Bree. Because that's who these people were. Assassins. The American solider, Gul, Handan, the Asker children—"

She tried to protest but he cut her off.

"There's no sense arguing. And if they are alive, you, of all people, are the last one who can go out and find them. Not in your condition. I need you to focus on recuperating." His voice softened. "And in the meantime, I'll try to figure out everything we can about Miss Margaret McCarthy. I need to think through how to do it without arousing suspicion, but there has to be a way. Maybe what we learn can help us unravel our current conundrum as well."

"But Dash, there are other things," Bree insisted. Now that she knew they were on the same side, she felt an irrepressible urge to tell him everything, to let the words pour from her mouth. She had yearned for someone to understand, someone to believe in her. "There were things they've said in interrogation that make me wonder."

He patted her hand. "In due time, my dear. Right now, we need to get you back. We've been gone for quite some time—they may get suspicious when they look at the GPS records. And," he added, peering out the window and the half-lit sky, "it looks like rain. We'll have plenty of time to discuss things further. But never at Jaguar House. You understand, Bree? We cannot take any chances. Certainly not with Susmita there."

"And what about Ruby?" she asked, feeling a stab of guilt.

He shook his head. "Not even with Ruby, I'm afraid. You saw how competitive she is during finals. She would stop at nothing to ensure her success. We can't be sure of what her motivations are right now. So until we know the truth, we must keep this just between us."

———

Margaret McCarthy. Susmita Hilvale. Judy Roberts. Three women of Norwood, shrouded in mystery. Did something link the three of them? Something from the past, its convoluted ribbons reaching out through time to entwine them together?

If there was something, Bree couldn't imagine what it was.

She rolled over amid the scramble of blankets and looked at her alarm clock. Two a.m. She sighed. Ruby had fretted over her like a mother hen all evening. She'd studiously avoided any discussion of Istanbul and the investigation, and Bree sensed her discretion had been motivated by concern for her feelings, rather than any desire to keep Bree in the dark. Bree had been touched, if perhaps a little annoyed at being bossed around so much.

She looked across the bedroom to where Ruby's form lay huddled, watching the rise and fall of her breath, punctuated every now and then by a gentle snore. A pang of gratitude gripped her.

Yes, Ruby was protecting her. It had almost been funny, the way she'd jumped down Dash's throat when he'd accidentally let slip that he and Ruby had both been cleared and put back on active status. Oblivious, he'd cheerily added that he and Ruby had been reissued their guns and might be getting another interim summer placement.

"Have you pudding for brains? Put that gun away," Ruby had savaged him while he waved his pistol, "and shut your trap. We don't need to be talking about any of that right now." She concluded with a harrumph that brought a definitive end to the conversation. "She shouldn't be thinking about anything but her recovery," Ruby insisted, eyeing Dash meaningfully.

Bree smiled wistfully, knowing Ruby could not shelter her from the reality of the situation for very long. Ruby didn't know about all of the threads that Bree was trying to disentangle. She couldn't know how it was all Bree thought of, day and night. Bree didn't want the realities tucked away, unspoken of. She needed to confront them in the bright light of day.

She needed to clear her name and, more importantly, find the children.

Frustrated by her inability to sleep, Bree shoved aside the covers and eased herself out of bed. The jolt of pain in her ribs nearly knocked her off her feet, but she gripped the edge of the nightstand, steadying herself, until she was able to shuffle off.

The short walk down the hallway into the common room was enough to exhaust her. The medication was wearing off, she could tell, but it would be hours before her next dose. She eased herself down onto the futon and curled into a ball. Through the barred window, she caught a glimpse of moonlight. Did that moon shine on the Asker children tonight? Where? Her mind took up the threads again, picking at the knots of the mystery until, bone weary, she collapsed into sleep.

A sound outside the door woke her, the sudden jerking of her body jumping to alertness, taking her breath away on a wave of pain.

Groaning, she limped to the front door and listened.

Someone was there. She could hear two voices murmuring, just beyond the door.

The adrenaline of paranoia and fear took hold of her in an instant. Everyone was in for the night—she was sure of it. She looked at the insistent blue lights of the digital clock on the stove. Half past four. Not a time for decent people, people with nothing to hide, to be out and about. Certainly not a time for people to be lurking about doorstops.

The voices rose and fell. An argument? Bree couldn't tell.

Cautiously, she felt her way around the room, leaning on the wall for support. She didn't even realize what she was doing until it was there, in her hand, stolen from the hiding place in Ruby's cupboard.

A gun.

It felt heavy and unfamiliar in her hand. Shaking, she checked the chambers and slid off the safety, making her way back to the common room. She could no longer feel any pain. All she could feel was the nervous energy pulsing through her veins, compelling her forward, until she found herself leaning against the front door, ear pressed to its surface, hovering; listening; waiting.

"What are you doing?"

Bree wheeled, holding the gun outstretched, and gasped. It was Susmita.

She stood not four feet away from Bree, illuminated by the moonlight, a ghost of a smile on her face.

"You shouldn't be out of bed, Bree. You haven't healed properly. Look at you. You're so weak, you can barely even hold that pistol steady." Her eyes gleamed speculatively.

"Don't come near me," Bree warned.

Susmita laughed. "What? Are you going to shoot me? Really, Bree. I know the doctors cleared you, but I wonder if you withstood a concussion after all. You're clearly not thinking straight."

She crossed over to the kitchen table. With one arm, she lifted the chair to the center of the room and took a seat facing Bree. A bright strip of light fell more directly on her where she sat, giving Bree a better look. She was dressed immaculately, as usual—a clingy wrap dress, stilettos, and heavy drop earrings marking her with sophisticated glamour. But her hair was disheveled. Her lipstick smeared. Her lips swollen and ripe. The collar of her dress hung a little too open, giving Bree a glimpse of mottled skin, bruised with fingerprints.

"You were with someone. With a man," Bree accused.

Susmita chuckled low. She cocked a speculative eyebrow, appraising Bree's reaction. "Yes. A man. A real man. Instead of that pushover, Dashiell. What of it?"

"Why? Why do it?"

Susmita shrugged. "Why not? I'm not stupid," she said bluntly. "I know Dashiell is just using me to annoy his daddy. He uses me, I use him. It's all the same."

"But what are you using him for, Susmita? What's the point of it?"

Susmita sighed. "You really can be tiresome with all your questions, Bree. Such naked curiosity is very American. And quite rude."

Bree waved the gun at her. "I have a right to know what's going on, Susmita."

"Yes, poor Bree. Kept in the dark all this time about everything. I understand your impulse to want to understand. But some of these things will simply never make sense. They will simply happen to you, and you will be left to pick up the pieces of your life and do the best you can."

Bree said nothing. She wasn't going to let herself be baited into a conversation.

"Oh, fine, then," Susmita said with an exaggerated roll of her eyes. "If I must. Though really, you must realize how tiresome you are, Bree. And how bad it is for you to be putting such strain on yourself. Look at you—you're breaking out in a sweat."

Susmita was right. Bree's whole body was damp with perspiration from the effort of holding herself up against the doorway. She'd clearly overdone it, traipsing all over Bath with Dash, and now her system was rebelling against her. Gingerly, she felt her way along the wall, bracing herself for support.

Susmita crossed her legs, her hair flashing silver as it caught the blending light of sinking moon and rising sun. She was enjoying having the upper hand, Bree could tell.

"Did you know that when my mother abandoned me, she left me in the care of my Indian nursemaid? Pooja was her name. She wasn't a real nanny, not like we have been trained to be. But she loved me with all her heart. It was from her that I learned the truth about my own family. About their selfishness. Their rejection of me. And she is the one who whispered in my ear each night, telling me the stories of the Hindu gods and goddesses, reminding me of my heritage, making sure I never lost sight of who I really was."

"And who are you, then? Who are you really, Susmita?"

"I'm someone who has been overlooked and pushed aside—no, not pushed. Ignored, like a bad smell in a room. *Hidden*. Forgotten. Someone who's been underestimated her whole life. Why? Because I was English, but not just English. I was English when I wasn't supposed to be. And yet I wasn't English enough. England, England, England. We sit on a dreary, rainy dump of an island. I honestly don't know what's so special about it. But it rejected me. At some point, Pooja made me see that. That all my striving to fit in, all of my longing to be loved, would amount to nothing. But it didn't matter. Because I could be strong when they thought I was weak. I could punish them for what they did to me."

She was speaking rapidly now, the glinting hardness in her azure eyes offset by an almost breathless giddiness—the lightness of unburdening. The relief of confession.

I just need to keep her talking, Bree thought. *Eventually, she'll tell me what I need to know.* Her knees were shaking with the effort of standing, but she couldn't back down.

"Punish who? How?"

Susmita leaned forward in her seat. Even in her frenzied confession, she couldn't resist batting her eyelashes, tossing her hair. She'd been trained to seduction—it didn't matter the audience. It was hardwired into her.

"Yes, that's the question of the hour, isn't it?" she purred, her eyes lingering coquettishly on Bree.

"Do you know it was my father who came up with calling me 'Susie'? He always hated anything that reminded him of my mother. And he wanted me to fit in. As if slapping an English name on me would cover up the facts of my birth and the embarrassment of his own corrupt life. He christened me Susie, but Pooja had another name for me, a secret name. Diti. I don't suppose you know what Diti means in Hindi?"

Bree shook her head.

"She's the goddess of revenge. Bloody and cruel, she is, adept at cleaving people and families and whole nations apart. Everything you need to know about me is in my name. Susmita, 'a pleasant smile.' Diti, 'revenge.' My whole life I've been fooling people. All so I could win in the end. And now I'm close. So close."

Susmita eased back in the chair and closed her eyes. The zeal of storytelling was fading as the sun rose. Bree could tell she was tired. So tired.

Bree cleared her throat. If she didn't get it out of Susmita now, the others would wake and her chance would be lost.

"Close to what, Susmita? I know you were the one who threw the operation. It's obvious, isn't it? What I don't understand is why."

Susmita opened her eyes and laughed derisively at Bree. "You're so dull. I practically spoon-fed you the answer. But that's what I loved about you. You were so trusting. So naïve. I kept testing you, to see if you'd wise up. The falling bricks at the theater in Shoreditch. The jab at you for being an orphan, with those ridiculous love-token things. The collapse at the Roman Baths was a bit trickier to pull off, but luckily, I was able to divert Rodney's attention away and get you two alone there. Of course, I had help."

She was preening now, reveling in Bree's shock.

"I knew it," Bree muttered. "Judy warned me, but I didn't believe her."

"Ah, Judy." Susmita shook her head. "You were right. You shouldn't believe her. Not a word she says."

Bree gaped. "What do you know about Judy?"

"A great deal more than you do. I know she lies like she breathes. Except, she was telling the truth about one thing: I do have my own agenda. Let me spell it out for you."

She paused. She was playing with Bree now. But Bree steeled herself— she would be as patient as she needed to be.

"Somebody at Norwood is running their own covert op to divert arms to Chinese rebels. But it is pointless. The PRC is unstoppable. The unfortunate wretches who are being armed by Norwood's operation will be swatted down like flies. But for me, it's the perfect opportunity to get back at England. To end this little exercise in modern colonialism, I'll stand with the Chinese. And I'll do whatever it takes to do it."

It was breathtaking, how a few sentences confirmed everything Gul had signaled on the hidden video. But the revelation only led to more questions.

"But why?" Bree asked, baffled. "Why do you care?"

"I hate this country," Susmita stated simply. "I hate that generations ago, its men raped my people. I hate that my mother's blood was considered so beneath the inbred nobility that she'd rather flee the country than withstand their judgment and stares. The whole thing needs to come crashing down. And now I'm inside. With connections in China and wherever else I want. Because my good-for-nothing father, bless his soul, was at least able to run in good circles. Meaning, every ne'er-do-well piece of Eurotrash, every dissolute Saudi, every ambitious Chinese diplomat and would-be African dictator regularly graced our dinner table. It was only a matter of time until I got my opportunity. And now, I've reached a new stage."

She reached swiftly under the chair and extracted a gun. In one smooth move, she pointed it at Bree's head.

"I've got everything in place. The colonel's children are pawns now, to bring Norwood—and thereby, England—to its knees. Your stupid poet, Asker, will do anything to save them. I will exploit that to its fullest. And I've got you to take the fall." She cocked the hammer. "Now that I know you're not working with Judy, you serve no purpose. Other than to wash my slate clean."

Bree's heart was racing. She pulled the hammer on her gun back, too, but knew it was pointless. Her hand was already so unsteady, her sweat making the handle slick and unsure in her grip, that it was clear she'd hit nothing, even at this range.

Bree licked her lips. "What do you mean?" she asked, voice hoarse. "What do you mean about working with Judy?"

Susmita rolled her eyes. "You really don't get it, do you? Who do you think is directing this whole covert arms thing? It's her. She's been running rogue for decades. Who knows what she really thinks? Or for whom she really works? She's the one who can't be trusted. Just ask your mum."

Bree gasped.

"Oops," Susmita laughed. "You can't, can you? Because she's dead. And that, too, was Judy's fault." She smiled a grin of faux innocence, enjoying twisting the knife in Bree's psychic wound. "Sure, she admitted things went bad on her operation. But did she tell you what really happened? Where they were when they died? What were they even trying to do the night their car blew?"

"What do you mean?" Bree asked, confused and angered to have someone speaking about the private pain she'd kept to herself for so long.

Susmita paused, a speculative gleam lighting her face. "Oh, you didn't know I knew about those details, did you? I know more than you think.

I know the whole story, Bree." She let her words sink like a rock in Bree's stomach. "Did Judy even tell you the truth about your father?"

"There's nothing to tell," Bree stated flatly, not wanting to believe Susmita.

Susmita laughed. "Of course Judy wouldn't tell *you*. And now you'll never know. Because you've run out of time. When Ruby and Dashiell wake up, they'll see that you stole Ruby's gun and they'll hear all about how you attacked me. Maybe you'll be tagged a counterspy. Maybe they'll chalk it up to head injuries and medication. It doesn't matter to me. Soon, the inquiry into what happened in Turkey will be closed and I'll be on my merry way, digging deeper and deeper into the heart of Norwood." She gestured wildly with her gun.

Bree bit back her bitter retort. *She's still talking*, she thought to herself through gritted teeth. *That's good. Keep her going. Flatter her. Underneath this hardness, there's still a needy child.*

"You've thought of everything, haven't you, Susmita? You've planned it brilliantly. All along, you had us fooled," Bree mouthed her flattery into the last vestiges of night, hoping her words—so bitter on her tongue— would find their mark. "We underestimated you."

"Do you think so?" Susmita breathed, lapping up the compliment. "It wasn't easy, you know. I'm not stupid," she insisted, her voice brittle. "I may not be witty, like Dashiell, nor experienced, like Ruby. But I have my own talents. I have instincts. I have determination. I have patience. Who else but me would bear the endless insults that have been thrown at me all year long? No one. That's who. But I grew up used to it. So, it was no great sacrifice."

"You've been more than patient," Bree averred, recognizing her flattery was doing the job. "You've been clever. It was very clever, stealing the Asker children right out from under our noses. Where did you take them, Susmita?"

Susmita laughed. "You'll never know. It's time for you to die. You'll die and be branded a villain. I'll be the hero."

She steadied the gun, pointing it directly at Bree's head.

Bree paused, waiting. Hoping.

"What? No begging? No crying? I'm disappointed, Bree. I thought you'd be upset at being unfairly blamed. You're not giving me the reaction I crave." Susmita pouted, her fleshy bottom lip jutting out. "You don't seem to really appreciate all the trouble I've gone to. Ooh. No, I know. I have an idea. A bargain of sorts, for you."

She clapped her hands with feigned enthusiasm.

"You want to know where the children are. That's understandable. Even though you won't be able to do anything with that knowledge, it will give you some sort of closure as you go to your grave. And yet . . . you have also spent your entire conscious life longing to know the truth about your parents. An equally understandable need to make sense of the train wreck that became your life. So, I'll make you a deal. I'll give you one dying wish. Your choice. I can tell you where the children are, or I can tell you the story that Judy will never, ever, divulge. The truth about that car crash and the mission gone bad. The truth about your parents. You choose."

Bree stared, dumbfounded.

"Don't make me wait," Susmita growled, recentering the gun on Bree's forehead. "Make your choice."

"No," Bree replied, disgusted by the injustice of it all.

Susmita smiled. "I knew that would get you in the proper moo—"

Susmita gasped, eyes rolling to their whites as her head snapped backward and an explosion of gore littered the room, spraying Bree from head to toe. Susmita's lifeless body slumped forward in the chair and then rolled to the floor.

Behind Bree, in the shadows of the doorway, stood Judy. She was still pointing the gun, its barrel topped with a silencer, at the space where Susmita had been sitting.

Bree slid against the wall, sinking all the way to the floor, where she landed in a heap. It felt like she was watching from miles away, disconnected from the pain, removed from the suddenness of death, distant from the coppery tang of blood in the air and from the reality of the gritty linoleum beneath her bare legs. Even so, she could see the neat circle where the bullet had entered Susmita's head, the blond strands of hair surrounding it smoking from the gunpowder.

A puddle of dark blood was pooling under Susmita's cheek, seeping across the tile toward Bree. Judy sidestepped it gingerly in her Chanel pumps to walk to Bree, hand outstretched.

"Give it to me," she ordered.

Trembling, Bree deposited the pistol in her open palm. Judy checked the safety and wiped it down, setting it on the kitchen table.

She quickly dismantled the silencer from the gun she'd used to kill Susmita, then thrust it at Bree. "Here. When you're asked, you shot her with this. It's Dashiell's." She checked her nails, then ran her fingers through her sleek bob, poised as ever, as if nothing had happened.

Bree numbly accepted the gun, turning her face, slick with tears, up toward Judy.

"She knew where the children were, Judy," she sobbed. "She was going to tell me."

"She wasn't going to tell you anything," Judy said dismissively. "Didn't you see? No, of course, not—not with the light shifting the way it was. She was already pulling the trigger, Bree. She was just toying with you, getting your hopes up before doing you in. Don't ever hesitate like that again," she chided. "You have to be prepared to use your weapon, Bree. This is the second time."

"The second time what?"

"The second time you could have died because you were too slow. The first was on the cargo ship. Don't let it happen again."

She arched a brow, taking in Bree's reaction.

"Of course I know all about that. Do you think I'd let you go out on your first mission without keeping track of you? But look at you. You're shaking. You're going into shock."

Bree shook her head vigorously, dragging her cast roughly across her tear-streaked face. "It's not shock. It's exhaustion. I'm still recuperating from the ship."

Judy cocked her head, appraising. "Very well. But I'll have my men check you out, just in case. They've been waiting outside, ready to clean up any messes. Move away so they can come in the front door."

Bree skittered across the linoleum, putting more distance between herself and Susmita's body. She tried to ignore the streaks and smears of blood she left behind her. Judy swung the door wide. Shoulders squared, back to Bree, she paused.

"What she said about your parents? It was nothing. There's no story to tell. She was only trying to get under your skin. You know that, don't you?"

She waited for Bree's answer, expectant. When Bree didn't answer, her eyes narrowed.

"Bree," she said flatly. "Remember that woman who tied you up in the barn when you were a child?"

Bree's head snapped sharply in surprise.

"She didn't disappear by accident. I made her disappear. I made sure she would never hurt you again. I watched. And as soon as I knew just how strong you could be, I got rid of her."

Bree let the realization of what Judy'd done to her childhood tormentor—and the knowledge that Judy had let the abuse happen, watching Bree's reaction before deciding what to do—sink in.

"Your high school counselor? She wasn't supposed to apply to colleges on your behalf. She even told you so herself—each student had to do their own application work, as a matter of fairness and ethics. But I convinced her to make an exception for you, for Norwood. I showed her that it was different in the UK—no essays, no personal statements, nothing but test scores. She wouldn't be misrepresenting her work as yours. What could it hurt? I'm the one who got the proof she needed of your real birth. But she couldn't be allowed to live, not with what she knew. She'd started asking too many questions—questions about you, questions about me. I did what I needed to. I will always do what I need to when it comes to you."

A wave of revulsion swept through Bree. She choked it down.

"I have always been there for you. I have always protected you. Then, and now. Now do you understand?"

"Yes," Bree whispered quietly, frightened and acquiescent. Her body shuddered, suppressing one last sob. "Yes, of course."

"What Susmita said about the arms diversion? A lie. But one that would be best to never be aired. It will just add uncertainty to an already confused situation. It would be senseless to prolong the investigation unnecessarily."

"I understand, Judy."

Judy nodded, her shoulders sagging slightly. Then she stepped out into the morning glow.

As Judy closed the door behind her, Bree pushed away her new knowledge, pushed away the horror of the evening. But she couldn't stop herself from lingering over one thought.

Judy's men. The fact that Judy even had them meant she was much more organized than Bree had realized.

And if they'd been waiting to clean up a mess, that meant Judy had planned to make one all along.

But just whom had she planned to kill?

In the end, it was just as Susmita had predicted, only the one who was fully exonerated—nay, deemed a hero—was Bree. At first, Bree had been under a cloud; after all, no one else had witnessed the exchange between her and Susmita but Judy, and Judy obviously could not come forward. But the evidence, circumstantial and otherwise, had pointed to Susmita having been at the center of the plot all along. That she was working for the Chinese seemed clear, given her confession. The Norwood administration chalked it up to an embittered childhood and mental illness—rumored to run in the house of Fewersham—and left it at that.

Nobody seemed aware that the arms meant for Syria were being diverted to China, and as far as Bree could see, it no longer mattered. The arms flow had stopped the day Handan and the children vanished. Bree and Dash agreed amongst themselves to keep the videotape of Susmita's suitor, along with Gul's blinking message in Morse code, to themselves— they had time to see how things played out. And if Judy were somehow involved in the plot, they could hardly afford to let their knowledge get into her hands. They'd seen how cold-blooded she'd been with Susmita. They couldn't take any chances. The stakes were too high.

It was only a matter of weeks until the official inquiries were completed. Neat and tidy, the way Norwood preferred.

Bree was reissued her gun, her laptop, and her phone. She was free.

Afterward, Judy requested Bree meet her at Poppins.

The chapel door seemed heavier to Bree, weighed down now by the reality of what she was becoming, the purpose of her life, so different from what she'd expected. She pushed through, admiring the way the late summer sun filtered through the skylights, piercing the dark of the anteroom, and the lingering cool of the stones beneath her fingertips.

She still ached—both body and soul—but here, in the stillness of the Memorial Chapel, she could find solace. She resolutely ignored the photos of the nannies who'd given their lives in service. Now that she knew the reality of their sacrifice, it was too stark a reminder. Thinking about it only drew her thoughts to Arslan, Gamze, Isra, and Eda.

Judy was waiting, seated quietly at Poppins's feet.

"You wanted to see me?"

Judy smiled—a taut pressing of her lips. She couldn't tell where she stood with Bree, Bree realized. That knowledge was a source of strength to Bree, but also a worry. For an uncertain Judy could be very dangerous indeed.

"I heard the administration has agreed that the rest of the summer is a wash for you. You have about three weeks until the start of term. No sense in putting you out in the field again. It's not as if you need more experience—you've garnered more than your fair share." Her lips twisted in amused acknowledgement. "Plus, you still could use some time to heal. The second year is very difficult, if I remember correctly. You'll want to marshal your strength."

Bree bowed her head in quiet acceptance that other people's decisions were shaping her life now, and that whatever Judy's methods, nothing about that life seemed private anymore. Judy's grip on her was stronger than ever, and there was seemingly nothing she could do about it.

That said, she'd been relieved to learn she wouldn't be forced into a live op, nor deposited in the midst of some household where she'd have to pretend to care about someone else's children. She couldn't muster the energy to care for anybody right now. She knew she wouldn't until she'd brought the Askers back to their father.

"I know it's hard for you to accept," Judy continued, choosing her words with care, "but for right now, you need to move on from the Istanbul operation. You need to trust that even though our operations will be, shall we say, running in parallel, I, presumably along with every-one inside Norwood, will be doing everything possible to determine the meaning of the Chinese interest."

"And to find the Asker children," Bree prompted.

Judy lit a cigarette and inhaled deeply. "Yes, yes," she said, breathing out a ring of smoke with impatience. "We'll all be trying to track down the children."

Bree drew her brows together, not finding Judy's pledge to be convinc-ing. Judy ignored her and continued.

"You remember, Bree, when I told you that there is something rotten inside of Norwood? This Chinese thing—it may be the first break we've had in ferreting it out. It's clear to me that Susmita could not have been orchestrating her countermaneuvers alone. Yes, we underestimated her," she acknowledged, "but the level of planning, the sophistication of the logis-tics—that took an experienced hand. She was at the center of disrupting your operation, but she was not the mastermind. There's someone else— maybe multiple individuals—still at large. And now we have a chance to find them. Thanks to you."

Bree felt herself blushing against her will, still not having gotten past her years of seeking Judy's approval.

"I don't think I really did anything. I just happened to be at the wrong place at the wrong time."

"False modesty does not become you. You were stoic under pressure. You kept Susmita talking, for example, when she had a gun pointed at your head. If you hadn't, she'd never have gone on rambling, providing us with what amounted to a confession. We'd never have known the truth."

Bree sighed. Yes, she had done that. But she'd had to, even if for no other reason than that she'd been too weak to pull the trigger herself.

"Anyway. I won't forget it," Judy concluded, stabbing out the butt of her cigarette against Poppins's pedestal. "And since the administration has agreed to give you a break, I think you deserve a reward. I'm sending you back to Florence, to the Shoals, for a couple of weeks' respite."

Bree's head snapped up. "What? You're helping me go home?"

Judy smiled, a genuine smile this time. "Yes, but don't get too excited. It's only for two weeks. But honestly, it's the safest place for you now. Since you seem to be on the mend, we shouldn't need to worry about your medical care so much. It will be a good break for you. A restorative, if you will."

Suspicions forgotten, Bree threw herself at Judy, wrapping her one good arm around her shoulder in a grateful hug while trying not to jostle Judy with her cast. "Thank you! Thank you, Judy."

Judy drew away, laughing. "Make the most of it. You will be staying at Thornton, of course. Rodney is expecting you. He's been told you had an accident, but not the details. You will tell him you were in a car wreck. That should be sufficient. He doesn't have a distrustful mind. He'll believe whatever you tell him."

Bree stepped back. Rodney. Ollie. All of them. She hadn't thought about the lies she'd have to tell, just to be back with them. Nor the danger in which she might be putting them.

"What if something happens there? After all, you said they used to send people there to check up on me. What if they keep spying on me? Or what if someone comes after me, and . . ." She let her worry hang in the air, her fear unspoken.

"It's natural for you to worry, but unnecessary. I've been visiting for years, incognito, and have never had an incident. And, most importantly, there is no evidence that anyone is after you, now that Susmita is gone. Unless there's been something that you haven't told me about?" She cocked her head, skewering Bree with that familiar look that demanded answers.

Bree shook her head. No more threats, imagined or otherwise. The lingering fear she had of the man who'd hit her over the head—the man who'd known her mother—she kept to herself.

"Well, if it makes you feel better," Judy continued, "you can take one of your groupmates with you, as well. It's easier to send one of them—they've had the same trumped-up summer as you and will be at loose ends, and there will be no need to explain anything, nothing odd about a college mate tagging along. In contrast, an actual security detail would stand out like a sore thumb. So, a groupmate it is. Perhaps Ruby? She's proven to be quite handy with the medical care, I hear?"

Bree shook her head again.

"Ruby was planning on seeing her family, if she gained permission to leave Bath," she explained. "No, I think I'd rather take Dash. His family won't miss him that much. And he seems eager to see the United States."

Judy frowned. "You're not getting too familiar, are you, Bree? I know you and he have been spending an awful lot of time together. It isn't wise for a spy to become attached. It drives too many complications down the road."

Bree blushed.

This could actually work to her advantage, she reasoned. If Judy thought she had feelings for Dash, Judy would never guess the real purpose of their marathon sessions and ramblings all over Bath. Regardless, she made a mental note to warn Dash—they could no longer assume their favorite internet café haunts were surveillance free.

"I just think it will be better for all if it is he who accompanies me to Florence. That's all," Bree said simply, hoping her logic was compelling enough to satisfy Judy.

"Then it's settled," Judy said definitively. "And while you're there, you can have a look at this. Another part of your reward. Consider this one a personal thank-you from me."

She laid a thick manila folder on the corner of the statue's base and rose.

Bree stared at it, breathless, listening to the insistent click of Judy's heels against the stone until the chapel door had slammed shut behind her and Judy was gone.

With shaking fingers, Bree picked up the file. It was heavy.

"Margaret McCarthy," it was labeled in bold letters, birth and death dates starkly marking out the shortness of her mother's life. She opened the folder and fingered its contents—three years of her mother's undergraduate experience, the entirety of her Norwood training, and then some.

Was it a simple thank-you, as Judy had said? A peace offering?

Or was it a bribe?

Bree didn't care. She took a deep breath, settled back on the bench, and began to read.

—THE END—

To be continued in book two of *The Norwood Nanny Chronicles*

ACKNOWLEDGMENTS

This book has been several years in the making, and as is common when one is tackling a difficult—but exciting—project, there are many people to whom I owe thanks.

The genesis of the premise for this series came during an extended brainstorming while on a car ride with my three children. Thomas, Reagan, and John are full of interesting observations about the world and exhibit a ton of imagination. They are wonderful partners, with whom I can riff and against whom I can bounce ideas. Thank you for sharing your youthful enthusiasm and unique take upon the world with me. You are all three an endless source of inspiration, and I am so grateful you are my children! Thank you doubly to Thomas and John, both of whom read different early versions of *The Agency* before nearly anybody else did, offering me detailed notes and suggestions. My other beta readers are a gift. To my brother, Jake Houle; my parents, Lorraine and Ray Houle; and my friends, Dr. Shami Feinglass and Beth Melendez—thank you, as always, for your willingness to plough through early drafts and push my thinking. Your observations on both characters and plot were invaluable—your support, priceless. To fellow author and friend Kathy Florence: You saw even more in Bree than I did, at first. Your prods to keep going, your follow-up inquiries regarding my status, and your ever-insightful advice played a large hand in seeing me through. I hope you love where this story has wound up! To Lesley Salmon—thank you for taking on the thankless role of policing my British colloquialisms and references. All errors, of course, remain my own. To Dr. Susmita Pati, who lent my character her wonderful name, imprinted me early in adulthood with the inspiration of owning your identity, and who graciously read with an eye toward cultural and ethnic sensitivity—you are the best, and I am so glad to have your friendship still, after all these years!

This is my fourth go-round with the good folks at Greenleaf. Your enthusiasm for this story was palpable, and your willingness to work around my crazy corporate schedule deeply appreciated. Special thanks in particular to Tyler LeBleu, Lindsey Clark, and Chelsea Richards for coordinating the production, titling, and marketing. Thank you to Elizabeth Brown for your intrepid proofreading and positive energy. Thank you to Mimi Bark for your inspired graphic and cover designs. To my editor, Ava Justine—what a true pleasure working with you! I have learned so much from our time together and appreciate your guidance as you shepherded this through the final stages. The book is undoubtedly different, and better, because of your touch.

The current events, history, and spy craft references contained in this book are culled from general reading, the Googleplex, and, of course, the ever-authoritative Wikipedia. For my background knowledge of human trafficking, used to inform the scenes in Calais and the escape from Turkey, I am thankful for my time with the fantastic people at Street Grace and ECPAT. To better understand issues of race, sexual politics, and intermarriage during the Raj, I am indebted to the works of William Dalrymple, specifically *White Mughals: Love and Betrayal in Eighteenth-Century India,* and *The Anarchy: The East India Company, Corporate Violence, and the Pillage of an Empire.* My reference for the classic Anatolian lullaby "*Fış Fış Kayıkçı*" (which the children teach Bree while in the shipping container) is Mircan Kaya's album *Bizim Ninniler* (I highly recommend the trippy video one can find on YouTube).

If I have inadvertently forgotten someone in the above, I beg forgiveness. Please know I appreciate all the help and support I get, from every quarter.

A final thank-you to my husband, Tom. Thank you for all the ways you help me, most importantly with your good humor and by your persistence in helping me find the space to create. If you are reading this, know I am making sunset heart hands, just for you.

QUESTIONS FOR DISCUSSION

1. Is there a book or movie you can think of that compares in terms of Bree's story? Do you believe there is a fascination with orphans in our culture, whether it be scientific, comical, or morbid? How does *The Agency* explore themes of orphandom, and what do you think the significance is there?

2. What was your initial reaction upon discovering that Bree would be forced to enter a lifestyle and career not of her choosing? Were you shocked, disappointed for her, curious? How did you feel about this by the end of the book? Is the author making a statement on the importance of being made to do something we don't want to in life, at least on occasion?

3. How did you feel about the idea of a nanny training ground designed to serve the elite? About the disparity of wealth and poverty shown in the novel?

4. Did you like Judy any less, once you discovered who she really was to Bree? Did it change the stakes or the way you read the book?

5. Why do you think the author chose to place the story in England? What sort of atmosphere and effect is created by using Bath as a setting? How would the story be different if placed in the United States? Would it be as successful?

6. What role do the English historical references play in the book? How would losing these mentions impact the reading of the book, in your opinion?

7. We uncover various "truths" as the narrative progresses, and much of what we do believe gets deconstructed along the way as we learn that Bree is not the simple orphan she thought she was. One reveal negates another, sometimes requiring work on our part to keep logistics in order. How did you experience the reveals that occur in the novel?

8. Can you see the author's political opinions shining through on the pages of her book? What sort of leanings might our author have, given the implicit commentary on global events and conflict?

9. Do you think adolescent readers could gain from reading this book, or should the audience be limited to adults?

10. How do you think the playful yet innocuous title could affect our reading of the novel, especially if we go into reading not knowing that Norwood is not exactly a school made just for aspiring nannies?

11. Bree is obviously our heroine, but, as a reader, do you have a preference for one of the four main group members, as characters? Which one do you relate to more, or have more empathy toward? Did it surprise you when Susmita turns out to be our true "bad guy"?

12. Relative to other prep or trade-school scenarios depicted in books and movies, or your own experience of such, do you consider Norwood College to be realistic? Were you able to suspend disbelief? What made it work for you?

13. Do you feel that, if Bree were an actual person, she would have accepted her fate as a chip-tracked spy and servant of the state quite so gracefully? How did you respond to the four main characters' reactions when they learned the truth of their situation? What would some problems be for you, if you were suddenly to encounter the same fate, and what is the author potentially saying about free will, autonomy, and choosing our own path?

14. Did you want to know more about Bree's life in the orphanage, before she came to England? Or do we get "just enough"? What questions would you want answered?

15. It is not very often in literature that we enter a world dominated by women, other than in an entirely domestic setting. How does *The Agency* play into these norms, and how does it upend them? Do you find the way characters such as Coach Shadduck encourage the spies-in-training to use gender stereotypes for their own purposes to be empowering, or something else? Why? What did you make of the only prominent male characters—Dash, Rodney, Arslan, and Colonel Asker?

16. The question of identity runs strong throughout this novel. The author continually confronts us with examples of the way people grapple with their own self-perception and how the world, on its own, may see them or classify them based on stereotypes. What were some of the ways this came to the forefront for you? Why do you think the author found this so important?

17. What elements of the "Hero's Journey" do you see evident in Bree's story?

18. How does the treatment of spy craft and spies in this novel compare to other examples in movies and literature with which you may be familiar?

19. By the end of the novel, do you have a strong sense of whom—if anyone—Bree can trust? Why?

20. How do you, as the reader, envision a sequel unfolding? Do we want to know more about Bree's past, or are you more excited to see the next adventure?

AUTHOR Q & A

Q: Readers may be curious to learn a little about your educational background and personal interest in world events, as *The Agency* is packed with interesting political and historical material. Can you tell us anything about your background there and how you go about researching and fact-finding?

MM: I was a government major as an undergrad, with a significant focus in international affairs, and have retained a personal interest in international relations ever since. I also love to travel and am especially drawn to the history of any place I am lucky enough to visit. I am very fact-based in my approach to most things. Writing is no exception! I tend to do a lot of research to make sure the details of a location, or of a timeline, make sense, even to those who may be personally familiar with the topic.

In the case of *The Agency*, my research has included time on the ground in Bath (including scouting for the building on which to base Jaguar House); deep dives into the politics of Turkey and China (both of which I have previously visited); reading up on the history of the British Raj; lots of listening to the music of Muscle Shoals; and, of course, delving into the wonderful story of Norland College, on which Norwood is loosely modeled. As I research, I document things on Pinterest boards to serve as ongoing inspiration. Readers can always check them out for themselves to get a sneak peek!

Q: Were your four student characters based, even if very loosely, on real-life friends or colleagues, or are they entirely fictional? Similarly, did you draw from your own school experiences when writing the book?
MM: I always warn my friends and acquaintances to be careful or I may put them in a book! In seriousness, they are largely fictional, with a few sparks of inspiration. Judy (before she turned into such an *ambiguous* character) was inspired by a fellow church member who was a supporter of a local orphanage and had herself been in M&A. I found her to be such a trailblazer and wanted to capture that in a character. Susie/Susmita was initially crafted upon a colleague who was particularly adept at using faux naïvete to get her way, but then evolved into more of an amalgam. Susmita's act of claiming her real name and deeper identity was inspired by two friends—one actually named Susmita—who went through an experience of embracing their ethnic origins after having "Americanized" themselves for convenience and assimilation. I thought their reclaiming of their true name was inspiring and wanted to bring that to readers. In today's environment, that level of authenticity and self-awareness is so important to celebrate.

Q: What inspired you to write the book, more generally? And were there any personal nanny stories that contributed to that inspiration?
MM: Honestly, I was driving in a car with my children, brainstorming ideas, and the concept of the real Norland College being a spy school popped up. I was immediately taken with it. As for personal nanny stories . . . let's just say that Penny, the virtual baby's, backward diaper, non-BRAT diet,

explosive-diarrhea-on-a-white-couch incident was inspired by a true story. With three children, I've had every form of childcare imaginable—and I even was a nanny briefly myself—so I had lots to draw from.

Q: Can you share any of your own feelings on why you chose the setting you did, as well as the political climate you chose to anchor the book in?
MM: Since the original idea was based on a real college in Bath, it just made sense to keep the location in England. It also gave me a great way to show the innocence of the main character and how she grows in a strange environment. As for the global instability—I felt it was critical to link the spying to something bigger than the characters themselves. I wasn't interested in corporate espionage, which would seem self-serving. I wanted to find a way to explain why these characters could ultimately become vested in what they were learning and doing—even if it involved a fair amount of coercion. The world climate is very volatile right now, which made it very easy to identify places where human and civil rights are at risk—places where spying might feel justified as serving the greater good.

Q: Was the theme of global instability and Bree's own instability an intentional pairing?
MM: The parallels to Bree's own situation were almost coincidental. What was a bit more intentional was the exploration of the personal and geopolitical threat of imperialism, colonialism, and its aftermath. Three of the roommates—Bree, Ruby, and Susmita—all have cultural or even personal histories imprinted by British colonialism in some way. Their identities and ways of interacting with the world are very much influenced by these factors. In parallel, in the background, is the political environment of instability created by these types of movements and histories. There are a few references to the unraveling of the British Empire and its aftermath, including the possibility of Chinese encroachment in parts of the Pacific

from which the British withdrew. A large part of the book is set against the backdrop of Turkey, which has moved between various empires for centuries and was occupied in some parts following WWI by the Allies, prompting the emergence of its own nationalist movement and eventual independence. I would say this novel teed this up for further exploration in the next book in the series, where it may feel a bit more in the forefront.

Q: Because your novel is the first book in a series, the construction of the narrative—which has a relatively complex plot—must involve some sort of careful planning or writer's organization. Can you tell the reader anything about the process of weaving the story, and advise any aspiring authors?

MM: This is my fourth original novel, following two novel-length works of fan fiction. I tend to write out the broad outline of the entire plot and then go deeper into each book, in turn. I spend a lot of time researching to get a grasp on the details, a lot of time thinking through back story and characters, and then I jump in. I write sequentially, and once I get going, I write pretty fast. I know others do not. My only advice to aspiring authors is to get something down on the page. You can always edit!

Q: The reader discovers truths gradually as the narrative progresses, and much of what we believe gets deconstructed along the way as we discover the reality around Bree's past and her parents' past. One reveal negates another, thereby keeping the reader on their toes. What challenges presented themselves to you as you crafted a plot structure containing multiple levels of reveals?

MM: It could get quite difficult keeping track of the reveals without a good outline! I also allow myself to change things up when a better idea strikes me. When this happens, inevitably I have to go back and undo some bit of plot or characterization—or embellish it—to make sense of it. I have literally woken up in the middle of the night with the sudden realization, "Oh no! That plot point is impossible!" I keep a notebook bedside for those eventualities.

Q: One of the truths we discover is that Judy is not the generous orphanage benefactor and role model Bree has held her to be. Judy plays a major role in the book, and there is a great deal of ambiguity surrounding whether she is a "good guy" or a "bad guy." Can you describe why you chose to paint her character the way you did, or speak about the significance of her character more generally?

MM: I personally found her to be a fascinating character. I began working professionally in business during an era when it was unusual to see women in very senior roles, so I loved having this character—supposedly with a really globe-trotting, successful track record in M&A—in the mix. There is a lot of good in Judy; you can't deny it. She has single-handedly kept that orphanage open. She has nurtured—even pushed—Bree to realize her potential. She seems to genuinely want to figure out what happened to Bree's parents. Is Judy Bree's guide? Or is she using Bree? I love that we—and Bree—can't tell. I love that Bree wants to believe her—because if she can't, what does she have left? From a writer's perspective, it's a wonderful dilemma, and it gives me a lot of options for how to further develop the characters, as well as the plot.

Q: When did you first realize you wanted to write a novel, and what motivated you to pursue this path?

MM: I like to say that I had a mid-life crisis, at which point I realized that while I was "all in" in this high-power career, and "all in" as a mom and wife, I had squeezed out all the little pleasures that were just for me. I had lost my creative outlets. That is simply not sustainable. It was then that I picked up writing again, after a long break. Fan fiction eased me into it and after some success there, my husband encouraged me to write something original. So here I am.

Q: Did any books or authors in particular inspire you within the genre of suspense and mystery?

MM: As for inspirations from the genre of suspense and mystery, there are so many. I am such a voracious reader that it would be hard to name one. This year I have focused my pleasure reading on classics that for some reason I had not ever gotten to read. There were a fair number of psychological thrillers and mysteries on that list, among them *Rebecca* by Daphne du Maurier and *The Woman in White* by Wilkie Collins. I loved them both and was particularly gratified to read the Collins, as it had been the subject of my college roommate's thesis! I couldn't believe I'd never read it.

Q: Was there a favorite chapter for you? Was there one that was especially difficult to write?

MM: I really enjoyed some of the funnier bits—the classroom antics and projects, for example. I needed something a little lighter after *The Archangel Prophecies*; the conclusion to that trilogy, *Dark Before Dawn*, was just really heavy. It was wonderful, but heavy.

I wound up loving the chapter detailing Bree's escape from Turkey with the Asker children, but it was also very difficult to write as I imagined what it would be like to go through that. The most heartbreaking part of the story, to me, is when Bree wakes up in the hospital and they break the news to her of what has happened. It just guts me, even now.

Q: Who supported you most in your *The Agency* journey, and how important do you feel that support was? Or was writing a solitary and individual act for you? Do you have advice for writers on how much

(or how little) to rely on support (whether from family or beta readers) during the process?

MM: I could do nothing without the support of my family—from giving me space and time, to brainstorming ideas with me, they are critical.

I also have my small circle of beta readers. I have been blessed with friends who are fellow writers and family members who are quite critical readers and they will not spare my feelings—they tell me what they really think. I truly value that. It can be hard to let go of something you have worked so hard over, so it is a gift to have people you really trust take the time to read and reflect and discuss their reaction with you. I am truly grateful.

Q: How essential are these beta readers to the process? Can you provide an example of an instance where a beta reader was especially useful?

MM: I would be remiss if I didn't acknowledge my wonderful "beta readers"—the guinea pigs upon whom I inflict early drafts, especially those who can offer a perspective on a location or culture which I am trying to capture. My lovely colleague, Lesley Salmon, for example, read a version of *The Agency* to catch all the British things I messed up (and there were many!). This is one of the most wonderful aspects of writing—with the need to research, I have been handed an excuse to travel and to meet and spend time with many interesting people whom I might never have met under other circumstances.

Q: Themes of world-crisis, global suffering, and injustice lend poignancy to the novel. Is there a humanitarian message you would like to relay to the reader?

MM: If there is a message, it is to be aware. Pay attention. Get outside yourself. There are bigger issues in the world out there.

ABOUT THE AUTHOR

Award-winning author Monica McGurk likes nothing better than weaving complex, multi-layered stories that bring contemporary issues and strong female characters to life through different genres of popular fiction. Her previous work includes three volumes of paranormal YA romance—*The Archangel Prophecies: Dark Hope, Dark Rising,* and *Dark Before Dawn*—along with numerous works of fan fiction under the name Consultant by Day.

A corporate executive, she now lives in Chicagoland with her husband, Tom, her youngest son, John, and their two dogs, Jack and Ellie. You can find her on Facebook, Instagram, Goodreads, and LinkedIn, or on her website monicamcgurk.com.

PLEASE READ ON
FOR A

SNEAK PEEK
OF
BOOK TWO OF
THE NORWOOD NANNY
CHRONICLES

Chapter One

BREE

Present day, Alabama

Late summer in the Shoals was just like its music. Sweaty, throbbing with an overabundance that made no sense. Teeming with life and threatening to burst up like kudzu and overtake everything in a chokehold so tight you might not ever hack your way through it, might even lose yourself if you didn't pay enough attention to the rhythm and the order and the rules that despite everything, did exist.

To her astonishment, Bree found that words failed Dashiell. Not words: imagination.

"It's hot," he muttered, wiping his patrician brow with a monogrammed handkerchief.

Bree laughed out loud. "You told me London was built on a swamp. You should feel right at home."

Dash shook his head, fanning himself with a sheaf of papers. "It's not a proper swamp. More of a floodplain. And it never feels as oppressive as this."

"Be careful!" Bree snatched the papers from his hand and added them to the pile next to her on the seat of the porch swing. She smoothed them out carefully, setting the swing in motion with an absent-minded push of her toe. "We want to keep them in order."

Dash sighed, staring at the pile with pained boredom.

"You've read them over and over, Bree," he said gently. "You've memorized them by now. Even I've memorized them by now."

"There's got to be more to it than is here," she insisted stubbornly. "Something we're not seeing."

"Well, let's sum up, shall we? But let's not stay on the porch. Let's go for a walk while we think."

Bree dragged a toe and let the swing swerve and skitter to a stop. It was hard to gain the motivation to move in this humidity, but Dash was right. A change of scenery might help her see what she was missing.

They'd been in the Shoals for over a week now, Bree installed in her old room at the orphanage and Dash, a member of the British aristocracy, squeezed unceremoniously into the little kids' bunk room, the only place with beds to spare. Ollie had taken a shine to him, insisting he get the top bunk over Ollie's—a position of privilege, Bree knew, even if Dash's feet dangled over the edge of the bed. The little boy had been their shadow for the first few days, clinging to Bree and rapt with fascination at Dash's English accent and formal manners, until Rodney, the administrator of Thornton Children's Home, had discreetly come up with some "summer school" work for Ollie, giving Bree and Dash some privacy.

"So you can recover," he'd said solemnly, scanning her once more as if he was afraid she'd fall apart right in front of his eyes.

Even now, as she limped along the hard-packed dirt path around the orphanage grounds, she could number her injuries: the pin in her wrist, the broken ribs, the contusions and sprains that left her feeling as fragile as an old piece of lace. That Rodney believed the story the administration of their college, Norwood, had shared with him—that she'd had a car accident while nannying her summer charges—was something for which she was grateful, because she didn't know if she could lie to his face. And she didn't want to have to tell him the truth.

The truth: that Norwood, the prestigious British college for nannies to which she'd won a scholarship, was a ruse for an international ring of spies. That the patron of the orphanage in which she'd been raised—the woman, Judy, who'd helped win Bree's admittance to the school—was one of them, a spy through and through, and had manipulated the whole thing, literally from the day Bree had shown up at Thornton's doorstep. That Bree and her Norwood friends—Dash among them—were now being trained to join this deadly cadre of spies. That her injuries were not from a simple car accident, but were inflicted upon her when she'd been placed in her first field assignment, during which she'd uncovered an international arms smuggling plot. The young Turkish children left in her care—the Askers—had been snatched away, held as collateral by the unknown people smuggling the arms. It was trying to unravel their disappearance that she and Dash had ultimately uncovered the fact that their own classmate and colleague, a young woman named Susmita, was a mole working for the Chinese.

It had been a disastrous operation. The four Asker children remained missing and, according to Norwood, their mother missing. Bree, herself, had almost lost her life. And two agents were dead—one, Susmita, at Judy's hand, as Bree had watched.

Bree and Dashiell now knew they couldn't trust Judy. The problem was they didn't know whom they could trust. Meanwhile, Judy had gifted Bree with the one thing she wanted more than anything else: information about her dead birth mother—one Margaret McCarthy, Norwood graduate and spy.

Once left to themselves, Dash and she had pored over the papers from the file folder Judy had given Bree, trying to piece together the story of what had happened to Bree's mother, and what, in turn, had led to Bree becoming an orphan. But they'd run into dead ends.

"Let's try again," Dash began in a hopeful tone, taking her by the elbow to slightly steer her to a shady part of the path. "What have we learned about Margaret?"

Bree began counting things off on her fingers. "Basics first. She was Irish American, from Chicago. Her father a McCarthy, a salesman. Her mother, Mary Margaret Kelly, an immigrant from Ireland proper—Bogside, in Derry, Northern Ireland, listed as homemaker. She never took US citizenship. Hence, Margaret's British citizenship and qualification for Norwood."

"And there is our first odd little clue. Why would someone descended from Irish refugees—for surely, Mary Margaret was a refugee from the Troubles—want to go back to the UK? Back to enemy ground?"

"You're assuming she sided with the Irish."

Dashiell shrugged. "It fits. The census records show her mother came over in 1971, right after the bombing of McGurk's Pub, one of the worst incidents of violence against the Irish up until that point. A young Catholic girl, coming over on her own from the hotbed of the IRA? She must have hated the British."

Bree turned to him as they continued walking.

"Maybe it wasn't that at all. Maybe her mother came over because she wanted to put that all behind her. Margaret's application to Norwood says she wanted to take advantage of the opportunity she couldn't get in Ireland or anywhere else. That she wanted to work with children. Could it be as simple as that?"

"You know it's not."

"Right, because we know, at least from her records, that she never went back home to Chicago. She stayed away on purpose. She even got special dispensation to stay on campus during holidays."

"And we know her father died after falling down the stairs of their flat, intoxicated, freezing to death in the middle of winter."

Bree grimaced. That her grandfather was a drunk raised all sorts of possibilities she didn't want to imagine.

"Right," she said briskly. "Possibly sympathetic to the IRA. Possibly just trying to get away from a difficult situation. In any case, no reason to go home again."

"What else?" Dash prompted, pulling a prolific vine of kudzu out of the path so they could pass.

"She was a goody two-shoes," Bree noted, pulling a face.

Dash snorted. "Whatever do you mean?"

"Her recommendations were from the parish priest and a bunch of nuns. Oh, and from the person in charge of administering her high school's honor code. She was valedictorian of her high school. She was top of the class at Norwood, too—perfect grades; you saw the report cards."

"Yes," Dash acknowledged, "perfect marks, even while taking Mandarin."

"She was Head Girl, like Montoya-Craig," Bree continued, her voice tinged with disapproval, "and sat on the Norwood Honor Committee, too. She was in the choral society, leading that treacly school song at every assembly. So a suck-up and possibly a snitch, with all that honor code business."

"Hmmm. You don't sound very sympathetic to her."

"She sounds just too . . . perfect."

"And yet, don't you wonder? Was she bullied, perhaps, for being Irish? And American? Was all that perfection so that nobody could find a chink in her proverbial armor? It is intriguing to consider. I doubt it was easy, coming to Norwood at the height of the Troubles. I'm sure everyone regarded her with suspicion."

"Why are you defending her?"

"Why are you attacking her? You seem intent on disliking her. Perhaps you blame her for getting herself killed?"

Bree stopped in a spot of shadow on the path.

"I don't know what I'm supposed to feel. I just know that I don't feel any closer to her now than I did before. I only have more questions."

Dash steered her on, tactfully shifting the conversation.

"The Mandarin bit. It's intriguing, isn't it? Especially given her trial placement after first term was with a visiting consul from Hong Kong, who was trying to negotiate an increase of visas and residency permits for people trying to flee before the handover of the island to the PRC. That China connection, again. It keeps popping up."

"It could be coincidence."

"As I've said before, coincidences are just the universe's way of birthing forth the truth."

Bree looked up. They'd wound their way back toward the orphanage's main buildings and now stood in the shadow of the abandoned barn.

She gulped.

"Let's go in," she insisted, rushing ahead before Dashiell could stop her.

She heaved the heavy door to the side, wincing as the rusty wheels whined against the track. As she crossed the threshold, she was instantly plunged into darkness. She waited for her eyes to adjust, her nostrils picking out the ancient smell of dusty hay and faded, oily cotton bolls. Eventually, the dust motes floating in the shaft of light from the upper window, the decrepit ladder leaning against the loft, and the forgotten hand cart all came into view. She swung her head around and saw it, then—the lusterless metal ring in the wall, a frayed length of rope trailing from it onto the ground.

She walked over and stared at it. Then, she grabbed an old plastic bucket, turning it upside down, and took a seat. Dash trailed in behind her.

"Is this it, then?" he asked softly.

She nodded, unable to speak.

"You don't have to do this, you know."

"I think I do," she whispered. "I haven't been in here since."

The dust motes floated down around their heads.

"I didn't tell you," she continued. "Judy knew. The whole time that Rodney was away, caring for his sick wife in the hospital, Judy was aware that the temporary person put in charge of the orphanage was abusing me. She let it go on because to her, it was a test—a test to see if I was strong enough to be a spy, like my mom. She only intervened once she had her answer."

She reached out to take the rope in her hand. Absentmindedly, she stroked its frayed strands.

She turned suddenly to face Dash. "Who does that, Dash? Who lets someone tie up a scared little kid in an empty barn? Lets that child strain and heave at their bonds until their wrists are raw and bloody?"

Dash squatted next to her and pushed the sleeve of her cotton shirt up, trailing his thumb over the shiny welted scars that still encircled her delicate wrists.

"Someone like Judy. Which is why you know, as well as I do, that she did not give you this information about your mother out of mercy or goodwill. She has a reason, Bree. Was it a bribe to keep you from divulging her existence to the Norwood leadership? A pat on the head to keep you in line while she readies you for her next mission? What does she want from you?"

Bree slumped on the bucket and threw the rope down to the ground in frustration. "I don't know. I feel like I'm further from the truth than ever. All I know is that she feels somehow this is her opportunity to fix whatever went wrong on that mission in which my parents were killed."

"Very well. Let's go with that, then. There's a very good chance your mother was IRA."

Bree drew herself up to protest, but Dashiell silenced her with a shake of his head.

"Look, the signs are all there. Catholic Irish émigré mother, father also of Irish descent. From Chicago, a hotbed of support for the old country's rebellion. If you were the brass at Norwood, would you take a gamble on bringing in a possible IRA plant in hopes of turning her? Or using her for your own purposes?"

"But to what end?"

"The Irish threat was one of the greatest facing Britain in that period. And what was her first assignment, Bree?"

I was so stupid, she thought to herself. "My father."

"And . . . ?"

"And he was MI5. British Intelligence. Which means he was probably focused on domestic terrorism. She was spying on him," she exclaimed, jumping up from the bucket and knocking it over in her enthusiasm. "Of course she was. Judy as much as told me. But for whom? The IRA or Norwood?"

"Maybe both. One thing's for certain. We need to see if we can establish a definitive IRA link."

"How? We've already searched the online emigration and family records. Mary Margaret Kelly must be the most popular name in all of Ireland. We don't even know who we are looking for, really. We're just spinning our wheels."

"Come now, it hasn't been all a waste. You did find out your grandfather was a close cousin to that paragon of anti-Communist virtue, Senator Joseph McCarthy."

Bree grimaced and wondered if that, in itself, was a clue.

"Maybe it's time to take a different tack," Dash suggested.

"What do you have in mind?"

"DNA."

Bree scoffed. "You're grasping at straws. No self-respecting member of the IRA is going to spit in a cup and help the authorities track him down. We'd be wasting our time."

"But don't you think it is odd for an Irish family to ship off a lone, young daughter for no reason? Maybe they were trying to protect her from the Troubles. But maybe, just maybe, she—or they—were in the thick of them. And it will take no time at all to take a swab from you and submit it to the genealogical sites. We can do it under a fake name and anonymized account so nobody will be the wiser."

He looked at her expectantly.

"No harm in trying," he nudged.

"Oh, fine," she said, throwing up her arms. "I suppose you're right. Again. I don't suppose you already have a swab kit back in the house?"

He beamed. "You know me so well, my dear."

"Fine. Let's go get this out of the way. As for this place . . ." She looked around the shadowy barn, pushing back the memories that threatened to encroach her. "I'll speak to Rodney about tearing it down."

Just then Ollie bounded in, running up to throw his arms around her. "Bree! Bree! Did you look up in the loft?"

"No buddy," she said, ruffling his shaggy hair. She worried about him—he hadn't seemed to grow much since she'd left for school in England. "What's up in the loft that's got you so excited?"

"It's a construction zone now," Ollie pronounced. "I'm not allowed to go up. But if *you* gave me permission, I'm sure that Rodney wouldn't mind. Can we? Huh, can we, Bree?"

Bree looked warily at Dash, who simply shrugged.

"Construction zone; is that right? Well, I'd better talk to Rodney about that before we go poking around. Come on back with us; I bet you there's some lemonade in the kitchen."

———

Rodney had aged a lot since the time he'd visited her in Bath, during the Christmas holiday. His slack skin had taken on an ashy tone. His tightly coiled hair was now completely white. His eyes seemed permanently tinted pink with weariness. She didn't know what was going on, just that it couldn't be good.

"You're working too hard, Rodney," she scolded, plucking a fresh peach from the basket that graced the countertop in the industrial kitchen. She tossed one to Dash, and another one to Ollie, before picking out one for herself. She probed, trying to keep it light while she sought out the truth. "Are these kids giving you trouble, now that I'm not here anymore to keep them in line?"

Rodney peered over his reading glasses at her. "Long arm of the law, you were not, Bree, and you know it."

Bree grinned and took a bite of her peach. Slurping through the juices, she continued to pester him. "You haven't answered my question. What's going on? It's not money, is it?"

Rodney busied himself in the cabinets, opening doors and counting, ticking things off on his shopping list. "It's nothing for you to be worrying yourself about, Bree."

"If it's my school expenses, I can take a break," she stated boldly.

He turned and put his notepad and pencil down on the gleaming steel counter. "You're just saying that to provoke me. And no, it is not money. For once, that is not a problem. I've got some new children coming in, this time with funding."

"I see. Ollie was telling me something about construction in the barn. Would that have anything to do with that money you've got coming in?"

Rodney shrugged. "Maybe. You know as well as I do that we need some modernization around here. And that barn has been sitting empty for years. We could put it to better use as extra housing and even a learning lab. One of the sponsors were here while you were out." He gestured at a half empty glass of lemonade, abandoned next to a pitcher on the counter. "Very exacting in their specifications, these folks. Want to see to every detail. Already lining up transfers of children for us, too, so we're on a tight timetable."

Ollie interrupted. "Is a learning lab like a school, Rodney? I don't want more school. Could we build a computer room instead?"

"See?" Rodney smiled. "We have no shortage of ideas of what to do with that space. And for once, no shortage of money."

Bree swallowed hard. "I was sort of hoping you could tear it down. Might be better to start all over."

Rodney was taken aback. "Now what would we do that for? A perfectly good building like that?"

"It might be stinky," Bree asserted, grabbing at straws. "From all the animals?"

Rodney scoffed. "After all this time? It hasn't been used in decades. There's nothing wrong with that place that some good lumber, insulation, wiring, and paint can't fix."

Bree looked imploringly at Dash, who was watching the exchange between her and Rodney like a tennis match. Seeing her look of desperation, he cleared his throat.

"Why don't you two take a walk to discuss it? Ollie and I can tidy up the kitchen a bit while you're out."

"There's not much to discuss . . ." Rodney said, his voice trailing off in doubt.

"Please," Bree said simply. "Let's at least go sit on the porch."

Dash pretended to busy himself while they stepped away. Bree could hear him chatting away, Ollie's bright young voice periodically interjecting with enthusiasm about whatever topic Dash had managed to conjure up, as they crossed out to the shady porch.

Rodney didn't wait for them to take a seat before he started questioning her.

"Now, what is this about, Bree? You never ask for anything, so something like this, out of the blue. . . ? It must be pretty important to you."

She looked at his dark eyes, now deep with worry, and knew she couldn't tell him. She tried to find another way, by changing the subject.

"Do you miss Beatrice, Rodney?"

He startled. "My wife? Yes. Yes, I do. It's been over a decade, of course, but I miss her every day."

"I always thought that this place would be frozen in time, like an ant in amber, after she died. That you wanted to keep it exactly the same as when she was here. With you."

He let out a loud exhale. After a pause, he eased himself onto a rocking chair.

"That's what this is about?"

She nodded, going with the unexpected opening.

He rubbed his hand over his face, contemplating her statement.

"Beatrice wasn't from here. I think you know that. She'd been places, seen things. How she ended up with me will remain one of God's great mysteries. But if you remembered her well, if you'd really known her, you'd know she didn't want to be remembered that way. She was vibrant and full of life. Changeable. She loved to try new things and was always encouraging me to do the same. For you kids. For myself."

"You said she'd been in Bath?" Bree prompted, suddenly intrigued by the way Rodney was describing his wife. She was, to Bree, a cipher, like so many other people and things in Bree's past: a shrunken form in a hospital bed in the middle of the living room; a feeble voice calling for ice chips; a grave they visited on holidays. Bree didn't remember the time before the illness. The cancer had blotted out everything else, like a cloud in front of the sun.

"You told me that, before I left for Norwood," Bree prompted him again.

He nodded, remembering.

"She'd been a PhD candidate there," he said. "At the University of Bath."

"Wait, what?"

Rodney nodded. "Neuroscientist, if you can believe it. A woman, in that day in age, working in that field, was quite unusual. She worked on memory loss. The university had a lot of pharmaceutical and technology expertise. She had some research program going on, something to do with aging. I met her when I stumbled across a paper she'd done with someone in the Child Psychology department. She'd done it on a whim. Can you imagine? Being so brilliant you can pick up research topics on things like the long-term psychological impact of being in foster care, for *fun*?" He shook his head. "But that was Beatrice. When I read it, I had to know more. I had to know *her*. The rest was history, as they say. She fell in love with you kids, just as much as I had. This place became her home."

"We don't honor her memory by keeping things the same," he added with finality. "And even if we did, tearing down that barn wouldn't accomplish it, would it? Now, where is that young man of yours?" Rodney segued smoothly, the barn and its destruction deftly left behind. "He seemed awfully eager to help you out."

Bree blushed, her aversion to the barn temporarily forgotten. "He's not mine. He's just a friend."

"A friend who accompanied you all the way to a teeny tiny bit of nowhere, Alabama. Hmm?"

Bree shrugged. "British aristocracy slumming it, I guess."

Rodney snorted. "I see. Does his definition of slumming it include doing the dishes and cleaning up after the children for me?"

Bree smiled. "He's weaseled into your good graces with housework."

Rodney waved a hand at her. "He sure has. And, young lady, I've seen how attentive he is to you. So, you'd best be sure he sees the best part of the Shoals before you go. You can't have him come all this way and just mope around this dusty old farm. That would not be up to the standard of Southern hospitality I'm sure he's expecting."

Bree ignored his comment about Dash's attentiveness. "I guess I could take him out to the Rattlesnake or FloBama, let him hear the sound?"

Rodney pushed his glasses on top of his head, staring at her in disbelief. "Now why would you go and do that? You know better than to take him to one of those touristy places. If you're going to take him anywhere, you need to take him to John's place."

Bree paused. John was an old friend of Rodney's, one of the best guitarists she'd ever heard, and had been like an uncle to her. But she'd never been out in the woods, to his makeshift bar, on her own at night. It tended to attract an unusual clientele. "You think?"

Rodney looked over his readers and pinned Bree with a stare.

"You want me to go out there with you? Might spoil the mood for you and your date," he pondered, a mischievous look stealing over his face as he settled into a rhythm with the rocker. Every time he swayed back in the chair, the old floorboards of the porch gave a groan, punctuating the awkward silence.

"It's not . . . he's not . . . I mean, no. I'm perfectly able to go on my own. It's just been a while. And I'm not sure if the English can stand that many mosquitos."

"What's a little discomfort in exchange for a glimpse of the face of God when John starts playing? John has known you since you were a little girl. He's practically family. He'll take good care of you both."

Rodney paused for a moment.

"You've lost your accent already, Bree; probably didn't even realize it. All the roundness, the softness, is gone away. It will be good for you to get a dose of that music, reconnect with your roots."

He looked her over with what Bree thought was a touch of wistfulness, before rising to head back into the kitchen.

And so Dash and Bree found themselves hunkered down at a grey, weather-beaten picnic table under the inky night sky. The dense pines obscured the stars. The soft glow from the pole shed and a scattering of string lights marked a tiny perimeter. In the shadows, a smattering of other guests lingered, talking low, nursing icy beers and Mason jars of something stronger, waiting for John—or whatever act he'd conjured up—to appear. They were a few hardscrabble locals, punctuated by bikers and truckers, obvious strangers, passing through. More were streaming in, emerging from the makeshift parking lots in the woods and canyon: a mostly rough, anonymous crowd.

Dash swatted at his face. "Are you sure these are insects? They seem large enough to be an avian species."

Bree laughed. "They like you. Drink your beer; maybe the hops will make your blood less sweet to them."

"Who am I to challenge a prompt to imbibe more alcohol? To mosquitos," he declared, raising the bottle in salute before taking a great swig. "Now, Bree, explain your connection to this place, again."

"John is an old friend of Rodney. I guess they used to play together, back in the day, before Rodney was tied up with the orphanage. Though, now that you mention it, I'm not sure how. Rodney is not from around here originally."

"That surprises me. He seems very much settled and of this place. Where did he come from, then?"

Bree frowned. She ran her finger over the splintered wood of the table, trying to remember. "Can't say. He doesn't talk much about the past."

"Hmm. Seems to be the theme with you people." Before Bree could protest, he pressed on. "Aren't you going to go see this John before the show starts?"

She shook her head. "He'll be busy. We can say hello later."

"Well, you've been promising me you'd explain this music ever since you shocked our little monster of a Head Girl, Montoya-Craig, with your delightfully inappropriate song at orientation. And I must say, your intriguing dancing on the tables at the bar in Bath only heightened my interest. What exactly is this music to which you are so devoted?"

"I can't explain it. It is just, well, soulful. People from around here used to say there was a ghost or a spirit in the river who sang songs to protect her tribe. Some people think the songs come out of the mud. You're going to have to listen for yourself and see." She nodded at the pole shed. Musicians were setting up, adjusting their chairs for the meager light, though in reality, Bree knew, they didn't need it. They knew everything by heart. It was in their bones.

There was no announcement. They simply started playing.

Bree closed her eyes and let the music envelop her. A funky, dirty mix of horns, saxophone, and guitar jumped out into the night, laced by the throaty, soaring voice of the woman gripping the mic. The steady beat commanded the very beat of their hearts, the blood in her veins whooshing to the swooping rhythms of the band, the staccato of the drums urging them on, faster and faster. Then the music shifted, the bass throbbing, intense and insistent, danger spilling out with every note. The words, heady and plaintive, pierced her heart.

She was swaying, letting song after song wash over her.

She felt Dash squeezing her fingers. "Look," he shouted at her over the music. She looked around. The crowd was on its feet, couples draped over one another, hips moving in unison, others swinging and rolling, loose limbed and oblivious to anyone around them.

"Let's go," he grinned, pulling her to her feet.

Before she could steady herself, he expertly twirled her about, then pulled her in, breathless, tight against his chest. She closed her eyes. She could feel his heart pounding in his chest, could smell his expensive cologne mixed with sweat and mosquito repellent.

He laughed out loud, the vibrations traveling through his chest and tingling her fingertips like little electric shocks.

"Look at me, Bree," he insisted.

She opened her eyes. His eyes locked with hers as he pulled her tighter.

"I think I like this Shoals sound," he whispered into her ear, his mouth up against her loose hair. "And I think I like what it does to you even more."

The music stopped, whooping appreciation and applause punctuating the sudden silence.

Dash let his hands run from Bree's shoulders down the length of her back. He wrapped his hands around her waist and then frowned as they came to rest.

"What's this?"

He arched his eyebrow, waiting for her to speak, his arms locking like steel bands around her.

"Bree! I thought that was you!" A heavy Southern drawl interrupted them.

Dashiell hesitated, then dropped his hands to let Bree turn.

"John," she smiled at the man who was approaching them. "Great show. You were incredible, as always. Rodney will be disappointed when I tell him what he missed."

John ran his hand through his wild mane of silver hair and laughed, his sweaty, tan face crinkling into a mess of smile lines.

"I wish I could say I believed you, but I don't know anymore. He won't come out, ever. It's almost as if he can't hear the music anymore, Bree." He shrugged, the words spilling out of him as he considered the strange behavior of one of his oldest friends. "I don't think I've heard him play in over ten years. But that second song in the set? You remember it? That was his, you know. He wrote that back in '79. Always had a talent for the groovy stuff. But come here, you. Let me give you a proper welcome home."

She folded herself into a great bear hug. He stepped back to inspect her. "Definitely older. Maybe wiser. Probably not, if you brought this one with you," he said, winking as he tilted his head toward Dash.

Bree rolled her eyes. "Dashiell, let me introduce you to John Hardy, proprietor and, as you've just witnessed, musician extraordinaire."

John grasped Dashiell's hand warmly between his two. "Dashiell, is it?" He looked him up and down, noting the pressed linen shirt and pants. "Definitely not from around here, are you?"

"I'm afraid not," Dashiell answered, laughing. "But I hope to be invited back again. Tonight was spectacular. I think I'm beginning to understand a bit about what makes Bree's home so special."

"If you come back, I'll expect a proper introduction. Bree, you hear? Listen, you two, I've got to run—I need to be sure everyone is watered and fed before the second set starts—but stick around. Enjoy it. Just mind yourselves. There's a group that has had a few too many over there," he added, shooting a worried look at a particularly loud corner of the audience, "and I wouldn't want you to get into any trouble. Rodney would never forgive me." He squeezed Bree's shoulder. "You kids have fun. I'll see you later."

He bounced off, slapping shoulders and shaking hands as he made his way through the crowd, back to the hum of the makeshift stage.

Bree and Dash stood awkwardly, unsure where to pick up. The space between them seemed too close now, the moment lost.

"You're a much better dancer than I remembered from the pub," Dash began, delicately.

"Um. So are you. I mean, better than I expected," Bree stammered, grateful that the black night would cover the embarrassed stain spreading across her hot cheeks. She hesitated.

"You know, maybe we should go. It's getting late," she added lamely.

"Of course," Dash said, retreating to formality. "It was entertaining, but it has been a long day. And we've a bit of a drive back to the farm." He picked up their empty beer bottles from the table and gestured ahead. "After you, my dear."

They picked their way through the crowd, winding their way through the press of bodies and into the cover of the woods. The small light of the makeshift music hall in the clearing gave way to darkness. "Stay close to me, Bree," Dash urged, trying to make out the path back to Rodney's ancient pickup.

"You can hold the chivalry. I'm not scared of the dark, Dash. I don't need you to protect me," Bree retorted sharply.

"Of course not. What have you possibly to be afraid of? Especially when, for some inexplicable reason, you're packing a gun in the waistband of your pants."

They walked in silence, Bree trailing Dash, feeling a unique blend of confusion, regret, and frustration.

"Hey! You there!"

A dark figure stepped out onto the trail in front of them, emerging from a clutch of parked trucks.

"You think you can get away with insulting me that way?"

The man loomed before Dash, sneering into his face.

"I'm sorry, chap, I don't know to what you are referring. But I'm certain I did not deliberately insult you. I don't even recognize you. Though I admit it is hard to see your visage through this obscuring darkness."

"You think big words can get you out of this?" The man shoved Dash, sending him stumbling back. He was hard to understand, his words slurred and strange. "You sure don't spill my beer and get away with it. Your fancy talk is just gonna make it worse for you."

Dash laughed uneasily as he steadied himself, positioning himself between the drunken man and Bree. "I see. I must have bumped you as we were leaving. Now that you mention it, I can smell the beer coming off you. I do apologize. Can I give you some money for your troubles, buy you another beer? Call it even between us?"

"Dash." Bree said it quietly.

"Not now, Bree. I've got it under control."

"Dash," she said more urgently. "He's not alone."

Another figure quietly stepped from the shadows.

"You just give us what we want and nobody has to get hurt," the second man began. His accent was honed sharp, with none of the soft curves of a Southerner. A stranger here, too.

"What do you want?" Bree demanded, stepping up to Dash's side. "You already got your apology."

"We want information." The second man continued talking, taking the lead.

"About what?"

"Not what. Who. We want to know about Roberta."

"Roberta? I don't know any Roberta. Dash, do you know a Roberta?"

"Not a one."

The first man chuckled. He let the fake drunkenness and the bad imitation of an Alabaman accent fall away. "We think you do. And until you tell us everything you know about her, we can't let you go." There was a burst of applause from the clearing. "They play three sets tonight. Nobody's coming this way for a long time. It'd be better if you talked. For your own good."

"How do you know about the sets?" Bree asked sharply. "You're not from around here—I can tell by your accents. And John doesn't publish a set list, or a plan. His shows are spontaneous. Always have been."

The first man shrugged. "We have our ways. Now, start talking."

Dash shrugged. "We can't help you. And even if we could, we wouldn't be inclined to do so, after such a display of atrocious manners. Just who did you say you are, again? Who are you working with? We'll be sure to file a complaint."

"You think you're funny, do you?" the first man sneered. "You won't think so when that old man at the orphanage pays for your smart mouth. Or those kids."

Dash squared off on the path and seemed to grow even larger with indignation. "That's not very sporting of you, is it? He has nothing to do with this, I'd wager. Though what *this* is, we have no idea. As I've said, we don't know your Roberta and have no idea what you're talking about. Now if you'll excuse us, we'll be on our way. Bree?"

In the darkness, Bree had stolen over and climbed into the bed of the closest pickup truck. She'd pulled her pistol out and now, with a satisfying click, placed one of the men within her sights.

"Like you said, the band will be playing long and loud into the night. Nobody will hear a thing if I need to use this. And since you threatened my family, I *will* use it, if I'm forced to. I'll hunt you all the way across the state line if I have to. Your choice."

"This isn't a game, little girl."

"Oh, you shouldn't have called her that," Dash shook his head. "You'll only make her angry."

Before the man could answer, Dash swept his legs out from under him, bringing him down to the ground. With his knee on the man's neck, he patted him down and stripped his pistol.

"Silencer, Bree. We are apparently dealing with professionals." Dash held the gun against the man's temple. "We seem to have arrived at a stalemate, my friends. Perhaps if you throw down the rest of your weapons, we can discuss this in a civilized manner."

"As you wish," the second man murmured. "Just step away so I know I can trust you."

"I've got him, Dash," Bree stated flatly. "You can get up. You—" she said, nodding toward the second man. "Slowly. Take your weapon out and throw it into the woods."

The man on the dirt path gasped for breath as Dash released his neck and backed away, the confiscated gun still trained on the man's head. Coughing, the man pulled himself up to his knees. His partner moved his hands slowly, reaching behind him for his own weapon.

Through the woods, the music crescendoed, the crowd screaming for more.

The man pulled his gun and dangled it in front of him, as if he were going to throw it. Instead, in one swift, terrible move, he aimed it at his partner and shot him in the back. Then, with a terrible smile, he put it to his own head and pulled the trigger.

His head snapped with a burst of gore before he collapsed to the ground.

The music stopped.

Bree and Dash stood, horrified, staring at the crumpled bodies.

"Well, that was extreme," Dash finally choked out. "It didn't really seem necessary, did it?"

"Whoever they were working for," Bree said, ignoring the nausea that threatened to overwhelm her, "they were willing to die for them rather than be captured."

"What do we do now?" Dash asked.

"Wipe down that gun. You have to remove your prints. Wipe it down now and throw it away."

Dash stood in a daze.

"But how did you know?" he asked. "What made you bring your gun tonight, Bree?"

"Dash," Bree commanded sharply. "I mean it. We don't have time. Do it now."

Bree re-engaged her safety and shoved the pistol back inside her waistband, her movements automatic as she kept reasoning her way through the mess in which they found themselves. She kept talking, the nervous chatter settling into a steadier pace.

"We'll just leave them. Hide them off the path a bit so it will take a while to find them. Nobody will be looking for them, so that should help. Dash." Her voice softened. "I didn't know. I was just nervous. But I'm glad I decided to have it on me. Now, we've got to finish the job."

Dash acknowledged her comment with a nod and wound up to hurl the gun.

"No! Wait!" Bree shouted.

Dash froze, confused.

"That won't make sense. They were fighting each other," Bree paced the back of the truck bed, telling herself the story. "They drew guns on each other. He needs it in his hand."

Dash hesitated.

"Do it, Dash! Put it in his hand. Wipe your prints off and put it in his hand."

Bree jumped down from the pickup truck. "C'mon, let's go. Before anyone else comes along."

When they'd dragged the bodies a few yards away, Bree patted down their pockets.

"Nothing," she spat with frustration. "No ID. Like you said, professionals. At least when they're found . . ."

"If they're found," Dash interjected. "Let's hope they're not."

"If they're found, it will be that much harder for the police to identify them. I'm guessing they won't show up in any of the normal criminal databases."

From the path, they heard the chatter of loud voices and drunken laughter. They crouched lower, waiting for the concert goers to pass by.

"We need to get out of here," Dash whispered urgently. "And I don't mean these woods." He grabbed Bree's wrist. "We need to get out of Florence, Bree. We're putting Rodney and the kids in danger if we stay any longer. Whoever these people were, they are part of something big. Something much bigger than we understand. So big they would rather die than be captured. There will be more of them. Which means this—" he gestured to the lifeless bodies—"doesn't stop with them."

Guilt surged through Bree.

"You're right. But how can we leave the orphanage unprotected?"

"They are only at risk as long as we're here. Whoever is after us will use them to get to you. But that's the only reason. That much is clear. It's time. We need to get back to Norwood and put the safety of distance between us and them."

"You're right," she murmured.

He clutched her wrist even tighter. "And you can't tell Judy. Not a word, Bree. We can't trust her. Not even with this."

The tight knot of worry in Bree's throat got bigger. "She could help protect them, Dash . . . "

"But what if she's somehow connected to this? After all, wasn't it her idea for you to even come here? We can't take that risk. The best thing you can do to protect them is to leave.

"We leave now. And we don't look back."